T0268379

ROBERT S WRIGHT

A NOVEL OF THE EVOLVING HUMAN SOUL

KING DAVID'S LOST CROWN

 ISBN 979-8-35092-233-2

Honoring the Memory of

Wendy Rae Wright

Sept 15, 1947 – Nov 17, 1986

Contents

"After Jesus was born in Bethlehem in Judea, during the time of King Herod, Magi from the east came to Jerusalem and asked, 'Where is the one who has been born king of the Jews? We saw his star when it rose and have come to worship him."

Matthew 2:1-2

Prologue

THE WOLF PRINCE OF PARTHIA

Year 52 (6AD) to Year 74 (28 AD) of the Calendar
of Pater Patriae Gaius Julius Caesar

CHAPTER 1

A WOLF CALLED MITHRA

THE PARTHIAN EMPIRE – THE CITY OF ECBATANA

The Parthians call the sun Mithra

If you squint just right, you can see him up there with his white horses as they draw his chariot across the sky.

Mithra is more than just our source of heat and light. Mithra is a living thing; he is the all-seeing eye of Ahura Mazda.

And Ahura Mazda is the creator of all things, the Unknowable that fills all time and space, from whose bosom is formed the earth and all creatures thereon, and the sky and all that resides therein, in much the same way that ice is formed from water.

When the time is right, say the Parthians, the boundless Ahura Mazda will cause his seed to be deposited within the womb of a virgin, so that she might bear a son. She is Eredat Fedhri, called also Visap-tauravairi, which means the all-destroying, for no evil can stand before her. Her son shall be called Saoshyant, which means World Savior, and his birth will be heralded by great signs in the heavens, and he shall be king of all the earth below and of all the sky above. It is written in the Bundahishn and the Avesta. So it shall be.

On a certain day, when Mithra was bathing the earth with his brilliance in an especially splendid fashion, two brothers were walking in the forest, one older than the other, both sons of the king. The king had sent them on a quest. He had sent them out to hunt the great wolf. One of the sons was called Orodes. A handsome lad, but with an arrowhead birthmark over his left eye and a scar that ran the length of his torso chin to groin. Orodes was different than the other boys, preferring books and study to the rough courtyard games the other boys played, and this concerned his father. What will happen when he becomes a man, the father wondered. Will he be too weak and kindhearted to be a successor to a kingdom? The king consulted the Magi, and it was suggested that the boy be entrusted to his older brother, who was the diametric opposite. The older brother was growing tall and strong, and excelled in all the games of wrestling and weapons training in which the younger son was deficient. His name was Gotarzes. He was approaching his mid-teens and nearly ready to be given a commission in the Parthian army. "Watch over the boy," the king instructed Gotarzes. "Teach him the ways of a man. Teach him how to hunt the wolf, for no animal is more cunning, and no prize is as valued as a wolf pelt. Such a great prize it would be, for a young boy, befitting a prince." Orodes was the favored son, and the one to whom the throne would pass, this because the Magi recommended him to the king as the one who would rule in wisdom and moderation. One such Magus, Belteshazzar, loved Orodes as if he were his own son. Belteshazzar was wise in the mystic ways of things and had taken it upon himself to mentor the young prince.

Mithra is a great hunter. Carvings abound throughout the city. They all show Mithra thrusting a knife into the neck of a giant wolf. And so must his son be. Would any father do less?

"A wolf pelt will soon be mine, then we will see who the king favors," joked Gotarzes, but he was not joking, because he was aware of his father's favoritism, though his father never spoke it.

"Not if my arrow finds its heart first," said Orodes. "I intend to hang its tail from my headband, so that all can see that I am the better hunter."

"Well, for truth, you are not the better hunter, my little one-eyed brother," put forth Gotarzes. He knew full well Orodes could see just fine out of that shaded-over eye. "That is why we are here," he continued. They were approaching what could only be described as a playground for sylphs and fairies – green so green it hurt the eyes, as people so often say of the forests of Ecbatana, and a pool of water from a creek-sized waterfall that settled so calmly beneath its fall that its basin could be seen with complete clarity. The pool was formed by a collection of gray snags damming up the creek and transforming its banks into new creations as dozens of tiny sprigs sent their roots through moss, wood, even solid rock, in search of the water and fertile soil underneath, as if a superior intelligence might be guiding them. "We are here because Father wants me to teach you the things I know, which may not be possible. Father wants me to transform you into a prince. Father may have given me an impossible task."

Without saying a further word, Gotarzes calmly raised his bow and let fly with an arrow, because he had seen something Orodes had not, in the movements of leaves and the flashes of light and shadow. The amber-red of the wolf's body blended so well with the foliage that Orodes had not noticed the young pup. An expert eye was needed to observe it, as its muscles tensed to run. But it hesitated, being too young to realize how dangerous it was to stand even at a distance from this particular enemy. Unknown to the young pup, this enemy did not need massive jaws to kill, did not need muscled legs to close distances quickly. This enemy was one that could kill simply by standing there. This enemy needed no reason to kill. The pleasure of the act was reason enough.

The wolf yelped and cried in confusion as sudden pain ripped through its body, and it ran, as if it could outrun the thing that was causing the pain, and tripped over its four feet that had suddenly stopped working and fell helplessly into the deep part of the creek.

The young wolf wasn't growling or snapping as the two predators ran toward it. All its strength was needed to keep its head above water. As the two-legged creatures approached, they did things the wolf could not understand. One of them slipped on the moss-covered rock and fell headlong into the water. The other waded in and gently lifted the little pup up and carried it to safety. The pup was not even half its full adult size. That was why young Orodes was able to carry it with such ease, and that was why it had not run when first receiving the scent of the two upright creatures its mother knew full well to fear.

"Fool!" yelled Gotarzes. "The mother is stalking you. She will rip you to pieces. Drop it and run. I speak what I know! Drop it and run!"

The reason the mother did not attack is one that can only be guessed at. Perhaps it knew that it could do nothing. Perhaps there were other cubs that needed to be protected. Or, with an intelligence beyond that of any other forest creature, perhaps the mother wolf knew her baby was in protective hands. Its eyes continued to follow and watch, as Orodes ran from Gotarzes. Gotarzes was slowed by an injury sustained in the fall into the creek, and limped as he ran, spewing his fury in words that resounded off the trees and cliffs of the dense forests that abutted the southern edge of Ecbatana, as the city rose upland from the shoreless Mazandaran Sea. And finally, as the forest came to an end and the king's castle came into view, the mother wolf said goodbye with her eyes, and slowly took backward steps into the denseness of the trees, and stood there for the longest time, ears pasted back. Then, trusting, hoping she was right in what was really the only decision possible, she loped away to care for and protect the rest of her litter.

Her instincts were correct. The human predator who had her little baby would protect it. It was a part of the young human's nature that even he had not known was there, until the moment it was tested.

"My son, my son, how can you wear a crown and become a warrior capable of defending a kingdom if you cannot kill even game?" said the king to young Orodes. Love seemed to be the measure of his words, as he looked upon his son. In a cage off to the left was the wolf cub, lying face between its paws. Its eyes were closed, except on occasion when it would open them to nervously look to and fro, with just the eyes moving.

Its breathing was fast and unnatural. Its sides trembled with each quick breath, partly out of fear, partly pain. When touched it vomited and peed, so great was its terror. Tied around its midsection was a white cloth with a red stain marking the wound. Said the king, "But we will consider that matter at a later date. For now we must decide what to do with the matter of the wolf, and to whom it belongs." He looked at Gotarzes, who stood on the left.

Gotarzes bent to one knee. "Your Majesty. The wolf is mine. My eyes marked it. My arrow brought it down. Orodes will not deny it."

King Artabanus could have decided the matter on his own without the convening of a formal court, but he was a king resolved to treat all matters in a fair way, especially when it came to matters of his own family. He spent long moments stroking the furrows of his square beard. He looked at Orodes. "Orodes, my son, is this true? Was it in fact Gotarzes' arrow?"

"The wolf should be mine, Father, because I am the one who saved it," Orodes replied. "Gotarzes intends to kill it and make a pelt of it."

"Answer my question. Was it in fact Gotarzes' arrow?"

"Yes Father."

"If I should decide in your favor, what do you intend to do with the animal?"

"I will care for it, and when it heals I will set it free so that it can go back to its mother and live among its own kind in the forest, as Ahura Mazda intended."

"So that it can then become a predator to our own animals and livestock, even our children?"

"Please Father, let me do this. Please."

"But why? I really do not understand. Help me to understand."

"I don't know. It's just, I just, I don't know – it's just, I need to do it." Young Prince Orodes almost grabbed the animal and ran with it, so strong was the protectiveness swelling within his chest.

"Your pardon, Majesty, good father," said Gotarzes, "We all know that a wolf is a wild creature and as such can never be trusted. True, it is a puppy now, cute and fluffy, but the time will come when he will mature. And a time will come when he will turn against us. Because you can never take the wild out of the wild. It was you who taught me this, Father."

"That is true, my son," said the king to Orodes, with kind eyes, but eyes of wisdom.

"Please, Father, let me do this," said Orodes, one final plea. "Let me have the wolf. It shall be my responsibility."

King Artabanus gave out an audible sigh, reflective of an obvious troubled heart. "Let the Magi decide," he finally said. "I am fearful that my son does not have the fortitude to be a king. Thankfully, the task of choosing a successor is not mine alone, for in Parthia it is to the Magi that the duty falls to nominate and install kings. That is why we call them the Kingmakers, for without their blessing even a prince cannot wear a crown. So in the same manner I will let the Magi decide this issue." He gestured to an old man standing in front of a Chaldean doorway, a square entrance to a darkened place wherein potions are mixed and spells are cast, wherein no common man or woman has ever dared venture. "Belteshazzar?" invited the king.

The elderly Magus stepped forward, a gentle smile on his face. He was adorned in the attire of a Magus, elf like, the striped and fluted trousers, shirt with puffy sleeves, and the high conical cap. They were clothes worn and faded from years of washings. Said Belteshazzar, in the guttural harshness of Parthian speak, but strengthened with the same gentleness that was in his smile, after first bowing to the king, "Your Highness, there is a story that is told of a prince in the land of the rising sun, the land of the fierce yellow-skinned warriors. This prince was called Siddhartha, who was the favorite of the king's sons. But like your son, Siddhartha was a different sort of child. His mind was filled with many questions. He wanted to know why life had so many cruelties, and why one creature must kill another to survive. Prince Siddhartha felt sadness even when an insect would die. 'What kind of a son do I have, that he be so kindhearted?' wondered the king, just as you are wondering, my Lord. 'What kind of a man will he grow up to be?' The story is very similar to ours. Prince Siddhartha had a cousin. His cousin was named Devadatta. Devadatta thought only of play and shooting arrows, so the king made arrangements for the two children to play together, hoping Siddhartha would mature in the same way. One day, when the children were out at play a single goose flew overhead, having been separated from its flock. It was very large and very beautiful. Devadatta raised his bow and aimed his arrow at the goose. Siddhartha called out, 'No, Devadatta, don't hurt it!' But it was too late. With a sharp cry the goose came tumbling out of the sky. The children ran up to it and discovered the bird still lived, and before Devadatta could react Siddhartha gathered it up and ran toward home, in the same manner as Orodes had done. The king and queen saw him running and were afraid something terrible had happened. 'What is it?' cried the king. 'Where is Devadatta? Is he all right? What are you carrying?'

"Before Siddhartha could answer, Devadatta came running up and screamed for Siddhartha to give back his bird. 'He stole it from me. It is my bird. It was me who shot it down.'

"'Is this true, my son?' questioned the king.

"'Yes, Father,' said Siddhartha. 'But it is mine now, because I plan to save its life. Devadatta plans to kill it.'

"The king was deeply troubled and unable to make a decision, so he called together his Wise Men, in the same way that you have called upon the Magi. 'I will let them decide the case,' he said. 'Their decision shall be final.'

"The Wise Men questioned each boy. Siddhartha admitted that Devadatta shot it down, but claimed that the bird should be his because he wanted to save its life.

"One of the Wise Men asked Prince Siddhartha what he planned to do with the bird when it was nursed back to health. Said Siddhartha, 'I will turn it loose to live freely among its own kind.'

"The Wise Men conferred briefly with one another then decided thusly, that the bird belongs to the boy who will save its life, not to the one who will destroy it."

"Pray tell, what became of this prince called Siddhartha?" asked King Artabanus.

"He became a great spiritual teacher, some say the greatest, the one chosen by Ahura Mazda to explain the good news of his future kingdom to the people of the Rising Sun. Some have compared him to the coming Saoshyant. In their land he was called The Buddha.

King Artabanus thanked the Magi and told them he no longer needed them to make the decision. "A king should have the courage to make his own decisions," he said. "My decision is this. The wolf belongs to Orodes, because he intends to save it."

Gotarzes began to protest, but King Artabanus raised up his hand. "It is decided," he said. "The wolf shall be given to Orodes."

"Yes, Your Majesty." While making a decision of law the king mandated that even his sons should address him formally.

CHAPTER 2

IN SEARCH OF THE BABY SAOSHYANT

THE PARTHIAN EMPIRE – THE CITY OF ECBATANA

Mithra. A fitting name for a creature so powerful, yet so gentle. Mithra and Orodes were the talk of the entire city, and of the countryside as well, as word began to spread. Soon the entire known world began to hear stories of "*Hyrcania*," *Wolf Country*, and of the Wolf Prince. The wound had not pierced vital parts, and had healed nicely, with the help in part of Old Belteshazzar and his herbal potions.

If there was anyone Orodes loved as much as Mithra it was his four-year-old sister Nahid, and Belteshazzar loved them both, and took it upon himself to school them in the ways of the mystic sciences. Like Orodes, Nahid was a child born with brilliance beyond her years, and with uncommon abilities, among them the ability to foresee future events, happenings barely to be noticed by most, but significant enough to catch Belteshazzar's attention, to make him think that here might be another advanced entity in need of protection and guidance. One day she was crying for no apparent reason. When asked why, she responded, "Because! I don't want my arm to hurt." The next day she stumbled and broke her forearm.

Nahid means Great and Beautiful Star. She had eyes that could gaze into your soul. A permanent smile was affixed to her face. In all her four years she had not known one day of sadness. There were of course those little annoyances that come with life – the broken arm, or going to bed at bedtime, or getting up at dawn – at which Orodes would laugh and say, "Dear sweet Little Star, with your hair as black as midnight and your eyes as full as the moon, if that is the worst thing you will have to suffer in this going-out consider yourself blessed," which would make Nahid cry all the louder. The thing that gave her the widest smile of all was when Orodes would take her to hear Belteshazzar tell the story of the Baby Saoshyant, and how they brought the baby their gifts of gold, frankincense, and myrrh. One day, while Orodes was charged with the duty of caring for her, little Nahid came up missing. Orodes spent the entire day looking for her, with his mind creating terrors of the worst possible kind of what could happen to a child lost in the forest. After searching the entire day, just before the setting of the sun, Orodes conceived an idea. He held one of Nahid's shoes to Mithra's nose. "Mithra, okay good friend, go find Nahid. Go now. Go find her." Mithra stiffened and pointed his ears forward. "Go now. Go find her. Go." Mithra whined, looked at Orodes, then pitched his ears forward again. "Go now." Mithra dropped his nose to the rocky soil and zigzagged forward, withers hunched like some kind of beacon device. Now and then he would slink forward in a sideways glide the way wolves do, looking ahead and sniffing the ground at the same time, on occasion stopping altogether when hundreds of scents were assailing him, to sniff the ground and redirect, with Orodes following behind. Orodes followed Mithra across the rock-strewn meadow, where moss and sprigs grew straight out of the rocks themselves, as if by the magic hands of the Magi. He followed him to the edge of the forest where the tall pines grew to pierce the heavens…and discovered Nahid walking along with purpose, no more than a hundred yards from the palace. "Sweet child, never do that again!" he scolded. "You scared me so! Where is it you think you are going?"

"I go find Baby Sunt," was the answer.

"Oh, sweetheart, no, that is too far away. Besides, that was a long time ago. The baby Saoshyant is all grown up now."

Time and time again Nahid would go trudging off into the forest to go see Baby Sunt. Belteshazzar would run after her and gently scold her, then reassure her that she would someday have a very special place in baby Saoshyant's life. "I have seen the future in my dreams," he would say. "It is ordained."

"Uh!!!" she spouted in protest. "I go see Baby Sunt! Like Brrr did!" Then she announced, with the supreme confidence that could only come from a four-year-old, that she was going to grow up and marry the baby Saoshyant. Orodes took her regularly to the forbidden Hollow of the Chaldeans, where Belteshazzar would tell his stories.

Belteshazzar was filled with marvelous tales of adventure – no one ever knew if they were true or not. He claimed they were, though they defied imagination – like the one about Shadrach, Meshach, and Abednego. King Nebuchadnezzar had passed a sentence of execution upon the three and threw them into a fiery furnace, after which he heard what sounded like singing and laughter coming from inside. The furnace was so hot that when the king peered inside to investigate, he singed his eyebrows. Of course what he thought he heard was not possible, given that the furnace was hot enough to melt iron. But when he looked a second time, singed eyebrows and all, what he saw was beyond belief. He saw four men, not three, unhurt and smiling and laughing, Shadrach, Meshach, Abednego, and a fourth, a Fravashi clothed in white, whereafter the three walked out untouched. Then there was the time Belteshazzar claimed he had been thrown into a den of hungry lions and emerged without so much as a scratch after remaining there for a full day and night. Nahid believed every word of those tales. Orodes himself came near to believing them, they were told with such conviction. The thing that made the stories so special was that Belteshazzar claimed to have been a personal witness, which, if true, would put him over 700 years old. He was in the process of committing the stories to the written word, in a scroll to be called The Book of Daniel, his given name prior to his service to the Parthian Empire.

Without a doubt Nahid's favorite story was that of Saoshyant, born in the far-off land of Judea and whose given name was Yeshua-ben-Yosef. "It is the coming of his time," Belteshazzar would say. "It is the ending of the thousand-year period."

"The Bundahishn predicted a sign would appear in the heavens to herald his birth," was how Belteshazzar would begin the story. "Year after year we among the Magi would watch the night sky, faithfully, night after night, scanning the skies east to west and north to south. For years we watched, and then one night there it was, the King's Star. We saw it merge with the Star of Renewal and Rebirth, to be joined by the Star of War. Three huge stars clumping together in the heavens! The Star of War is the one called Mars by the Romans. It symbolizes the day when the Fravashis will descend and claim victory over the forces of evil. The mighty three, Mars. Jupiter, and Saturn, the most powerful of the hosts of the night sky, came together within a collection of stars known to represent the land of Judea. Somewhere in Judea, the heavens were telling us, the child had been born. There could be no mistake about it. The Most High had taken on a cloak of flesh and blood to walk among men. We set out to find our king, and to lay before him our gifts. Our journey was long, lasting many days."

"Where is Jewee?" the wide-eyed little girl would ask. And Beltshazzar would each time answer in the same way, a shine of adoration sparking in his eyes, for he did so love little Nahid. "Judea, my child, is way far away," he would say, "beyond the mountains, beyond the desert, close to where the earth ends and falls into a great and boundless sea. It took us many nights to get there."

"How come you didn't get lost when you went to see him?" she would ask.

"We had the big star, remember?" he would answer. "As we traveled another star came to guide us, a great heavenly body that moved slowly across the sky. It looked like an upside-down teardrop. Its head lay high, and its tail fanned out toward the earth in a manner most spectacular, in translucent fashion, fading lighter to merge with the night. With each setting of the sun the star moved further westward, and each night it dropped lower in the sky, coming closer and closer to touching the mountains and the earth. As we traveled, we could see it even in the daytime, an upside-down teardrop of barely visible white brushing against the blue. As we passed into Judea, the silver mist of the star's tail had touched the horizon, and the city of Jerusalem.

"So then we inquired of the people there, asking where was he who has been born king of the Jews? No one understood what we were talking about. A strange sight it must have been, the Parthian Kingmakers coming from the East claiming to have followed a Divine star in search of one they would install as king. As king of the Jews? As king of Parthia? As king of both, though Judea be a state of Rome? Some of the people must have thought us possessed with madness. Some probably thought that Parthia was planning to invade and conquer Judea, which may not have been far from the truth, among the minds of some of the Parthians at least.

"Herod was concerned as well and summoned us for an audience. Herod told us that certain Hebrew writings also spoke of the coming of one sent by God, to be known as the Anointed One, the Messiah. Herod told us that when word came to him that Magi were searching for a king born in the land of Judea he called together the priests and the teachers of the Law, and inquired of them if this was true, and if so where the child had been born. The priests pointed to the writings of the Hebrew prophet Micah, in which was declared that a future king would be born in Bethlehem, a king great and powerful. One of the priests had the passage committed to memory:

But you, Bethlehem Ephratah,
Though you are small among the clans of Judah,
Out of you will come for me
One who will be ruler over Israel,

Whose goings out are from of old,
From Days of Eternity.

"Herod seemed as excited as we were about the king's birth. He asked us when the star had first appeared. 'We began our journey the very instant the heavens revealed themselves,' we told him, 'and we have been traveling many days, many months.' Herod sent us in search of the child, to Bethlehem, so that he could worship him too.

"It was late in the evening when we set out once more. The star was there again. We saw that its resting place was not Jerusalem, but in fact Bethlehem, six miles beyond. We saw that the entire town of Bethlehem was enclosed within the bottom of its wide cone. As we watched and marveled at the sight, there gleamed from the middle of the star's head a narrow stream of its essence, silent and pure, a twinkling within the cone of the softer light, spearing down to rest upon a certain rooftop. Then it was gone. But we remembered, and we marked the house. As we moved closer, the star and its cone moved further away, as happens when one comes close to the spot touched by a rainbow. But we had marked the house wherein lay the child, asleep in his bed under the protection and care of his father, the Great and Holy Ahura Mazda. It was a happening that was recorded in the journals of a Chinese stargazer, who had made note of a large comet that had appeared over the valleys and mountains of Hyrcania at the time of the child's birth, and whose course over the days and months had taken it westward to pass over Judea, so that doubtful future generations may read and believe."

"What did you do then, after the star found the house?" she asked. She asked the same questions each time she heard the story.

And each time Belteshazzar would answer in the same way: "Why, we approached the door and asked the man who came out if there was a child in the house."

"What did the man do?" she asked, as she did each time she heard the story.

"What would you do, if you looked out your window and saw hundreds of Kingmakers from the land of the Magi claiming your child was their future king?"

Nahid laughed. "I would tell them, Noooo. No baby here."

"Exactly! And that is what the man said!"

"You know what I would think! I would think you were robbers!"

"Mmm. Standing outside his house were hardly thieves. Standing there were Magi, kingmakers, dressed in expensive linens and carrying gifts. 'We are looking for the child who has been born king of the Jews,' we said. 'Born of virgin woman from the seed of the Most High.'

"The man explained that we had made a mistake, that his son was not of royal lineage.

"'There has been no mistake,' we told him. 'We have seen his star. It went before us and led us here.' We assured him we would not harm the boy, that we wished only to honor him and present him with gifts."

"So what happened then?"

"The man was very protective, refusing steadfastly to let us see his son, suspicious of our intentions. After all, imagine your thoughts as a father; you are aroused in the middle of the night by a contingent of royal priests from a country with which your country maintains an uneasy peace, and they announce that your son is their king. More than a king, a king sent by God."

"Ohhhh, I would say, 'No baby here!'"

"Yes. But! This father knew his son was no ordinary boy. This father knew what the answers were, when we asked our questions: When was he born? Did your wife conceive the child while still a virgin? Does the boy display unusual abilities? Does he have intelligence beyond his years? Were there visitations from angels?"

"Yes! He knew!" she stated, as if she could tell the story herself.

"So why don't you tell me what happened next," said Belteshazzar.

"Baby Sunt came running around the corner to stand right in front of you!"

"Yes! That is what happened. The child came toddling out followed by his mother. We told the father, 'Let us at least leave gifts. They are expensive gifts, among them gold that could be used for the boy's care and well-being. Please. Take them.'

"The mother pleaded with her husband. 'We have been praying for a means of survival,' she entreated. 'This gold might be the answer. Let us take a chance and let them in.'

"The father gave a nod of his head and the mother gestured for us to come forward. At that moment we knew we had found our Saoshyant. When the child looked up at us we knew. We were filled with the essence of God. It caused us to drop to our knees, for indeed this was a king, and more."

"Then what happened?"

"We laid our gifts before him. And we left, but we sent back servants to keep a distant watch on the child and his family, so we would know where he went and what he did, the things he taught, so that when he was ready to accept his kingship we would be ready. We tried to persuade the mother and father to come with us, to bring the child to Parthia so he could be properly trained and guided in his development. The father and mother of course refused. We accepted their decision, though we had the power to do otherwise; with us were guards waiting outside, and servants and soldiers who could have forced them to go. 'Ahura Mazda has chosen to place the child in the care of this man and this woman,' we reasoned. 'We must respect their decision and their authority.' The others finally agreed that yes, this was the right thing to do. We all agreed that the child should grow in the environment in which God had chosen to place him. Let the child, once he has matured, make the decision for himself of how and when he is to lead, we decided. After all, he is Saoshyant. How much greater is his wisdom than ours? Beyond this we were divided. Some thought he would be a physical king, leading armies of bone and muscle to gain the kingdom with force. Others, myself among them, argued that his purpose was a higher one, an inner one, and that the kingdom over which he was destined to rule was something other than that of mortar and stone."

"So then you went back."

"Yes. We returned to Parthia without telling Herod of our discovery.'

"Because of the Frah-shee."

"Yes, because a Fravashi told us in a dream not to trust Herod."

"What is a Frah-shee?" asked Nahid, the same as she would ask each time she would hear the story.

Belteshazzar would answer, "Fravashi, child, Fravashi. Say it, Fra-vah'-shee."

"Fra-vah'-shee," Nahid would repeat.

"Very good, child, very good. A Fravashi is a servant of Ahura Mazda, having great white wings."

"Like Sunt?" she said, pointing, meaning Saoshyant the eagle, perched on his pedestal, eyes closed.

"Yes, child Yes, child, wings like Saoshyant, except a Fravashi is not a bird. A Fravashi is like a man, but with wings. Some people call Fravashis angels."

"How come the eagle has the same name as baby Sunt?"

"My my, but you are just full of questions. Well, I'll tell you why. In years gone by, the Magi of ancient times envisioned Ahura Mazda as looking like an eagle. In truth Ahura Mazda is much more than an eagle, but it is as good of a symbol as any, because the eagle flies free, and the eagle protects its young with its powerful yet gentle wings. And Saoshyant the child comes to protect us with –." Belteshazzar stopped and smiled, nearly chuckled, in seeing boredom creep into the child's eyes.

"Oh," said Nahid.

It seemed as though the bird too was bored, having heard the story himself a thousand times. But the boredom didn't last long, thanks to Mithra. The wolf rolled over and opened his massive mouth, an invitation for the bird to spread his wings and lower himself to the floor so he could pick out food particles from between Mithra's teeth. It was the oddest of symbiotic relationships. The two were fast friends. When the eagle wasn't riding on Old Belteshazzar's shoulder he was riding atop Mithra, who was always walking next to Orodes, the animal's withers tall to the waist of even a tall man. Surely such relationships were signs that spirits of the divine abide within animals as well. Some feared it to be the opposite, that it might be the spirit of Ahriman possessing them both. None drew conclusions of the obvious, that it was natural animal behavior, of which man on earth could be enriched, if he would only observe, if only he would allow experience itself to define the behavior and not superstition. Over time it would become commonplace for Saoshyant to be seen riding atop the massive shoulders of the dire wolf called Mithra.

"Where is baby Sunt now? Still in the land of the Faraway?" she wanted to know.

"The land of Pharos – Pharos are great kings – but no, he is not there anymore. He lives in the kingdom of Judea."

"I go Ju-dee."

"Someday child. But not right now. Judea is way far away. It is too far even for me. Someday you shall go and learn from him. Oh, that I could go as well, and hear the things he says…."

"Is Sunt our king?"

"Yes, child, and much more."

"But, but, why he there and not here?"

"Mmm, a very good question, child. Truth, I do not know, other than to say there has to be a reason. Ahura Mazda always has a reason for the things he does. Perhaps he chose Judea for the birthplace because it is a center of commerce. Travelers to all parts pass through Jerusalem. The Lord Saoshyant's works will spread quickly to all corners of the world. Perhaps he chose Judea because among the Jews there exists detailed and disciplined methods of record keeping. Perhaps because among the Jews there exists an advanced system of ethics under which he could better grow to understand his true nature and purpose, for one comes into a new going-out with a mind like an empty vessel. For all these reasons, perhaps it is, that Ahura Mazda has chosen a Jewish maid to receive the seed and to be the holy mother Eredat-fedhri."

"But he is our king. He should be here."

"Yes, he is our king. He is also their king. He is everyone's king. He is the king of all people everywhere. He is the World Savior. That, my child, is what the word Saoshyant means, World Savior."

"I don't understand."

"Nor does anyone else, so don't feel bad about that one." Belteshazzar took an aging finger and placed it on her nose, as if with it he intended to impart wisdom, but more than anything it was a simple gesture of love from an old man to a little girl. "But I will try, if you will listen."

"OK." She was listening, but barely, because crawling beside her on the table was a horned beetle that had most of her attention. She was pushing it back from the edge where it wanted to go, and making it crawl on her hand, then putting it back down again, guiding its movements, she being the god and the tiny creature her subject.

"Well, OK, let me go on to explain," said Belteshazzar. "You have heard in your classes that Ahura Mazda made us, and that he also made the animals that roam the land –"

"Like he made Mithra?"

"Yes, child, like he made Mithra. And the fish in the sea, and the birds in the air, and the stars in the sky. But – that is not quite correct. What I say is this. I say that Ahura Mazda, the Supreme Architect of all that is and all that ever will be, he who was, is, and forever shall be, is not yet finished with his creation."

"You mean he's still making things?"

"He is still making everything, and that includes you, and me, and all of us."

"He's still making me?"

"Yes."

"Why?"

"Only Ahura Mazda knows the answer to that question. He is not done with any of us yet."

"How will we know when he's done?"

"At the end of all of our lives, after having been molded into the children of his perfection, we shall sit in his high court. As his sons and daughters we shall claim our inheritance, which he holds for us. The hand of Ahura Mazda will have destroyed us, and raised us back up. But that is not the end either. Even after that we shall grow and advance."

"What does Ar'Maz look like?"

"What does who look like?"

"Ar'Maz."

"Ah, you mean Ahura Mazda."

"What does he look like? Is he big and scary? Father says that if I ever did see him I would go blind, he's so scary looking."

"Well, I don't know about that. Let me see if I can explain. He's like this huge machine – if one can define such vast intelligence in terms so limiting. And each one of us, even that nasty little girl you keep fighting with, even people you don't know, are all a part of the machine. We're all cogs in that machine."

"What's a cog?"

"Cog. You know. A little wheel with teeth that's connected to another wheel. All the wheels together make the machine work. If even just one of those little wheels breaks down, the machine breaks down. The machine won't work."

"You mean Ar'Maz looks like a bunch of wheels?"

Belteshazzar's sides shook with laughter. "Oh child, you make my day special, do you know that?"

"Hmm hmm."

"OK, all right, look." Belteshazzar reached for a nearby bucket of water that sat beneath a dripping vent. Bobbing along the top were thin slivers of ice, left over from the overnight frost, making it cool and refreshing for those that dipped in a ladle for drinking. "OK, imagine the water in this bucket is Ahura Mazda, existing everywhere, having in it the potential of all form and all existence. Mmm? And the ice here? Imagine that it is you and me. The ice and the water are of the same substance, only in different degrees of manifestation. So it is with you and me, and everyone else that exists, and everything that exists. We are the ice, Ahura Mazda is both the ice and the water."

"I thought you said he was a machine."

"Yes, I did, didn't I? So I did. And so he is. Sort of. To know exactly what he is is beyond our comprehension. But that is as good of an explanation as any. So a machine he will be. And so are we all cogs in that machine, vital parts to its functioning."

"Oh." She pushed and prodded at the beetle, and tilted her head sideways, as though perhaps she was listening, as though maybe she truly was absorbing these intangible concepts elusive to even the adult mind, for they are in fact beyond our grasp, in the same way that calculus is beyond the ability of the human mind to conceptualize. Without the crutch of mathematics, even the simplest of calculus would be beyond one's mental grasp. The number one-third is an example. The number exists, because you can cut a thing into three equal parts, yet it doesn't exist, because it can only truly exist if the number 0.33333333333 is carried out to infinity, which is not possible, yet it is possible because one-third of an object does exist, yet it doesn't. So it is with these concepts being attempted by Belteshazzar, and of all things to the mind of a child!

"Life is evolving," Belteshazzar continued, after a brief pause and a smile, "Humankind is evolving. All of the millions of stars in the sky are evolving. If a creative intelligence exists, must it not also be evolving? Or is Ahura Mazda an absolute? But if Ahura Mazda is an absolute, who made the absolute? And is that absolute evolving? It must be, for to be perfect a thing must also possess the ability to improve itself. But if it can improve itself, then it is not yet perfect."

Belteshazzar nodded his head up and down, as though to examine and then agree with his own hypotheses. "The enigma of existence," he went on. "To be perfect, a thing can never be perfect. And suppose we as human creations are an inexorable part of this evolving entity, as the ice is to the water, and vital to its advancement, as the cog is to the machine." Belteshazzar was now well beyond the conceptual mind of a child, though who knows what a child can and cannot absorb, other than the child itself? "And suppose that each act of evil, each thought of malevolence, causes this component to break down in its purpose, causes therefore the great machine to stall in its purpose and progress. Now, suppose that each act of kindness, each moment of forgiveness, allows this omniscient, omnipresent intelligence of which we are a part to go forward in its never-ending progression, in our never-ending progression."

"Oh," said Nahid, in complete distraction, lifting up the beetle to her eyes, examining its glossy blue green shell, of far greater interest than anything Belteshazzar had to say.

"...I have named him Farhad," she said. "Father told me it means handsome boy. Don't you think he is handsome?"

"Mmm? What? Oh, why yes, of course he is handsome. Sorry my child, in my old age I forget who I am talking to, that I am speaking concepts beyond you, concepts beyond most grown-ups. I'm afraid I cannot remember what it was like to have been a child. It has been a long time. Surely I must have been one. Mmmm? Ah, but that was an age ago. But what is an age? An age to us is a moment in time to Ahura Mazda, the Knower and Maker of all things. An entire lifetime could very well be but a mere day to Ahura Mazda. The sun rises, our hearts beat. The sun sets, our hearts are stilled; and we rest, until he sends us out again, to refine us more, as one purifies a metal, again and again, until at last that creation has met certain death…and a new one has risen from its ashes, a creation in its completion, one sitting in the high court of Ahura Mazda, forever. The Right Hand of the Father, as those in the land of the Israelites would say. And even that is only the beginning. For when eternity is the endpoint, any point in time is only the beginning. And thanks be to our Lord Saoshyant, he who loves us beyond measure, he who is perfect, he who is refined and pure, who is the past and the future, he who has no beginning, who has no end – for without the light he is to bring to the world we would remain in the darkness of our infancy, instead of moving to stand with angels, on the threshold of things to come."

"Ohhhhh," said Nahid, chin on the table, nose to nose with her little buddy The insect was now completely motionless in front of her, as they both stared into each other's eyes.

"There I go again, droning on. Sorry child."

"Do you think Farhad is a part of Ahura Mazda too?"

"Farhad? Who is Farhad?"

"Farhad! The beetle! I have named him Farhad! Haven't you been listening? One of Father's servants is named Farhad. It means handsome boy. Don't you think he is handsome?"

"Yes child, he is very handsome."

"Is it true?"

"Is what true?"

"'Bout the machine. Is it really true? Is Ahura Mazda really a machine?"

"Mmm. Someday perhaps we shall find out."

"I saved Farhad's life. Cause you didn't see him. He was on the floor. You almost stepped on him. So I helped the machine."

"You have been listing! What a dear child! Yes, yes, of course, of course. You helped very much! And yes, Farhad is a part of the machine as well!" He kissed her on the top of her head. "You have been listening! My precious, precious child!" And this tender old man everyone thought was doddering and confused, but within whose mind blazed the secrets of life and immortality, droned on again about concepts beyond comprehension…until the child yawned and looked as though she were about to fall away into sleep. "I think it's true," she said.

"What? You think what is true?"

"'Bout the machine. That we're a part of the machine."

"Here's the funny part," said Belteshazzar. "It doesn't matter if it's true or not. What matters is that we love one another, and help one another, and forgive one another, and lift one another up. That's what matters. Because that is what makes the machine work. Even if there is no machine."

"I think so too," she said. And Farhad crawled off to pursue his own unique role in the machine, if the machine exists.

CHAPTER 3

CALIGULA

THE PARTHIAN EMPIRE – THE FORESTS OF HYRCANIA

The king was cursing and throwing things on the floor, and against walls, in search of his dress gloves. "By Mazda I had them, I had them right here," he thundered. "They were right here." He thrust a finger at the table. "Right here."

"Where did you have them last?" responded the helpful queen.

He pointed again to the table. "Are you deaf woman? I told you. Right here, they were right here," whereupon Mithra popped up from where he had been lounging in observation of the curious exchange – head between his paws beneath the open window where the morning sun had been warming him, where the summer breeze had swirled and caressed his golden fur – and loped long-legged out of the room, that semi-side-ways glide specific to Mithra, and returned moments later with the very gloves and dropped them at the king's feet. There was no look of shame on Mithra's face, only that open-mouthed smile huffing out charm, tail straight out and whipping around like a windmill. The king roared out his pleasure. His sides fairly shook with his laughter, and he rubbed Mithra's head. Unlike dogs, wolves rarely express a need for affection, though they do love and show love, with pupils large and black and ears pasted back like they have none at all, so when King Artabanus rubbed the animal's head and said, "Good boy," Mithra cast back one of those looks and loped off to the sunshine and settled himself back down again. "That animal, better than a servant," the king bellowed. Mithra fanned his tail again, as though he understood what had been said, as though a duty had been fulfilled, then curled it back around him. The king had resisted the inclusion of a wolf into the family, but now was growing to love the animal. He still considered it foolish and unnatural to make a pet of an animal considered a predator, and spoke openly of it, yet when Mithra ate the pillows of his favorite lectus he laughed it off, saying he needed a new one anyway. When Mithra adopted a litter of baby squirrels – why he didn't have them for breakfast one will never know – King Artabanus picked them up one by one in his giant and scarred hands and spoke to them as if he himself was nursing them. Maybe that was why the king loved Orodes so much, because there was a part of the king that was just like him, gentle and compassionate, though he was afraid to admit it, even to himself, because the part everybody saw in the king was the part that allowed him to protect the kingdom and keep the warring Persian sub factions at peace with one another. It was the part the people depended upon, the part the people wanted. It was also the part that abused the people.

King Artabanus soon became known as the Wolf King and Parthia as the Land of the Wolves, Hyrcania. Mithra was an anomaly of nature, made so by Ahura Mazda and by love. He was as large as he was gentle, and as gentle as he was large. Images were imprinted on tapestries and carved into stone, on doors, on balustrades, on walls, even in the hills on cliffs, of a wolf with golden fur and penetrating yellow eyes, of Mithra, the king's fierce companion and protector. The king still worried, and vocalized it from time to time, wondering if a time would come when Mithra would turn, because "you can never take the wild out of the wild," as Gotarzes warned that first day when Mithra came into their lives.

Now and then Mithra was put on a leash, for show only. One such time was a morning when a visiting dignitary wanted to experience the forests of Wolf Country and wanted to see the wolf firsthand. "This particular visitor is a very important person," King Artabanus told his son. "We must all be on our best behavior."

"What is his name?" inquired Orodes.

King Artabanus laughed and smacked his lips, and stroked the whiskers that tended to mat themselves upon his mouth, whereupon a smile curved upward. "His name? Who can say it? The Romans and their names! Gaius Julius Caesar Augustus Germanicus. The Romans have a flair for complexity. He is known by the common name of Caligula, which means 'Little Boots,' because as a youngster he would visit his father's army camps and clomp around in his father's oversized boots."

"How old is he?"

"He is only 13. Even though he is younger than you, I am hoping you two can be friends. Remember what I told you, about how important it is to be honorable toward our Roman guests? There could come a time when he will be emperor."

"That amuses me," said Orodes. "The Romans are our enemies, yet they are our friends. The two countries are threatening war, yet entertaining their dignitaries as if they were visiting royalty."

"Ah, but this one is royalty. His father is Germanicus, the adopted son of the emperor Tiberius and a prominent general in the Roman army, and most beloved by the people. The reference to Julius Caesar comes because Caligula is of the Julian dynasty, and the reference to Augustus honors the great Caesar Augustus, to whom he is a grandson-in-law and great-nephew. And that, I believe, makes him the nephew of the current emperor. Does it not? I lose track of all the nephews and sons and grandsons and sons-in-laws. At any rate, he is royalty, and will be treated as such."

"Why not just love them and be done with it?" young Orodes mused. "Then they would no longer be enemies. Imagine for a moment what kind of a world it would be if there was nothing to kill or die for …"

The king interrupted him with his laughter, and put a hand on his son's shoulder. "Ah my son, my son, if only life were that simple. Someday you will grow up and understand the world. Here you are, eighteen years old, and still you have the idealism of a child. My son, my son."

"You need not worry about me, Father. I will be cordial to our guest."

"Yes, I suppose you will. It is not in your nature to be otherwise. Which is good, because soon I will be sending you to Rome."

"Rome? Me? But why?"

"Why indeed. For the furthering of your education, and for culture and refinement, as was done with Vonones. But we must be careful and send you there under the cloak of secrecy. Vonones was rejected by the Parthian people after returning. They referred to him as Caesar's bond slave. That is the reason I am king and he is not. I do not want that to happen to you."

"Then why send me at all?"

"There is much that can be learned from the Roman people. Trust me when I say this. Future governments will be patterned after the Roman system."

"Little Boots" was not at all what Orodes had expected. Orodes liked him instantly. In some ways Caligula was a lot like Orodes, shy, polite, and much more reserved than the other sons of visiting kings. King Artabanus insisted that Mithra be on leash during the boy's entire visit, for the sake of the king's image. Guests expected the king's wolf to be ferocious, and great effort was made to convey such an image. Among other shrewd tactics, the "fang game" was employed, where Orodes or King Artabanus would grab Mithra's two longer fangs with their forefingers and play tug-of-war. Mithra loved the game. He would growl and twist and pull and display a terrifying façade, but one look at his face, ears pasted back and pupils wide with affection, would reveal that the gentle animal was having fun, and was understanding the power of his jaws. Of course no one but a wolf expert would know that.

The forest was particularly green that day, and the tops of its bare and rocky upper mountains were ringed in low lying clouds, enough to encase the entire valley in softness, letting just enough of the sun through to paint itself upon the trees of the forests and the wildflowers. "A well-kept secret," Orodes told his guest. "Most think of Parthia as being no more than barren rock and high desert. As you can see" – Orodes swept the valley with a wide gesture – "It is not true."

"Everyone thinks the same about the land of the Jews," said Caligula, "that it is nothing more than barren desert, but in the north, where the Jordan has its beginning, where the god Pan lives and plays, it is like this, filled with trees and forest creatures. I have been there many times. It is one of my favorite places. I am told you are a Jew by birth."

Orodes looked at his guest with bewilderment.

"Ah, perhaps I should not have said anything" said Caligula, an apology veiled in shrewdness.

"What do you mean? What are you talking about?"

"I'm sorry. I should not have spoken. I thought you knew."

"Knew what?"

Caligula spoke at a level far above that of the thirteen-year-old that he was. "…that you are not the natural son of your father and mother. Have you not wondered why you do not look like your brothers? Have you not wondered why you look more like a Jew than a Persian?"

A mischief maker. This he had been told, about the young Caligula, and he was prepared for such, but this he had not been prepared for. He felt like slapping the little bastard, for Caligula himself had questionable birth, and Orodes had his mouth half open ready to say so. No bigger around than a poker, was this boy called Little Boots. And his face was pocked with pimples, and he was afraid of even the smallest of forest creatures. When a hyrax came scampering across the road he stiffened with fear. The low-lying clouds to the east flashed with a jagged stripe of lightening, and it caused him to jump. Rather than jabbing with a mischievous comment Orodes kept silent, remembering his promise to his father that he would be courteous to this bizarre guest of royalty.

After walking for a few moments in silence Orodes asked a question, forced by his need to know. "What are you saying? Are you saying I'm adopted? That the king is not my real father?"

"Ask him. Everyone knows but you, apparently. Even the beggars lining the streets of the Esquiline in Rome know that Prince Orodes of Parthia is not the true son of King Artabanus, that he was rescued from the slave cages as an infant. But evidently the rumors are wrong. You should know more than me."

With each beat of his heart a great emptiness thudded out from within Orodes. Could it be true? He hated Caligula for telling him, yet if it was true, should he not thank him? It was his adoptive father he should hate, yet, if it was true, should be not thank his adoptive father, for saving him from the slave cages, for giving him a life no other slave would ever know? So why then did the emptiness exist? Why should he even care?

"Well, I can tell you right now, the rumors are wrong," said Orodes. "Perhaps we should walk back."

"Let's sit awhile," said Caligula. "Rest a bit. I'm tired. And I'm enjoying the forest. They were right. The forests of Hyrcania are greener than any other kind of green." He settled himself on a fallen grey snag, in itself beautiful, for our of its rotted-out pockets grew sprigs of young trees. Caligula commented on it. "Life growing out of death. It is a strange world, where life feeds on life, where life grows out of death, where life creates death, where death creates life."

Orodes had been warned; he had been given instructions to indulge Caligula's curious whims, but that was before he knew that those curious whims included sexual proclivities, because Caligula's hand kept going beneath Orodes' tunic and under his loin garments to fondle his genitals. Then Caligula's lips pressed against his ear.

Even then Orodes was careful in what he said. "You are very attractive," he told Caligula, though he wasn't, with a nose thin and small, arms far too long, and a torso that tended to fall over before his spindly legs could catch up to it. "...but I cannot. I am committed to another."

"Another man, I presume? How'd you get the black eye?"

"It's not a black eye; it's a birthmark. I've had it since the day I was born."

Caligula's smile spread wide. "Tell me," he said. "– how would this other man you are supposedly committed to find out? I certainly won't tell." Caligula was continuing to press against him, attempting to kiss him, caress him.

Orodes was continuing to push him away. "I would know, and I made a promise to be true to this person."

"If I were Caesar I could order you to submit to me."

"Even then I wouldn't."

"Perhaps you would if it meant your life."

"Not even then." Orodes was being firm now and was holding Caligula at a distance. "I am being polite, as I was told to be. But truly listen to me when I say, you are testing my patience."

"I wonder what would happen if I told everyone what I have discovered, that you are not only a Jew, but are also of the other sort, and that you were attempting to force yourself upon me. What then?"

"I would simply deny it. The dirty deed would reverse itself and land upon you." How Caligula could possibly have known about his sexual preference was a surprise and a mystery. Except for the man to whom he was committed, he had not told anyone.

"Perhaps you would be more cooperative if it meant the life of someone you love? Your precious wolf?"

Orodes ignored the threat. "My man-friend and I have agreed to be fair to one another, that's all there is to it," he said.

"Your religion tells you this?"

"It is a simple matter of right and wrong, and of responsibility. Religion has nothing to do with it."

Orodes could tell that the rejection was angering Little Boots, and that his green eyes were hiding dark thoughts. "It's time for us to return home," said Orodes. "Come, Mithra." Mithra jumped to his feet at the command.

"Ohweee," said Caligula. "Look at that animal! Look how he obeys! Too bad you don't obey as agreeably." Neither spoke to the other as they walked.

A hyrax scampered by and Mithra took off after it, jerking the leash out of Orodes' hand. The king had insisted that it be a chain leash – Mithra could effortlessly bite through anything less – so when it became caught in the crevice of a split rock formation he had not the ability to free himself. Even a wolf's teeth are not as strong as iron.

Mithra was not howling. No need for that. He knew the human protectors who had always kept him from harm would come and set him free, and in fact one was there, right there in front of him. The skinny one. But why wasn't he doing it? Why was he walking away, this strange friend of his master's? No need to worry; he would be back. Of course he would. And if not, his master would come. Someone would come. It was the way of the world. Mithra knew of no other possibility. Unlike his forest siblings he had never known hunger, had never known danger. He never had to fight for shelter. He had never learned to fear man. Mithra's needs had always been provided for by these great and wonderful creatures that walked on two legs, that had wisdom beyond his own, that would protect him always.

"There he is," pointed out Little Boots, gesturing with his outstretched arms in a direction opposite the one in which he had caught site of Mithra, sitting, waiting.

"Mithra, come!" Orodes went running in the direction Little Boots had pointed. The wrong direction. And of course Mithra was not there.

Orodes kept calling, unconcerned, expecting him to come bounding out from the underbrush at any moment. And when it didn't happen the worst kind of fear gripped Orodes. Because he knew something had gone wrong. It was a fear every bit as strong as the terror that comes to a parent searching for a lost child, or a shepherd searching for a lost lamb. It gripped him so hard it robbed him of breath.

With senses heightened Mithra heard the call and responded with a deep and low howl, but it blended with the rush of a nearby creek and the approaching thunder of a storm and simply could not be heard, at least not by the one person who needed to hear it.

One will never know what caused Caligula to do such a thing. There is a darkness within some people, that's all. It's rare, fortunately. It's rarer still that such a person comes into power. But destiny *would* yield to the dark side. Little Boots *would* possess power. In ten years he would succeed his great uncle as the emperor of Rome. And the world would tremble.

The Parthian royal family did not know how attached it was to the wolf named Mithra until he was gone. They were all thrown into a panic as they searched, then into dismay when the searches turned up nothing. Each family member participated. The king eventually called out the army. "Comb the forest inch by inch," he instructed his soldiers. "I want that animal found!" For days they searched.

"Begging your pardon, Your Magnificence," said Arsaces on the seventh day. Arsaces was general of the king's eastern forces and was a great hunter and understood forest creatures. "Mithra is a wolf. Could it not be that he responded to a longing within to rejoin his pack?"

"Did you not remember what I told you?" shouted the king. "He is dragging a chain around with him!"

"Yes, Your Magnificence, yes," said the general.

So yet again they searched.

On the tenth day Mithra was found, or at least the place was found where his chain had become entangled. A broken section of his leather collar lay on the ground, having marks that could only have been made by powerful teeth. The other end was still wedged within the rock crevice. A small patch of blood was there also, imprinted with multiple paw prints, more than could be made by one animal.

After that, the king gave up the notion of ever finding Mithra, but still continued with the search. At one point the Parthian army spent an entire week, day and night, in the forest in search of Mithra. But a wolf pack is as elusive as it is cunning. At night the moon lit the way, large and ornate in the fog filtered sky. Still Mithra and his pack was not found. The search did provide Orodes with a chance to connect with his father the king. When they would sit beneath that moon and before a fire that snapped and popped with sparks that melded with the stars, and sip beer, they would sometimes hear wolves from a distance, mournful sounds echoing above the treetops. Sometimes, reflected in the firelight would be sets of eyes. Large or small they could not tell. A bear? A hyrax? A wolf? Mithra? Sometimes Orodes would shout into the darkness. "Mithra? Mithra? Is that you? Come Mithra! Come!" But nothing would happen, other than the cracking of twigs and underbrush as the calls frightened away whatever animals that had been there.

Once, in the clear light of early morning, while standing upon a cliff overhang, King Artabanus waved his arm as if to pass it over the entire Parthian landscape. "All this will someday be yours to administer," he said to his favored son.

Most children would give their weight in gold to hear words like that, but Orodes was not such a person. His mind was on what he had just been told, the truth about his adoption – his father the king had admitted to it – but it was a truth that came tinged. King Artabanus told him that his natural father had been a traitor and a criminal, because that was what he had been told, those ten and more years ago when the child had come to them from the slave cages. There was even a rumor among the Parthians that the traders had saved the child from the sacrificial altar, at the last moment, at the very point of the raising of the knife. The Jews were believed at the time to have practiced child sacrifice, because of a story of a man named Abraham, a thing particularly detestable to Mazda. The king assured Orodes that they had raised him as their own, and that it didn't matter to them that he was not blood offspring, in the same fashion that it didn't matter to Augustus Caesar that his stepson Tiberius was not blood offspring. "The government was Caesar's to pass to whomever he chose," was the king's example, "just as Parthia's government is mine to pass to whomever I choose, with the endorsement of the Magi of course, and trust me when I say, the Magi will support me in my choice to name you. Belteshazzar will see to that."

But the silence reigned, as they both looked out at the land from the high cliff top.

It was the king himself who broke the spell: "Worry not, my son – you are nothing like your father."

"And what is my father like?"

"I have already told you. He sold your people and their land to the Romans, and nearly took your life, the life of his only begotten son. The slave traders saved you from the sacrificial altar. Prior to that I don't know what had transpired."

"No, I mean you. What are you like? You are my father."

"I would like to think I am a strong king, the man who holds the warring factions of the Parthians together."

"Sometimes late at night I hear the screams of men. There are rumors that you torture those who disagree with you. It is said that you sometimes torture and kill your own guards."

Artabanus hung his head, as though to speak of it gave him pain. "There are times when you must do things that are unpleasant, when you are a king" he said, and let it then be known by holding his palm up that he would speak no further on the matter.

"We must return," he said. "For you must make preparations for your trip to Rome, for the furthering of your education. You will stay with the emperor himself."

"I have no desire to go to Rome."

"Mithra is gone. We all have to accept that fact. It is difficult, I know. It is difficult for me as well. But he's gone. Your mother will help you prepare. It is a long trip."

"But what about what we sometimes see on the eastern ridge?" Orodes was referring to the ridge that overlooks the city, and the wildlife that comes to gather there, wolves sometimes, and there was always one off by itself, as if it did not quite belong, too far away to know for sure. "It could be Mithra. He's bigger than the rest, just like Mithra, and it does seem to have the golden brown coloring of Mithra."

"It's not him," said the king. "And if it is him, it's clear that he has made his decision."

"It is him. I know it is."

"Then he has made his choice, and you should leave him be."

The logic of it was sound, but to accept it was hard. It was as if Orodes had lost a lover. Mithra had gone everywhere with him over the years as he grew up, had slept with him, had listened to his deepest thoughts and understood them. Orodes truly believed that.

Everyone had given up. But not Orodes. Orodes walked the hills and valleys daily with his broken heart.

And Gotarzes assisted. The two brothers had become close during the past three years of having Mithra in their lives. The animal had been a type of bridge between the two of them, a commonality that bonded them. Also bonding them was the diametric opposite sides of their characters, softness, hardness, gentility, strength, so that together as a unit they were made stronger than their individual parts. For it was Gotarzes who was the committed paramour that Orodes spoke of, his own adopted brother.

CHAPTER 4

LOVE AND LOYALTY

THE PARTHIAN EMPIRE – THE CITY OF ECBATANA

It *was* Mithra up on that eastern ridge. He had made his choice. He had chosen the wolf pack.

He was thin and his fur was matted and balled up in clumps, unrecognizable from the silk-coated and muscled animal of before. The only thing that remained the same was the caudal mark on the upper part of his tail, the perfect shape of an hourglass. The perpetual smile had been replaced by a look of desperation, of deep hunger that was pacified now and then by the taste of a grub, or of a mouse, or sometimes from the leftovers of a kill that another wolf would bring him.

And that other wolf – recognizable by scent – was the one that used to shelter him and allow him to suckle. He tried from time to time to latch onto her underbelly, as faded memories prompted him to do, to get the milk that used to appease the hunger, but she would not allow it anymore, could not allow it, because she was old and long past her time. Mithra himself was old.

He had made his choice. Still, he could not forget the protectors down below. None of them had done him any harm. The opposite was true – they had fed him and kept him from harm – so he was torn in his loyalty. The ideal would be for the pack to expand and include both the wolves and the protectors who moved on two legs. But of course that was impossible.

At times Mithra would go to the ridge by himself to look down, in hopes of seeing one of those protectors. Sometimes he would start to go toward them. Sometimes one of them would yell his name and start to run toward him, and in his uncertainty he would lope away to the pack. In time he learned to hunt for himself, small game, like the hyrax or the shrew, both as abundant as ice in winter, fish occasionally too. And as his mother aged, roles came to be reversed. Mithra brought her food, the hyraxes and the shrews…and as such he could not leave…

…until a time when the old girl failed to get up. Mithra pushed at her with his nose, tried to lift her. She was cold and stiff. It was confusing to him. He had never experienced this before. He stayed there with her for days, bringing her the grubs and the shrews, and chasing away circling buzzards in the daytime and scavengers in the night, and biting at the flies that buzzed furiously everywhere. Perhaps he would have understood if he would have grown up a wolf, but he had grown up as a human in a wolf's body, with a wolf's mind, with a wolf's ability to comprehend. As each day passed, her body rotted more in the sun and the open air. Eventually her stomach began to rise and fall – life? – he bent in his excitement to sniff it, and as he did the carcass burst, and a white oozing mass rolled out. Life indeed, but of a different sort, thousands of them, hundreds of thousands, each no bigger than a toenail, feasting, bubbling. And so he began to understand, and he began to spend more time on the high bank of the ridge, longing for a life that used to be.

One day, as he was lying there on the ridge, panting, looking below, he saw something that didn't make sense. The other wolves had seen it too. They too were on the ridge, a distance away. What they all saw was a child off by herself quietly singing and picking flowers and arranging them into a basket. Mithra recognized the scent, and the sweet voice, though the scent was hidden by perfumes and oils. He had not seen Nahid the entire time he had been gone, not even from the ridge. But the scent was the same, and it reached up to the ridge and the long and highly sensitive nose of Mithra, and it caused him to react. It caused him to remember. He remembered that whenever Nahid would enter the room where Mithra was, he would spring to his feet and run to her. It got to be where it was a reaction of his muscles to the sight and the scent. He could smell her before she came visible. Belteshazzar used to laugh and say it was because Nahid was such an advanced entity. And so it was on the ridge that Mithra's muscles tensed and sprang into service. He was running toward her before he realized he was doing it.

Mihra's approach was misunderstood by the pack. A hunt begins with one wolf, usually the alpha, though not always, that identifies the prey then stalks it, while the others follow from a distance. He spots the prey. Rarely is it human. Typically it is a weaker or injured member of a heard of some sort, a straggler. Then he initiates the attack. The attack is timid at first, hardly identifiable as an attack. The others mimic. They gather in a circle around the straggler. And quickly the animal is down and bleeding to death, but not before its soft entrails are devoured before its still living eyes.

As Mithra ran up to Nahid and jumped on her and began licking her face the pack thought it was an attack. The people watching thought so too, as they ran to help with rocks, sticks and whatever else they could procure as weapons. They thought it was six wolves attacking the girl. In reality it was one wolf protecting her from the other five. The snarling and the gnashing of teeth was so furious that to discern friend from foe was not possible. Even Nahid herself did not realize what was happening, that it was Mithra keeping the other five away. Because wolves don't snarl when they bring down prey and eat. They snarl and bare teeth when they fight. The snarling was from the lone wolf fighting the others, and it was furious. But nobody knew that.

It was over quickly. The confused pack retreated to the ridge, and Mithra came sliding in to sit on Nahid's feet, confused as to why he was being chased away, and why rocks were being thrown at him. He ran away to a certain distance, then sat, panting, confident that his decision was the right one, confident he was one of the humans, knowing that now he could never go back to the wolves.

Nor could he go back to the humans.

He had protected one of them, saved her, and for that he would pay a price.

One of the humans that had come to the child's rescue was none other than Orodes himself, believing also that it was all six wolves that had attacked.

There were tears streaming unabashed down Orodes' face as he stood before his father the king, his beloved Mithra by his side. "I will do it myself, Father," he said. "It is my duty. It is my wolf. I will do it. It must be done. Gotarzes was right. You can never take the wild out of the wild."

The two of them, Mithra and Orodes, walked into the forest, Orodes with a solemn look on his face, knowing it would be only him that would return, Mithra with a look of utter happiness on his face.

King Artabanus sat on his throne, and upon his face was a look of pride, and with compassion in his heart, as Orodes and Mithra disappeared into the woods. This surely showed courage, the deepest kind, where duty supersedes wish. Perhaps he is a man after all. Perhaps he would make a good king.

CHAPTER 5

AN ARROW FOR MITRHA

THE PARTHIAN EMPIRE – THE FORESTS OF HYRCANIA

It was good for Mithra to be back where he belonged, back with his true pack, the ones who protected him, the ones he would protect. They were different, these animals that walked on two legs, different in look and sound and habit. They made different and unusual sounds. But they were the ones. They were his pack.

Long ago he had begun to realize that these complex sounds have meaning, that it was the way these creatures interact with one another, and most of these sounds he had come to understand. It had been no accident that he found and brought King Artabanus his gloves. He would have been able to do more had he the ability to articulate the sounds himself, even perhaps carry on rudimentary conversations. As it was, all he could do was try, and hope that the grunts, growls and whines that substituted would suffice. Sometimes they would. And then sometimes the sounds grew so complex he couldn't follow them at all, and couldn't even begin to mimic them. And he learned that he must never use low throated sounds in his efforts, that they would be misunderstood and would bring fear and anger. He could often communicate with Orodes using no sounds at all, using nothing more than his body and his eyes.

He had learned long ago that the simplest of sounds – Stay, Come, Stop – were all directives from a higher intelligence that he must trust for his own wellbeing. So when he heard the word "Stay," when Orodes led him to a certain flat part of a meadow, by where Orodes had dug a hole in the ground, he did not question it.

But this was the most confusing of all. Why, after Orodes had administered the command of "Stay," did he kneel with tears in his eyes and hug him around his neck and say, "Goodbye faithful friend"? He knew what goodbye meant, and he knew what friend meant. But the words did not mix with one another. What his alpha-friend said next was one of those things that lost its meaning altogether to complexity. *"I wish it didn't have to be this way. This is the hardest thing I have ever had to do."* But he did know that something was terribly wrong. Because he knew what a bow was. He knew that when an arrow was locked in place on its frame it would fly and strike with great devastation. Why then was it locked and loaded and directed at him?

And he did not understand why his alpha-friend at the last minute screamed to the sky and moved the bow to the right so that the arrow thunked its devastation into a nearby fallen log. And he did not understand why his alpha-friend began picking up stones and throwing them at him. Nor did he understand why he was saying the words he was saying – "Go! Go!" – words he understood. He just did not know why his leader, his friend, was saying them, and attempting to hurt him, a thing he would *never* do to him, regardless of circumstance.

So with a heart broken into pieces Mithra loped away, stopping now and then to look back, only to experience another volley of rocks. Then he vanished into the underbrush, with that sideways glide specific to Mithra.

CHAPTER 6

THE LORDS OF THE WORLD

ROME

The Lords of the World, they called themselves, the people who strolled the streets there. While he was in Rome two things happened that would forever change the life of Prince Orodes of Parthia. First, he received a letter from his father delivered by private courier. Second, he was invited to the games by the emperor.

Our good friend and your teacher Belteshazzar is dying, the letter began, and desires your presence. I have written to Tiberius requesting his assistance in preparing for your long voyage home. Belteshazzar told me to tell you that he has something important to speak with you about, and an item he wishes to bequeath to you. He is not wealthy, so I cannot imagine it is anything of value. The foolish old man. But we do honor him. I promised him I would tell you.

Then the letter warned of a conspiracy afoot that could result in the overthrow of the Roman government. It involves offshoots from many standing governments, it went on to say. The battle will be furious, and it will be impossible to know friend from foe. Rumors are already beginning to circulate, and if such a rumor reaches the emperor's ears my fear is that he will have you executed, so your return must be with haste. I have been given assurances that once the coup has taken place the current governments will remain. Rome, Parthia, Armenia, and the four Palestinian tetrarchies all will be held intact, but all will operate beneath an overall umbrella government ruled over by Him, the one called Saoshyant by the Parthians, Messiah by the Jews. I have been given assurances by the conspirators that I shall retain control over Parthia, and that you shall be given the government of Cappadocia, on the condition that you can demonstrate your military leadership. Say nothing to Gotarzes about this. He shall also be given a territory, but it needs to come from me. In Rome you have been afforded the opportunity of learning much to prepare you for the task. You have learned the languages of all the governments, a necessity, and have gained an understanding of their cultures and their religions, also a necessity. As regards your military training, I have appointed you general of my forces in the northern regions, where Armenia is under threat from invading forces. You will be apprised of the situation upon your return to Ecbatana, and will leave in the spring for your post. I pray for your safety, my son, but if you should die in battle, remember that to die by the sword is an honor above all honors, and is rewarded in the next world with possessions fit for a king and virgins the beauty of which transcend description.

I beseech you in the strongest terms, say nothing of this to Tiberius. Say nothing to anyone.

Be well, my son. When you have read this give these tablets back to the courier, who has instructions to destroy them forthwith. I shall ever remain,

Your Loving and Devoted Father
King Artabanus III
Of the Ruling Arsacid Dynasty
So ordained by the Magi
And by their seal made so.

Orodes handed the tablets to the courier, then asked him to return the next day at the same place and time, whereupon he would have a reply for his father. But there would be no reply, because Orodes would not return. His father's deepest fears would be made manifest.

Because the following morning an invitation would come from Tiberius to sit in the emperor's box at the games. Such an invitation is a tremendous honor. Orodes could not refuse. To do so would be tantamount to treason, though he detested the spectacle of men and women fighting to the death for any reason, let alone be it for no reason. Further to incite his disgust was the pre-gladiatorial "Beast Hunt," promoted as the "spectacle of a hunter armed with nothing more than a knife fighting a hungry lion – which one will win? – and an angry bull elephant pitted against a bear brought to frenzy by salt-tipped arrows slung at non-vital parts, plus a surprise the likes of which has never been seen by Roman eyes –" as the advertisements read, posted at eye level throughout the city, ending with: "– starvation-ravaged Hyrcanian wolves, the most ferocious of all beasts, pitted against the winner of the contest between the bull elephant and the bear."

CHAPTER 7

REUNITED

ROME

So often the emperor's guests drew as much attention as the games themselves, as people tried to figure out who it was occupying the guest seats, but none so much as the venerable Wolf Prince of Parthia. Rumors and tales had circulated throughout the kingdoms, told and retold by those in the traveling caravans, and had grown into a mystique. King Artabanus the Wolf King and his son the Wolf Prince could transform themselves into wolves, it was said, which they often did to scour the countryside at midnight and avenge their enemies. Now and then a mysterious death of a farm animal would turn up, with internal organs removed as though for a sacrifice. The people knew what had happened, that it was the Wolf Prince transformed, or the Wolf King, and fairly quivered at the knowledge of it, for they knew that one night it might be their desecrated remains found at the side of some road. A new story was soon to be told, of what happened on a certain day in Rome when the prince attended at the games. It was during the "Beast Hunts" that the prince stood and with nothing more than the power of his eyes stilled the souls of the beasts.

Only one other person had been able to do such a thing, the Galilean Rabbi, the Sorcerer Jew that wandered from town to town in the land of the Hebrews, tales of which had even reached Rome, of how he could heal the sick and raise the dead, and could calm the hearts of storms. Once the

Galilean Rabbi defeated an angry crowd with nothing more than the power of his eyes, as they were about to throw him over a cliff.

And so did the Parthian prince speak to the animals, in a way that could not be possible, with only his eyes. But the people saw. The Romans had a saying, that if ten or more people bear witness to an event, the event is true. Thousands bore witness to this event. They saw the Parthian Wolf Prince stand and call forth one of the wolves that had been captured in the forests of Hyrcania. The largest of them, given power by the prince, ran toward the stands and leapt a full forty feet through the air, over the barricades and into the stands, and scattered the people to the left and to the right. Looking almost as if it had a smile on its face, the wolf bounded straight for the prince, attacking him with a fury. It was then that the people realized how big the animal was. With its forepaws on the prince's shoulders it was at least a full cubit taller than the prince, and its head twice the size of a man's head and shaped like an almost perfect isosceles triangle. Prince Orodes charmed the animal in the very midst of it tearing at his face, with fangs like stilettos. In less time than it would take to utter a single word, the animal was in complete submission, whining and licking the prince's face, made so by the prince's demonic stare. What the prince then did was truly startling. He drew his sword and turned against Caesar's guards who were advancing upon him – though he did not need the weapon, because under the prince's gaze the guards submitted and backed away and opened the gates, so that the prince could lead the remaining wolves and the bull elephant to freedom.

That was the legend, the way the tale was told, or variations thereof. What happened in reality was something far less akin to the supernatural. Mithra recognized his young alpha, his deep and committed friend, that's all, at about the same time that his human alpha recognized him. Orodes had drawn his sword because he had fully intended to have to fight for his beloved pet – more friend that pet, more brother than wolf – but the guards were so dumbfounded by the incident, already believing there were unnatural forces at play, that they backed away of their own accord. And they opened the gates out of nothing more than their own fear. Orodes did have to use his sword, but it was not to fight; he used it to cut Mithra free from the protective netting below the emperor's box. Mithra's aging leap had in truth only been about fifteen feet and he had slipped into the netting. The snarling and snapping, the baring of fangs, had been nothing more than the fang game Mithra was so fond of playing, where Orodes would grab his two lower fangs and the two would play tug-of-war.

And Orodes, fully expecting to be stricken down by someone somewhere with a weapon, took a life-or-death stand, and did indeed free the other animals and lead them from the arena when he saw that the gates were being opened for them by the frightened and confused guards. The instinctive natures of the animals led them to trust this solitary human being, among all the others that had acted toward them more as beasts than the beasts themselves. Whether or not the animals survived is not known. Perhaps not, not being in their natural environment. It could be that Orodes had not done them a kindness at all. On the other hand, whatever lay in store for them beyond the gates of their freedom, it had to have been better than their stock in captivity, where they were caged, whipped, beaten, fed only part of the time, left in their own feces, unable in the confines of those cages to even sleep, often barely able to stand or turn in a circle, and abused to the point of insanity before their entrance into the arena so that they would fight and kill. It was only Mithra's recognition of Orodes and his remembrance of the love he had been given that broke through the insanity. So certainly, Orodes had done the right thing by Mithra, because never again would he be mistreated. Never again would Orodes allow the animal to be ripped away from him, for any reason. He was his own man now, not controlled by family, by royalty, by law, by nation, by religion, by culture. He was his own man, doing what he deemed right, gleaned from within, not without.

When he and Mithra were alone in the safety of the forests east of Rome, the foothills of the Apennines – or what he thought were the foothills of the Apennines; in reality it was only the forested part of a senatorial estate – he sat and composed the letter he was unable to write previously. He wrote a letter to the king and queen telling them he would not be relying on Rome to assist in his return, because he had broken Roman laws. He would return to Parthia, he assured them, if and when he was able; he hoped it would be before Belteshazzar passed. He was not sure when he would be able to find passage, or even if he would be able to find a courier to deliver the letter. At least he would have the letter and be prepared.

He had stopped to procure writing instruments and papyrus at a villa visible from the forest's edge. He assumed the man opening the door to be a senator, because of the expensive weave of his tunic, and because of the purple stripe running shoulder to waist, and because the home was vast and spoke of wealth. Orodes offered to pay for the writing utensils, handing the senator a handful of sesterces. The senator handed the money all back except for one sesterce, saying even one sesterce was too much. "I would have thought you would have gone to the games?" queried Orodes, fearful he might be recognized, fearful the Senator might have been to the games and seen what had happened. But no, said the senator, he had not gone to the games, seeming not to notice that there was a wolf five feet away, an animal acting more like a dog than a wolf, reclining head between its paws, patiently waiting. But he did notice the dog that didn't quite look like a dog – the long nose, the triangular head, the long legs, the square back, the tip of the long tail swishing the ground. "I detest the spectacle of violence created by the games," the senator had said. "There is a veil of evil crowning the skies on those days," is what he said to Orodes, "A thing that enwraps men in cocoons of their own failings."

"May the Lord be with you, young man," the senator finalized, an odd way for a Roman to bid farewell, given that a Roman likely would have said something to the effect of, "May the Hearth Goddess go with you and bless your footfalls as you travel." Then the senator handed him money, a handful of denari. "Keep it," he said.

"I cannot," protested Orodes. "I am about to embark upon a long journey. I may never be able to return and pay you back."

"It is all right. I expect no such remuneration. Keep it."

"What is your name, in case I am able to return the sum? And let it be known that it will be with interest."

"You will never find me," said the senator. "I am a visitor only. I am from a place a long journey from here."

"Tell me anyway, because the future is never known to us."

"Mahlir," he said. "My name is Mahlir-of-Mathias. I am staying here in this home temporarily, as a guest of the emperor. I am to be wed in the morning."

Orodes grew pale at the revelation, but not because of the name – he had never been told the name of his birth father – but because the man was a friend of the emperor's. "Say not a word to the emperor, I beseech you," trembled Orodes, in tones that surely betrayed his fear. "For if you are a friend of the emperor, and the emperor finds out where I am, it surely will end in my death. Because I am being sought by the very same." He regretted saying it as soon as it passed his lips. Of course the senator would tell the emperor.

But instead the senator said, "You have my word, young man," realizing full well that serendipity had placed him face to face with his own son, the child he had lost a lifetime ago, for whom he still grieved. The birthmark over the left eye in the shape of an upward pointed arrowhead, the scar that ran from chin to groin, the top of it barely visible, the wolf – it could be no other. "Go, and may God go with you."

CHAPTER 8

THE BEQUEATHAL

THE PARTHIAN EMPIRE – ECBATANA, THE HOLLOW OF THE CHALDEANS

Prince Orodes of Parthia knelt and took the old man's feeble hand. Beside the bed were jars of urine. Belteshazzar was too bedridden to relieve himself in any other way. Orodes emptied and washed them. A nearly spent flame struggled out of a lamp on a nearby table, the same lamp that had been on the table as long as Orodes could remember. "Is this the time you spoke of, when you will finally be going home?" Orodes asked.

Belteshazzar's eyes brightened, and he opened his mouth to speak, but closed it again before the words came out, as if the concepts were simply too vast. Instead he nodded his head. Someone somewhere must have been caring for him, since several logs were ablaze in his stone fireplace and were sending out waves of welcome warmth. A tear traced its way down Orodes' cheek.

"Now, now," said Belteshazzar. "Do not be sad. You will be joining me soon." Belteshazzar laughed when he saw the concern in Orodes' face. "No, no no-no. I don't mean now. Seventy years from now. Perhaps a hundred. But even a thousand years is a blink of an eye to Ahura Mazda, who has no end, no beginning. Be happy for me. I go to see friends." He was waving a bony finger as if to emphasize. "I will tell you something. Glories beyond explanation await us at death – I use the term death only because of its common usage – in truth it is birth. Entering the womb – that is what truly is death, because we do so with all memories cloaked."

"I am going to miss you, my old fellow, my teacher…"

The conversation lay there for a while, stalled, with a faraway look occupying Belteshazzar's eyes, and a barely noticeable rising and falling of his chest. I was told you have something for me, was what Orodes wanted to say, but it didn't seem appropriate. It would carry the wrong connotation.

Belteshazzar spoke again, with a great effort, because with each passing moment his body was growing closer, weaker, heavier. But what came out of his mouth had nothing to do with a bequeathal. "And you returned with your beloved Mithra!" He had not noticed the wolf until now, and laughed, a laugh that turned into a frightful coughing fit. "They tell me you took on the entire Roman army," he said after composing himself, "and freed all the animals in the process."

"The story is exaggerated."

"Then tell me how it happened. I love a good story."

"It's a peculiar story," Orodes said, and told of how he rescued Mithra and freed the animals, and of how he grabbed Mithra's fangs and played the fang game, Mithra growling and wagging his tail – no one noticed the tail banging back and forth, whirling like the windmills of the Greeks – and of how Orodes held off the entire Praetorian guard with barely more than a sneer, and of how he ended up in the dark of the forest surrounded by hidden sets of eyes that came visible only when they caught firelight in just the right way. And he told of how Mithra had been curled in a ball by his feet, ears picking out the sounds and scents of the forest and the curious creatures that came to watch and investigate, when the animal was suddenly on its feet, back hunched, stepping backward, a low steady rumble coming from its mouth.

"A cowled figure emerged," Orodes went on. "A man? The hooded garment reached all the way to the forest floor in a way that suggested he was gliding on air. But it was a woman's voice that spoke. 'Your Highness,' it said. At its sound Mithra realized there was no threat and settled back down again. The woman handed forth a bag she had been carrying and told me there was a traveling pass inside with the emperor's seal on it. She gave me instructions to be at the Tomb of Turia at first light morning after next to meet a trade caravan which would be passing through. She said the caravan would be expecting me, and that it would be a long journey, with the final destination being the principal city of Ecbatana. There was also food inside the bag."

Belteshazzar smiled broadly. "I enjoyed it," he said of the story. "Quite a tale. Good story indeed. Was the mystery solved? Did you ever find out who the woman was?"

Orodes shook his head. "A mystery never to be solved, it appears. Very strange. Almost as if someone were watching over me."

Belteshazzar smiled and nodded his head, in a way that signaled he might have the answer. But before Orodes could ask, Belteshazzar changed the subject. "Now," he said, "– I must tell you something, before I leave you, for the time is now near."

Belteshazzar closed his mouth then opened it again – the process alone was an effort of will – and spoke the last words Orodes would ever hear from his mentor and friend. "I have something to give you," he said. "It is something of immense value..." Another broad smile spread across Old Belteshazzar's face, and froze itself in eternity. Belteshazzar was dead.

Mithra, head lowered, tail dragging, went up and sniffed the motionless form, sniffed it up and down, and cried softly as he further tested the confusing scent with his tongue.

Orodes pressed his lips against the cold and lifeless forehead of his friend, his mentor. Belteshazzar's face seemed thinner than it did when there was life in it, and way too fragile, like a gray and brittle stick found on the forest floor. He fell to both knees and wept. When a man cries – men are highly sensitive creatures, a fact unknown to all except another man – a massive amount of energy is consumed. It caused him to fall onto the floor in a deep slumber, within which was a vibrating type of paralysis that hurtled its way downward to a stunning moment of causeless fear, like someone had pulled the entire earth out from under him and left him suspended in a place where there was a cacophony of activity, voices, a loud buzzing sound, where before there had been nothing but silence…and it startled him "awake."

"Here, over here," came a voice at nearly the same instant, which in itself would have roused him had not the buzzing already done so. Another Magus? Indeed! Standing there all along apparently, in the shadows back by the scroll shelves. The Magus stepped forward and bowed and also kissed the body, and untied and retied its Holy Waist Cord, and uttered: "We worship the Fravashi of the Ashasavah; and we thank you, time-worn form. You have served me well."

Then the Magus raised his head and continued on with Orodes, as if nothing out of the ordinary was afoot. "Talk to him if you have things to say, he said. "He will hear." The Magus nodded at the body and moved his head up and down for emphasis.

"You think so?"

"Yes, I do."

"Belteshazzar and I used to have these conversations," said Orodes, speaking to the unknown Magus as if he too were a friend. "…these arguments about life and death, and whether or not life survives death. There is a sect of the Jews called the Sadducees. While they believe in God, they do not believe we go on after death. They believe death ends it all." Orodes tipped his head toward the dead body. "Belteshazzar would tell me about all the wonderful things that would happen after death, how we would take stock of our previous life and of what we learned, and of the mistakes we made and what we must do to correct them, and what we must still learn. All nonsense, I would tell him." Orodes laughed, but it was a laugh of respect. " – and I used to say to him, prove it to me and I will believe. I used to say, show me something I can see, touch, taste, smell, then I will believe.

'You cannot touch the sun,' Belteshazzar would argue back. 'Yet you believe in the sun's existence.' And I would answer back –"

"– you would answer back this way," finished the strange young Magus. "– that you believe in the sun because you feel its warmth. And I would remind you that you cannot see the wind, and you would say, 'Ah, but I can feel its force on my face!'"

Orodes stood in muted confusion and stared at the young Magus, and moved closer, and thrust his head out like a turtle from its shell to study this strange man. The light fell on his face in an indistinct sort of way, so he was not sure at first. It was an odd profusion of light, not the kind that would come from a fireplace, and certainly not the light of day provided by the sun, dimmer than that, yet brighter in a way. It was like he could control the light, make it brighter or darker by simply willing it so. "Is it you?" asked Orodes in a raspy whisper. The face he was looking at was younger, fuller, but yes, unmistakable, yes – could it be? Yes! It was the face of Belteshazzar, Daniel, Magus Supreme, one-time ruler of all Babylon. "Is it really you?"

"Yes," said Belteshazzar. "It is me. My gift to you, my bequeathal to you, the only thing I have to give since I am not wealthy, is the proof I promised you, the proof that life goes on, that death is really birth and that birth is really death. But even at that I do you a disservice, because there is so much more to God's kingdom. One would be stunned at its vastness and how many hearts beat within its sphere. Words limit me. And the one who holds the key is Yeshua-the-Saoshyant who walks the earth in the land of the Jews. I want you to go there. I want you to stay there, and study under him. It is his destiny to take the sins of the world upon his shoulders. He is coming just now into the full awareness of who he is." Belteshazzar pointed to the wall where the scrolls were shelved. "If you would, there, right there, find the scroll for the 58th Yast. Behind it you will find a loose brick. I have hidden a bag of coins there. It is not much, compared to what a king can give you, but if you are careful it should be enough to sustain you during your study."

"My study? What study?" He wondered if Belteshazzar had taken senility with him. "My study with whom? What are you talking about?"

"I have already told you. Have you not been listening? Saoshyant. Yeshua as is his given name. The one who can give us the key to free ourselves from the illusions of mortality and the cycle of birth and death, so that we might reign at the right hand of Ahura Mazda in Mazda's kingdom of magnificence." Orodes began to tingle in a way indescribable. Every appendage was suddenly afire with bliss, every nerve, every vessel. He looked over at the dead body, still there, then he looked at the man standing. The man standing, smiling, looked like Belteshazzar, more so than the dead body. He also saw his own body, its chest rising and falling, mouth open rasping in and out somnambulistic breaths, as though benumbed in a deep trance on the floor beside the dead body of Belteshazzar.

"So much more," reiterated Belteshazzar. "So much more."

The bliss burning inside Orodes was bringing the illusion of a strange type of consanguinity to all that surrounded him, to all surrounding objects and to all people. And there were other people in the room who had not been there before, he suddenly realized – a young woman with long raven hair and a man with a white beard, and a man with a black-streaked silver beard. A bald eagle floated down and perched itself on Belteshazzar's shoulder.

"Uh, Saoshyant?" guessed Orodes.

"Yes, it appears Saoshyant has joined us as well," said Belteshazzar. Then he pointed to the young woman with the raven hair and said something remarkable. "And this stunning beauty, dear boy, is your mother. In her most recent going-out her name was Rachel, but we all know her as Silva. Your father was a lucky man. If I was five thousand years younger –" Present upon Belteshazzar's lips was the sparkle of a smile that revealed the charm and wit that was so typical of him. Indeed it was Belteshazzar.

And gone were the wanderings of senility that had begun to obfuscate his brilliance, as the physical brain was winding down.

Happiness veritably blazed out from Rachel. She opened her arms to her son.

It was more than an embrace. Mother and son quite literally melted into one another and formed a fire-like pillar extending into the earth in one direction and up into the heavens in the other, and the bliss burning through Orodes increased by exponential proportions, frightening it was so powerful.

Saoshyant-the-eagle floated over to where Mithra was lying head between his paws, one eye closed, one eye open. "Ah, my dear bird," soothed Belteshazzar. "I am afraid you will have to wait awhile, before you will be able to play with your good friend the wolf. I am sorry, but he cannot see you." It was clear that Mithra was looking at an empty room only, that his physical eyes were not seeing the three people and the eagle. He twitched an ear and gave a whine, being nonetheless aware that something was not quite right in the room.

"Is all this real?"

"It is the only thing that is real," said Belteshazzar. "Life in the body is the illusion, and what limits us by the reflection of light"

"I think I might be beginning to believe that."

"It is true, but it matters not whether you believe it. Now, if I might focus for a moment. The one thing you must do, and I cannot emphasize how important this is, is to go to the land of the Jews and study and learn under the man who is the Saoshyant, born Yeshua-ben-Yosef. He is the one who knows. He looks young, but he is ancient. His goings-out number as many as there are stars in the sky. As your prophet Enoch wrote – he is the Most High, come to take on a cloak of flesh and blood in order to teach us by word and by example. Willingly he does so, because no sin is found in him. He is as pure as the driven snow. You must learn from him."

"I am afraid my father the king has other plans for me."

Belteshazzar shooed away the objection with a wave of his hand. "Pooh on the king! A greater king has greater plans. I have made arrangements for you to travel to Judea. I did so before I discarded my body. Yeshua divides his time between the compound of the Essenes in the Judean Wilderness and the Temple in Jerusalem. One of those two places is where you are likely to find him. Now, there is to be a summit of leaders from the kingdoms of the known world at a place called Macherus near the Dead Sea. I have arranged with your mother and father for you to be a part of the Parthian delegation. Gifts are expected because a banquet will be held in honor of King Antipas, tetrarch of the Galilean regions. You will be traveling there with your mother and father, the King and Queen; that will be your passage, and your excuse to travel to the land of Judea."

"But I have instructions from my father to report to the Armenian front."

"He expects you to leave for Armenia after your return." Belteshazzar had a peculiar glow in his eyes that might as well have said, if you return. "Your sister Nahid will be coming with you. Do you remember how she always used to run away pretending to look for him?" Belteshazzar held his stomach as it shook with laughter. "Oh how that used to anger you. Now the fantasy shall become reality. Because she too will be learning from the Saoshyant."

The eagle stayed behind to play for a time with an unawares Mithra, but the rest of them, Belteshazzar and his entourage, disappeared through a set of double doors into an explosion of light, yellows, reds, blinding white, shades of blue and purple. Orodes whistled for Mithra and tried to follow, but his eyes popped open and he was back in his body, where he was left to view life once again through the limitations of the flesh and what could be discerned from sound-impacted air against the ears and the reflection of light upon the eyes, and to wonder if what had happened had happened at all. Had it only been a dream? The bliss was also gone, and the brilliant colors were replaced by the ghostly dimness of dying fireplace embers.

And the cacophony of cheerful activity and all it's wonderful people was replaced by the foul emptiness of a cold room and a dead body.

Mithra popped up and stood tall and pointed his ears forward, and looked at something that wasn't there, at a tiny whiff of air, and howled, mournful and low. Mithra's howls consisted of three octaves, low to high and low again, the middle sounding almost like a child screaming, the low at the end akin to a baritone. It was a cry that could be heard for miles, over ten miles in the open forest.

"or else I am awake for the first time, and
all before has been a mean sleep."

Walt Whitman

Part I

MAHLIR-OF-MATTHIAS

22 Years earlier

Six years after the speculated birth of the Christ Child
Year 46 of the Calendar of Pater Patriae Gaius Julius Caesar
Year 0 of the Gregorian Calendar (0AD)

CHAPTER 9

THE HAPPENING NEVER TO BE SPOKEN OF

ISRAEL – THE NORTHERN KINGDOM

In a time of human turmoil, when men and women did unspeakable things to one another in the name of God and goodness, when power was measured by the ability to control and dominate, when masculinity was defined as a man's ability to inflict injury on another man, when gods slept with virgins and sired demigods, when men and women envisioned Deity as a creature demanding subservience and the sacrificial blood of living things, a young man walked alone on the road to Caesarea Philippi. He was dressed in the habits of a Jewish Temple priest. If he stopped and listened he could hear the Dan off to his right, from down an embankment hidden beyond the green risings of trees and papyrus thickets, rushing silent and deep and green to join with other rivers and creeks to form the holiest of them all, the River Jordan. Smoke was rising from somewhere in the distance to create a haze along the long upward-sloping ridges of Hermon. It would have almost had a beauty to it, had it not painted of death with its hues of filtered sunshine, of subtle colors.

A flock of birds burst into the air from within the papyrus thickets. Something was in there. He should have kept going – nothing good could come from investigating whatever creature it was that made those birds fly like that – but curiosity forced the young man to stop and look. The reeds were bunched together as tight as the trunks of trees, forming a virtual wall of green, and fanned out at the top into sprays of millions of tiny needles, giving a rolling soft appearance. A surprise awaited him as he carefully parted them. The thing that had caused the birds to swarm was a woman, young and raven haired.

She must not have been familiar with the northern regions, otherwise she would have known she was not safe. She would have known that the swamps of the Hula Valley were replete with inhospitable creatures, some as large as oxen, others small enough to fit within the palm of your hand. She would have known she was entering the lair of Leviathan, the worst of them all. The sun was hot and the air cool from a wind blowing in from the coast, having in it no hint whatsoever of peril, carrying in it only the essence of the upcoming season change, a dampness, a freshness, and the feel and smell of the good earth about to renew itself. So often that is the way it is with danger; it comes when one is least expecting it.

The young man watched as she waded ankle deep into the film-covered and stagnant water, watched as she parted more of the tall reeds and disappeared into them. He followed, and found that beyond the papyrus, beyond the fortress of green, was deep water, freshened by the backwashing of the Dan. He watched with the quickening of his heart as she dropped the veil and loosed her long black hair, watched as she stepped from her gold-embroidered purple garments and hung them high on a cluster of reeds.

He watched as she slipped into the slow-moving swirls, as she began stroking with surprising skill out into the middle, with an unexpected look of strength displayed in the suppleness of her bare arms and legs as they powered her through the smooth current.

He watched as the eyes of Leviathan broke the surface, just the eyes, like two stones sticking up. A smooth wake traced the beast's path as it followed her. The attack came swiftly. The water in an instant turned to a churning boil, then lay quiet. The woman's blood rolled up to the surface in a single surge of crimson bottom water, turned up by the monster's attempts to hide her in the mud. The young man was not possessed of great courage in that moment. He simply did not take the time to think of how utterly foolish it would be to dive into that water. Armed with nothing more than a Roman short sword he carried for cutting tree branches and digging roots, he swam toward the cloud of black at the bottom.

Leviathan is three times the size of a man. He is as a snake but is armored and has legs, and is stronger and far more cunning. His head is long and his nose flat, and when he opens his mouth it is large enough to swallow a man whole and is filled with a thousand fangs.

The young man wrestled the enormous crocodile, come inland from the Great Sea as some of them didd, attracted by the still waters of the swamps. This one was bigger than most. Someone had tried unsuccessfully to catch it. A frayed and decaying rope, short, broken at the end, hung from its neck, no match for the mammoth strength the thing possessed. The creature probably had been intended as an exotic treat for the games, where the fiercest of animals are matched up. The young man had once seen a carving on a lamp stand of a lion and a crocodile tearing at one another.

He looked in the crocodile's eyes and held on as the beast thrashed him about. With lungs ready to burst, trying to think, prepared to die, he plunged his sword into the huge underside of its neck.

Blood poured out.

With sudden hope he fought harder. He thrust the sword again and again, until at last Leviathan floated away.

He felt around in the darkness of the blood and the billowing mud, and found nothing. He kicked around in a circle, fighting against the current, and reached everywhere, and still found nothing.

He surfaced.

The weakness in his limbs and the terror of breath choked off by sprays of water only fortified his determination. He tried again…and again found nothing.

Again he dove. This time he found her. The last place he dared look, in the mouth of the beast. Leviathan was dead, his grip loose. The young man was able to pry her free, hearing her flesh rip on the creature's teeth.

He must have fallen faint for a time, because the next thing he remembered was the woman lying beneath him, coughing and gasping. He didn't remember how he got her to shore, or even how he himself made it to shore.

Skin and bone on the right side of her face had been torn away, having ripped with it her beauty. Her ribs were broken and crushed, her organs visibly torn and punctured. He cradled her head in his lap and stroked her hair, and talked to her. Because he didn't know what else to do. Not even the finest of Caesar's surgeons could fix the damage that had been done. His first inclination had been to go for help, but she stopped him. "Stay with me," she said. "If you leave, I fear I will be dead by the time you return," she implored. Drips of water falling from his head made her twitch. Each sensation seemed to cause her pain – the simplest thing, the breeze, a tiny crawling ant, the very act of breathing. Though – she did not complain. She seemed content to hear him talk. It was someone to hold her as she died, a friend to comfort her as she passed into the terrifying unknown, strangers a moment ago, now bonded, fused by a horrific trauma. Using half-formed and halting words, uttered after first taking sputtering breaths for strength, she told him as best she could about her life, and asked him about his. She was the daughter of a wealthy widowed grain merchant, she said. She and her father were staying close by in Mallaha, she told him, a town older than Abraham. The young man knew the town well; it brushed the foothills of Mt. Hermon on land rolling and fertile that rises to hills on the west and drops down to swampland on the east where flows the Dan. Their home was in Caesarea on the coast south of the Sea of Galilee, she said, but they were in the northern sector because of the trouble in the south, the rioting that had been ongoing in the wake of Herod's death, and because her father had land holdings here in the north. She swims in the morning, she said, because that is the time one can be closest to God.

The young man told her he was a priest, serving mostly in the Temple in Jerusalem, but traveling at times to the synagogues of the towns and cities, as he was this day.

She allowed a smile to form, even though to do so caused pain, and with a raised and trembling finger pointed to his forehead. "That is why the box?" Though the beast had stripped away part of her face it had left her mouth intact so that she could still speak. Likewise were her eyes spared from the mauling, so that she could use them to view the chambers of the young man's soul, for in fact she seemed to be looking that deep.

He reached up. He was surprised it was still there, his phylactery, the small square pouch bound to his forehead by a thin strap, as is required of a priest, containing writings of the prophets, close to the head, never out of mind. "A priest is also required to wear one on his sleeve," he said. "I'm afraid that one is gone." Half his tunic was gone, the rest clinging to him like a shroud of ice, shivering him, though the air was warm.

She tended to dip her head and widen her eyes before speaking, as if hoping the expressions themselves could convey the words in case she was unable to push them forth. "..are you a Sadducee or a Pharisee?"

"Politics don't concern me much. A Pharisee if you must label me. Which annoys my father, but then what doesn't annoy my father. Unlike the Sadducees, I believe in life after death, and in a resurrection. And, unlike the Sadducees, I am not wealthy. That, I expect, would make me a Pharisee. I am a simple man. I study the Law and the inner mysteries, and I teach the children in the Temple courts. I copy scrolls; my hand is good. And I write letters."

"My father is a Sadducee," she said. Each word came with care, artfully; it was important to her that she be understood. "You and he would certainly make a pair." She would have laughed, had her trembling body permitted it.

They talked about many things – he didn't know how long, minutes, it could have been hours – then he interrupted himself with his own tears, because he realized that death was upon her, perhaps with her next breath. And he said something foolish. Maybe it was just compassion that caused him to speak the last words she would ever hear; maybe it was only a moment of supreme empathy, perhaps only a strange lapse in the thought process, an illusion born of the trauma. Whatever the reason, whatever the illusion, he seemed connected to this woman, with a type of unexplainable bliss transcending rationality, as if saying goodbye to a love of many years, as if they had lived a lifetime together. "I do believe I might be falling in love with you," were the words that came out of his mouth. It caused a smile to cross her lips.

"I am pledged to another," she said, upon breath barely present. "By my parents at my birth."

"As am I," he said.

"I don't even know your name."

He told her that his name was Mahlir, and that his father was Matthias, the high priest under Herod who pulled down Caesar's golden eagle from over the great gate of the Temple. "King Herod had installed the eagle in defiance of the law that forbids us to erect images of living things. My father and some of the other priests and leaders pulled it down and hacked it to pieces. The king had him burned alive for the deed, or at least that's what the king and everyone thought. Herod's guards were supporters of my father, and believers in his way, and were able to spirit him away under cover of darkness. It was another prisoner who was burned. My father lives in exile in a faraway place."

"I am a priest of the highest order," he continued. "I am of the line of Bilgah. I was born during the ninth year of the reign of Caesar Augustus, at the tenth hour of the fifth day of Elul, to Jewish parents in the Holy City of Jerusalem. My lineage can be traced all the way back to the first priest. It is written down in the scrolls of our family. My father was Matthias. His father was Margalothus. His father was Nashon. His father was Berekiah. And on it goes, back thirty-one generations to Bilgah.

"Bilgah, as you know, was one of the twenty-four descendants of Aaron selected by King David as keepers of the Ark of the Covenant. For all these generations my father and my father's fathers have kept watch over the tablets, and have offered the appropriate sacrifices and incense, and prayers of atonement for the people, and have done so honorably and without defilement. After the tablets were lost during the Exile we kept watch over their resting place, knowing someday they would be found. There are thousands of us who have come down from the original 24. All are priests, a few serving permanently in the Temple, like me, most serving in the various synagogues and ministering in the Temple on a rotating basis."

Her motionless lips, the whites of her eyes, her half-closed lids, let him know that she may not have heard any of it, that she was somewhere else, that he was now alone. Had she lived but a moment or two longer she would have heard him speak the name of his father. She would have recognized it. Her own father spoke it often. He was proud that his daughter would someday marry the son of the high priest who pulled down Caesar's golden eagle.

Neither did Mahlir know that the dead woman in his arms was the one to whom he had been betrothed at birth.

A short time ago his body was shaking because it was cold; now it shook because of desperation. He wanted to reach down and mend her, to somehow put her together. His muscles may have even twitched in efforts to do so. Instead, he simply looked skyward into the vast emptiness, and spoke to it, asking, wishing, demanding that this tender and gentle angel whom he didn't know be restored – the foolish impossible – promising he would care for her and protect her if it be done, and never do her harm.

Then he brought his eyes back to reality, back to her disfigured body, motionless, stilled of breath, and tried to think of what he should do next, who he should seek out to come for the body.

He suddenly realized why his tunic had been so continuously wet. It was not from water. It was from her blood, now turning sticky, itching his skin. He looked up again, into the emptiness of the approaching night, but saw through the film of his moist eyes no angels, no god, only shaded ruffles of pink and red, gentle fire rolling across the sky. Between the fire and the hilltops were ribbons of sapphire blue. It surprised him, that the hour was so late. She had been in his arms the entire afternoon and evening.

He felt tranced.

An odd scent came to his nostrils, tangled in amongst the odors of the river. It was an unfamiliar scent, yet familiar in a way. A fresh smell. Like alabaster? The way an empty anointing jar smells? Akin to the clean powdery smell of a craftsman's shop, though mixed with a touch of perfume.

He began to stare ahead at the things in front of him, the clumps of high grass poking out of the mossy, matted soil, the blooms of the white squill, the winged water insects darting in and out of the foliage. He was seeing but not focusing, and soon became aware that he was looking at the face of a child peering nervously out of the reeds.

At first Mahlir thought he was looking at an apparition of his mind, the kind that tends to come to those under the stress of exhaustion.

But this apparition was no apparition This was indeed a child. The child jerked, like he was preparing himself to run, rustling the reeds and rippling the water into which dipped the ends of his crudely made cloak and tunic. Of mixed wool and camel hair, the garment looked to be. Mahlir spoke harshly, annoyed at being startled. "Away with you! If you are lost I am sorry. But I am not able to help you. The road to Mallaha is up on the rise in back of us. You can find someone to help you there. It is well traveled. Go"

The child simply stood there, a look of sadness upon his face. He could not have been any more than five or six.

"Go!" Mahlir shouted. "Before I take a stick to you. Then you will not only have a smarting backside but will be ceremoniously unclean as well, because I have touched the dead."

Still the child remained immobile.

"Do you not hear? I said off with you. Now go. You are intruding on a very private moment."

Still the child did not move.

Again Mahlir shouted, louder. "Now! Out of my sight! Go!"

The child jumped and began to cry, little sobs that caused his body to shake.

Mahlir was suddenly filled with shame. His sorrow should not be such that it harms others. The boy was far too young to be alone on a road beset by thieves. Mahlir shook his head and smiled. "Hey, I'm sorry little one. Come here. I – I'm really sorry. I shouldn't have said those things. Come, come. Sit. I will care for you and see that you are reunited with your family. Do you have family? Come, come over here."

The child affirmed he did by nodding.

"Where are they?"

The child shrugged.

"Can you not speak?"

He shrugged again.

Comfort then came from Mahlir's mouth. "Hey, little one – it's all right – there's nothing for you to fear. I won't hurt you. Neither will the woman I hold. Yes, she is dead, but the dead cannot hurt you. This I know, for I am a priest of Yahweh. She was killed by Leviathan, which is all the more reason for you to do as I say and come out of that water. There may be more of them in there. Come here and sit by me. I will help you."

The child looked at Mahlir eye to eye, still not moving. Mahlir was even more ashamed. Because the gaze stirred within him protectiveness overwhelming.

"Come child," Mahlir repeated, so softly, so very powerfully that he was surprised mere words could carry such force. "Please."

The tenderness must have reassured the boy. He stepped from the water and walked toward Mahlir.

"At's a child. Here. Sit by me. Right here. Until I can determine what should be done with this situation of ours."

There was a grass clump next to Mahlir. The boy sat on it and waited obediently.

"I suppose we should take care of you first," Mahlir said.

So, ever watchful for the eyes of Leviathan, Mahlir laid aside the unknown woman and waded into the water to bathe himself free of the blood, and to wash it from his clothing. But his tunic would not come clean. Large blotches continued to obscure its holiness, its white purity. The embroidered gold and purple band running shoulder to hem was so stained that its separate colors were indistinguishable, and all four of his tassels were soiled. "I fear I cannot help you," he had to tell the boy. "I have broken a law. I have touched the dead and have corrupted myself with its blood. For a priest to touch the dead is forbidden. It is written in the commandments laid down by Moses that if a priest makes himself unclean by touching one who has died, he must immediately cleanse himself with water, and must immediately wash his clothes. He will remain unclean until evening. Then he will be free to touch and be touched. As you can see, I am unable to cleanse myself." Mahlir looked at the child, then at the sun, a ball of yellow sinking into the hills, casting out its red glow. Above was blackness. "It is nearly nightfall. If only I could wash out the blood. Now I must wait another day."

He walked over and knelt in front of the boy. "I have no choice. Before I am allowed to move among people I must be clean. Until I cleanse myself and robe myself in clean garments, and remain unsoiled for a day, I cannot walk with you and lead you. I cannot even touch you. It is the Law. What I must do is this. I must travel to Mallaha, maybe as far as Kadesh, to obtain new garments. It's not far. I will return tomorrow. I will bring food, and stay with you until evening, until I am clean. Then we will look for your family, and for the family of the dead woman. Now – you must promise me – while I am gone you will stay here. You will not move. And you must not touch the dead woman's body."

Mahlir climbed the rocky hillside to the road and left the child alone in the dark, with Leviathan lurking, with jackals howling, with the cold of night descending, with roadside thieves prowling.

And an uneasiness settled inside him for having done so. It grew with each step. He marked the place in his mind, a place just to the north of the Dan's merge – papyrus thickets, a circular grove of trees, a rock shaped like a hammer – so he could find it again.

By the time he reached the road, marking his position by noting a Roman milestone twenty paces to the north, the uneasiness lay in the bottom of his belly like a parasite.

There were sounds of men at a campsite, laughter and drinking and fighting. Bandits, likely, who would think nothing of enslaving a young child for the rest of his life, or worse, of killing him for no more than the pleasure of it. Since Herod's death the entire countryside had been set upon by bandits and would-be kings. Travelers were reporting that Sepphoris was in flames, just fifty-five miles to the south near Nazareth, at the hands of Judas-of-Ezekias. The southern sky verified it with its film of hazy smoke.

Mahlir nearly turned around, then scolded himself for putting thoughts of the boy above the laws of God. He had blasphemed by even daring to do so, by even suggesting to himself that he go back and help the boy while still unclean. Away, foolish thoughts! Act like the priest you are. Obey the edicts of God and of the Law. Obtain the garments. Then go back for the boy. Obey what is written by God. Put the fears aside. God first, the boy second. God above all else.

Once on the road, upon coming closer to the torches and fires of the bandits, Mahlir realized that it was not a campsite at all, and that the men were not bandits. They were shouting the name of a lost child.

Mahlir made a decision. He would break the law of God. He would take whatever punishment Yahweh should choose for him, even death, as befell Uzzah for breaking a commandment and touching the ark. For the child, yes, he would trade his own life.

Unclean and soiled in blood, he approached the group and inquired who might be the boy's father. "I know where your son is," he told the man who came forward. "He is safe. I can lead you to him." The man was large and burly, with the eyes and nose of an eagle. His tunic, like his son's, was brown and coarse, of wool and camel hair, breaking another law, where it is written that one must not wear garments woven of two different kinds of materials.

Were these Nazarenes? They were indeed, Mahlir came to realize, by their accents and their crude manners of speech. A Nazarene would sooner crack a skull than listen to an explanation. Always fighting and drinking, the Nazarenes, menial workers the lot of them. Not a wealthy nobleman in the bunch.

With the group hurrying behind him, Mahlir retraced his steps – to the Roman mile marker, to the hammer shaped rock, to the Hula Valley below it, to the circular grove of trees and the papyrus thickets. He was half running, afraid the boy might not be there. Should the boy be gone, and with Mahlir covered in blood, his father and the crowd would think the worst. But Mahlir's concerns were larger than that. His concerns were for the boy.

The boy was there, washed in the light of the moon that hung barely touching the distant snow tipped ridges of Hermon, purifying the entire valley in silver. The boy was kneeling by the body. Touching it!

He had taken the bottom of his wool and camel hair tunic and had dipped it into the water, and with it he was wiping the dead woman's face.

The father did not react, apparently not realizing the woman was dead. His only interest was that his boy had been found. He put his arms around him and reprimanded him for wandering off, then came to Mahlir to express his gratitude. "Thank you, good man," he said, and moved to embrace Mahlir as was the custom.

Mahlir withdrew. "Did you not see that my clothes have been defied by the blood of the dead?"

The boy's father looked confused, as though not understanding what Mahlir had said. Then Mahlir saw. His tunic was no longer blood stained. It was gleaming white, pure, radiant. In the moonlight the tunic seemed to be its own source of light. And the gold and purple sash was once again awash with color.

Mahlir's first thought was that he was losing his mind. He rationalized that he had been mistaken about the discoloring. Perhaps he had washed the blood out after all, and it didn't seem so at the time because the fabric was not dry. Which was another curiosity. There had not been enough time for it to dry. Yet here it was – completely dry.

Again the father smiled in gratitude. "Please accept my thanks. If there is anything I can do, offer you my hospitality, food perhaps –"

"No. I am happy you are re-united with your son. That shall be my reward. But you should see to it that he bathes, after having touched the corpse."

Confusion returned to the man's expression. "Corpse?"

Mahlir motioned to his left – and saw the impossible. The dead woman was sitting up.

Mahlir's beating heart came close to bursting. She had not been dead after all, was the only explanation his mind could put to the happening. Yet, there was one thing about which there could be no confusion, no mistake of perception. A short time ago half her face was torn away. Now there was not so much as a blemish. And she was once again wearing the clothes she had placed in the tree.

Said the boy's father before parting, "I wish also to express my thanks to your wife," whereupon he turned to the dead woman and gave a slow and prominent nod of the head, a sign of greeting and respect. "May the Lord richly bless you both."

The dead woman was looking around at all the people, perplexed, like she was not remembering any of what had happened, if indeed it had happened.

"I'm sorry for the trouble the boy has caused you," the father continued. "You must forgive him. You have my word he will be disciplined. He is an inquisitive and curious child, always asking questions, always wanting to see things he has not seen, always wanting to understand things he could not possibly understand. You see, we have been living afar in Egypt since the boy was two. He remembers nothing of his homeland, and is, you could say, overanxious to explore it. He loves to hear stories about the countryside. He makes us tell them to him over and over, about how barren and dry it is in the south, how rocky and forested it is in the hills, how green it is in the north, how on a clear day you can see the snowy top of a big mountain, and about how someday he will be able to play among the folds of the hills of Nazareth. We have told hm about the graceful Ibex that can climb the sides of a steep mountain, and about the fox and the jackal, and the colorful birds."

"And about the wolf, Father," reminded the boy. He was clinging to his father's coarse robe, walking around him in annoying circles. It was the first time Mahlir had heard him speak.

"Yes, child," said the father, laying a hand on the back of his son's head. "The beautiful and graceful wolf. And about the River Jordan, and about how good it feels to bathe in its clear waters. And about the behemoth that lives and walks upon its bottom. Hmmm?"

The boy nodded, still circling.

"I'm afraid he got carried away in his excitement. If it had not been for you and your wife, I shudder to say, we may never have found him. If there is anything we can do –"

A noise came. A lapping, a subdued splashing. Heads turned. An enormous crocodile was easing its way into the water. The father pulled his son close. "That, my son, is one of God's creatures that is not so beautiful. That is a creature we must stay far far away from." He turned again to Mahlir. "All the more reason for me to express my gratitude. You have saved my son's life. Again, if there is anything we can do."

"Nothing," Mahlir assured, probably giving the impression he was only half attentive, which in fact was true, so bewildered and shaken was he. "I am happy to have been of service." He thought he saw the frayed end of a rope lap into the water with the crocodile, adding more confusion to these things that could not possibly be happening. The crocodile he had killed? It also had a broken rope around its neck."

The man motioned again to embrace Mahlir. This time Mahlir did not resist. "I am Joseph-son-of-Jacob," the man said. "And again, I thank you."

"I am called Mahlir."

"Tell me, Mahlir, is it true what we hear? That Herod is dead and that his son Archelaus rules in his place? And that Judea is full of robberies and seditions?"

"Yes, all true."

"Then the matter is settled. We will return to Nazareth, to be as far from Archelaus and the trouble as possible. We were unsure where we should go, to Nazareth where we lived before, or to Jerusalem where my trade as a carpenter and stone mason would doubtless bring me more work. For the boy's safety, we will return to Nazareth."

"Approach it from the west," said Mahlir. "Even Galilee is not free from the discord. It spreads and seeps like the poisoned waters of a flood.

I am told that Judas-of-Ezekias and his band have taken hold of Sepphoris. Nazareth is untouched."

"Thank you. It is fortunate truly that our paths crossed."

"The Lord be with you," Mahlir said.

"As with you. I could not help but notice that you are a priest of Yahweh. I am fortunate. My son has been in good hands."

Mahlir acknowledged with a slight bow.

The father looked at Mahlir powerfully. "Until we meet again." Folding his cloak around the boy's shoulders, he made his way up the rocky slope to the road. Waiting above were more people – friends from Egypt, likely, or people he had befriended along the way, people traveling together for protection, who had fanned out and had been looking in other directions, until realizing the boy had been found – women, men, and children. One of the women must have been the boy's mother, because she ran and threw her arms around him.

"He thought you were my wife," Mahlir said to the dead woman. He forced a laugh. "If only it could be."

"It cannot be," the dead woman said. Sadness weighed upon the beauty of her face, upon the beauty of her soul. "For I am pledged to another."

"As am I," he said.

CHAPTER 10

THE WEDDING

ISRAEL, CAESAREA

A veil of clouds obscured the wedding of Mahlir-of-Matthias. It was befitting since clouds also covered his heart. His heart belonged to the woman at the river.

But he had been pledged to Rachel. Such was the way of his people. The agreement between the families had been made at birth. The contract had been signed and witnessed years ago and blessed and made holy by God. Mahlir had no choice. It was the way of his people. It was the way of God.

The wedding was held in Rachel's home in Caesarea. Normally there would be a procession from the bride's home to the groom's family home, and the wedding would take place there, at the groom's home, symbolic of the transference of protection from one home to the other, but the groom's family was not present. Mahlir's father was in hiding in a city beyond the northern reaches of the Great Sea, beyond the isle of Cypress, for fear of retribution from Herod's son, and Mahlir's home was no more than a tenement room in the Temple. So the procession began at home of the father of the bride, and ended at the home of the father of the bride, after having wound throughout the streets of Caesarea, and through the theatre and the hippodrome. A wedding procession must be a public event, as is set forth in the Mishna, in order for the townspeople to be able to testify to the legitimacy of the marriage. Thousands came that day to be a part of Mahlir's procession, the son of the great Matthias who pulled down Caesar's golden eagle. The bride, the daughter of Eli-the-Sadducee, esteemed member of the Sanhedrin, was carried in an apiryon made of wood from the cedars of Lebanon, as had Solomon's bride been carried in her litter, made also from the cedars of Lebanon. Both bride and groom wore garlands of many-colored flowers, elevating them on that day to kings and queens. Oil and wine were spilt on the path before them, anointing the ground upon which their feet trod. A king and queen before God.

Eli's house sat on the rise of a small hill of solid stone, on the southern edge of the city, next to the seashore, to Mahlir a palace. "Modest," Eli maintained. Compared to the way some of the wealthier citizens and officials lived, it was indeed modest.

The long-stepped porch, of limestone and shaded by fruit trees, and the sectioned rock walls of the home, soft-yellow and porous, the color of the beach, blended so well with the terrain that to an eagle flying overhead the compound was no more than a large swell of wind sculpted sand. It was the very last piece of Caesarea to the south, and one of the few parts of it not built by Herod when he constructed the maritime monument as a tribute to Rome's ruler ten years ago. Within its plain looking walls were palatial gardens and polished mosaic floors warm to the touch from hypocaust blown air. The décor was Jewish, but it was a décor adorned with Roman fountains and peristylium gardens. Grumbled Mahlir to himself, "It is a home that encompasses as much of the culture of our conquerors as it does of our own." Eli must have heard, and the comment must have amused him, because he glanced at Mahlir with a twitch of a smile forming through the white of his beard.

The wedding was of three parts, as were all holy weddings, the first being the procession, the second the consummation, and the third the feast. The beginning of the second part, the consummation, was held in the central peristylium, a garden of exquisite beauty in the very midst of

Eli's blasphemous mansion, open to the sky but enclosed by the four walls of the home itself. Mahlir took the slow walk to the Chupah, the flower and vine-covered archway under which his bride stood, in strides measured and pained. It was held up by four posts and was open on each side, symbolic of the tent of Abraham and Sarah, giving welcome to all, at all hours. Mahlir's heart grew heavier with each footfall, for he loved another. The woman God had chosen for him was not the one that filled his heart. The woman that filled his heart was the woman at the river.

Rachel was being presented to him for the first time on this the day of their wedding, virgin eyes upon virgin eyes. He had always been told about her, but had never seen her, other than those two or three times when they were children, but that was a very long time ago. The first time he would see her face would be upon the lifting of the veil.

He could tell that Rachel was looking at him through the veil. He could feel the pierce of her eyes. He thought he heard a tiny squeal come from her mouth. Of delight? So strange; why would she do such a thing? He could not see the form of her face, only shadows through the gossamer of the veil. Rachel, however, in looking out, could see clearly the images in front of her. "This was my mother's favorite place," she said. She reached out and stole a gentle squeeze of his hand, as though trying to impart a secret.

"It is beautiful," Mahlir said, though he didn't think so, though he was offended by what surrounded him. Other than the items brought in to decorate the mansion, the Willow and the Myrtle to hang from balconies instead of tapestries of the eagle, menorah stands instead of busts of family members, scrolls of the books of Moses instead of altars to Vesta, the place was Roman. Its architecture, even its smell, was Roman. Roman homes always had a strange smell, a large and lonely type of smell. The entire city was built like a Roman city, in honor of a Roman emperor, by a supposedly Jewish king.

The seven blessings were given, the Sheva Brachot, and the second cup of wine was consumed. She circled him seven times, symbolic of the seven times in the Torah that the phrase "...and when a man takes a wife..." appears, and symbolic of the wholeness that cannot be attained separately. As Adam and Eve were one, a part of the same flesh, one having been formed from the other, both having been formed from God, so had the bride and groom been an inseparable part of the Whole, brought forth from the fiery bosom of the Creator and divided into man and woman, soon to be united again, but stronger this time, made from the flesh of the Flesh, melded together once again, man and woman, Adam and Eve, Wisdom and Understanding, powerful when separate yet more powerful together, as it is meant to be. And woe be to the person who puts a barrier between them, for a firestorm will erupt as forces work to correct themselves.

The marriage contract was signed. With the placement of his name on the papyrus Mahlir promised to feed and clothe and shelter this person he did not know, but felt like he had known since time everlasting. It was his promise to God. On this day all his past sins would be forgiven; it was a day of atonement, a day on which to begin anew.

A sudden calm swept over him, and he lifted the veil...to confirm the truth of what Rachel already knew, that his wife-to-be was the woman at the river, was the one to whom his heart was bound.

At that same instant the sun came out. It was at her back. It burst through the clouds at the point of the lifting of the veil, streaming down to obscure her face in the shrouds of its brilliance, hiding for a moment the confirmation that he was marrying the woman he loved. He could make out just enough of her face to tell that the corners of her mouth were turning upward, blending shadows and sunshine. As her full lips spread wide to show the perfect white of her smile, to show that she also knew, as her eyes blinked away the substance of all her doubts and all her past miseries, as tears ran down her face, he lifted his own face skyward to thank God for the incredible gift, for the answer to the foolish prayer he made that day at the river, the impossible made possible, a happening so epic that neither of them would speak of it, not even among themselves. It would come to be known as the happening never to be spoken of.

A cheer went up and nuts were scattered by the crowd, to be trod upon and cracked open by the feet of the bride and groom, symbolic of a man and a woman in marriage breaking through the outer shells, the outer layers of beauty, of personality, of doubts and fears, to view and commune with the naked soul, which is now blended one with the other.

They were led to the marriage chamber, and while the guests waited outside the marriage was consummated. The Yichud, it is called. It is a union set apart, different than any other. None on earth will know the true intimacy of what two people share within the sacred environs of the Yichud. It was even more so with Mahir and his wife Rachel. When their lips touched their souls were already linked; when the coolness of their bodies came together they were already bonded; when his penis sank inside her, numbing their minds, stopping their breaths, stilling their hearts, they were already fused as one. The outer was an extension of the inner. It is an extraordinary experience, to lie with one's wife for the first time after having loved her for a lifetime, after having twice lost her, to discover that she was not lost at all, that the loss was only an illusion, that they were bonded anyway.

The moment of their penetration was the moment of their marriage, the moment they were declared man and wife, a pronouncement made not by the lips of man, but by Almighty Yahweh, the only witness, the one out of whom all creation is begotten.

In the chamber there was bread for them to eat, unleavened, and wine for them to drink. They had fasted the entire day. It was the finest meal of their lives, though it was nothing more than bread. A single sip of the wine's sweetness swam in Mahlir's head like sparkling dewdrops before the sun, and branded therein the memory of his wife's visage, of her long black hair, of her femininely muscled limbs, of her face full of devotion, of her eyes that spoke of unshakable commitment. When such a creature gives her heart it bestows upon her husband an even greater responsibility.

The first bite was taken by the bride and groom simultaneously, a symbol of fertility, of the children they would have, sons and daughters blessed by God, sent to earth in chariots of angels, descended to do great things. It was the beginning of the feast, the beginning of things to come, the beginning of a lifetime. After they ate they joined the others, so that the others could begin eating.

The feast lasted seven days.

They were married. They were one.

But the wellbeing extended only as far as the walls themselves, for the entire countryside was in disarray. Thieves and would-be kings were everywhere. And the couple would soon be caught up in its sway.

CHAPTER 11

THE SHEPHERD MESSIAH

NORTHERN ISREAL – THE PLAINS OF MEGIDDO

It had been nearly a full year since the marriage of Mahlir and his wife Rachel, and five years since the death of Herod-the-Great and the dissolution of the government's iron fist, and the countryside suffered still from the thieves and would-be kings. Upon his death bed Herod had divided the kingdom and given each of four parts to his sister and his three sons, and it threw the people into confusion and provided fertile ground for revolutions and seditions, the most prominent of which was spearheaded by one called Athronges, known to the people as the Shepherd Messiah. The province called Judea, the heartbeat of Israel wherein stands the Temple, had been given to Herod's son Archelaus. Galilee went to his son Antipas. The northern most region was bequeathed to his eldest son Philip. It is beautiful in the north. It is a place where the River Jordan has its beginning, emerging from the very stones of the earth, a jeweled piece of Yahweh's creation that sparkles forth in the form of creeks, waterfalls and all things green. Curiously, it is an area of the world also considered sacrosanct by the Romans as the home of their god Pan. Further complicating the political landscape was the fact that it was the age of the predicted Messiah, and all were waiting, expecting the arrival of a king greater than David. There were no less than a dozen claimants to the title, Athronges among them. The people thought it probable, that it could be Athronges, because of his uncommon size and strength, and because of his heroic deeds and relentless pursuit of justice. Whenever the robbing and plundering of a caravan preceded the giving of anonymous gifts to the poverty stricken, Athronges was suspected. Whenever the daughter of someone of royal ancestry was kidnapped and ransomed, and magnanimous gifts to the needy followed, the name of Athronges the Shepherd Messiah was rolling off the tongues of all those who heard of the deed. Whenever a criminal went unpunished for an act of evil, the people soon could depend upon some type of misfortune befalling the purveyor via the righteous hand of a ghostly rider at midnight.

It was far too late to be traveling. Mahlir was making his way along the Damascus Highway in search of an inn when two men approached. The moon was resting atop of westward rolling hills and was strong over the Plains of Megiddo and illuminated enough of their dress to reveal that the two men were common hill people. Their voices could be heard before they could be seen. The halting pace of their walk and the way their eyes shifted back and forth between the two of them suggested their intentions were not pure. "Hold there," one of them shouted out. "A shekel for the cause."

Mahlir ignored them and attempted to pass by without meeting their eyes. One of them blocked his way. "Hold, Priest," he said. "No one passes without paying the toll."

Mahlir squared his feet. "What toll? There is no toll on this road."

"No one passes without paying the toll."

"I've passed this way many times in service of the synagogues and have never been asked to pay a toll. How much money is this toll? And for what cause?"

Both men laughed. The one blocking the way said, "How much do you have? That is how much the toll is. And it is for the cause of the two people who might let you pass once the toll has been paid."

Mahlir's Roman short sword flashed; it had not been visible beneath his robes, and it caught the thieves by surprise and delayed their reactions. Its arc slashed one of them across the face. But a surprise also awaited

Mahlir. Things were happening in fractions of seconds, as the two thieves also displayed weapons, as the two dueled against the one. Mahlir's only experience with weaponry had come as a child when he would pester the Temple guards for swordsmanship training. He was energized and terrified all at the same time. The sword had become so heavy he could barely grip it, and his lungs heaved for air. You cannot be angry, the guards had taught him; you cannot be frightened. You have got to be thinking, strategizing. It's a game. The moment it ceases to become a game, the moment you allow anger or fear to overtake you, is the moment you have lost the fight. And here in this moment he had lost the fight. Something came down hard on the back of his head. In the next moment he was looking up at both men, a sword point pressed firmly to his throat. One of the thieves was searching the folds of his cloak. "Ah, what is it we have here?" he said, holding up Mahlir's purse. "It appears you have money after all."

There was a hum and a thick sound, and the one holding Mahlir at sword point dropped the sword and stood stiff, then collapsed under legs that crumpled beneath him. An arrow was protruding from his back. It was followed by great purple robes riding upon the wind, and thundering hooves tearing at the road and throwing bits of night into the air. The man riding the lead horse was so big his feet nearly touched the ground. A round platinum moon danced with subtleness on a golden diadem fashioned upon the big man's head. Golden rings adorned every finger. The bow that had delivered the arrow was still in his hand.

The arrow must have pierced a lung – the thief lay face down, gasping – and it left Mahlir with a weakness the Temple guards warned about. It occurs in battle, an impulsive need to help your enemies. You must harden your heart against it, they had warned. Your duty is to kill your enemies. If you help to heal them they will recover only to kill you, and instruct their children to kill you. It is the way of the world; it is the way of God.

The riders reigned in their horses to form a circle around Mahlir and the thieves. The thief with Mahlir's purse placed his feet as if to run, looked right, looked left, as the riders nudged their horses inward to close all pathways of escape.

The dying thief had momentary hope in his eyes. Tales abound about thieves helping other thieves. But such was not the case here. The big man, with arms large and hanging like those of an ape, slung the spent bow over his shoulder and dismounted, which took no more than the simple swing of one enormous leg over the head of the horse and thumped in heavy strides over to where the dying thief lay in the dust of the road and with his bare hands broke the thief's neck. Even then the unfortunate soul did not die right away. He struggled ever the more for breath, until at last his face froze in silence. The horsemen had their bows loaded and aimed at the standing thief's chest, close range, strung back to cheek level, the bronzed tips of their arrows catching glints of moonlight.

The big man lumbered up to Mahlir, who was by then sitting up, catching his breath, holding his throat as blood collected on his hand and seeped through his fingers. The big man knelt. "Let me see" his voice rumbled out. It came from a triangular opening in a thick silver and black beard. It came as a gentle sound. "Now, now, it's all right, let me see." He moved Mahlir's hand and caught the blood with his purple robes. "There, there now. It's all right, young priest. Superficial only. There we go. Let me just see." Mahlir felt like he was a child again, and that he was in the care of his father.

Who is this man of power?, he thought.

"There we go. It's all right. It's all right now. It's but a tiny bit of a scrape. Courage now." He reached out with his enormous hand and touched the wound. "Say something. I want to hear you speak. Anything. I want to see if you are able."

Mahlir shook his head no.

"Now, now. It's only blood. Say something. I think you are able, but I want to make sure your throat is not damaged." The big man was speaking in Hebrew, the language of God, understandable to Mahlir, though the accent was thick, being a strange kind of Hebrew, not at all the formal and proper linguistic singsong of the Temple hierarchy. It had more of an easy quality to it, folksy, with an intonation common to the Judean hill people who spoke it, tinged with its own mix of errant words, as if the language were evolving. It was not likely that the remaining thief could understand it – Mahlir could barely understand it – the common tongue being Aramaic, the mix of Babylonian and Hebrew that grew out of the Exile and the mixing of races, of theologies, of languages. "Thank you," Mahlir finally said, after a full and patient period of effort.

"There we go now," said the big man. "Good. You can talk. Good." The opening in the beard seemed as if chiseled from stone, a sort of pasted-on-upside down smile, the only evidence of a mouth being the bottom lip, the bottom of the triangle, sunburned and crusted.

"I'm not much of a warrior, I guess," said Mahlir. Every appendage in his body seemed to be trembling.

"To the contrary," said the big man. "We were watching from the hilltops. You did admirably well." He gestured with an enormous hand. Mahlir had never seen a hand that big. "Your swordsmanship was quite impressive. Where did a priest of Yahweh learn to handle a sword like that?"

"My good sir, you give me too much credit, I fear. My father is Matthias, the high priest who pulled down Caesar's golden eagle from over the Temple gate. The Temple guards taught me. They were Macedonians."

"Truly? You are the son of Matthias, the high priest who pulled down Caesar's golden eagle and hacked it to pieces?"

"Undeniably," said Mahlir proudly. "Mahlir is my name. Mahlir-of-Matthias."

"You are then a descendent of Aaron, brother of Moses, the first high priest?"

"For certain," acknowledged Mahlir. "My father's father was Margalothus, who was a descendent of Bilgah, who was one of the 24 original offshoots of Aaron."

"I am humbled to be of service to the son of the great Matthias." The voice rumbling out of the opening paused, then took on the tone of a reprimand. "However – let it be understood that the proper way to address your Messiah is with the title of Lord, not 'my good sir.'"

Mahlir was stunned. The man who had rescued him was Athronges, the Shepherd Messiah. Of course! The purple robes, the crown, the enormous hands, the man who was more of a god than a man. Who else could it be? "My apologies, my Lord. I didn't know. Truly, it is I who am humbled."

Athronges again rebuked Mahlir. "There is one other thing you need to know. It is a punishable offense to refer to that mixed-blood offshoot of Herod who now sits on the throne as king. He is to be spoken of by his given name only, Archelaus. He is no more of a king that you are. There is only one king, the Shepherd King, the Messiah, the one foretold by the prophet Micah, the true king of the Jews, and I am that king. I am the one destined to be anointed."

Mahlir bowed. "My Lord."

At hearing the adulation Athronges turned kindly in his expression, and it was overpowering. "Calm yourself now – it's all right," he said. "You had no way of knowing. But to those who know who I am, and do not acknowledge me, and who dare not bend a knee to me, a curse it shall be that shall lie over their heads. It is the unforgivable sin. He who denies me I shall deny him before God, and God will thenceforth deny him from this day forward into eternity."

"My Lord, it shall not happen again. And I thank you, my Lord Athronges, for saving my life. Had you not come along I would surely be dead." Mahlir could remember only one time in his life when he had felt such overwhelming relief, and such dependence on another human being. He had been a child barely past infancy. A bantam rooster had attacked him. Humorous now, but terrifying to one so young, as the bird came at him screeching and squawking, feathers batting, talons slashing. His father shooed the creature away, with no more than a calm voice and two hands the rooster respected. Everyone watching was laughing. Except his father. His father squatted low to be eye to eye with his son and said, "Are you all right, my son?" The young Mahlir nodded that he was, and his father's next words were reassurance, as he pointed to the men laughing, understanding that there was a wound deeper than the scratches given by the rooster: "Don't you worry about those men over there. Truth is, those roosters give me a start too." He patted Mahlir on the back and nodded toward the men. "Someday you will be a man twice what they are." His father had no way of knowing it at the time, but that pat, that moment, had been one of the most powerful memories of Mahlir's boyhood. It was a moment that sealed the two of them as father and son, that established his father as protector and mentor.

Athronges stood up, and it was then that Mahlir saw how truly large he was. The legendary Goliath could not have been any taller. Athronges put both hands down and helped Mahlir struggle to his feet, then turned to the remaining thief, still standing, purse still in his hand.

"My Lord Athronges," the thief said, and bowed. "King of the Jews."

"Now –," said Athronges. His eyes were hard, and that frightened the thief more than the bronze tipped arrows of the archers, "– perhaps you can remind me what it is that must be done with a thief, by the Law of Moses. I can't seem to remember. What was it now? Something about an eye for an eye and a tooth for a tooth? Perhaps you can refresh my memory."

The thief bowed a second time, trembling visibly. "My Lord, I, I," he stammered. "...please, this is not what it seems. I am fortunate that it is you, my Lord Athronges, who came upon this incident. For you will be fair above all others. Everyone knows that the Shepherd Messiah has the wisdom of Solomon. You are the one who has been anointed by God, the one who will free us from the bonds of Archelaus and Imperial Rome. And as such I am sure you will be able to see through the error of appearances." The thief held the purse out. "This is my purse." He pointed at Mahlir. "The young priest stole it from us. We were only attempting to recover what is ours."

"Do you know what happens to those who lie to the Messiah?" Tiny gurgles of laughter were coming out of the Messiah's mouth, a malevolent chuckle that could barely be heard, that sounded like little belches.

"My Lord –" The thief pointed to Mahlir. "You must believe me. It was he who took the purse from us. We were simply taking back what is ours."

The chiseled upside-down smile widened, and the tiny gurgles grew louder, hardly recognizable as laughter, sounding almost like Athronges was coughing or clearing his throat. "So –," he said. "You are a thief and a liar? Is that what you are telling me" His hair was full and wavy past his shoulders, befitting a Jew of holy prominence, but the top of his head, most of it hidden by the diadem, was hairless, and the weak and wiry strands that struggled out of it were all the more noticeable because of it.

"My Lord, please, you must believe me."

Athronges moved forward and stood a forearm's length in front of the thief. The thief tried to move backward, and turned his head to make movements to run, but there was no place to go, only into the midst of the encircled horses and the riders with their loaded bows, all aimed at the thief's chest. Athronges spread his feet then crossed his arms. His body parts did not quite fit together the way they do with most people. His torso was way too thick for his legs, and his arms too long, and his hands too big, and his head too small. He swaggered when he walked, but not out of arrogance, more out of necessity, as if the upper couldn't move without first being initiated by the lower. Words of authority came out of the opening. "Return the purse to its rightful owner."

"But my Lord –" The top of the thief's head came barely to chest level on Athronges.

Athronges nodded his head to secure the demand. The very power of the gesture compelled the thief to act, and he handed the purse back to Mahlir, his arm shaking.

"Very good," said Athronges, and stretched out his hand to the thief, as if offering forgiveness. At first that's what Mahlir thought it was, a conciliatory gesture to thank the thief, and to let him know that things had now been equalized.

But the thief knew otherwise. His entire body shook in fear. "Please, my Lord, I have returned it. There is no need for this. He has his property back."

"Your hand," said Athronges.

"Please. My Lord."

"Your hand."

Athronges' hand completely enclosed the thief's hand. The thief grimaced. His knees quivered. There was the sound of bone crunching, and more of the silent gurgles from Athronges' mouth.

In Athronges' face there was no indication of effort or strain, only the chiseled-out smile and the malevolent spurts. He was two people, defender of the innocent, ruthless arbiter of justice. Athronges released his grip to reveal a crumpled right hand, twisted, with fingers poking out at awkward angles from a swollen mass of purple. The thief held it, moaning, and dropped first to his knees, then to the ground altogether, moaning and rolling to and fro.

Said Athronges, standing tall above him, a symbol of righteous authority, "Moses said, if your right hand offends you, remove it."

Recompense having been given, the riders lowered their bows, and Athronges turned to Mahlir. The triangular opening and the strong eyes exuded compassion once more. "My young priest, my good fellow, it is by no accident that we met."

"Indeed?" said Mahlir.

"Yes," said Athronges. There was a large flat rock close by; Athronges sat on it to be at eye level with Mahlir, and put his hands on his knees. "You see, I am in search of an ancient artifact," he said. "This particular artifact contains power greater than any on earth. It possesses the ultimate power. It is a crown meant to adorn the head of the Messiah. And you can get it for me."

"Me? I know of no such object."

"Ah, but you have access to it. You are a priest of Yahweh, are you not?"

"Yes, but –"

"You are a priest of the Temple, are you not?"

"Yes, but –"

"The lost crown of King David, I am told, has been found, and resides in the Temple's inner chamber. You shall get for me."

Mahlir was stunned. "There is no such thing," he said, when words finally came. "The lost crown of Kind David is only a legend. Even if it does exist, I could not steal it from God's holy presence, not for anybody."

"The crown exists. It waits for the Messiah. It waits for me."

"Forgive me, my Lord Athronges, but you expect me to steal from God?"

"You are not stealing. You are retrieving. This is no coincidence, that you came here to us. Don't you see? God has sent you to me. It is God's will that you retrieve the crown, so that it may reside where it belongs, on the head of God's messiah."

"Forgive my boldness, but it is a child's tale. My father used to tell me that story when I was a boy. The crown was lost the very day King David lay with Bathsheba –"

"It is much more than a child's tale," broke in Athronges, "As the story goes – well, you know the story. You're a priest and a scribe."

"Yes, I've copied it and recopied it many times. I could probably recite it word for word from memory. The things King David had done, his adultery with Bathsheba and the murder of her husband, displeased the Lord so greatly that he sent the prophet Nathan to David with a story. 'There were two men in a certain town' the story begins. 'One was rich, the other poor. The rich man had a very large number of sheep and cattle, but the poor man had only one little ewe that he had raised from a tiny lamb. It had grown up with the poor man and his children, even slept in his arms. It was as a daughter to the poor man and his wife. Now one day when a traveler came to the rich man, instead of preparing a meal for the traveler with one of his own sheep, he took the ewe lamb that belonged to the poor man and prepared it for the traveler.'

"David burned with anger at the story, and said to Nathan, "As surely as the Lord lives, the man who did this should die! He must pay for that lamb four times over, because he did such a cruel thing and had no pity.'

"It was then that the prophet Nathan pointed an accusatory finger and cried, 'You are that man!'

"And as the story goes, the mighty king withered under the rebuke. God's punishment was that David's wives be given over to the one who was closest to him, and that the child given him in sin by Bathsheba should die, which in fact came to pass in seven days.

"That day of the prophet Nathan's visitation was the last day David saw his crown. The Lord took it away, it is said, because David no longer deserved to wear it, it being a symbol of fairness and purity. And that was the day, they say, that the Lord cursed the crown with the Shekinah Fire to protect it from those who would use it for purposes of evil bent. But to those with a pure heart, those whose souls are free from sin, those who would use the crown's power only for righteousness, and there is but one, even more power will be given.

"Another crown was made for the king, but it was forged by the hands of man. It was heavier, prettier, hammered out of solid gold, but it wasn't the same. And it had no power. To this day the real crown waits to be discovered. It waits for the Messiah."

"The man to whom you refer, I am he," said the mighty Athronges.

"But it's a child's tale, a metaphor only. It does not exist."

"It exists. And it belongs on my head."

"But my Lord, if the story is true, and if you are not – "

Athronges' eyes stopped Mahlir in mid-sentence as they focused on his implied impudence, but then softened and became fatherly once again. "Bring it to me," he said gently. "And I shall make you a general in my army in the conquest of Rome." He clawed at his beard – it was what he did when puzzling over an issue – and pointed an enormous finger at Malir. "Yes, that is what I am going to do. I am going to make you a general. The son of the one who pulled down Caesar's golden eagle deserves no less an honor." Then he rose and put his hand on Mahlir's upper back, a gentle hand. "Courage now, you will do fine. God would not have chosen you for this task if you were not up to it." And he stood and embraced him and kissed him, both cheeks, to seal the arrangement.

"You wish to conquer Rome?" asked Mahlir.

"In time. All things in their own time. For now we will be content to drive the invaders from our land, and to restore Israel, and to displace Archelaus with Israel's true king."

"Meaning you?" asked Mahlir, with a touch of the impudence returning, regretting it in the same instant.

Athronges let it slide. "Did you know that Archelaus is not even a Jew? Yet he holds the title of king. He is the son of Herod-the-Great, no more, no less. And Herod-the-Great was the son of Antipater of Idumea, no more, no less. By blood Antipater was no more a Jew than is a Roman. Antipater was a mere servant to the Maccabees and ascended to the throne only because of his allegiance to Pompey. Pompey put him on the throne, not the Jews, not God."

"My Lord, forgive my insolence – it is not intended as such, only to help and inform – but whoever sits on the throne sits there by approval of Caesar. Even if one were successful in displacing Archelaus, still, in the end, it must have the endorsement of Caesar."

Athronges' eyes opened wide and he pointed upward with his index finger as emphasis. "Ah! See? You are already proving helpful. This is to be a conquest done with both intelligence and power. You shall help me with the intelligence, with the strategy. The crown shall give the power. It possesses the Shekinah Fire, the very breath of God. None of my enemies will be able to stand before me."

"Forgive me, my Lord Athronges, but it is foretold that the true king of Israel will come from the line of David."

Easy tones of reassurance passed through the triangle. "King David was my grandfather twenty-six generations removed. His crown should be mine by ascension."

Mahlir bowed. "Forgive me, my Lord, there is one more question I must ask, before giving my allegiance and stealing the crown for you."

"Retrieving the crown," corrected Athronges. "Remember. It is mine by birthright." All the while the thief was on the ground writhing in pain. Mahlir cast him a nervous glance, but all others continued to ignore him, because the Mighty Athronges had dispensed justice.

"If I may, my Lord," continued Mahlir, "Judas of Ezekias is also from the line of David, and also claims to be the true king of Israel. How do we know which of you speaks the truth, which one of you is the one anointed by God?"

Athronges gestured toward the horizon, visible in the night only because it was illuminated by an eerie glow. "The false messiahs, you will know them by their fruits. As we speak, Sepphoris is in flames, at the hands of Judas of Ezekias. Ask yourself. Would the true Messiah burn your cities?" Athronges was one of those rare souls that captures passion with every word, simply because the eyes will it so. They wrap their target in comfort. The opening in the beard widened in softness. "Be a general in the Messiah's army. Change the world. When history writes itself of our causes, the name of Athronges the Sheppard Messiah will grace every page, to be read ten thousand years from now by ten thousand people. Let the name Mahlir-of-Matthias be there alongside it." He put his hand again on Mahlir's upper back. "Hmm?"

Mahlir pondered in silence before answering. "My wife is with child. I must consider my responsibility to my family. I am only recently married."

"God will protect you, when in the service of God's work."

"Perhaps. But I also have Temple duties requiring my attention. And my father-in-law has entrusted me with duties of his estate while he is away in Jerusalem on matters of the Sanhedrin."

Athronges stroked his beard. "Hmmm. Your father-in-law? Truly? A member of the Sanhedrin, the governing body of Israel? This gets better and better. So, he is one of the 72 that dispenses Hebrew law and justice? It is indeed fortunate we met. What is his name?"

Mahlir hesitated, but the eyes of Athronges were strong. "He is called Eli," Mahlir finally said.

"Eli. Hmmm. I have heard of this Eli. He is very wealthy. You married well. God has indeed blessed us, by directing you here so that our paths would cross. It will be good to have such strong connections. Return to settle your affairs, then bring the crown to me, and be a general in my army." Athronges pulled from one of his fingers one of the golden rings. "Here. Take this. We conduct our warfare from hidden places in the forests and the hills. Show this, and you will be taken safely to me."

As Mahlir was walking away Athronges turned his attention again to the thief. The thief was still there, but no longer writhing, no longer whimpering. A measure of relief had settled in, after the initial pain and shock, leaving the misshapen purple mass to throb in rhythm with the beat of his heart. Such secondary pain is almost a pleasant thing in comparison. Mahlir did not look, thinking of it as superstition if he did. A Temple priest is taught not to revel in the misfortune of others. He nonetheless listened intently to what Athronges was saying to the thief: "By the Law of Moses, if your right hand offends you, it must be removed," and heard renewed screams from the thief.

Finally Mahlir did stop and turn and look. Athronges, though a sword hung from his belt, though the sword would have been the most effective way of removing the thief's hand, had chosen a different method, one to better serve his reputation for great strength. As Mahlir turned to watch – anyone would have done so; the human mind forces itself in its macabre curiosity to watch the horrific – he saw Athronges gripping the thief's wrist and wringing it as one would a chicken's neck. It caused the little spurts to come from Athronges' mouth as full-blown laughter, as bone, and muscle, and flesh tore and popped.

In less time than it took to draw a second breath Athronges had the appendage loose and was waving it in the air like it was a victory branch. Blood was pouring from the jagged stub of the thief's forearm. "Take care of that thing before he bleeds to death," Athronges told his men, having in his voice a casualness that was chilling, and he threw the hand for the jackals to take. It went twisting through the air trailing beads of blood behind it, forming little concentric patterns in the moonlight before thumping down somewhere in the darkness, fifty, sixty feet away. The thief again screamed, but it was a different sound, not of pain, but of seeing the jackals coming to eye it, their formless shadows circling, making cautious movements toward it. One of Athronges' men began to unwrap his tinder and flint to start a fire so the wound could be sealed by hot metal, while another dismounted and began to tie tourniquet bandages to the stub.

Said Athronges, in addressing those who stared in disbelief, "It is not so hard to believe, that I can do these things, for God has given his own strength to me. And once I have the crown my strength will be greater still, greater than that of the gods of Rome, and the cause will be unshakable." He gestured for the others to dismount and gestured for them to make a circle around him. "Come, let us gather together and pray." He waved Mahlir over to be included in the circle and motioned for the man starting the fire to come as well, and the one who was tying the torniquet, though the tourniquet was only half completed, though the stub would continue to spurt blood. "Come. For a moment." He stuck his sword in the dirt and dropped to one knee and bowed his head. The others knelt and bowed. Mahlir did the same, as the thief's life essence collected on the ground. "Lord, we come before you in humility, for none is greater than you. Goodness has triumphed here today. Evil has been adjudicated. In like manner we ask for your strength to drive out the Romans and take back the land that is yours, that you gave to us, your chosen people. And give us also the strength to take the land of the Romans, and make that also our land, as did Joshua with the land of the Canaanites, the very soil upon which we kneel. With you, O Lord, at the head of our army, how can we lose? If Moses, leading a weakened group of slaves, can kill a thousand Egyptian soldiers in their flight to freedom, and if Joshua can kill six million Canaanites in the conquest of the Promised Land, and if David can slay a giant twice his size with nothing more than a stone, should we worry about a simple Roman eagle? Nay, we worry not, for you are with us. And we thank you, O Great Lord, for we know we are your chosen people. El melekh ne' eman. God our Faithful King."

"El melekh n' eman," rumbled the men in unison.

Then it was that Mahlir-of-Matthias, the man who took a vow never to bow before any false god, walked over and sank to one knee, and said – "O Lord Athronges, the one anointed by God, I give to you my full allegiance and service, however you see fit to use it. From what I have seen today, you could be none other than the Messiah. I am your servant." – and became one of many who recognized the Shepherd King as the incarnation of the long-awaited Savior of Israel. Some of the Israelites had gone so far as to assert that their Shepherd Messiah was of the direct seed of Yahweh and that his mother had received that seed in her sleep, not to be outdone by the Romans and their claims of Caesar Augustus being of divine origin, his mother Atia having received the seed of the god Jupiter while she slept.

Before mounting his horse Athronges stretched out his hand so that Mahlir could kiss the ring that was most prominent, the messianic symbol, the interlaced triangles, Involution Evolution, descending matter, ascending matter. Mahlir did so without hesitation, and without touching Athronges, because he was unclean having just battled with the two thieves. It would not do at all to touch the one anointed by God while unclean. "The crown," reminded Athronges, looking down from his horse. "Do not disappoint me."

Mahlir nodded in the affirmative.

The thief was crying out in what was the worst of his agony, because Athronges' men were completing the cauterization. They had cut off the hanging strands of muscle, tendons, and blood vessels, and were laying the flat side of the heated sword against the evened-out stub. Out there in the night, in the dust, flies were gathering and buzzards were circling, their black wings like flecks in the moonlight. One of the jackals lunged forward and grabbed something and loped away. And the buzzards screeched and fought with one another over a piece of it that one of them had managed to snatch. And Athronges and his men merged with the shadows of the night, ghosts into the blackness of the trees and the rocks, leaving the thief now to fend for himself, without a right arm. A man without a right arm is a man useless. And for some reason that bothered Mahlir. So he did something completely out of character for any rational human being, something utterly foolish. He gave the thief the contents of his purse anyway, not all of it, but enough so that the maimed man could establish himself in safety without having to depend upon those who would abuse him.

The thief hobbled away down the road in the opposite direction, weak from blood loss, humiliated to the point of ruin, limping as though it were his legs too that had been mutilated, and confused beyond measure at this deed of unrequited kindness, and Mahlir made his way to Jerusalem to procure the crown. He prayed as he walked, asking All Mighty Yahweh to take away this strange weakness that had overtaken him, the cowardice that had caused him to give money to a man that had nearly killed him.

CHAPTER 12

THE REVOLT

ISRAEL – JERUSALEM

"The crown is not there," Mahlir had to tell Anthronges.

Athronges ran his fingers through his beard's length with a gesture that said he was near to laughing. Still, everyone knew it was not laughter augmenting the expression. "Did you search everywhere? The Inner Chamber?" His voice thundered and the people trembled. He was as a god standing with his arms folded before the snapping and popping of the midnight fire. It threw its sparks into the black night with the smell of oak and pine and drove flashes of itself up to meld with the stars and become themselves a part of the firmament. Mahlir was privileged. Not many had ever seen the campfire of Athronges-the-Shepherd Messiah.

"It is impossible to enter the Holy Place," replied Mahlir. "The Holy of Holies is guarded day and night. But I spoke to my uncle – Joazar is his name – who is in line to become High Priest. I approached the subject delicately, with the ruse that I had concerns about someone stealing the Crown. He told me I need not worry, because it is not there, though an empty pedestal waits for it, for the time when it is found."

To Mahlir's surprise, Athronges was not angry. "Brilliant really," was his response. "To protect the Crown by letting everyone believe it is lost. No matter. We will take it during the revolt."

There was a sound coming from the blackness beyond the campfire. Mahlir's eyes kept wandering toward it. It was a wailing, low but loud enough to be heard by everyone. Yet they were not looking. They knew better. Because Athronges had once more dispensed justice. "An execution has been carried out," Athronges volunteered, upon realizing he would not have Mahlir's full attention until an explanation was given. He gestured for Mahlir to follow him into the blackness and look for himself. So he did, following the big man's footsteps, tripping over stones until his eyes adjusted, and viewed a disgusting sight. The stones were littering the ground in an uncommon way, some stained with blood. One had brain matter stuck to it. A figure was crouched in front of a mound of the rocks. A woman. Her frame trembled with her grief. Said Athronges, stopping in front of the figure, speaking softly in a kind way, "This woman's son was found lying in a sexual way with another man." Beneath the mound were the headless remains of two men that had been buried up to their necks. Their bodies would be dug up the following morning and carried to Gehenna, to be lost forever, no remembrance, no shiva. Just gone. Forgotten, except by the woman crouching. The leftover small chunks of skull and brain matter would be raked into the dirt.

Explained Athronges, in seeing the revulsion in Mahlir's face: "It had to be done. The commandments laid down by Moses are absolute. They were given to Moses by God. And they are exactly that, commandments, not suggestions. You cannot pick and choose. You cannot obey one and not the other, simply because one feels good and the other does not. You understand." Athronges was nodding, expecting Mahlir to respond with a similar nod, which he did, but the revulsion was still there, the pain at what God expects men to do to other men.

The revolt was to take place in Jerusalem, Mahlir learned, against the might of Rome, for it is Rome itself that protects Jerusalem. "Will you help us recruit from the citizenry?" Athronges stated. Athronges never asks, he states. "We need more soldiers. Will you help us?" Again a statement, not a request.

Mahir responded that he would. No other answer was possible. "I am in your service," he said, and suggested that Athronges dress as a common tradesman so that he would not be recognized by the Roman soldiers. "Dress plainly, perhaps as a carpenter or a stone mason. Carpenters and masons abound in and around the Temple due to its ongoing restorative efforts. Perhaps even sprinkle yourself with stone dust." And so with Romans posted on every street corner, with the great Messiah cloaked in the guise of a common carpenter, they both silently and without suspicion recruited their soldiers. Some would not believe, without seeing the messiah with rings on his fingers and clothed in fine linens and riding behind fine steeds having halters of silver and gold. But many were willing, even those who had no business in the business of war, old men, women, children, because that is how the Maccabees had done it, their name a cognomen for the phrase Mi Kamocha Be 'eilim Hashem, "Who is like you, O God?" – Mac-ca-bee, when spoken fast. The Maccabees brought down the forty-thousand soldiers of Antiochus Epiphanies with nothing more than ordinary citizenry. "And the Jews celebrated," Athronges said to the people, reminding them of their history. "And future generations, in remembering the conflict, would celebrate the celebration, not the victory itself, because when the Maccabees rededicated the Temple with the lights of the Lord, they had oil enough only for one day, yet their candles burned until a new supply could arrive eight full days later. That was the miracle to be remembered, not the fact that a handful of untrained Jewish field workers faced off and defeated the empire of the Seleucid kings. Thereafter the candle stands of the Menorah were built with nine receptacles instead of seven, eight for each of the eight days the lamps burned and a central ninth candle used to light the eight."

"In like manner we will take back Jerusalem from the Romans and their puppet king," Athronges told them. "With you we will win," he declared, "an army consisting of the people themselves, like the Maccabees. And in the process I will find and wear the crown of King David, heavy with precious stones and a full talent of gold." Athronges was persuasive. He gathered his recruits with remarkable success. The followers truly believed the words of their Messiah, that God would be on their side – as he was on David's side when he fought Goliath, as he was on Joshua's side when the Canaanites were plundered – and that the Romans would be caught off guard, never believing in a million years that the people they were protecting would be the ones to rise up against them.

And it almost worked, except that the Romans were wise in the ways of war, more so than the hap-slap soldiers of Athronges, and the Jews were all but annihilated, and their Temple nearly destroyed. For a time it had seemed the Jews might prevail. The Temple walls were high and sturdy, and the resolve of the Jews strong. They had slings and bows, and fired their stones and arrows from the highest points of the walls. The Roman arrows, being fired from below, fell short, or if they did reach their height, they simply hung in the air harmlessly before their return to earth, or fell upon the flats of the parapets to be gathered up and used by the Jews.

But the Romans had capabilities beyond those of the Jews. They secretly brought in one of their catapults, disguising it within the marching throng of a century of soldiers, and began to launch pots of fire up onto the esplanade. It was the beginning of the end for the Jews. Some of the pots fell upon the esplanade. Others landed on the roofs of the open sided cloisters, and the wood and the pitch and the wax fairly exploded under the barrage. The Jews were unprepared for such a disaster and were thrown into confusion. And the Romans rushed in and struck them down. Worst of all, they seized upon the treasury where the sacred money was deposited, and where the Crown of King David lay, if it was there. It was not.

It was by pure change that Mahlir survived, chance and perhaps by skill, from his boyhood days and his swordsmanship lessons from the guards. As Macedonians, the guards had fought Romans many times, and knew their tactics and strategies, how Roman soldiers bunch together with their shields to make fortresses of themselves like the scales of a reptile, and how their body armor is constructed to deflect blows, how the only way to inflict any kind of damage at all to a Roman soldier is to come from above or below the breastplate. He found himself on his back beneath one of the cloisters. Its roof was in flames above him. Fire was the enemy now. The heart of the beast seemed directly above, formless, roaring, almost a thing of beauty, slithering along the center beams with its scales of gold sending down wave after wave of crushing heat, exploding now and then into glitters of sparks, each in itself a firebrand of stinging pain.

Also standing over Mahlir was a Roman soldier, arcing high with a spear to drive through his heart. But something happened between these two men, an exchange of the oddest sort, amongst the chaos, amongst the seconds that passed as if hours, amongst the absolute and utter pandemonium. Mahlir looked into the eyes of this complete stranger, and the complete stranger looked into his. A mistake in war, to look your enemy in the eye, the Temple guards had always said. For then the combatants so often discover that each is not so different from the other. And, but for an obscure concept called patriotism, they may even come to conclude that it's no affair of theirs, and that all they are trying to do amidst the chaos is stay alive. So it was with the stranger with the spear in his hand, the stranger that was hardly more than a boy. And so it was with Mahlir. The Roman should have done his duty. He should have driven his spear. Instead, he took the time to question the reason why. "Why do this?" he seemed to have been thinking. "I'm not even angry; I don't even want to be here," because the muscles in his face began to relax, and the flex in his arms and hands eased. And the two enemies made an unspoken agreement with one another, with only their eyes, as if their minds merged, that there was nothing embittering between them, and that if the one let the other live it would have no bearing whatsoever on the outcome of this immense and insane conflict born of the human condition. No one would be the wiser. The soldier began to lower the weapon...and lost his life. Mahlir's Arabian sword – the weapons of the Jews were varied, from whatever they could lay their hands on, swords to rocks to pitch forks – found its way up under the breastplate of the young soldier, just as he had been taught by the

Macedonians, and into the flesh of his enemy and up under the rib cage, more by reaction than anything else, almost like it was an accident, something Mahlir did not intend to do, though he did intend to do it, though he didn't know why anymore.

A moment ago he was furiously committed to his cause. Now, not so much. As he was pushing the sword into the flesh and vital organs of the stranger – it went easy, far too easy – the Roman soldier's mouth was moving in surprise. "We had an agreement," it seemed to be saying, though no words were coming out, only the movement of lips. Mahlir began quickly to pull the sword out, hoping it wasn't too late to undo this thing he had done, hoping it wasn't too late for the two of them to do what they had agreed to do in the intensity of their silence, to just walk away unharmed, to let one another live and tell no one about it. The sword thrust was a mistake, Mahlir wanted to say. Here, let me undo it, let me turn back time. The soldier stood stiff and turned, and began walking in the opposite direction, then sat down, hard, legs out like a toddler sits when he can't quite negotiate the next step. And while sitting, the soldier looked away at seeming nothingness and began to convulse and vomit blood. At which point Mahlir scrambled to his feet and fled, fleeing not from fire and sword, but from the revulsion of his deed, an act that ran counter to every component and every wheel in the human engine. It occurred to him in that moment that perhaps even the most minimal act of harm is an unnatural force that could stymie and stall the cogs of that engine, and perhaps the cogs of a larger engine to which it belongs. Maybe that's why when someone trips and falls the instinct is to reach out with assistance. Maybe it wasn't just an anomaly exclusive to Mahlir, a weakness of character, that caused him to have empathy for his Roman enemy; maybe it's the nature of the species to protect one another, just as it's the nature of a spider to spin a web, the same web every time, the same symmetry, the same geometry, or of a bird to build a nest, the same nest every time, one being identical to the other, though its makers have never conversed with one another or have never received instructions on how to do it. He heard the crash of a burning beam behind him. He stopped and turned. The beam had exploded into an echo of sparks upon its impact, in the exact spot where the soldier had been sitting. And another thought came. Maybe he did do the right thing. Maybe the soldier would have taken his life after all, or the life of another Jew, or three or four, maybe the life of someone he knew. The insanity of it all, the efforts to make sense of something that makes no sense, can drive a sane man mad, often does, if one takes the time to think too much about it.

Mahlir continued to run, and more Jews died. And he became aware again of the ultimate enemy. Fire. Heat. Smoke. It was searing itself into his lungs to make breathing impossible. He felt his legs crumple beneath him as he struggled to make his chest work. He was not worried about running anymore; he just wanted to make his chest work. And he did, somehow, in those seconds. He figured out how to do it, right before a curtain of black was beginning to envelop him. If he wheezed in the air slowly, bit by bit, then his chest would allow the air to pass, not much, but enough to keep him conscious, enough to terrify him beyond reason. Soon he was coughing and gasping, gulping in the air by the mouthfuls. Still he was unable to move. Still he was lying face down on a smooth paving stone in a street completely deserted. The citizens of Jerusalem had long since gone into hiding, even the animals. Nor were there birds in the sky. Nor insects crawling. No life. The Temple was behind him, roaring, exploding, rushing, the way fire does when it is massive and uncontrolled. And the smoke was above him, like a low cloud cover. The paving stone on which he lay was so hot he was sure his skin was being seared off. So he had no choice but to lift himself up, and to continue running, past the silence of dead bodies, multitudes of them, hideous in the contortions of their last moments. Eventually the roaring fire came to be nothing more than a menacing sound in the distance. He looked over his shoulder, in the same way Lot's wife looked back. The clouds were high that day. The dark plumb of smoke had risen to the heights of those clouds and had merged with them to show an eerie sort of marriage between heaven and earth, good and evil. And in their shapes he saw the image of the young soldier, sitting with his feet out, like a toddler, with his mouth open and forming the words, "We had an agreement." Mahlir ran some more, then turned again; he could not help himself. The clouds had drifted and stretched, giving the face and the mouth a sudden fierce and vengeful look. The smoke continued to roll into the clouds, slowly, majestically, as if it had a purpose, as if it were stretching the face into laughter to welcome to the fold all those on earth who would kill for a cause.

All of the Jews in the revolt died that day. No need to tell Rachel. No need at all for her to know that her husband was a run-away deserter. His duty had been to return to the camp of Athronges. He did not. He had a greater duty to return to Rachel. He would not ever be returning to Athronges. It was his first taste of war. It would be his last. And Athronges would view it as desertion. Athronges had been seen retreating as well, but that was to be expected, demanded. The Messiah is to be protected at all costs. If the Messiah dies, the cause dies.

The revolt accomplished nothing. The Temple was rebuilt and the Romans remained, and Archelaus continued on as king. "It was because I didn't have the crown," Athgronges would tell his people. And he would blame Mahlir, because Mahlir had deserted, and the penalty for desertion in any army is death. Not only did Mahhlir desert, he failed to find and turn over the crown. Someone told Athronges he thought he saw Mahlir carry it off. And the more Athronges thought about it the more he began to believe it.

Mahir had done more than desert; he had turned his back on God's messiah. A grand heifer was needed for such a sin, the entire animal, one pure and unblemished. Then perhaps Yahweh would forgive.

But perhaps not. Because a curse had fallen upon the family, even given the sacrifice of the heifer. One day Eli failed to return from one of his many business trips into Jerusalem. Rachel was constantly pleading with him not to go into the city anymore, at least for a time, until the rioting had subsided, until all the would-be kings had given up their notions of wearing diadems on their heads and of being called royalty.

But Eli would not hear of it. He went anyway. Without guards or escorts.

He prided himself on his perfect attendance record with the Sanhedrin, and on his punctuality. He would always return on the promised day and at the promised hour. Except this day. This day the promised hour came and went. And the day came and went. And another day came and went. Then another. And another.

Then there was a thundering of fists at the door.

CHAPTER 13

THE RANSOM

ISRAEL – CAESAREA

The pounding continued. There was the clattering of metal and the hurried exchange of heavy male voices from beyond the carved timbers of the barrier that kept them safe. "They are Romans," whispered Rachel.

Mahlir stood motionless. "Maybe," he said. Crimson was sweeping up from his neck into his face. Blood vessels began to bulge on his forehead. It was what always happened when he was angry or frightened, or when he felt threatened. Rachel loved to tease him about it – it was how she got him to capitulate whenever they would argue, by mocking him until he finally started laughing – but here it gave her comfort. Here she accepted his protectiveness as he moved instinctively in front of her, muscles tensed. She could see it through his tunic. Though he was gentle on the inside, he was powerfully built, and his face could look threatening to anyone who didn't know him, as if it had been hacked out beneath jutting cheekbones, the way a statue might look before being smoothed out and refined, and it made her feel a little safer.

Shammah was making hand gestures for them to open the door. Shammah was Eli's mute servant, an aging Samaritan with the wisdom of Solomon, so said Eli. It was Rachel who spoke first. "Shammah's right. We should open the door. The Romans are not our enemies. They are here in added numbers on orders from Caesar, to act as our protectors from the marauders. Maybe they have information on Father."

The doors, thick and reinforced with iron strips, were obscuring understanding of the shouts beyond it. The surf and the wind were further clouding the meaning of the words.

"All right," Mahlir said, and together with Rachel and Shammah he unbolted and drew open the weighty doors. They were double doors the height of three men, and opened inward from the middle. Standing there were soldiers.

There were two of them. The helmets and the gear were mismatched and ill-fitting, and when one of them spoke his voice lacked the accent common to Romans. "Is this the home of the merchant Eli?" one of them queried. He had a scar that parted his lips in such a way as to give dominant authority to each word spoken. Mahlir recognized him instantly. They had been tricked into opening the doors for soldiers of Athronges.

"You are correct," said Mahlir. "This is the home of the merchant Eli. But he is not here. He is away on business concerning the Sanhedrin."

The reply was immediate. "You are partially correct," the one with the scar said, amused by what he was about to say. "He is certainly away on business, but it is business that concerns the Shepherd Messiah, not the Sanhedrin."

"What are they talking about?" asked Rachel.

"What have you done with him!" demanded Mahlir.

"Father? Are you speaking about Father?" Rachel breathed out the question with hope and confusion all at the same time. "Do you know where Father is?"

"The Lord Athronges is not an unreasonable man," said the man with the scar, in tones of dripping sarcasm directed at Mahlir. "We have instructions to tell you where your wife's father is once we have within our possession the Crown of King David, which we all know you have, and funds for the cause, which we also know you have. Fifty thousand sesterses is the sum the Messiah asks."

The other soldier quickly added, "But we must hurry." His voice was helpful in its tone, rather than that of delivering an ultimatum. It made it seem as if he were a reluctant participant in the affair. "He has been set within a watery place. It may already be too late. I am instructed to give you this." He handed Mahlir a piece of parchment, whereupon was written a ransom demand in two languages, Aramaic and Latin. Mahlir read it aloud, his voice lowering to a near whisper at the end:

> *If you want to see the master of your household again, you will follow these directives without compromise. You are instructed to bring an amount of fifty thousand sesterces to the base of the aqueduct on the shoreline, as a contribution to the Messiah's cause of liberating the people of Israel, and there you shall also surrender the Crown of King David.*

Rachel shook her head in confusion. "The Crown of King David? Mahlir! You told me you didn't have it. What's going on? What are we going to do?"

"We'll give him the crown."

"What??"

Mahlir explained in an undertone of near silence, as though his thoughts alone were good enough to answer the question. "The mythical crown of King David. It's not a myth. I have it."

"Mahlir?"

In a guttural and barely audible whisper Mahlir answered her. "I do. I have it."

"Why didn't you tell me any of this?"

"Because I didn't want you involved. Because a very dangerous man wants it."

"I thought you said he was the Messiah."

"That is the very reason he is so dangerous. Rachel, think about it, this is the man anointed by God." Mahlir's tones were unnatural, and loud enough to be overheard, as if he were an actor in a play, as if he wanted to be overheard. "If he truly is the Messiah this is a man who has been singled out by the very hand of God. A man with that kind of power is indeed a dangerous man, especially when you cross him, which I do not intend to do. A man like that doesn't forgive and forget. And he has odds against me. I stole the crown, and I ran like a coward while other Jews died horrible deaths."

"If he has that kind of power, what does he need the crown for?"

Mahlir was stumbling over his thoughts, because half of what he said was true. He did believe in the power of the Messiah. Obviously Mahlir did not have the crown, but he needed them to believe he did. He was thinking of how he would answer the question when the one with the scar answered for him. He had indeed overheard. "With the Crown of King David the Messiah's power will have no limits. Power even to crush Rome. With the same ease that David slew Goliath. Power even to raise the departed souls of the righteous. It is enwrapped by the Shekinah Fire itself. Now where is it?"

"It is here. Hidden. Well hidden."

"Go get it, along with the money."

"How do we know you really have my father?" asked Rachel.

The reluctant one laid his bag on a nearby table and pulled out a ring, handling it like it was a precious stone that might slip away and be lost forever.

Rachel snatched it up. "It's Father's. What have you done with him?"

The reluctant one looked into Mahlir's and Rachel's face. "There is not much time. Your master has been bound hand and foot and has been set within a cluster of rocks that will soon fill with water at the rising tide. We are instructed to deliver this message to you, and to lead you to a place on the beach by the hippodrome, where another of Athronges' freedom fighters will meet us and exchange the funds and the crown for exact instructions on where to find your master. It must be fifty thousand sesterces." He looked at Mahlir. This was a soldier older and wiser, spoke the lines in his face and the tone of his voice, wiser in the way of life's experiences, caught between two worlds, his own that something good inside was forging, and the one on the outside that mankind had created. "My Lord, you must do exactly as he says. I am bound by my promise to tell you that it must be exactly fifty thousand sesterces, and that you must also deliver the crown. I am also bound by my promise to remind you that you have chosen the wrong side, and that it is never too late, that he will forgive and forget."

The one with the scar quickly finished the thought: "...for once he has the crown he will plunder Rome. Under the all mighty banner of Yahweh, the god of the Jews, he will gather his followers and dispose of every last living thing that is Roman, wives, children, even oxen and sheep," – He was speaking as though he had been given the words and had committed them to memory – "as well as those sympathetic to the Roman ways, just as Joshua did to the nonbelievers of Canaan, for here is the long awaited Messiah, come to us at last to slay a great beast, an evil empire. It is so written. It is in the prophesies." He began to chant in Aramaic. "Elaha Akbar, Elaha Akbar. God is great, God is great." The reluctant one joined in, eyes glazed over. Mahlir knew then that nothing more could be done, except to procure the crown. Both were prepared to die for their cause and their god.

"Fifty thousand!" Mahlir whispered to his wife. "Do we have that much?" He didn't know why he was whispering. The soldiers could still hear. "I don't even know where your father keeps his money."

"I do," she said, steady and sure. "I think I can get it together. It will take me awhile." She said it while turning to walk away, and was quickly stopped by the one with the scar.

"Ah! Not without us," he said. "We will come with you."

That was what Mahlir was hoping for. It gave him the opportunity to find something to approximate the weight of a crown of solid gold. While Rachel led them in one direction, he went in another, to Rachel's bedchamber, where he emptied her jewelry box and placed a brick inside. The box had carvings of Moses and the Pillar of Fire, the Shekinah Fire, the very power purported to enwrap the crown. The perfect receptacle. They would not look inside. Their superstitions would not allow it. They were well familiar with the story of Uzzah who touched the Ark of the Covenant, possessed also of the Shekinah Fire, and fell dead upon the spot.

The money and the box were placed in a satchel. Mahlir was forced to carry it. It must have weighed as much as a full-grown goat. He was barely able, its weight at times causing him to collapse under it, at one point striking the ground so hard it caused his mouth to bleed, as they made their way to the secret rendezvous point where it was promised the Shepherd Messiah himself would complete the exchange, and probably also take Mahlir into custody. No one escapes justice, not anymore, now that the Shepherd Messiah rides.

Strange is the way the mind works. Now, facing the possibility of actually losing his father-in-law, the arguments with Eli, the philosophical and religious differences that seemed to form a chasm, were of little importance. All that mattered was getting him back safely. Even Eli's gentle dog knew something was amiss. Jesus-of-Sie was prancing back and forth, a golden Canaanite with a tuft of white on his curled-up tail. Mahlir patted him on the head to calm him, as he had been doing during the ordeal, lest the animal attack, in which case all would be lost. Mahlir remembered the first time he saw the bothersome beast. It had been right after he and Rachel were married, when they first moved into their portion of Eli's mansion. Mahlir had gone outside to assist Shamah and Eli after they had returned from a buying trip. The dog bounded out from seeming nowhere. Eli reached in his pouch. The dog halted, ears perked forward, tail arched above its back.

Eli held out his hand. A morsel of dried beef was in his palm.

The dog barked and half lurched.

Eli stopped him. "Ahhh! Tell me first, is Jesus a good boy?"

The dog titled his head inquisitively.

"Tell me, is Jesus a good boy?"

The dog finally conceded to the demand, curled back his lips and bared his teeth, but breaking the snarl a time or two with an impatient yap, causing Eli to withdraw the offering. "Ahhh – now – is Jesus a good boy?"

The dog resolved to obey, and set firm his stance and hardened his eyes, and gave a most fearsome growl.

"That's it, that's a good boy," whereupon Eli delivered the morsel.

Jesus gulped it down, and, duty done, returned to his imposing, smiling, yapping self, his body shaking with delight as Eli and Rachel stroked his head and shoulders.

Mahlir whispered his disapproval to Rachel. "Your dog is named after the high priest?"

"It's Father's private protest. He doesn't have much use for the Temple priesthood."

Mahlir was taken aback and began to wonder if his father had made a good decision in promising him in marriage to this woman, to this family where blasphemy abounded.

But he loved his wife, and he loved Eli, and he loved life. Every single day brought newer and deeper meaning to his existence, and to the relationships with which God had chosen to bless him. He could not let Eli die. He would not.

Mahlir was right; superstition forestalled verification of what was actually within the box. The two soldiers led them to a place on the beach within full view of all parts of the half moon bay of Caesarea, never once looking inside the box. Mahlir was confused. It was where the aqueduct came down from the hills. It was a public setting, with people coming and going in full view of one another. There would be no place to hide a kidnap victim. Where could Eli possibly be?

As if in answer to his confusion, the reluctant one, unseen by his more warlike comrade, gave a furtive wave of his head toward the aqueduct, its geodynamic archways and smoothed out bricks crawling down to the beach from Mount Caramel and the Spring of Shummi ten miles away, delivering atop its smooth elegance a ribbon of cold and pure mountain water. Something was in there, some kind of blockage. Bits of the water were spilling over the side.

At the direction of the one with the scar Mahlir threw down the satchel.

"Open it," he demanded.

Mahlir hesitated, then went to the satchel and untied the rope and drew it open, and stood back, feigning fear.

"You know what I mean. The crown. The box. The box that is inside the satchel. Pick it up and open it. Let us see the crown."

Mahlir took another step back.

"Did you think we would not check?"

"I don't know if the crown is in there or not," said Mahlir. "I did not look."

"Why not?"

"You know very well the reason why," Mahlir told him." For the same reason you have not opened it yourself. It possesses the Shekinah Fire, the most powerful energy under the sun. It is the very breath of God. That is why."

"Open it," he repeated.

"I did my job. I took the box from its pedestal in the Temple's Inner Place. It is up to you to verify its contents."

"Open it."

Mahlir picked up the box, and with an almost imperceptible nod at Rachel said, "Turn your eyes away everyone, lest the fire blind us all." The nod had been a signal to Rachel. He was about to make his move.

The one with the scar thought he saw something shining from within the box, as the lid was being ever so slowly drawn back. "A light!" he shouted out in fear. And he too turned his eyes away.

His imagination, obviously, because nothing was in there but the brick. But all were able to see Mahlir's knees quiver and give way, and blood come gushing out of his mouth. All were witnesses as he screamed out words in Hebrew and fell unconscious into the sand.

Rachel and Shammah knew and understood the tongue of the Lord; the others did not. Gibberish, words of nonsense, was the way Mahlir's scream had come to the ears of the others, because Athronges alone understood the Temple dialect of Hebrew, and Athronges was not there.

"Your father is in the aqueduct; run to him there!" was the way the Hebrew words were heard by Rachel and Shammah. And they did exactly that. They ran to Eli's rescue while the captors in their superstition were staring in horror at Mahlir's prone body, and deciding whether or not they should risk picking up the thing responsible for it. When Mahlir had fallen earlier he had bitten his tongue. That was all there was to it. The tongue is a sensitive organ. It bleeds profusely even with a minor injury. He had allowed the blood to accumulate in his mouth for when the time was right.

The coins had spilled out upon the sand. As the captors were gathering them up – they would deal with the box later; for now they just put it back in the satchel unopened – they failed to notice that Mahlir too had run to the aqueduct. The three of them – Mahlir, Rachel, and Shammah – were scaling its wall like soldiers in battle, finding hand and footholds between the basket-sized blocks of stone, at the place where the water was spilling over the side, all without being yet noticed.

Eli had been gagged and bound hand and foot and was struggling to keep his head above the icy water. He was shivering with convulsive force, nearly unconscious from the cold itself. It was approaching the time of the Feast of Sukkot, an annual commemoration of the forty years the Jews had wandered in the desert, a time when more flow would soon be released through the channel. That had been what the reluctant one had meant by the term "rising tide." Eli would have drowned in minutes. When his gag was removed, shivering and near death though he was, the first thing Eli did was to look at each of his rescuers and thank them, with a touch on the cheek from a trembling hand. "My daughter, my prized and precious pearl, my only heir, my legacy – thank you. Ah, and good Shammah. What would I do without my most excellent Samaritan servant? And my son-in-law, blessed it be, the day you became yoked to our family."

The three of them – Rachel, Shammah, and Mahlir, half carrying Eli – were hurrying in an effort to put distance between themselves and the soldiers, but escape was not possible, they realized, when horses came lumbering out of the forest, well able to overtake them. It was a single rider leading three empty horses, his ribbon of red trailing, an obvious accomplice, a monstrous form of a man, nearly as big as Athronges. The rider shouted for them to stop, and Mahlir signaled compliance to Rachel and Eli. They had no choice. The forest rim was too far, and Eli too weak. Even if they could get to the forest, they were well within bowshot range. They'd never make it.

So Mahlir and his wife and father-in-law, though they were so close to freedom, simply stood and waited for the captors to once again surround them.

"Is that where the crown is, inside?" the rider shouted at the one with the scar, hovering over him, pointing to the satchel, which he now carried. "Open it!"

The one with the scar dropped it, but did nothing more. His terror was etched into his face.

The rider shouted again for him to open it.

With trembling fingers he picked up the satchel and drew open the cords.

"You know what I mean," clarified the rider. "The crown. It had better be in there, or Eli the Sadducee dies, and you shall die along with him."

"It's in the box," said Mahlir calmly, amused that this grizzled warrior was afraid of a brick, though he didn't yet know it was only a brick. Mahlir was also amused at his own cleverness.

The one with the scar reached in the satchel and took hold of the box, but dropped it and cried out in fear, warning of the fire.

It was the reluctant one who finally took the box and opened it, and as he was unlatching the lid he promptly fell over dead, gripping his chest in the process as though trying to tear out his heart, letting the box fall to ground only half opened. There was a strange look frozen into his face. He seemed to have been asking a question in his last moments of life – is there a purpose to it all, a journey, a road upon which we are traveling, destination unknown? – and he left the confines of his body in almost the same instant, to find the answer elsewhere. Never fully opened, the box lay on the ground for quite some time, until the one with the scar, his misshapen lip trembling, was ordered by the rider to pick it up, latch it, and put it back in the satchel. "Never mind looking inside," the rider said. "I am satisfied it is in there. We will let the Messiah open it. Clearly, the power the crown possesses is meant only for him. It is evident that it is only safe in the hands of the Messiah." As he was carefully placing the box back in the satchel, the one with the scar kept whispering audibly that he had seen a type of light escaping from the partially opened lid, a type of hot light. His imagination, since there was nothing in there but a brick. Had it happened in future times everyone would have understood that the dead man had died of a heart attack. Simple heart failure. And the fact that it had happened at that particular moment in time had been nothing more than a coincidence.

The rider drew forth an Arabian scimitar he had been carrying bare-bladed in his leather waistband, and, after announcing he was the brother of Athronges eased his horse forward and claimed the money and the box; no more was there a need to open it. He raised his clenched fist skyward in a silent salute, a militant gesture that meant, O God, who is greater than you? The horse, unencumbered by the harshness of metal in its mouth, was obedient to the rider's every command, being no more than a nudge of the knees here, a nudge there, a gentle and loyal animal that knew nothing of the deeds it was empowering.

The Brother of Athronges then threw down an additional weapon. Its steel clunked in the sand. The one with the scar grabbed it up and touched the deadly blade to his disfigured lips in a peculiar type of kiss. It was a sword that looked like a Greek dagger, though longer and thinner, stiletto type, sheathed in a makeshift leather scabbard. Like so many others of provisional armies and counter revolutionaries, these men had no uniformity, no standard of weaponry or dress, other than the red ribbon that marked them as soldiers of the Messiah, and the untrimmed beards that identified them as servants of God. Their weaponry was what they could steal. The ritualistic kiss seemed to take away the fear and replace it with a feeling of strength and power, as if it too possessed some type of energy. The misshapen lips took on a sneer as he tied the death instrument onto his back, positioning it so it could be reached with an easy swing of the hand, and mounted one of the empty horses. It was effortless, the way he leapt astride the saddled and waiting animal. His duty only partially complete, and in seeing that Mahlir was among the living, he edged his mount forward toward his former general, smiling, to let him know he was going to particularly enjoy this part of his assignment, now that he was the powerful one, for he now had the things that make men powerful, a horse, money, steel that can end a life, and the Messiah as his lord and master. And God was with him, as it was with the kings of old. And if God is with you, who can stand against you? So said the smile as he moved toward Mahlir. It caused Mahlir's muscles to twitch. The deformed smile curved upward, seemed to invite him to try. It was a horrific look, animated by the scar, exposing discolored and misshapen teeth. In his eyes were reflections of the insane lawlessness that pervaded the land, sect against sect, tribe against tribe. Oddly, it was Herod's iron fist that had kept the warring factions together in peace. Now, not even Roman soldiers could keep order, especially when some of the soldiers themselves were corrupt. "One of the empty horses is for your wife," he said to Mahlir. "I am afraid she must come with us."

Mahlir suddenly realized that his wife was no longer by his side. He looked around. There came a scream. Rachel! The color crimson flashed into his face as he saw that the Brother of Athronges had snatched her up, that he held her in one enormous hand and the Arabian sword in the other. The horse was backing away, prancing with controlled steps, nervous at the commotion happening on its back, because Rachel was struggling violently against this man's powerful arm. The Brother of Athronges laughed. "The plan worked," he said in the common tongue of Aramaic. "It was the only way we could lure the daughter of the famed merchant Eli away from the safety of enclosed walls. I am Josiah, one of four brothers of Athronges." The arm that held Rachel seemed the size of a rain cistern. "Soon Athronges will be recognized by all as the Messiah and be heralded as a ruler more powerful than the Caesars," he said. "More powerful than the Macedonian. He will be a king to rule over kings, subjugating even the fierce yellow-skinned warriors of the Far East." He was addressing Eli. Eli was half standing, half sitting, trying to stand, but shivering so violently he could not find footing. "And you shall help us finance our efforts, old man. You think we would be satisfied with a handful of sesterces? We know what you are worth. And we know how much you love your daughter. Your own life means very little to you. We know that. But your daughter? For your daughter you would give your entire fortune, if that be the price." He glanced at Mahlir, as though delivering an insult, then brought his eyes back to Eli. "Answer me, what do you think your daughter is worth, if you were asked to put a price on her?"

Eli's trembling turned into sobs. "Please. Anything. Just give her back. Please."

"Ten talents? Yes. I think that would be an appropriate amount. Ten talents. Two hundred and sixteen thousand sesterces. When the Lord Athronges has it in his hands she will be escorted safely back to Caesarea."

"Ten talents! I haven't got that kind of money. I'd have to sell my farms and my ships."

"Let us know when it is done." Josiah pulled Rachel into him, struggling as she was to free herself from his grip, and bent forward to look directly into her frightened eyes. "In the meantime, I am quite sure your daughter and I can find ways to pass the days and nights. We did bring a horse for her – let us spare no comfort for our guest – but for the moment I have given her permission to share mine." Her arms and feet were flailing. The horse was fighting an urge to rear up at the tumult and was being calmed by the soothing voice of this man called Josiah. The same voice that was tormenting Eli, laughing at him, was also cooing the animal with gentle tones and warm touches on its neck. The animal surely needed the reassurance, surely was already uncomfortable under the added weight of Rachel and of the large satchel of coins and the brick bearing down upon its neck, tied to its rigging. It was Roman rigging. The horse had at one time belonged to a Roman soldier, a particularly commendable souvenir for a warrior of the Messiah, for it was useful as well as commemorative. Some insurgents took scalps or fingers as souvenirs. God frowned upon such practices because it provided nothing of practical value.

The one with the scar sat comfortable now on a horse of his own, and watched with amusement this drama that was unfolding in front of him. Both his hands were idle in front of him. He was using them to lean forward on his mount. He would have no need for them. Nor would he have need of the Roman short sword that was a part of his stolen uniform or the dagger hanging makeshift on his back.

"How will I know where to find you?" stammered Eli, barely able to stand, barely able to speak.

"We will find you," said Josiah. Josiah indeed was a Goliath of a man. His neck alone was equal in size to his huge head, leaving one with the thought that God was running short on time and stuck it there on his shoulders without shaping it. Even given his strength he was having difficulty holding Rachel, so aggressively was she struggling and screaming. They were screams more of hatred than of fear. She would have spat in his face and torn it to pieces with her bare hands, had she the opportunity. The screams amused Josiah, and to show his power he freed his other hand by sliding the sword into his leather waistband – or so he thought; it fell to the ground instead – and violently shook her, then lifted her colobium and ripped off her undergarments, and did to her, by the force of his strength, right there on the horse, right there in front of Mahlir and Eli, what no man should do to a woman, what no father should see done to his daughter, what no husband should see done to his wife. Rachel jerked at the pain of the first thrust. The surprise of it showed in her face. She collapsed into the rest of them. The anger and the hatred in her face changed to show the overwhelming crush of defeat. Because now she had been defiled. Now she was useless as a woman.

Josiah was half laughing during the foul deed, and half succumbing to his passion. He was looking at Eli the entire time, with the sudden control he had over this powerful man of wealth and influence. But there was another man he should have been watching, that he had let slip from his sight. A dangerous man. The husband of the woman he was tarnishing. The man he had erroneously dismissed as a weakling and a coward. Where was he? Josiah realized his mistake and looked around for him.

Too late. Mahlir had picked up the Arabian sword. He swung it at Josiah's horse, crippling its leg, and brought the same single motion to cripple the horse of the one with the scar, then impaled him with it as he came tumbling to the ground. The sword caught him twice, first in the abdomen above his hip, the second just under the chest bone. It must have pierced his heart because life had gone out of him instantly. Both horses were down and struggling to get to their feet. Josiah should have run. But he was furious. He had been humiliated, by of all people a Temple scribe and a coward who had been given a military position of authority purely for political rcasons, where he, Josiah, bore the scars of many battles and deserved it far more. He needed recompense. He advanced empty handed and on foot toward this wretched and pitiable priest who was the lesser man. He would squash him with one bare hand.

He laughed as he walked toward Mahir, laughed and mocked him, with words like, "Babies shouldn't be walking around with things that are sharp," and, "You better give it to me now before you cut yourself." Those were the things Josiah was saying, unaware that his comrade lay dead in the sand at the hand of Mahlir, unaware of what was about to happen to him from behind from a second attacker, one he had not thought of as a hazard, a mere woman, the woman he had defiled.

It showed first in his face as surprise, then anger as he whirled to confront whoever or whatever had given him that huge sting. Rachel had plucked up a broken arrow that lay in the sand, a remnant from some battle of an era gone by, and had plunged it into Josiah's back. The arrowhead was not attached. It was merely a broken shaft, but sharp enough and stout enough to pierce flesh. He was angered to the extreme, and would have killed her in the next instant, had not his next breath been cut short by the edge of his own sword, held now by Mahlir, giving so deep of a cut that it nearly decapitated him.

Josiah had cut the throats of others many times. Now he knew the horror of it.

Rachel knelt on the ground beside him. Compassion was on her face. She reached out to comfort him with both hands on his chest. He gripped one of her forearms. It looked like he was mouthing the words, "Help me."

But it was not compassion the dying man saw in Rachel's face. It was something else. Her hands were not there to help. They were there to manipulate, to push and twist, to cause the spurting blood to gush out faster, to pump every last bit of it from his body. The face of this now powerful woman he had violated was the last thing the feared bandit Josiah saw before returning home to take stock of how terribly he had handled this going-out, and to face the judgement of a god he thought he understood.

Eli and Mahlir stared in disbelief at Rachel, at what she had done. Though – it was not the deed of what she had done to Josiah that caused them their alarm. "You didn't scream," said Eli to his daughter. "Why did you not scream?"

"Yes, why did you not scream when he was abusing you?" echoed Mahlir. "It almost looked like you enjoyed it."

She was still looking down at Josiah, covered in his blood. She knew what they meant. According to the Law given to Moses, if a woman is forced by a man to lie with him and it is in a public place where others can see and hear, and she does not cry out for help, it is a sin, and she is to be stoned at the city gate. She turned to her husband. "My Lord," she said, though not apologetically, not begging, looking forcefully at him, stating her wishes matter-of-factly. "The Law says that if the attack occurs in the country where no one is around to see and offer help, then only the man who committed the offense should die. Clearly my offender has paid that price. While it is true we are in a public place within the city, look around you. It is obvious that no one has seen. The people go about their own business. If they did see, they clearly did not care, or they were afraid. No one would have come to my aid even if I had screamed. Therefore, if you think I have wronged you, what I ask is this, that you have mercy and give me a quiet divorcement, and say nothing to anybody. No one need know."

"Except Yahweh," said Mahlir, "who knows all."

The horses were galloping away with empty saddles. They had been wounded but not completely crippled, and had managed in their terror and bewilderment to scramble upright, carrying with them the ransom money. The heavy jingling and clanking of the bag could be heard among the louder sounds of the hoof beats…disappearing sounds.

Eli looked in the direction of the horses, now almost to the cover of the forest, and mouthed a prayer to Almighty Yahweh, that the money find its way into worthy hands, someone who has need for it, someone who will use it wisely.

CHAPTER 14

THE POWER OF FAMILY

ISRAEL - CAESAREA

"It is true? Do you have it?" asked Eli, casually, not at all accusingly.

"Do I have what?" answered Mahlir

"The crown," said Eli. "The Crown of King David. Do you have it?"

"You know I don't. I'd have given it to him if I did, to save your white-haired ass."

"Fifty thousand sesterces. And the crown of a ghost." Eli smiled another thank you through his beard, damp with food particles and wine. "That's what my life is worth."

All five were reclining for their late afternoon meal, Mahlir, Rachel and Eli at one table, the servants at another, Shammah and Benjamin. Eli had purchased Benjamin as additional protection for his family. Benjamin was enormous, as big as Athronges. And like Shammah, Benjamin was of mixed blood, though Benjamin's other half was Egyptian. His given birth name was Imhotep. By changing the name to one of Jewish ancestry Eli was again making a statement to his associates in government about what he called the evils of drawing divisions between men because of blood and heritage.

"We think your life is worth a lot more than that, Father; we think it is priceless," Rachel said, hiding as best she could her silent confusion. Should the shame of the rape be hers? Or should it be visited upon her husband and her father, because of their soaring lack of sympathy? Her tension was thrusting outward – it was in her voice; it was in her face; it was in every movement of her body – as she wondered silently which of the options would be chosen for her, death or divorcement. Nothing had been said of the matter, by either of them, the two men who owned her life. Silent judges, speaking of things trivial, speaking not their verdicts.

Joked Mahlir, "My beloved father-in-law, your life is worth at least half the amount we offered to pay, brick included." Eli was feeding pieces of his meal to Jesus-of-Sie, making the animal first perform the required growl. "Ah, is Jesus a good boy? At's it, at's a boy." Mahir had not spoken of it until now, but the blasphemy still prickled at him. "One ought not to name a dog after our holy representative of God," he finally said, and it began another of the inevitable political "discussions" between the younger and the older, the Pharisee and the Sadducee, the Pharisee who believed in life after death, the Sadducee who did not, the liberal young Pharisee who accepted more than just the five books of Moses, the Sadducee who did not, the Pharisee who believed in the coming of a messiah who would rescue the Jews from the imperial bond of Rome, the more practical Sadducee who believed that the threat was not from Rome but from the tyranny of Archelaus, their own king. Eli's beliefs were partly those of the Sadducees, partly his own. He was fanatically independent in his thoughts. Eli liked to speak in Greek during their "discussions," purely to annoy his son-in-law. Mahlir would answer back in Hebrew, because the Holy tongue was the most complex and the least comfortable for most, even for Jews, with intricate and multiple meanings for as little as a single word. Aramaic was what was commonly spoken by the Jews as their everyday language, the language that evolved from the Exile when the Jews intermarried with the Babylonians, when languages merged, when philosophies and beliefs melded, when blood mixed with blood to fuse and form a new race of people. Samaritans. Eli, though, handled the Hebrew easily and charmingly, with a victorious dip of the snowy eyebrow.

"The high priest ought not to be mocked," Mahlir went on. "He is a man of God, appointed by God to act in our behalf, and we ought not to mock him by naming an animal after him."

Eli lifted his eyebrows at the challenge, quickly finishing his food morsel and slopping down more wine that dribbled down his pure white beard, and drove his black eyes at his opponent. "Appointed by God, you say? Tell me. Perhaps you were there. Did the fiery cloud descend and speak the name of Jesus-of-Sie?"

Eventually in their relationship Mahlir came to realize that Eli, though furiously committed to his beliefs, simply loved to argue, with Mahlir in particular, because Mahlir he could intimidate. It was sport to him. "I shall tell you exactly what happened," Eli said. "Jesus-of-Sie was chosen by Archelaus, our jackal-eyed ruler, for this post of High Priest that is supposed to be a lifetime position, because the previous high priest displeased him." Eli grumbled and belched. "And Jesus-of-Sie will soon be cast aside and still another will be named - maybe it will be your uncle, maybe it won't - by this king who is no better than his father, who has yet to be confirmed king by Caesar, six and more years after his father's death. That is how confident Caesar is in our leader."

"Who is Caesar, that he should have the power to dictate who should or should not rule over us as Jews?"

"Caesar is the man who is going to step in and save your hairless chin, if we can convince him to do it." There was a hint of a smile on Eli's face, now that he had succeeded in rousing his son-in-law to frustration.

The reference to Mahlir's sparse and thinly spired beard would have been hurtful had not the part about Caesar overshadowed it. "There is only one person I will give allegiance to," Mahlir blurted out angrily.

"And who might that be?" came Eli's sarcasm. "The Anointed One? Athronges the Shepherd King? The man who almost killed me? Or maybe it's Judas of Ezekias, the man whose cowardly band is burning our cities and raping our women."

Mahlir's eyes met Eli's, and stayed there until Eli looked away.

Rachel too had been listening. Where was his concern for her?

"Babbling on about a messiah, typical of a Pharisee," Eli spouted, then belched and held his goblet out for more wine. Shammah rose and poured it with both hands from a heavy stone carafe. Servants in any other household would be standing in wait. Shammah always reclined and ate with the family – Shammah was family – a slave past his seventh year that chose to have his ear pierced on the doorpost with the awl, a sign of lifetime servitude, more personal friend than slave.

Mahlir sat in silence, and it confused Eli. Usually by this time Mahlir's face would be bright red and pinched up like a dried fig, but here today, it was dark and distant. Eli poked again. "Is this the same Messiah that Jews have been waiting for since the time of the ancients?" Still no reaction from Mahlir. Eli dug deeper. "You have perhaps met him?" Eli was a skilled Sanhedrin debater, and honed his skills on Mahlir, at times taking up the opposite opinion for no other reason than the challenge of it. "Is he Simon the Slave King? Let us hope not, because if he is, he's dead. I'm told Gratus cut his head off last week in yet another skirmish between the Romans and the Jews. Though I doubt God would bring the Messiah into the world only to allow him to be killed by Romans, so he must be Judas, the son of Ezekias. Or one of the other dozens of crackpots putting diadems on their self-serving heads, pretending to be kings, killing and robbing our own people. Fighting even among themselves."

There was a long and deliberate pause before Mahlir spoke. "There was a time not so long ago that I knew a lot more than I know today," he said. "Now I'm afraid I don't even know enough to allow you to engage me." Ever since the incident at the river reality had a shaky edge to it, and with each day that passed, and with each perplexing atrocity held within each of those days, man against man, man against beast, it became more so. He lifted his goblet and took a mouthful of wine, and rolled it around with his tongue before swallowing, as though with the gesture he was trying to decide how to formulate his response. In the end he said nothing, because the conversation had brought to mind once more the staggering circumstances of the "incident at the river," often thought about, never spoken of.

CHAPTER 15

A GUEST FOR DINNER

ISRAEL – CAESAREA

"Eh?" prodded Eli. "This messiah to whom you give allegiance? Who is he?"

This time Mahlir answered by looking Eli squarely in the eye, and the two of them dueled that way in powerful silence.

It was Eli who yielded, after the quiet had reached its intolerable peak. "The prophet Micah once said, of the coming of the Messiah, that when he comes, a man's enemies will be within his own household. Am I to count you among my enemies?"

Mahir's response was from the heart. "There is one to whom I give allegiance above all others, above even the Messiah. It is my wife, as the future mother of my children, and to you, my Lord, as the father of my wife. Have I not proven this? When forced to choose between the Messiah and family, I chose family. I still choose family. I will always choose family."

It took a while for Eli to process the unexpected answer – he was seldom caught speechless – then he smiled and tipped his head forward in a gesture of humility. It was the first Mahlir had seen such an expression in his father-in-law.

Mahlir looked down at his goblet, and ringed it with thumb and forefinger, and looked into the wine's dark swirls, as if therein he would find answers, like some kind of soothsayer. Eli's expression of love and acceptance was harder for him to look upon than the disdain and arrogance that was so typical, though there was another reason for the strange disquiet that had shrouded Mahlir's temperament. The men he had killed back at the aqueduct were weighing on his mind. It was the same type of disquiet that had come in the wake of the Roman soldier's death, that seemed to have imprinted itself on his soul. At the aqueduct he had been given no choice. But still it was there, the vacuous and dark inner thing that refused him all but shallow breaths. He had done the right and honorable thing. His wife and his father-in-law would still be captives, perhaps dead, had he not taken the lives of Athronges' men. Still it was there, the humble disquiet, as if another cog in the engine had been jammed.

A guest was also present for suppler, a friend of Eli's, one more intimidating than Eli, not because of the words that came out of his mouth, and not because of the condescending way an eyebrow might rise at Mahlir's liberal thoughts, as with his father-in-law, but because of just the opposite. More often than not this prestigious guest would defend Mahlir's viewpoints, or at least soften them with an acceptance of them as an opinion of intelligence that deserved to be respected, though it be different than his own. This guest was a man of the Temple, friend to Eli. His given name was Joseph-of-Marmore, known now as Joseph-of-Arimathea, since his move to Arimathea, a small town about five miles to the north of Jerusalem. Hence, Joseph was known to answer to as many as three names, the most common of which was Joseph-of-Arimathea. Joseph too was conservative, holding to the views of the Sadducees, but was even more skilled than Eli in the art of verbal warfare, having the unique ability of presenting an opposing view without offending his foe, and doing it powerfully. Joseph-of-Arimathea was a man in the latter of his years, approaching the age of Eli, one would guess, from the streaks of gray and white in his beard, though Mahlir never asked. Joseph's long beard, thick and untrimmed, required of a Levite since the days of Moses, and the wrinkles around his eyes, gave him as much a look of wisdom and distinction as the most learned priest. Mahlir wondered if his own youthful beard would ever be so full, if ever he would appear so wise in countenance. Joseph was far his superior. He too was a respected and influential member of the Sanhedrin, the 72-member council that interpreted and administered Hebrew law and justice, second only to Archelaus and Augustus, in some ways more powerful than both. Many in the Tempe were frustrated by Joseph-of-Arimathea, because no one really knew what his beliefs were, whether he was a Sadducee or a Pharisee. He was just as passionate about the writings of Isaiah and David as he was about the scrolls of Moses, and conversed learnedly on both. His black high turban gave the silver streaks in his beard all the more wisdom. He had been listening intently the whole time. Finally he spoke.

"You speak the truth," he said to Eli. "But your young son-in-law also speaks truth." He said it with a smile and a nod of his head, as if to say he knew full well that Eli knew it too. "We should not give blind allegiance to a leader simply because he is a leader, be that leader the High Priest or the coming Messiah. We should test his leadership with the logic and the morality that exists within our own souls. It is also true that a messiah is expected. It is not just the wishings of dreamers." With this he turned to Mahlir. "Although I would imagine that it's quite possible we won't recognize him when he does come. A messiah sent from God certainly would not be robbing and raping and pillaging. That much we can agree on. It is quite obvious the Messiah is not Athronges. Would you not agree?"

Mahlir kept his eyes fixed on Eli's eyes, unwavering, though in delivering his answer he was speaking to Joseph. "Yes. I am ashamed for allowing myself to be taken in by his silver tongue and his powerful ways."

The young wife of Joseph-of-Arimathea was also there at the supper. Jael. She was a friend of Rachel's. Jael also smiled at what her husband had said, and then turned that same smile toward Mahlir, a glance that was simple support for the fact that her husband had rescued Mahlir and had admonished him all in the same breath. The glance lasted more than what was typical for such a momentary expression. Mahlir smiled back then turned away but felt it necessary to look again because of the surprising intensity the glance held. Jael perceived it and looked up again. A bigger smile curved upon her lips, and almost turned into a laugh, as if to make an apology for its boldness. Mahlir looked away again from her strong eyes, looked instead to the safety of the colorful whites, blues and purples of the garments that flowed over her head to cover most of her black hair. A flash of gold from an ear lobe caused him to look away altogether.

Joseph was intent in his efforts to make his point. "But –" He gestured with an index finger and his eyes danced with efforts to transfer the full meaning of his thoughts. "Will we recognize the Messiah when he does come? Or will his truth bring things unsettling to us? Angering us? Because if he is coming to save us and to give us wisdom, as are the predictions, surely he won't be teaching us in the ways in which we already live, for if we were already living in ways of righteousness he wouldn't need to come in the first place, now would he? It is quite possible that the trouble facing us as creatures of God is deeper than that which can be assuaged with threats and rules. Consider this. Could it be that we have no idea what righteousness really is? Could it be that we have no idea what rules there should be, in order to govern that type of righteousness?" Joseph gestured with his goblet before putting it to his lips as a final profundity to what he hoped would be words absorbed and savored. "As it is now, we have defined our concepts of righteousness. We have set down rules, and threats of punishment and reprisal if those rules are not followed. God will do such and such if we don't follow this and that rule, strike us with a palsy, or visit upon us a famine, or kill our first born, and we become creatures who conform because of fear. Could it be, with all our concepts and rules, that we are traveling full speed in the opposite direction? Could it be that this is why God is sending us a savior? Because we are completely and utterly blind? I have a feeling we as creatures of God are sailing into an uncharted sea, one as vast as time itself."

Joseph was well known to Mahlir. Over the years he had been both friend and mentor, and had often defended, even encouraged Mahlir's independence of thought. In one's search for truth, he had always said, as one explores the mysteries, self-direction is crucial. After all, he would say, the teacher may be wrong.

Eli grumbled, saying something unintelligible, something intended for Mahir's ears no doubt.

"I have confidence that the Messiah will make himself known, somehow, whoever he is, whenever he comes," finalized Mahlir. "When the time is right. He will bring to us righteousness and he will bring to us lives of freedom. Then Rome will fall. No more will we be subservient to a pagan authority."

"If you truly believe Rome is so evil," jabbed Eli, goading, looking for a weak spot, "Why aren't you out there fighting right now? Why aren't you out there organizing your own army?"

"I will fight. If the true messiah makes himself known and asks it of me."

"You will not. You're a coward."

The crimson fairly gushed into Mahir's neck and forehead, because Eli was right. He was a coward. Eli of course did not know it. He was only trying to get a rise out of his son-in-law. But he had scratched open a sore. Mahlir had run during the Temple battle, while the others stayed and died. Not only that, his constitution had weakened with thoughts of pity for a Roman soldier, an enemy of God. "It was my first battle," he said to himself, as his private apology to God. It will not happen again. It is common for one to have a weak stomach during one's first battle, he kept telling himself. The Macedonians had told him this.

"When the Anointed One comes," Mahlir said, speaking aloud now. "I will be there. In his army marching on Rome, if that is what he asks."

"You will not. You're a coward. That's why you're a priest."

"When he comes."

"You and the others like you, you've been waiting hundreds of years for another David to come along and save you, and you'll be waiting around with your long robes and your little black boxes, spouting your pieties, until your beards fall out and your teeth rot, until all the messiahs have killed us all, ruined our nation."

The mere mention of his phylacteries made Mahlir want to reach and touch them, the one on his sleeve and the one on his forehead, just to make sure they were still there, newly oiled and filled with fresh writings. "When the Anointed One comes," was all he said. "God will see that we recognize him, and he will be a king greater than any king or emperor who has ruled on earth. Everyone will follow him. Even you, Eli. And once again we will be a great power."

"Well – in the meantime we need to take practical measures to secure our safety. At this point, Caesar is the one with the power."

Again Eli was alluding to the unthinkable. Mahir asked him about it. "Do you truly believe that Rome can solve our problems?"

"The entire countryside has been in a state of violent disarray since Herod died. Riots everywhere. For years this has been going on. Thugs wanting to be kings, never gaining more than several hundred followers at a time, never enough to gain a monarchy, but enough to do damage – fighting with each other, fighting with us, and murdering our loves ones, robbing from us, raping our women and our daughters."

Rachel dropped the goblet she was drinking from.

Eli ignored the spillage. "Caesar is the only one who can restore order."

"Archelaus is our leader," Mahlir countered, oblivious to Rachel and her anxiety as she was bending to assist Shammah in wiping up the spill. "He is Herod's son. Let us leave it to him to restore order. Let us give our allegiance to him. At least he is a Jew."

"He is a Jew because his grandfather was forced to convert and be circumcised at the sword point of the Maccabees. But it doesn't matter. Jews or Gentiles, the Herods are not effective leaders. The rioting continues. Archelaus isn't even here. As we speak he is on another trip to Rome, while his country burns at the hands of its own people. But the worst of it happens when he *is* here. He is a tyrant. Like his father. Someday the soldiers of Archelaus may knock on your door and drag you away in chains, simply because you are an innocent man. Trust me. It has happened to many a Jew. We not only have to worry about the bandits in the hills, we have to worry about our own king." Eli had dropped the condescension, and was now speaking low and serious, leaning confessionally forward on his ailing elbow, as though Mahlir was now a confidant. "I intend to travel to Rome with some of the other landowners to petition to have Judea annexed to Syria. We intend to ask that Archelaus not be confirmed as king and that a procurator be named to govern in his place. This before I too am burned out. By my own people."

Mahlir was horrorstruck. He could not believe what he was hearing. Eli could read it in his face. "Annexation is not a new idea," he went on. "Nor is it mine alone. It was first proposed five years ago, a year after Herod's death, following a year of living under the intolerable oppression of Archelaus. Fifty of our people, myself included, traveled to Rome and petitioned Caesar for that very thing, that we be made a part of Syria. We told of how he betook for himself the authority of a tyrant and put upon us such abuses as a wild beast would not have done. We told Caesar we desired no more to live under the government of a kingship. Archelaus was there and spoke in his own defense. Others were there, friends of his, and offered testimony on his behalf. Caesar decided in his favor. He decided to continue to honor the elder Herod's deathbed wishes and allow the country to stand divided into its four parts, with Archelaus continuing on as tetrarch of Judea and Samaria, on a trial basis, conditioned upon him ruling over us virtuously. This has not happened. I intend to return, and to again petition the emperor."

"You can't be serious. You wish to live in complete subservience to a foreign power?"

"Maybe under Rome we will finally stop warring with one another. Maybe then."

Mahlir could take no more. In a burst of anger he bounded to his feet and strode from the room, and from there he left the home.

In passing the security of the gate, between the two guardian lamps, serenely burning pans as large as ox-carts on tripods higher than a man's head, he felt suddenly alone, the anger washed away by the blackness beyond which was the Great Sea, whence blew an easterly wind that tossed his hair and batted about his phylactery, wind rich with the scent of salt and of the open sea, and of creatures fantastic, and of the intrigue of the unknown. A storm was coming. Above him was an opening in the cloud cover, as if someone had peeled back a window to the stars, an almost perfectly square hole in the sky. The wind was cold. Had it not been for the cloak Eli bought him in Tyre, he would be shivering. The sand was still warm, holding in the heat of the day. Its color, yellow by daylight, silver by night, had been given a luster ever the brighter by the unique illumination from above, from the moon hiding behind the chiseled edges of the cloud opening that seemed to be its own source of light. God's compluvium. It was tranquil, peaceful, while the wind below was whipping itself to a roar. It was as if Yahweh himself was looking down, shaming him for his childish outburst.

He felt something brush his side.

Jesus-of-Sie. He bent down, hands on knees. "Is Jesus a good boy?"

The animal forced the obligatory snarl and happily wagged its arched tail.

Mahlir rumpled the dog's head, feeling a little less lonely, and made his way further down toward the water to seat himself against a solitary tree sprouting out of the sand.

Soon there came something else familiar – Rachel's touch on his shoulder, and a voice that filled him with warmth. "Let me tell you a story, something that happened years ago," she said. "Then perhaps you will understand Father a bit more." Her hair, normally covered and veiled, was long and loose, and gleamed under the shine of the moon. The moon was now fully visible through the opening. It brought enchantment to everything it touched, the gold in the rings of her bracelets, the spindles of her glass-encrusted earrings, the cresting tips of the distant black ocean swells, the falling foam of the surf.

She rested herself beside her husband and rolled her hands inside her long blue and white pallium, and dug her feet, enclosed in lace-up Roman buskins, into the warm sand.

"Why are you wearing jewels and things of the Romans and Greeks?" Mahir asked, in protest to what was really quite appealing to him, something he dared not admit in the sight of God, the way the jewelry quickened the beat of his heart, and the way it gave rush to his senses. Coming also, dancing inside his head, was the soft aroma of perfume, pagan also, likely.

She looked at him in frustration and snared his head between her hands. One corner of her mouth lifted, concealing laughter. That's how she smiled, with one corner of her mouth, but somehow it always came out charmingly, instead of as a sneer, the way it would with anyone else. "My Roman shoes –" She lifted and wiggled one of her ankles in front of him, as if to admire the footwear. "Father bartered with the goddess Diana for them. He took them right off the feet of one of her nymphs. No, come to think of it, I think they were taken from the very feet of Diana herself. Beautiful feet. And the jewelry? Worn at one time by the ancient Temple prostitutes of Jezebel. Maybe by Jezebel herself. They are items that have powers to sway the minds of young men."

"Do not trifle about such things."

"Would you be still with your words?" she ordered, and placed a kiss on his lips. " – while I tell you my story?"

"First there is something I must tell you –" he said.

Everything alive inside her became corpselike. Because she knew. She knew what it was her husband was about to say, was bound by law to do. He was going to announce the divorcement, or perhaps even her execution at the city gate. "Please," she whispered. "Not now."

"It's important. I've been waiting to get you alone."

She touched two fingers to his lips. "Not now, not yet. This you need to know. It's about family. Because if you speak first, to tell me what you must tell me, I may never tell you this, and this is far more important."

He relinquished. And with her hand in his, looking out at the sea, darkened now by the closing over of the hole in the sky, she began. "Haven't you ever wondered why I have no mother? Haven't you ever wondered why it is that only Father and I and the servants live in our large house? Have you never been curious why I have no brothers or sisters? It is because my mother is dead. It is also because my baby brother is dead."

That much he knew. It had been a tragedy of some kind. A mass slaughter by outlaws, some said, Romans, others speculated. A few suggested in hushed whispers that it may have been Herod himself who had decreed the massacre, though no one dared speak such an accusation openly, as long as any one of the Herods remained in power.

"Let me tell you how it happened. More than four seasons back we lived in Bethlehem. It was suitably located for Father's business. It was the hub of his travels, connecting the Temple to the east, his fields to the north and the port cities to the west. One normal morning shortly after we had risen for the day, the world erupted in evil. Soldiers swept down upon us from the surrounding hills. The children of the city were at play; some were being bathed by their mothers; a few were still asleep; the youngest of them were suckling at their mother's breasts. Some were still in their mothers' wombs. I remember the aroma of the breakfast fires.

"My brother was three and a half. He was playing with a pile of rocks, building a house for his toy soldiers, his tiny heroes. Suddenly there was the feeling that a thousand eyes were upon us. I was on my way to the well for water, when my brother pointed to the east. A row of soldiers had appeared, every tenth one on horseback. His heroes. Then the horizon to the west opened up with soldiers, then to the north, then to the south. They remained there for the longest time, ringing us, studying us, our own soldiers. It was such a strange sight. At first I thought they were there to protect us. Or, the thought occurred to me, they were there to gather forces for a mighty assault on Rome. That's probably what my brother was thinking. He probably thought the Messiah was among them, come at last to select good men from each town and village. Always, when my brother would play with his stone soldiers, he would choose the biggest one and make it the Messiah. Then he would have great battles in the sand of his playland.

"The soldiers, after waiting in silence for the longest time, began thundering inward, swords held high, the foot soldiers close behind to kill those that had escaped the cavalry. I couldn't believe what was happening. I saw a bearded horseman wield his sword at a fleeing child, hunting it down, passing adult men and women by. The terror in the child's eyes I still see, as the blade sliced off the top of his –" Her words fell off into a trembling mumble. She drew in a breath, held it, then let it out, along with the rest of what she needed to say. "– I remember his body bouncing off the ground. I, I remember his arms and legs flopping then going still. I remember the contents of his skull spilling out."

She was shaking horribly now. "Lord help us, they were after our children, with purposes unknown. The images blur in my mind. I tried to grab my baby brother, but it happened too fast. A sword came slashing across his face. Right through the eyes. A line of red appeared and dripped down his face. I think I saw one of his eyes fall out." She looked up, like she was trying to figure it out. "But you know what? He didn't cry. He just had this look of surprise. His mouth was open, but no sound was coming out. Then he slumped to the ground." She pointed eastward. "Somewhere out there are the bones of my baby brother, unmarked, unsanctified…no Shiva… somewhere…"

For the longest time she didn't speak.

"My brother had a round little face," she finally went on, needing to talk more about it. Her voice was now barely audible, so softly did it come. "He was proud of himself because he was four. He was only three and a half, but he used to like to think he was four. He would always say, with such force in his tiny voice, "I'm four!" He used to cry when I'd hug and kiss him, because he was four, too big to be hugged and kissed. Everything was an adventure to him, building his houses with his rocks, building his roads, just like the Romans. It was all an adventure. The birds of the air, the crawling insects, everything filled him with excitement. Each word the child spoke came with enthusiasm. He saved each one of his rocks. They were his playthings. Each night he would save them in his special corner. He used to sleep with me at night, because he was afraid of the dark; he knew I would protect him. I used to lay my hand on the top of his head as we both slept, and I'd feel warmth inside me, traveling through my hand. My brother, my love – I shall miss you. With every breath I take, I shall miss you, for as long as I live and love."

"Are you sure they were not Roman soldiers?"

"I am sure. I know full well the difference between a soldier of Augustus and a soldier of Herod. These were not men adorned in burnished breast-plates with capes of red and purple. These were the hired mercenaries of Herod, outlaws, paid bodyguards and assassins."

"Maybe they were simple marauders, desert bandits, not sent by Herod at all."

"They wore the black of Herod's guards. And they wore the symbol of our people on their breastplates. Their faces and the varied colorings of their hair and beards showed how different were the origins of their births, as is the mix of the King's army – Germanic tribesmen some, some looked to be from lands as far away as Gaul, some may perhaps have been Romans, by the fairness of their skin. Some looked like they were Jews, Arabs others, Parthians, Macedonians. Any who would fight for Herod at a price, any who would do Herod's bidding, the misfits of the world's societies, any who would put money above conscience. The soldiers of King Herod."

"Why would he have done this? It makes no sense."

"Many things Herod did made no sense," Rachel replied. "It is said that upon his deathbed he gave orders that all heads of families be taken to the hippodrome and killed at the point of his passing, so that the country would mourn. When he died his sister Salome had the men released."

"It should be remembered that some of his deeds were of noble character," Mahlir said, because it was dangerous to speak out against the government, even within families, so out of habit he recounted some of the good things done by Herod-the-Great, this human paradox of good and evil. "When the Jews living in Rome were pressed into military service he appealed on their behalf and got them excused, because the law given to Moses prohibits us from taking the life of another. And he succeeded in gaining them official military protection under Roman law. In the days of your father's youth there was a drought that brought a terrible famine to the land. So withered had been the crops that there existed not enough seed for the planting. Herod melted down his own jewelry and purchased grain from Egypt and had his soldiers distribute the food. His bakers cooked for the sick and elderly. And let us not forget that he rebuilt Solomon's Temple, and brought water through the aqueducts, and modernized the cities and towns. He made life easier for us."

Rachel remained silent, a lonely look inset deep in her face. She said, at long last, "It is clear that my husband is more interested in defending the late King Herod than he is in helping ease the pain in my heart. Worse still, it is clear that he is more interested in holding to the traditions of the Law than he is in –"

She was about to speak of the rape, and the Law of Moses that would have her stoned, but Mahlir interrupted her. "Rest easy, my love," he said. "My allegiance is only to God, and to you."

She stood and faced the angry sea and spread her arms as though inviting the roar beyond the darkness to sweep over her and take her into its depths. "That's nice," she said, drinking in the wind, seeming to prepare to fly over the washing waves coming closer and closer. Her blue and white cloak flew off her shoulders and into the night, leaving only her tunic to protect her from the storm, drawn in tight around her waist by a cord of gold, to flap furiously around the solidity of her legs. She was strong against the wind, and it stirred desire within him. The blue and gold of her embroidered neckline looked ink black, as black as the night that surrounded her, and it gave her a ghostly look, as though her head floated above her body.

Jesus-of-Sie was barking furiously.

Mahlir could hear the roar of a mighty wave starting to break above their heads, could feel it, sense it. The devil must have been giving her courage, for if she would have stood a moment longer the wave would have caught her, would have caught them both. Mahlir glimpsed its enormous black wall and grabbed her around the waist and ran backwards with her, so that all they faced was the unsettling rush of sand and surf around their knees.

He gripped her shoulders and looked into the hollow of her eyes. "Are you all right, my love?"

"Yes," she said, her voice even more distant. "The water barely reached my ankles."

"No," said Mahlir. "I don't mean that. I mean because of what happened this afternoon. Because of what the brother of Athronges did to you. Are you all right?"

She began to tremble, and tears came, and she gestured yes with a quick wave of her head.

"Because I spoke with your father. It is what I have been waiting to tell you. We will get you to a physician. Your father and I are united in this. It will be private. No one will know."

She shook her head. "I am all right. I have some pain. Not much. And some bruising. But I'm fine. And I purified myself with the doves."

"But please understand, good wife. You need not fear me. No harm will come to you from my hand, nor from your father's, nor from anyone else."

"You will not have me stoned?"

"Of course not."

"But what about the Law? The word of God binds you to do so."

He shook his head in stiff motions. "Know and believe that I would not do such a thing. Nor will your father. Nor will anyone else. Nor will God himself, if I have the power to stop it. Your father and I are united in this. God could come down and stand right here in front of me and order me to have you stoned and I would refuse."

"So then it is decided? You will simply grant me a divorcement instead? And ask God for forgiveness?"

"It is you I am asking for forgiveness."

She looked at him in surprise and said nothing."

"We shall live a long life together as husband and wife," Mahlir said. "Providing you can grant me the forgiveness for which I ask, for what I said to you on the beach, and for allowing you to think even for a moment that I would bring to you such abuse. I am the one who deserves to be stoned."

"It is granted," she said.

He nodded. "Thank you. I needed to hear it, that you have forgiven me."

"I didn't mean that," she said. "I meant that it's granted you be stoned." And she picked up a pebble and with a little flick of her finger bounced it hard off his forehead, like one would flick a marble, and smiled broadly as it brought up an immediate knot.

Laughter forced its way through the stone silence of his lips, in spite of his efforts to counter it. He threw out his hands to show his tangled amusement. "Whatever in God's Holy Name possessed you to do such a thing as that?" he said, then he bent over and bared his backside. "Go ahead. Give it your best throw."

One whizzed by him, missing him completely.

He laughed and taunted her. "One more. Put a little aim into it this time." He slapped his bare bottom. "Right there."

Instead she rammed her foot, bedecked in one of the sandals that had one time graced the foot of the goddess Diana, soundly into his bare flesh. It sent him sprawling.

"Now I forgive you," she said, and jumped on top of him with huge kisses, in complete defiance of tradition and law, where women are supposed to ask permission before engaging in affection.

"I cannot believe you did that!" he said, half laughing, looking up at her, spitting out sand, moving hair from her eyes so he could see up into them. The hole in the sky was still there, still illuminating that which was below, and it encased her in an aura of dusty white. "You know what? You and I shall have many children. And they shall all be blessed by God. For to honor you, as I did under the Chupah, is to honor God. To place you above all else, is to place God above all else."

Another wave came. They scrambled to their feet and ran from its deadly path. There is sometimes humor in danger, for reasons not at all logical, and they both laughed. And a pang of fear came, as he realized the dog was not there beside him. "Jesus!" he yelled out. "Where in the name of Bacchus did that animal go? Jeeesus! I don't see him. Jeeeeeesus!"

"He's right there." Rachel pointed toward the sea.

"Where? I don't see him."

"Right there." She pointed again. "He's looking away from us. There. Right there. You can see his curled-up tail and his little winkie-eyed butt hole."

Sure enough, all that was visible was the little nugget sized button of pink below an arched over tail. He was sniffing and yapping as the foam sizzled up onto the sand to engulf his feet, jumping back and barking again, a sound lost to the roar of the wind. The yellow and white fur blended so well with the silver and black of the ocean that the two were nearly indistinguishable, save for the little button of pink.

"Jeeesus! Get over here."

Though he was ignoring Mahlir's commands, all it took was for Rachel to slap her knees and click her teeth. "Come Jesus," she called out sweetly, after which the animal complied, happy to be free of the overbearing duty he had assumed for himself of saving the ones he loved from this dragon the sea had become, with its gaping jaws of water and its breath of ice. Moments later an enormous black wall crashed onto the very spot.

The tops of the date palms were beginning to lie sideways, and the wind was now full of stinging water. It had blown out the guardian lamps of the gateway. Mahlir and Rachel were running for the doors, still laughing. She had picked up her cloak along the way – it had wrapped itself around a leafless bush – and was waving it over her head like a banner.

Jesus-of-Sie was now beside himself with confusion, barking, running, yapping, twisting in circles. The doors moaned as they pushed on them, slabs of iron and wood three times the height of a man. The cylindrical wood pivots shook, and soon the two lovers and their dog were inside, dropping the bar in place behind them. A rush of heat greeted them, rising up from the mosaic floor. It prickled his skin.

"Good," she said. "Shammah has the fires going."

She took his hand, like she was a mother and he was a foolish boy. "Tonight, my love, we will sleep like Greeks and Romans. With hypocaust heat. And I don't want to hear any complaining about it. Let the winds fly and skies wail."

The storm whirled and howled above the compluvium but did not enter. The entire atrium area was protected, other than an occasional leaf or tree bough falling through to disturb the water of the pool below. The inner torches were still burning, casting yellow light upward to show the reason the pool was so calm – a sheet of water, smooth enough to walk on, was being blown over as if it were a part of the roof. Mahlir could hear the cisterns overflowing from the rush of channeled rainwater. He could hear the crack of thunder distant in the sky.

Though not yet the time, Mahlir was half expectant that Rachel would conceive for them a son, so sweet was the wine of their union within the calm of the storm. He could hear it continue to rage as he lay in bed beside his wife, letting the rise of the heat from the hypocaust steal into his bones, letting it drug him. A pedestal lamp calmly burned and cast itself upon the walls in shadings of yellow and black, upon intricately painted depictions of the Holy City and the Temple and the olive-groved hillsides. Living vines and plants adorned the bed-chamber's inner corners, able to be nourished on cloudless days by the sun creeping and bending its way inward from the compluvium opening once curtains were parted. There were no windows, just a span-thick wall of man-made stone, the Roman invention of hardened ash, limestone, and water. It was what kept the storm from entering. Only its sound could be heard, its moaning, its thudding and scraping as the wind and rain and sea swells assailed the two of them. The comfort within, the high platformed bed with its carved posts and rolled head and footstones, the cushions of pillows, the embroidered covers, seemed to taunt the storm. And the storm seemed to be answering back, whipping itself into an ever-greater frenzy. It seemed the entirety of the ocean and sky was being set against them.

But there was nothing to fear, as long as they stayed within the walls. There is beauty even in the midst of chaos, as long as one does not open the door. Together they were protected. The lingering of their passions reassured them of this. It was a cool fire in their hearts. As long as they did not open that door they were fine, as long as they left the darkness to itself and left the storm in its own world, no matter the temptation, no matter the curiosity. And indeed there is a curiosity in the darkness, an attraction to the barbaric. There is a demanding by the senses for fulfillment, as the sea crashes around the fortress. "Come, open the door," cry the sirens. "Come to us. We will make evil your bedmate, and sooth your wounds by making deeds of ill will just as conscionable as acts of virtue, and no more shall you want."

But they stayed and slept – with Jesus-of-Sie curled up below them in pleasant slumber upon the warmth of the stone floor, his sides rising and falling to the tender rhythm of his dreams – and somewhere in the morning as the first light of day began to creep in from beyond the curtains, as the fading heat from the hypocaust was giving way to a slight chill, the storm withdrew, and the good scent of a Palestine dawn drifted in, fresh with things anew.

Mahlir could hear the gentleness of wife's breathing. He opened an arm and let her curve around him, and it warmed him. It was early still when she finally did awaken, well before breakfast. They lay together and talked, this couple set apart for one another by God. They talked mostly about their very different views of the world, she mirroring those of her father, those of a Sadducee, Mahlir holding to the more youthful and aggressive ideas of the Pharisees. "We are so opposite, you and I," he said, and smiled and touched her cheek. "Are we a match, my love?"

"It is true we are opposite," acknowledged Rachel, seeming to be proud of the fact. She took his hand in hers and looked into his eyes, and got up and led him to the doorway and drew back the curtain. A wave of swallows was seesawing in the air over the shrubs of the peristylium, changing direction on a whim in complete unison, as if of one mind. The skrawking of seagulls was beginning to emerge from somewhere. Where could such delicate creatures have taken refuge in a storm so violent? Fresh droplets of crystalline water were falling from the edges of the compluvium onto the marble sides of the collection pool. Through its roof top opening Mahlir could see the dawn, scatterings of clouds, purple fragments of the left over storm, disappearing pieces of a no longer angry sky that seemed to not quite know what to do with itself. Beads of heavy dew hung everywhere.

"Do you see the loveliness of the peristylium? How it charms?" She gestured to the garden, its shrubs and vines and trimmed-back flower stems, its couches and benches of rolled gold and stone. "It was my mother's favorite place. So many opposites. Silver and gold. Green vines, red berries. White fruit, red fruit. Water, fire. Lamps, fountains. Yet together it becomes beauty."

Here, more than in any other part of the house, was evidence of the massive Greek and Roman influence on Jewish society – the open-air gardens in the midst of one's home, the master's office with its columns and curtained walls, the frescoes and mosaics – but in the center of it all, instead of the alter to Vesta, the spirit fire of human existence, was a tall and sturdy menorah, its tender flames having held strong through the storm. Alongside it, on a table of polished marble, was the ram's horn. All of Judea, all of Samaria and Galilee, all of Idumea, was blending with the culture of the Romans, which had blended with that of the Greeks. The Romans were absorbing the Jews, little by little, as the Greeks of Alexander had done, as the Babylonians and the Assyrians had done. At least, as had been the wisdom of Nebuchadnezzar and Cyrus, the Romans allowed the Jews their religion and their worship. In exchange for that, the Jews chose to accept, even embrace, the Roman society, the modern buildings and fountains, the gardens, the roads and aqueducts, as long as the Romans allowed them their autonomy, and as long as they kept their symbols and their statues free from sight and as long as they did not force upon them their detestable games with their naked athletes and their prizes of graven images.

"My mother and father, they were also of different political views," she said, "yet they cherished one another." She seemed for a moment like she was going to burst out in laughter. "My mother would have been a good match for you. She would have found agreement in all of your arguments. My father is like me; mother was like you."

Yes, Rachel and her husband were a match. Opposites entwined. Stronger together than separate.

CHAPTER 16

THE DEMONS OF THE STORM

ISRAEL – JERUSALEM

Replied Mahlir, in response to his wife's question of what was heavy on his heart, right before her departure to Arimathea for another visit with Jael, "Since we moved to Jerusalem, it seems you spend as much time with Jael as you do with me." Mahir rarely complained to his wife, but he was losing a piece of her. She sometimes spent days on end in Arimathea, now that her friend was so close. God had chosen a good life for Mahlir-of-Matthias, and Mahlir cherished it, and he missed it when it was incomplete, when Rachel was away. He shared with her things husbands by tradition never discussed with their wives. Politics. Theology. Even the secrets of the Temple were things they shared. They truly were as one, agreeing, disagreeing, but always as one. They had the rare ability to be able to argue different viewpoints without getting angry. It was a bonding in itself, this ability, a twinkle-eyed smile present on both their faces, like a game was being played, especially with Rachel. With Rachel, the more powerful her argument, the more powerful her smile, with a now and then burst of unexpected profanity festooning her speech.

The rioting and the uprisings in the land continued, though the insurgents were lessened in their numbers because of the increased presence of Roman soldiers, supported in their efforts by the strengthening of Archelaus' own military. And the frequencies of the burnings and rapes and kidnappings were tapering off. Jerusalem, at first the heart of the trouble, was now the safest place to be, or so reasoned Eli, because of the fortified walls, and because of the soldiers. Their numbers were most massively reinforced in Jerusalem. For that reason he had purchased for the four of them a house in Jerusalem, one close by the Temple, not as big as the one in Caesarea, but much safer, with three chambers facing a long courtyard, and with thick walls to keep out the bandits and the heat, and to keep the heat contained during the winter. It had a hearth, a charcoal stove of masonry, a bronze brazier for cooking and warming food, a roof garden where they slept on hot summer nights under the sparkling immensity of God's heaven, and of course a mikvah, smaller than the one in Caesarea but effective, nice, all of it. The move was particularly pleasing to Rachel, because she was now close to Jael, the town of Arimathea being only an hour's walk away. They rented out the use of the mikvah during the festivals, as did many in Jerusalem, though in time the Sanhedrin mandated that the pilgrims were not to be exploited, that all had the use of God's city, that no one had the right to take money for lodgings and baths. Eventually it was decided that the people could charge, but only up to a certain ceiling as reimbursement for expenses. Rachel laughed with the moistness of her large brown eyes. "You're not jealous of another woman, now, are you, my love?" She knew he hated the emotion of jealousy. She knew he viewed it as a demeaning and domineering quality, one unworthy of a priest, a quality unworthy of their relationship.

He could have forbidden her to go. He was within the Law to do so. Eli sometimes would advise him to do just that. "The Law states firmly that a man should rule his household," Eli would say, "and the Law is from God. Yahweh knows what is best for his children. He knows that a home should have a leader, a husband who leads with courage and wisdom, for the benefit of his family, just as a monarch, for the benefit of his kingdom, leads with courage and wisdom, and sets forth rules and delivers edicts." But such control seemed contrary to this special and unique relationship Mahlir had with his wife. It would have weakened it somehow.

"Maybe I am jealous, a little, but more than anything I'm concerned for your safety, as is your father. The reason we moved to Jerusalem in the first place was for safety. Jerusalem has the soldiers and is further protected by the walls. Beyond the walls you lose that protection. It simply is not safe." Mahlir put a hand on his wife's stomach, swelling more each day with the marvel of life "We have a third person to think about now." Their only sadness, the only unfulfilled part of their lives, had been that they could not conceive children. Until now. After five barren years the Lord blessed them, and Rachel was found to be with child. The little one filled Mahlir with joy as it grew in its unborn state, as he watched Rachel walk under its burden, as he felt its movement on his back while they slept, as he watched the love in her eyes.

"Arimathea is only five miles away," said Rachel. "It's little more than an hour. And the soldiers are on the roads as well. There is an abundance of protection. Come with me this time. See for yourself. And besides, I would better enjoy Jael's companionship and friendship if you were there too. Perhaps you can develop a friendship with her as well. She's a very special person. I love her deeply." Her smile came to reassure. "But of course not as much as you." Then she nodded toward the man towering above her, bare-chested and cut lean from hard work and the struggles of life, with bands on his enormous arms to accentuate their power, and with flowing trousers of wool patterned from the land of the Pharos. A curved Scimitar in a jeweled case was attached to his waistband to further intimidate. "Remember too that I have Benjamin for protection."

And Mahlir truly was grateful that she did. "I intend no disrespect, Benjamin –" he said to the loyal eyes of the muscular sentinel. "But one guard is no match for a band of thieves, no matter the power of that guard."

Benjamin was silent. He was too new to realize that in this household a slave could converse openly with the masters and mistresses. He nodded to indicate he was not offended.

"Come with me to Arimathea," urged Rachel. She was bouncing on her toes with the excitement of it. She most often walked on her toes. It was probably what gave her calves the unique muscularity most women lack. "I will be doubly protected, and I will have the pleasure of your company. I'm sure Joseph would appreciate the added security too. Jael is alone in that big mansion, now that Joseph is needed so much of the time in Jerusalem for the Sanhedrin deliberations."

Benjamin again said nothing. But it was obvious by the way he looked back at Mahlir that he also thought it wise that Mahlir come along.

"All right, my love." Mahlir pressed a kiss on her forehead. "I have Temple duties, but they are ones that can just as well be done in Arimathea. Allow me first to go to the Temple and gather my materials. I am copying scrolls. I'm sure they will let me take these scrolls with me, since they are only copies of copies."

And so it was done. Mahlir would come as well, to ensure her safety. But what was waiting for his precious wife was something worse than a roadside thief, worse than a rapist, worse than a murderer. It was the last thing in the world she would expect. It was a thing no bodyguard alive could protect her from. It was a thing from the shadowland of nightmares, evil perpetrated by the very man she trusted most, the man God had charged to be her supreme protector, who had vowed to be so. Because beginning with this trip, starting innocently enough, Mahlir-of-Matthias would embark upon a subtle and deceptive road that would lead him to do the unthinkable. For reasons he would not understand, for reasons he probably never would understand, he would open the door and walk out into the storm.

And the Sirens of the sea would be there. They would gather him in and make him believe that he was in love with this woman who was his wife's best friend, who was the wife of his father-in-law's best friend, this woman who at first he little more than despised. In their deception the Sirens would convince him that he could not live without this woman, that he was in love with both women, that he now had responsibilities to both.

It started off slow, the opening of the door – with another smile, another glance, an innocent conversation, one too many moments alone with her – little by little, inch by inch. Inch by harmless inch the door opened, slowly, the curiosity allowing it still another inch, the attraction to the darkness drawing it open further, until suddenly, in one crashing moment, the door became impossible to shut against the force of the storm.

And Mahlir found himself in its full fury, disbelieving of it, ashamed, fearful, sickened, yet unable in the enslavement of his senses to do anything about it. He was like a leaf in a hurricane.

Or so he thought. Had he the presence of an oracle to show him future events he would have stopped it immediately. He would have in an instant swept aside the hurricane. Then he would have been able to protect his wife; he would have been able to take her away before the soldiers came.

Over many trips it happened, many weeks, trips he kept telling himself were only for his wife's protection. Then suddenly he was there, looking back at this monster that was himself, that had mutated from such innocence.

And Rachel knew nothing about it, though it was obvious from the vacant look that sometimes crept within her eyes that things were not as they used to be, that she was beginning to experience an unknown type of discomfort, moments of distrust that were never there before, that erupted for reasons unknown to her, that she dismissed as a weakness inside herself. Once she even apologized to Mahlir for it, a time when she felt guilt for admonishing him for not being there beside her when she woke up one morning, when she found out that Jael was also gone. "Fi, woman," Mahlir had said. "It was nothing but a simple early morning walk, one that Jael accompanied me on, because she happened to have been awake at the same time." A simple early morning walk, a simple explanation, a lie that placed yet another stone in the wall being built between them. "Forgive me," she said, "for ever doubting you." The moistness was back in her eyes. She patted her bulging stomach. "Matthias is sorry too," she said. She always included the baby in her conversations. It was always "we" instead of "I." She had already chosen a name, Matthias, in honor of Mahlir's father, the priest who pulled down Caesar's golden eagle. She was convinced the child would be a boy, and that he would do great things for the world.

Nor did Eli know of his son-in-law's enslavement. Mahlir was his friend, his son-in-law, his guardian, defender of the family against all evils, a man to take his place as patriarch to carry on his legacy. He and his son-in-law had become close, though their differences remained, Eli a Sadducee, Mahlir a Pharisee, and though Eli still loved to make sport of intimidating him. They would journey regularly to the heated bathhouses and discuss things, sometimes in agreement, sometimes arguing. Mahlir was far from being high priest, and probably never would be, but he served his duties to the best of his abilities. And Eli continued his campaigns in the Temple for the annexation of Judea by Rome, appealing to anyone who would listen, held he high position or low, often to Mahlir's embarrassment. Any time Mahlir would introduce him to someone new, particularly a person of influence, Eli would launch into his political diatribe against Archelaus. Mahlir would sometimes express concern over Eli's safety, because Eli spoke so openly on the matter. "My safety is immaterial," Eli would boldly answer. Then he would state some variant of the following: "Why should I act as a coward? Cowards never change anything. If the ways of government are to be changed, people must speak, surely, dangerous thought it to be. One thing history has taught us, from the Macedonian to the Maccabees to the Caesars. The only way government can stand is if the people allow it to stand, no matter how powerful the government."

Nor did Jael's powerful husband know of the evil that had crept into his household. Jospeh-of-Arimathea loved Mahlir. He looked upon him as a son. He had taken him into his confidence and was training him up in the ways of things sacred, showing him the secrets. He even shared with Mahlir personal thoughts, such as how blessed he was to have Jael as his wife. "To walk in the ways of righteousness surely does bring its rewards," he once said. "Jael could have any man she wishes, being beautiful and twenty years my junior, yet she has chosen me. How good God is, and what a blessing it is that he has given me one who is loving and loyal. It is not so much that she is beautiful – a side benefit only – what matters is that she is a true and deep friend. I love her dearly." In Joseph's mind the only threat to his family came from without, from the unrest in the land. To question otherwise would be absurd. Many an hour did he spend as mentor to the youthful Mahlir, teaching him, explaining the mysteries, interpreting dreams, which is so often the way God speaks, he would say. Joseph in his wisdom always knew what a dream meant. "Someday," he kept saying to Mahlir. "You too will have these lines of age and wisdom etched into your face. You too will be able to read a dream."

There was only one time when Joseph-of-Arimathea was puzzled over a dream. It was a dream of his own. "At the end of the dream an angel appeared," Joseph told Mahlir. "Ask young Mahlir what this dream means," the angel told me. "He will know." Joseph laughed. "Now there is a switch. The student teaching the teacher. So I am asking. What does it mean?"

Mahlir did not know, he told Joseph. But he did know. And its truth shuddered inside him. "My dream was this," Joseph had said to Mahlir. The elder's eyes were like reservoirs of reflected fire in recounting the vision. Wisdom was in them. Power was in them. Kindness was in them. And it terrified Mahlir as much as the dream itself, though Joseph intended it not to be such, for his heart was pure. "I dreamed of days gone by," he began. "The dream was of you. You were a young child. I was charged with your care, and we were walking through the olive groves. I dreamed that on the rise of a hill there was a great bear in a cage. It was a loving animal with a docile face. You were saddened that it was caged. I was saddened as well. I too saw the docility of its expression. You reached in and stroked it, and it responded by rubbing its head against your hand. It was clear that the bear had been unjustly caged by the cruelty of men, as is so often the case, for entertainment most likely, for the games, who knows why, perhaps for no reason at all. Compassion poured from your young heart and you withdrew the peg – only a simple wooden peg no bigger than a finger separated this huge animal from its freedom – and opened the cage door a crack, just a crack mind you. It poked its nose through and curiously sniffed the outside, the way animals do, then rubbed against your hand. The touch of its fur felt good to you, and you opened the door a little further, only a little. Again the bear rubbed against you, and you opened the door further still, not much – but it was enough – and the gentle giant turned ferocious. The soft hair in an instant stood to bristles and the harmless face transformed into a raging mass of teeth that could crush bone. Eyes glistened with hatred. We tried to shut the cage, but it was too late. The bear was halfway through. In another instant it was free. We tried to catch it. Such a powerless feeling it was, such an empty feeling, as we watched the bear bound away to tear to pieces everyone and everything in its path. It wasn't a bear at all; it was destiny itself, released to destroy things held precious. To chase him was of no use. He was fifty times the size of a man."

"If a sage such as yourself doesn't know, how do you expect someone like me to know?" Mahlir asked jokingly, trying his best to hide the nervousness disguised in his voice, for of course the bear was the destiny he was creating with his adultery, of the future he was altering, of the lives he was shattering.

Mahlir's father-in-law had also been forewarned of danger, though not in a supernatural way. Shammah had been in the baths of the Xyxtra and had overheard some of the king's servants speaking of how the king was preparing to take revenge against those in the Temple planning a sedition against him. "I want you to go away for a while," Eli told Mahlir and Rachel. "It may be nothing, but just to be safe, pack your belongings. I am sending the two of you to Rome for a time. Until things stabilize. I have a villa there."

"But Father, what about you?" Rachel asked.

Eli tried to soften the seriousness of what was clearly a weight upon his mind. One could always tell the depth of Eli's concern over an issue by how much the left part of his white-bushed brow dipped with the squinting of an eye, as though he were looking inward and speaking as much to a presence there as to the one on the outside. "Me? I will be fine. In any case, if I abandon my cause now, even momentarily, what would be the chance of succeeding ever? If Archelaus is worried, it is simply because he should be.

It is because I *am* succeeding in my efforts to gather support against him; he indeed should be worried. No, I must stay. You both must go. You have yourselves to think about, your family, your unborn child, your future children, my legacy. You have no part in this. You must go. For *me* you must do this. For my legacy."

Mahlir agreed. "We will leave tomorrow afternoon. Before the sun sets."

"No, today, within the hour," Eli said, narrowing his left brow further.

"But I cannot. I have duties in the Temple tomorrow morning. I have been chosen to enter the Holy Place. I have responsibilities to God."

"No. Go now. Abandon your duties to the Temple. It is too dangerous to wait."

"But I cannot. They are my commitments to God, and to the people."

"If you must. But tarry not a moment longer. Leave then in the morning, immediately after your obligations."

"It shall be so. By the time the sun stands at its mid-point tomorrow we will be on our way to Tyre. The day after that we will be on board a ship bound for Rome." True, Mahlir had been chosen to present the atonement at sunrise, a once-in-a-lifetime opportunity wherein a priest is selected by the casting of lots to enter and view what few human eyes have seen, in the inner chamber, the resting place of King David's Crown and the Ark of the Covenant, both lost but soon to be found, wherein is gathered the power and the might of Yahweh, and from where the prayers of atonement for the people are offered, wherein a sinful man is not welcome, where the measure of a man's sins will be doubled if he is not clean when he enters. But that was not the real reason he wanted to delay his departure. The real reason was so that he could be with Jael, so that he could have one last moment with her, to break it off in a gentle way. An excuse for one more encounter? Perhaps. But it was the kind thing to do. It was what his heart demanded. He was relieved that the affair would soon be over. The burden of his deception had been at times more than he could bear. In less than a day he would be free of it, and he and his wife would be on their way, he and the one set aside for him by God, and their unborn child. He would listen to the dream. He would push the bear back into the cage and put the peg in place while he still could. And then, upon their arrival at their destination, he would make a final atonement with an expensive and blemish free heifer. He was thankful for the dream, and he was thankful for circumstance. Events unfolding had offered him a way of escape from the trap he had made for himself. Mahlir would never return to his old ways. He would not so much as allow himself a temptation. He would never return to Jerusalem as long as Jael lived close by, and as long as Archelaus remained as king. What he didn't know, what he could not know, was that mid-day tomorrow would be too late. The soldiers were coming in the morning.

Rachel believed her husband, when he told her he was going to spend the night in the Temple in prayer and preparation; the people and the Temple officials believed him when he said he would be at home in prayer and preparation.

Mahlir was strong in his youthful body and could run the distance between Jerusalem and Arimathea in less than half an hour's time. It was how the poisoned affair had come to be conducted, with Mahlir running as a disguised messenger to meet his illicit consort, during the times Joseph was meeting in Jerusalem with the Sanhedrin, during the times Rachel had decided to stay home to be with her husband. He would say he was going out for an early morning walk, or that he had early Temple duties. Only a loin covering girded his body during the run, the attire of a messenger.

On this day Jael knew immediately something was wrong, that it would be their last day together. She knew it before words were ever spoken. He sat beside her instead of embracing her. His eyes had no passion in them. Fear instead, swirled within the structure of his thoughts, fear that he would not get back in time, fear of being attacked on the way, fear that he should have listened to Eli and never come at all – and Jael saw it all.

He reached and took her hand, as if to be compassionate.

"What is it?" she asked, even though she knew.

There was no effort in what he was about to do in ending the affair, no self-sacrifice, because on this day there was only revulsion within him. The mind of man and its emotions are like the winds of the earth. They blow on the surface, and they change direction in the blink of an eye. Sometimes there is passion in them, sometimes there is not. Truth, love, the eternal, is beneath, and it is a world apart from what most people call love. This day the winds had changed to wag a huge finger of shame at Mahlir-of-Matthias. Other days the winds had done just the opposite; they had held him blameless, and had whispered words of comfort, and had convinced him that he had done no wrong, that all he had done was to fall in love with another woman. It happens all the time, whispered the winds, even to good people. It had happened to King David. After all, were it not for King David having fallen in love with Bathsheba, King Solomon would have never been born, and the world would never have known his wisdom. All was part of the plan; all was in good order.

But beware, declare the mysteries. It is the Scoffer that is in the wind. And somewhere beyond, or beneath, or above, or within, lies truth, love, a thing immutable, a fire that burns without consuming, yet consumes all, the bush on Sinai that transformed Moses, the bush that speaks if one has ears to hear.

When he didn't answer her question, she reached for him. The strong lines of her face and the fullness of her lips would stir passion in any man. But not within Mahlir, not that day. That day beauty had been transformed into ugliness. As her hands came to caress his cheeks and his neck, he shook his head in loathing. He grabbed her hands and pushed them back. He knew that tomorrow the winds might change so that he would again be filled with desire for his lover, but no matter, because tomorrow he would be safe. Tomorrow he would be away with Rachel, safe, on board the cargo vessel *Destiny* en route to Rome. Circumstance had provided him with an escape. "I cannot be with you anymore," he said, in the soundlessness of a guttural whisper.

She looked at him with as much surprise as if he had struck with his fist, even though she knew.

"Tomorrow I must leave," he said. "We cannot see each other again."

"Why?" she finally said, forcing the word out in a barely to be heard murmur.

"Archlaus has targeted Eli as the one who is seditious against him. Eli has fears for the safety of his family and is sending us away."

"Who are you to be made a little boy by your father-in-law? Are you not a grown man who can make his own decisions?"

"I choose to go as well, for the safety and protection of my family."

At hearing the phrase "my family" Jael's face flushed red. She swallowed his hurtful words with a breath that barely showed, and said, affection present again in her profound Jewish eyes, "Then let us share our final moments together with beauty."

But Mahlir could not. He could not have done it even if he had wanted to, not even to be compassionate. Because there was no beauty in it. There was only the fear, the ugliness, the shame, and an image of Rachel. A powerful silent need for his wife flared up inside him. Jael knew it, could see it, though no words revealed it. She ripped away from his hands and struck him with a closed fist, knocking his phylactery askew and ripping a gash in his forehead with a ring of gemstones Joseph had given her only a few days earlier. He had given it to her for no reason, only because he loved her.

She pointed with the forefinger of the same hand, stained in the blood from his forehead, and screamed for him to get out.

But he didn't want it to end this way. He wanted her to see it like he saw it. He told of the dream, and he told her of the mysteries, of how the mysteries revered the structure of marriage, of the bonding between a man and a woman, that it was a bonding welded together by forces from realms divine, and that it cannot be broken without serious consequences. If Mahlir could have only known how very serious those consequences would be, he never would have walked into the storm.

She finally did see it, or said she did, because the anger in her face subsided, and the affection came back. "All right," she said, speaking so softly now he could not hear her at all, but knew that she had said it, from the movement of her lips. She reached for him again, and was powerful.

Supreme confidence reigned, surrounded her, permeated her. "But right now I need to touch you," she said, still speaking soundlessly. "One more time."

He allowed it.

She reached to undress him. He allowed it.

She disrobed and presented her naked body to him.

He allowed it.

She pulled off his waist clothing; he didn't resist.

And she pressed her body to his and reached to his loins to unify herself with him, one final time.

He allowed it.

He was late; his arrival at the Temple in the morning did not come until the breaking of dawn. It should have been hours earlier. Rachel was among those gathering in the Court of women, he was sure, as he hurried through the streets already beginning to fill with Passover visitors. The weeklong festivities were nearly at an end; still people remained, enough to clog the roadways. Rachel was proud of his accomplishments, keeping records of them, all written down on expensive papyrus and tied in a cedar box. She would be there surely, hoping to catch a glimpse of him from the balconies where the women are allowed.

He had forgotten. She would be preparing, packing and loading the animals.

Sweat was burning his brow, a foul potion coming from within, burning, itching, chafing it red where the strap of his phylactery lay, where beneath was the gash given him by Jael, drawing a line in his forehead, not bleeding now, but festering. A reminder forever of his deeds? Because in the black box, inside his phylactery, properly on his forehead as it should be, carrying in it writings of the prophets, was an excerpt from Isiah. *"I will make justice the measuring line and righteousness the plumb line; hail will sweep away your refuge, the lie, and water will overflow your hiding place."* Words of his own choosing written in his own hand before his fall, now cursing him, burning its white-hot message into the skin of his forehead. He ran, stumbled around corners and through side streets, taking the shortest route – to the shop on Clothes Market Street with the red awning where the old woman with no teeth sold steaming corn cakes every day; left and over to Tyropoeon, the street skirting the west Temple wall; down Tyropoeon and under the giant archway over which the main road enters the Temple from the Xyxtra and the King's palace, past the many shops and offices on the left and on the right, past the entrance to the Chamber of Hewn Stone wherein the Sanhedrin sits in council…to the great Portico Archway. The Portico Archway is a hundred steps high, as high above a man's head as the cedars of Lebanon, vivid, foreboding. In minutes sunlight would be shaving the oxen-sized bricks of the south wall, some of which were bossed in the middle to cut defining shadows against the soon-to-arrive glittering whiteness. Mahlir was wishing it was there now. Warm sunshine had a way of making him believe everything was all right in God's world.

The streets of Jerusalem were wide with nothing built over them, unusual for a city in Israel. But then Jerusalem was no ordinary city. Its curb-stoned thoroughfares, designed to accommodate the throngs visiting the Temple daily, those coming to pray, to sacrifice, to atone, to renew, were forty and fifty spans in width, often opening to large public squares, and were constructed on foundations fifteen spans in depth, sixty in the vicinity of the Temple where the larger paving stones were used, a span being the breadth of a man's hand finger to thumb. A single paving stone was large enough for a man to lay across and still not touch the other side.

Visitors were beginning to climb to the Portico. Mahlir felt their stares as he ran up the steps past them. Could they see the insanity in his face, and the perspiration soiling his garments, and the itching sore on his forehead beneath his phylactery? Could they tell that God was punishing him by marking him with his sin? It had transformed itself into something worse than a cut. He had stopped to look at its reflection in a pool of water. It was enlarged with red bumps and blisters. Leprosy? The thought of it stilled his heart. He made sure it was covered by the phylactery strap.

Inside the Portico, all of it restored since the fire, the most magnificent enclosure in all of Palestine, merchants and money changers were beginning to set up their booths, among pillars so thick the arms of three people were necessary to enwrap just one, pillars so tall they would have spired to the stars had a roof not covered them. Those visiting from far off lands would exchange coins there for ones bearing the inscription "Yehud" or for the Roman denarius, or for the didrachma of Tyre, any of which could be used to purchase clothing, food and wares, or to pay the Temple tax, or the tax to Archaleus, or the tax to Rome. Such was the Temple, the heart of Jerusalem, the center of commerce, the center of social life for the elite and penniless alike, and the center of all things sacred. And Jerusalem was the hub of the world, the gateway through which travelers from all four corners of civilization passed, bringing with them their money for exchange, and their goods, and their gods and goddesses and their religions, and their cultures. It had been that way for generations. Perhaps that was why in Palestine there existed such a blending of cultures, and so many different beliefs. Over the span of the years, bits of those cultures and beliefs had mingled with and even helped to form the belief of the Jews. That, perhaps, is an explanation of why within the walls of the Temple, within the ranks of the priesthood, there were people with so many different variations of that belief – those who believed in life after death, those who did not, those who believed in an eventual raising up of the gathered souls of the righteous, those who did not, those who believed in the regeneration of the soul through successive births and re-births, those who did not, those who believed in following the laws of the Torah to the letter, those who did not, those who were committed to the violent overthrow of Roman oppression by an army led by the coming Messiah, those who were not.

With money exchanged for acceptable currency, the travelers would then purchase wares and food from the merchants. If they were of the belief of the Jews, followers of Yahweh, they would buy from one of the venders an animal pure and unblemished for sacrifice. Those selling animals were the most abundant of the Temple merchants, and, as Mahlir passed, they were setting out their cages – doves and pigeons for women unclean from their menstrual cycles and from childbirth, so that they may be cleansed with the blood of something innocent, lambs for atonement of sins, heifers if the buyer had the money, to be slaughtered with kidneys cut out and washed and burned, an aroma pleasing to the Lord, their blood sprinkled on the alter so that Yahweh would forgive. The cages were large and bulky, and lay over much of the floor. The Portico, lit now by lamps, would soon be illumined by sunshine. The sunshine would momentarily be breaking through the archways of the hundred or more ceiling high windows, its beams crossing from heights to bounce off the gold-gilded sides of the glittering green walls.

He hurried across the floor. It was a breadth of mosaic second only in size to the hippodrome. A mouse was also scurrying to cross its expanse. An expensively dressed woman tried to catch it under her jeweled sandal, for no more than the amusement of it, but missed; the poor creature would be half the morning completing the perilous journey. After elbowing and excusing his way through, Mahlir walked out into the open air of the esplanade. The bluish light of early morning was beginning to paint away the stars. The people were beginning to stir, those asleep that had nowhere else to go the night before. Gentiles. That part of the Temple, in itself the size of a small village, was a gathering place for non-Jews, a haven for travelers from afar, a place of safety watched over by priests in the corner towers, or simply a place for relaxation, often times a meeting place, a place to buy and sell, a place open to all.

Mahlir walked toward the balustrade, the barrier between the Court of Gentiles and the upper-level terraces. Its low pillars seemed to speak to him, to tell him he also was unworthy to enter. Between each pillar were sections of waist-high walls carved alternately with the unfolding Flower of Knowledge and the Greek inscription forbidding non-Jews to pass.

No outsider shall enter
the protective enclosure
around the sanctuary; and

whoever is caught will
only have himself
to blame for the
ensuing death.

A nightingale settled itself upon the section in front of him above the inscription. It was properly surprised at its solidity and had to dance about to assure itself that it was firm. The stones of the Temple were so white they looked soft, and often sparkled like they were formed from bits of gemstones. To touch them was an urge irresistible. From this level, high above the street, the world was still, the soon to open marketplace being nothing more than the distant murmurings of another world. The only distinguishable sound was the hushing of the aqueduct, shaming him for his betrayal of a woman whose only fault was believing him when he said he would love her and honor her and protect her. It carried water as pure as Rachel, as pure as that which fell from the sky, entering the Temple one level below, flowing all the way from Solomon's Pools in Bethlehem.

Off to the east, above the marbled awnings of Solomon's Porch, one could see the rise of the Mount of Olives. Sleepy sheets of fog were entwining the trees, trees massive and old, some old enough to have been seen by the eyes of King David. Twisted and unsightly, they were, but also strong and compassionate, ready to offer comfort, standing like gentle sentries above the fog, a mist whitening by the second under the emerging dawn. Oh – would that he could take wing like the nightingale in front of him, with no cares, no sin, and catch the free wind and fly to the solace of those trees and disappear in the embrace of their branches. Just then a stream of lavender sunshine broke over the eastern ridge and burned a pathway through the fog. It startled him.

In the same instant a sound came from somewhere. He spun around and saw a priest pushing a cart of tools toward him. The noise made by the wooden wheels was deafening. Mahlir wanted to silence him. The priest looked up. Mahlir saw that he was barely more than a child. Twelve. Thirteen at the most. A man by law, but a child nonetheless. Mahlir put a hand on the cart and stopped him. "Where do you go? Who are you? What are you doing here? Why do you wear the white robes of the Temple?" Mahlir was spewing the words in a guttural whisper – he was angry – though all he wanted was for the boy to stop the wretched clattering.

A scent came to his nostrils, intermingled with the drifting fragrance of the mineral-laden Dead Sea air, an unfamiliar scent, yet familiar in a way. A fresh smell. The way an empty alabaster jar smells, the kind used in the anointing of those in the service of the Lord. The smell was not of the perfume itself, but of the vessels, of the porous stone from which they are carved, the alabaster, which after a time gives off its own fragrance, unique unto itself, having drawn in the oil, having mixed it with its own essence. Of a subtler nature than the oil, is the smell of this alabaster, like the clean powdery smell of a craftsman's shop. Such was the scent that dangled in the air that morning, but with a hint of jasmine, maybe also of rose, and of the wild wind, and of the breeze that floats through the pillared curtains of a late evening banquet with the flowers of the hillsides still upon it. Strong. Yet gentle. Replied the boy, politely, innocently, in Hebrew, with a maturity of speech beyond his years, "Sir, my apologies – I am doing the bidding of His Holiness. It is my duty this morning to prepare the gardens in the Court of Women. I go there now. As are my instructions."

"Why are you here? Why have I not seen you before today?"

A most strange thing did he then say. "I am in my fathers' house," he said. He stated it quite matter-of-factly.

The boy was trifling with him, was Mahlir's first thought, until he realized the magnitude of what he had just said. The boy was of the Herodian line, perhaps Archelaus' son, some close relation to the Great Herod, builder of the Temple.

"Go then –" Mahlir said, and smiled, forgetting for the moment the depths of his desperation. "Be about those duties of yours. Know you, though, that you are lost within your father's house." Mahlir gestured forward, beyond the balustrade, to the walls surrounding the courts and the Temple proper, all built on the surface of the esplanade, a fortress on top of a fortress. "The Court of Women is opposite the direction you are going. It is there, in the very area where you procured the tools. I am on my way there also. Please don't follow me closely. I'm late for my duties and wish not to attract attention."

The boy seemed to want to speak with him, but Mahlir was too obsessed with his purpose to pay him any mind and hurried away, up the seven steps and through the balustrade and across the Chosen Level to the Court of Women, all the while hearing the wheels of the cart behind him.

Mahlir walked quickly through the Court of Women gateway. He passed two priests, Neamiah and Shelomoth. They took no notice of him. They were engaged in discussion, intent only on each other – "...nay, you are wrong, a symbol only," one was saying to the other. "It is not a flesh and blood creature. Properly translated by Yahweh himself, 666 means mankind, that which is human." – calm and stoic in their long blue and black robes and their sashes of silver, and their belt-length gray beards, powerful, godly. Never would they have allowed themselves to become entangled in sin as Mahlir had done.

Once through the gateway, once inside the Court of Women, one beholds the true beauty of the Temple at sunrise. Above the pillared archway is the Court of Israel, and spiring higher still is the Temple proper, gold latticework encircling its roof line, flashing brilliant in the sun. Priests were gathering to sing on the 14 circular steps. People were beginning to file in to fill the courtyard, elders and those of high position in front, women with their children viewing and pointing down from the balconies and porches above. Mahlir looked for Rachel, forgetting for a moment that she was not there.

Of course she was not there. She was preparing for their journey into their new life.

The sounding of the ram's horn was splitting the morning silence, a signal that the priest was ready, beyond sight, inside the Holy Place, hidden from all eyes, prepared to give the absolution and offer up the sacrifice. But the priest was not there. The priest was late because he had been in sin with the wife of a man of God.

The clattering of the cart behind him was maddening. Mahlir turned. *Stop; return home*, the boy said. Or did he? Because his lips did not move. Mahlir's imagination. *Return home immediately*, the boy said. Or did he?

Mahlir was almost amused. Presumptuous little devil. The most bothersome people alive can be the sons of king and monarchs, old enough to wield power, too young to be mellowed by the flavor of life's experiences. Who does he think he is? Ordering me, a priest of Yahweh to abandon my duties.

Go home; there is still time, he thought he heard the boy say again, louder this time, yet too soft to be really sure.

Mahlir answered as if the boy had said it. "I don't have time to explain all this to you, about the importance of atonement. The blood of the lamb is not for me. It is for the people I serve. It is something I have an obligation to provide. It is for their redemption." He pointed to the crowd that was beginning to gather on the esplanade, waiting to have their sins washed away for the day. "All these people. I would be cheating all these people of their absolution if I went home."

Funny thing. Mahlir almost did do it. He almost did go home. Because of something hollow inside that was growing, something that was bursting out with a need to caress and hold his wife, that left him with an ache to feel her against him – not to have her sexually – well, yes – no, more than that – it was more like he wanted to melt into her so they could be like two clouds floating, merging, like sometimes is seen on sunlit carefree days. When he got home he would do it. Yes, by Jupiter, he would. He would take her in his arms and they would be clouds. But for now the people needed their absolution. To abandon the people in favor of his wife would be misplaced responsibility.

What the people would soon see, if Mahlir could get there in time, would be the rising of the incense through the roof, drifting into the day's first light, placed upon the inner altar by the chosen priest, by Mahlir, son of the great Matthias, if he could get there in time. Then the people, the men below in the Court of Israel and the women above on the balconies, would see the doors of the Temple proper swing open. Those closest might be fortunate enough to see the curtain wherein the priest, Mahir, the one chosen that day by God, would read from the scrolls. From behind the curtain, in tones loud enough for everyone to hear, he would utter words from the prophets, chosen by prayer to reach the hearts of those present. Then the curtain would part for a moment – perhaps someone might even glimpse the forbidden inner chamber – and the priest would emerge and walk out into the courtyard where the 49 steps of the main altar ascend to the heights of the Lord's Holy Fire, burning always. There he would offer up an animal to God, splitting it open, spilling its blood, burning its entrails, an aroma pleasing to the Lord, so that the Lord in his benevolence might forgive.

Soon Mahlir arrived. While the echoes of the second Shofar were ringing through the valleys he was putting on the vestments. Soon he would burn the incense and offer the reading, and the sacrifice, and the prayers to absolve the people of their sins, while he fairly dripped in his.

The soldiers were taking Rachel to the Tower as he was putting on the vestments – the Tower was an attachment to the Temple, a stone's throw from where he stood – taking her there to be stripped naked and tied to a wheel four times the size of an ox-cart wheel, as he was putting on the Ephod, and the breastplate, and the robes and the turban. The Ephod was of a cloth of finely twisted linen, gold and purple and blue and scarlet. He draped it over his shoulders front and back and fastened it with its gold clasp. The weight of its onyx shoulder stones gave him power, filled his limbs with strength. Braided chains of pure gold hung rope-like from each stone, clinging to him, calming him.

She was crying out for Mahlir as he was attaching the breastplate, crafted of the same material as the Ephod, gold and blue, purple and scarlet, and embroidered with inset gemstones representative of the twelve tribes of Israel. Upon the breastplate lay more loops of gold, calming him, energizing him.

She was being lashed to the wheel, calling his name, pleading for his help, as he enclosed himself in the blue robe, hemmed with pomegranates of purple and scarlet yarn, and with gold bells that tinkled at the slightest movement, vestments kept locked in the Tower but given for use at Passover.

As Rachel's screams echoed from somewhere – Mahlir did not recognize them; he thought it was someone else who needed help; he thought she was home preparing for their new life – he slowly placed the tall turban on his head, with its engraved plate of gold. Holy to the Lord, it read, high in view of all, so that the wearer might bear the guilt of those for whom he prays.

He stepped into the Holy Inner Place, as only the most holy and pure of men are able to do, into its solitude, and looked around at the walls, a sight few have seen, or ever will see, high walls reaching many times the height of a man, sculpted in intricate tracings of gold palm trees. The floor was wrought in mosaics of God's creations, of birds and trees and all manner of creatures. It was seamless and smooth, like the reflected beauty of a green countryside on still waters. Above loomed winged seraphs, enormous, hammered flawlessly out of solid gold, gazing down at the place where the Ark and the Crown will rest when found, and gazing down at the insignificant human creature called Mahlir-of-Matthias.

He removed his sandals, realizing he was on Holy Ground, and walked to the altar and scooped up incense and put it on the fire. The flame flashed, and the smoke rose up and through the opening. The pungent smell nearly made him cough. Then came chants from the priests on the steps outside as they saw it, and there came the sounding of the ram's horn. Mahlir repeated the process and waited again for the chants, and the ram's horn. A third time he did it.

Now it was time for the reading of the Torah, loud enough to be heard beyond the curtains and through the open doors into the courtyard. There was no time to pray and search for a passage, something he should have done and marked the night before. But of course he had been elsewhere.

He simply united the scroll and rolled it open to let his eyes fall where they may, to let chance choose for him…and trembled at the words. He thought he had picked up the Torah. But in his haste his hands had fallen upon the scroll of the prophet Isaiah. He didn't realize his mistake until it was too late, until words were already being spoken. *"I will make justice the measuring line and righteousness the plumb line; hail will sweep away your refuge, the lie, and water will overflow your hiding place."* The words of his phylactery! Cursing him. Rotting his skin. Making him a leper. He reached out, half in anger, half in terror, and rolled the papyrus forward to a new passage, one that would not curse him, and read again where his eyes fell. *"I will go before you and will level the mountains; I will break down gates of bronze and cut through bars of iron. I will give you treasures of darkness, riches stored in secret places, so that you may know that I am the Lord, the God of Israel, who summons you by name."* It was what he wanted, a passage of blessing and hope, a prophetic promise of splendor and beauty. Still he was terrified, still he was angry. He threw the scroll against the Holy walls. Its inner spine cracked and lay crooked.

The ram's horn sounded again, and the midpoint of the curtains parted, all ten curtains, of tightly woven fabric, of gold and blue, and purple and scarlet, two sets of five hooked together with golden clasps and heavy loops of blue. They were pulled away by a cord so small it could not be seen. What the priests and the assembled Holy men of Israel saw, from the other side, was a glimpse of the Most Holy Place and the Zadokite who was representing them before God. A tremor ran through him, and he forgot for a moment his burdens.

He put his sandals back on and stepped forward through the opening. The curtains closed in back of him, floated together as if by a will of their own. The assemblage chanted, "Holy to the Lord." In hearing it the people outside in the Court of Israel repeated, "Holy to the Lord." The priests on the steps of the Court of Women repeated, "Holy to the Lord." And the harmonious chants of the women on the balconies echoed, "Holy to the Lord." But of course Rachel was not among them.

All who saw Mahlir bowed as he walked past, and intoned, "Holy to the Lord."

Mahlir wondered in his ecstasy what it would be like to be the coming Anointed One, the Messiah, and to have the entire world bow before him. Except that the gold of his turban and the braids of his ropes would be brighter, if he were the Messiah. By ten times. A hundred times. And the colors of his robes would be richer. Tenfold. A hundred times. And the stones of his breastplate would catch the sun a hundred times over. And it would be he who would be wearing the Crown of David with its full measures of gold and its precious stones, not some blowhard shepherd who looks more like a gorilla than a messiah.

Such a sight he would be, if he were the Messiah.

And he wondered, will he ever meet him, if in fact the Messiah does come? Will he be one of the ones to serve him, the true Messiah? The true Messiah would be one who would not steal from his own, as Athronges had done, or rape his own. The true Messiah would be one who would focus his might against only the Romans and the Gentiles, not against his chosen people.

Mahlir was adorned with more pomp than the High Priest himself, whom he faced, his mother's brother Joazr, toward whom he advanced as he walked out into the Court of Israel, as he walked through a corridor of his piers toward the 49 steps of the Mighty Altar of God, its flames leaping into the morning sky in a furious roar. Joazar, his uncle, Archelaus' most recent appointment, was standing at the altar's base, holding the vestments of the sacrifice, white linen to collect and purify the stains of death, which he placed upon Mahlir in return for the robes.

Priests were already in place, standing near the flames, standing high on the altar, one holding the lamb, others carrying bowls in which to catch the blood to be sprinkled. Mahlir walked the 49 steps and faced the lamb, and bent low and stroked gently the creature's forehead, holding the death instrument in his other hand behind his back, honed to such sharpness it could not be touched in even the slightest way without bringing blood. The chanting intensified – Holy to the Lord – his eyes felt hypnotic. Instantly fear in the animal changed to a simple wriggling for support beneath its feet. And with a large-eyed look of animal innocence, like a puppy dog with implicit trust in its master, an ill child looking to a parent, so did the lamb watch as the glistening blade came to cut its jugular. Its face jerked with surprise as it felt the sting. Life spilled willingly from the deep wound, gushing forth with the gurgle of breath stopped short. The mouth of the young thing opened in its last moments of life, in its confusion, just a little, as if to show trust still. Even as its eyes glazed to emptiness they communicated trust.

The volume rose louder – Holy to the Lord – the monotone of the heavy male voices seeming to vibrate the walls, the stones themselves.

The ram's horn sounded again.

The people had been redeemed.

And – the thought occurred to Mahlir – perhaps he had been redeemed too. Perhaps God had accepted the lamb for him as well.

Now he would go home to Rachel. Now he would go. And they could begin their new life together. There was a passageway he could take that led directly to the Court of Women. In its midst the sounds of bells tinkled. A robed figure stepped out to obscure the dim torchlight.

"The gold and scarlet looked good on you today, my young nephew," said Joazar.

"Uncle!"

Alone in the tunnel with Mahlir was the high priest, his mother's brother.

Mahlir's heart began to race anew, and breath became hard. The air was heavy anyway in the Temple underbelly that day, straining his lungs, flickering low the wall lamps, causing the draining cisterns to echo harsher, bringing stronger the oppressive smell of the animals and their feed and manure.

Joazar was there to chastise him for his lack of preparedness and his ineptness, surely. Perhaps he even knew.

Joazar embraced Mahlir on both sides and kissed him, as was the custom. Feeling Mahlir's rigidity, he spoke to reassure. "You did exceptionally well, my young nephew. You have a great future in the service of the Lord. Come. Walk with me to the Portico?"

Mahlir nervously followed Joazar upward – he was always uneasy around his uncle – and emerged behind him into the Court of Women and the sunshine. The sun, full in the sky now, was blinding. He shaded his eyes. Maybe Rachel would be there. Maybe she had come to meet him. Maybe the animals were packed and ready, waiting below with Benjamin, so that they could leave right from there. That would be just like her, always the practical one, the organized one, born under the sign of Parthenos, fastidious to a fault. What would he ever do without her! He was looking above the heads of the other women for the shaved head of Benjamin. Where Benjamin was, so would Rachel be, ever under his watchful eye. Mahlir was thankful that Eli had acquired Benjamin, that he would be going along with them on their journey.

But of course they were not there.

On the distant hills – the Temple sat upon one of seven – he could see the long caravans of Passover visitors returning to their towns and countries, caterpillars, multicolored, ambling lazily over the spring-green of the boulder strewn and terraced terrain.

Said Joazar, adorned in his priestly garments, the gold and blue, the purple and scarlet, "The late king's son requests your presence."

"The Tetrarch? The most high and revered Archelaus?

To refer to Archelaus in any other way was unwise. One never knew what may reach back to him of thoughts spoken openly.

"I spoke to him yesterday. He directed me to have you escorted to the palace immediately following your duties here."

"An escort is not necessary. I know the way."

Joazar gave a slight bow. "As you wish."

"But why should he seek me? What could he possibly desire of me?"

"The high and mighty Archelaus is not to be questioned, when asking to see a priest."

"I only meant I was curious. I was hoping you would know."

Mahlir's uncle smiled reassurance through the cloaking of his long, gray beard. His aged eyes opened wide. "Worry not, my young nephew. You are a Zadokite. Your family is of the priestly line. It is only natural that the Tetrarch should want to develop a relationship with you. You should be wanting to do the same with him. After all – it may be you one day who will wear these robes."

"Of what things did he speak, in requesting my presence?"

"He inquired about your duties here at the Temple, and about your knowledge of the Law; he asked about your wife, and gave his best wishes to her in the upcoming time of her birth-giving; and he asked about your father-in-law the Sadducee."

The spot on Mahlir's forehead flared. He scratched at it furiously.

"My father-in-law? Eli? Why? For what purpose?"

"I have learned some lessons in my many years of walking with the Lord," said Joazar. "One of the greatest of these is humility. If I must humble myself before an earthly king to do the deeds of a greater king, to do the deeds of the God of Abraham and Isaac, before whom no graven image shall be placed, then let it be so. If the Tetrarch demands my presence, I obey. If Archelaus desires that I meet him in the baths of the Xyxra, though it be a place for the training and exercise of the naked athletes, I accommodate him, as long as he keeps it free of the graven images of Caesar and of the eagle. If we allow him the little things, the things that are important to him, then perhaps he will allow us the big things, the things that are important to us."

Said Mahlir, in remembering his encounter with the gardener, "I may have already done damage." He explained his confrontations with the tetrarch's son, how he had been short tempered and rude to the boy.

"His son?"

"The boy. The son of Archelaus. He said you set before him the duties of beautifying the Court of Women."

"His son?"

"The boy. The son of Archelaus. I met him on the esplanade pushing a cart load of tools."

"Ah – yes – the boy." Joazar came close to laughter. "But how did you conceive the idea that he was the son of Archelaus?"

"He said so. He told me he was in his father's house."

"No, my nephew. No. His father is a carpenter and stone mason."

"A carpenter? Why is the son of a carpenter here? And why is he dressed in the tassels and white robing of a priest?"

Joazar's smile widened. "We have taken him under our care – adopted him, you might say – for a time, until his parents can be located. We gave him clothing while his own is being washed and purified."

"A stray child? In the service of the Temple? Draped in the robings of a priest?"

"He is quite a remarkable young man. He displays an understanding of the Law far beyond his years." Joazar squinted against the sun, higher now in the mid-morning sky, warming the stones of the Temple, whitening and softening them. "He came to us at the start of Passover, with the most penetrating of questions. While his parents were tending to their business he spent his days with us, often answering his own questions with a profundity that gave us all pause. We put him to work cleaning and polishing the stonework. Being the son of a mason, he knows quite a bit about various stones and their absorption properties, and how they need to be cleaned in order to bring out their true polished beauty. That one stone near the aqueduct? The one where the iris was chipped? He carved a replacement block. It was better than the original! And he did it in less than an hour!"

Mahlir did not respond. Joazar must have perceived his emotions. "The boy is not threat to you. He is not a Levite. His name is Yesua-ben-Yosef. He is from the line of Judah, of the house of David, so he could never be High Priest, as you someday may be. He could never assume your position. He could never enter the Holy Place, as you did today.

"Where are his parents?"

"The family is from Nazareth. He became separated from them when Passover ended. They must have left without realizing he was not with them in their caravan. I am sure they will return for him soon."

Mahlir and his uncle were nearing the Portico.

Mahlir rubbed and scratched again at his forehead. Blood ran through his fingers and down his cheek.

Joazar stared, part in disbelief, part in fear.

Fear seized Mahlir as well. He had done it without thinking. The lesion had been hidden beneath the phylactery.

"Remove your hand," demanded Joazar.

"It is nothing, Uncle." Mahlir tried to conceal his anxiety, tried to think of an explanation.

"Remove your hand!" shouted Joazar. "It must be examined."

Mahlir did as he was asked. "It is nothing – I bumped my head in the corridor." He put his hand back over it, in fear that Joazar might see scabs and blisters.

"Then cover it until it heals, lest someone think it otherwise." Joazar was satisfied. The priesthood had pronounced him clean, the final authority in such matters.

With Joazar as a witness, Mahlir purchased a wrap from a vender setting up at the Portico entrance, and gave it no more thought. He could not. Any other reality was unthinkable.

Joazar gave his peace and walked away into a doorway to attend to duties elsewhere, saying as parting advice, "It is not wise to keep the king waiting."

Mahlir nodded and purchased a gift for Rachel from another one of the venders. He had no intention of going to see Archelaus. By this time tomorrow he and Rachel would be boarding a ship in Joppa. From there they would travel to Tyre where they would dock to replenish water and pick up more passengers. Tyre was under Syrian rule. There they would be able to breathe a little easier. From there it would be on to Rome.

The Portico was now resplendent with reams of sunshine blasting in through the windows, and it was filled with people, the buyers and the sellers and the dignitaries, and the common people, and those from far lands.

Mahlir had much to be grateful for. He had been lauded by the High Priest himself. He was tall in the eyes of men. And the blood of the lamb had redeemed him of his sins as well. Sins past, because there was no sin anymore. From this day forward he would begin anew, with only his wife as his lover and companion, as it should be. Although – a strange thing – as he was pushing his way through the crowd a feeling of discontent began to grow, a bitterness undefined, an emptiness in which all was not well. Even though he had been redeemed. Even though he would not be returning to Jael.

The more he walked the more it grew, magnifying, doubling, tripling itself, beginning as a tightness in his stomach then expanding to a pounding between his ears, an actual physical noise, pounding, booming – until – halfway through the Portico, amid the laughter, the arguing, the bartering, the multitudes of lively discussions, at a point where the noise had grown to a storm inside his head, an answer came. In an instant Mahlir knew what must be done. God was speaking to him. Mahlir knew from his Temple studies how to listen to the voice of God. The "inner voice," it was called, an urging that cannot be ignored. To ignore it is to cast one's fate to chance. For his redemption Mahlir needed to do more, so great was his sin, worsened by the fact that he was a priest, a man of God, an example before men, darkened further by the fact that he had harmed one of God's creatures using God as his alibi. He whirled around to go back to where he had come from, nearly bumping into a man doing business at the table of a moneychanger. The man was a dignified and comely gentleman of a foreign tongue, clothed in the colors of the Orient, and had just been given three denarii in return for a gold Parthian double of Phraataces and Mousa. He had given the moneychanger a coin worth ten times the amount of the three he had received in return. Mahlir would have intervened at the injustice, had he not been in such a hurry, had he not been in the service of the Lord's bidding.

Obsession moved his steps, determination formed his expression. Quickly he walked, half running, his eyes defining his purpose. He walked to the Court of Women, just to be sure Rachel had not come there to meet him, up its steps and into its terraced enclosure. No one was there, except the young gardener, tending the gardens of stone, for it is set down in the Mishna that no green thing is to be grown within the Holy walls. The things of God's creation, the vines and the petals of beautiful flowers, the intricacy of a leaf, the sturdiness of the stately date palm that reaches to the sky, are all carved into the stone of the Temple, into the cornices and columns, into the stools, benches and railings, and are washed and polished daily by the "gardeners," priests whose duty it befalls that day, or in this case the young son of the carpenter from Nazareth.

The boy looked up. Mahlir felt the pierce of his eyes and refused to return the look. Let him annoy one of the other priests. Let him find his mentorship elsewhere. Mahlir had needs of his own.

Mahlir kept on walking and caught again the scent of alabaster. Again it seemed as though the boy wanted to say something. Mahlir refused him, looked straight ahead and walked on past, feeling all the while an urge to return, feeling strangely protective of the boy, powerfully so, like he had turned his back on his own well being. But he had concerns of his own.

And the alabaster scent began to fade.

The burning on his forehead was worsening. He resisted the impulse to scratch it again, to ease the pain of the deepening itch, and walked on. Perhaps if he didn't touch it, if he didn't think about it, it would go away.

He was looking for a door to the under chambers. His steps were slowing, because to get there he had to pass a place he always took pains to avoid. It was a place the mere presence of which turned his stomach foul, one wherein a thing lay festering worse than the boil on his forehead. He forced himself not to think of it. He forced himself to focus on the beauty of the Temple itself. The Temple had been rebuilt since the fire, ever the sturdier, more appealing to the eye, if that be possible. The wood smelled of fresh pitch and cedar. The pitch on the roofs of the cloisters was covered over with gold ornamentation, and the roofs themselves with clay tile, never again to be susceptible to catapulted pots of fire, a lesson learned. There was no evidence whatsoever of what had transpired five years earlier, of the destruction wrought by the fire and the battle, except for a black smudge on the floor beneath one single cloister, the one by the door to the under chamber, charred blood and grease that would not come clean no matter the scrubbing, remnants of a young soldier whose essence impressioned even the surrounding air with words of ever-present malicious intent: *"Why do you do this? We had an agreement."* Mahlir stopped and turned – there were other doors he could take – it was not as if this was the only one to the under chamber – he even considered abandoning altogether his plans for absolution, this that the Lord was telling him to do, and saw again the eyes of the stone gardener, the boy from Nazareth. The boy had followed him – wretched child – with those pompous eyes. The boy was about to say something. Mahlir could see it on his lips, though they were yet unparted. The boldness of it! Mahlir turned away before the absurd thing could be spoken, whatever it was, and went back to his own purpose, to do the bidding of the Lord, and passed through the cloister anyway, with its foul spot on the floor. It would not defeat him.

He procured a torch and touched it to flame, and went down again into the belly of the Temple, to do the Lord's bidding, to take a goat from the vaults, a goat pure and unblemished, to deposit three times its value into the Temple treasury, and to release it into the desert to thirst and die, in the same manner that Mahlir deserved to thirst and die. This was what God had told him to do. The animal would bear his burdens, his sin, Holy to the Lord. Mahlir's scapegoat. And great were his burdens, the greatest of which was what he had done to Rachel. He found it odd, that he should suddenly come to think of his adultery as the worst of sins, because adultery was not even a punishable offense, unless of course the adultery were to be perpetrated by a woman. More than being wrong, Mahlir's adultery was made worse by the fact that he had done it using God as his alibi, and he was so very very sorry, and relieved that he was finished with it, and that he had escaped it without having done harm.

He found an Ibex doe, one pure and without blemish, long haired and white, silken, smooth. Her face was soft with the tenderness of maternity, for she had only several months ago given birth. She was blessed, because her children had been offered up to the Lord.

She cried out as Mahlir led her through the tunnel to the gate, because she had not been milked and her udder was full. Mahlir was fearful somebody would hear, though no one came. He walked out the gate unnoticed. Access to and from the Temple was unrestricted in the weeks before and after Passover, day and night. The Hairy Goat Gate, it was called. It led toward the desert from the stables. It was the one always used for scapegoats.

He walked into the valley and up to the top of the Mount of Olives, called by some Olivet, leading the doe by a white woolen rope. The sloping length of Olivet's peak was in itself a tiring walk. On the other side was the sudden white and yellow of the Wilderness, terracing and rolling and cutting its way into oblivion.

The hills of Judea - splendid with trees and all types of flowering bushes, except on the northern sides where the winds never carry the rain - come to a point eastward where there is a monstrous hole in the earth. This is the Judeean Wilderness. The creatures that live in its depths are of a hostile nature. The land itself is unforgiving. Many a fated wanderer has become lost while walking a simple straight line to the Dead Sea. Other than the Dead Sea, where nothing lives, where an occasional spring or oasis pops up, the only water in the Wilderness is that which flows beneath the surface upon a rock water table. The roots of some of the sturdier trees reach it from dry riverbeds cut by wintertime flash flooding.

For one to walk to the bottom of this gorged out valley would take an entire day, if one could make it at all without falling to one's death. So Mahlir went partway down, and in a lifeless ravine released the doe. But she refused to stay. The beautiful creature continued following at his heels. At one point he threw stones at her. Still she followed, bawling, bleating, because she had never known freedom. Until being given to the Temple she had known only the gentle hand of a master, the protection of a herder who would give his own life for hers, who would milk her when the pain came, who would find grazing grass when she hungered, who would provide water when she thirsted. So when Mahlir tethered her with the rope around a stone, she expected he would return. She had been tethered many times, and each of those times the herder had returned. There was no reason to doubt that this time would be any different. She would watch moment to moment, patiently, in anticipation. Even at the point of her death she would be watching, knowing he would return.

Mahlir looked in her eyes before leaving – and he almost didn't do it. He almost changed his mind and took her back with him.

He should have, because she suffered in vain, he soon discovered, as did the lamb at the altar. Neither did any good. Change had already begun, be it due to providence or by chance, or by Mahlir's own folly. Life would never be the same.

When he arrived home, instead of finding Rachel, he found their front door sealed with multiple layers of wax, still warm from its application. A plank with the inscription

Property of
The Tetrarchy

was nailed across it, carved once in Aramaic and again in Latin as notice to the Romans.

Benjamin was there as well, in a helpless sitting position, dead, impaled by the shafts of three oversized arrows. A large mechanical crossbow of some sort had pinned him to the door, the kind carried by oxen on a war cart. He would have given his life for his mistress, and he did.

Mahlir's mind sat frozen, pulsing with its confusion.

He called Rachel's name in screams of terror, and pounded on the door, and dug his fingers into the wax. The only people to hear were those outside who gathered to point and whisper, some of whom used to be his friends. He ran up to them, only to see them turn and hurry away. In his madness he grabbed one. "What has happened here?" he pleaded. "Where is my wife?"

Said the man in fear, "O Priest, servant of God, the Tetrarch comes to arrest you. Now release me before I too am bound over for execution as one who knows you. As we speak his army searches for you."

Mahlir shook him as though the man were his enemy. "Why? In the name of Abraham. Why? And where is my wife?"

"She has been taken to Antonia. They say she and you are accused of seditions against Archelaus, of conspiracy with the merchant Eli for the overthrow of the government."

In his blind insanity Mahlir went there too, to the tower. What he was thinking he could do, he did not know. He merely ran mindlessly to the feared Tower of Antonia, to the woman who was soon to leave this world without ever knowing of his sin, and without ever allowing him to make amends.

Like Benjamin, he too would give his life for Rachel.

CHAPTER 17

THE TOWER OF ANTONIA

ISRAEL, JERUSALEM

The Tower of Antonia, it is said, is such that if a man sees the insides of its walls, he will never see sunlight again, or if he does it won't be as a whole person. But Mahlir went there anyway. Because that's where Rachel was, taken there by the soldiers.

He was seized before he reached the gate, by the soldiers, and dragged, half carried, to somewhere within its bowels, to a place where darkness smells of the rot of corpses, and of feces and vomit, a place where fear and evil hang in the air like an actual physical thing, an invisible cloak clinging, as if poured out from somewhere. The bricks of Antonia are smaller than those of the Temple proper, and each one has a slightly different hue of gray, from dark to light, as if each carries its own varying degree of human misery, in contrast to the stones of the Temple where the bricks are of soft rose, occasioned by periodic rows of white.

Along the way he had been beaten and chained, with a shackle locked around his neck so that he could be led like a dog. He heard moaning, and voices, and hideous laughter. Darkness was his veil. Between the sounds, in the midst of the Tower's unnatural stillness, he heard the tiny screeches and squeaks of rats.

The Tower of Antonia, called by some the Praetorium, was the isolated northwest corner of the Temple, four mighty turrets driven far down into the earth, rising skyward above the Temple, guardians in days gone by. In itself unholy, it was the oldest part of the most holy of places. It was built by John Hyrcanus as a defense fortress during the Maccabee reign, and rebuilt by Herod the Great to house soldiers, offices, storage vaults, prison cells… and torture chambers.

When Mahlir's eyes finally adjusted, they beheld a thing no man should see. His wife had been lashed to the outer rim of a wheel. A treadway of iron spikes was beneath it. No words were coming from her mouth, whimpering moans only.

Her face was focused upward, away from Mahlir's. She did not realize he was there.

He screamed her name and ran for her, but there was iron around his neck. He had forgotten. His feet flew out from under him.

He leapt up and charged again, unmindful of the restraint. Again the chain clinked taut. Again the dungeon floor slammed into him.

He grabbed at the chain and found that there was a man at the other end holding a triple-tailed flagellum.

Mahlir was like a wild beast, maddened beyond sanity. He ran at the man, needing to tear at his face, his eyes, his mouth, and was met with the sting of the flagellum, its spiked stones ripping through clothing and slicing into flesh and bone.

Again Mahlir fell, not from the chain this time, or from the flagellum, but from knees that refused support.

Again he rose.

Again he was struck down.

Exhausted, he cried out to God, and stood and looked at his wife. He could have ripped the iron collar from his neck and saved her. He truly felt he could have. Somewhere within him was the power. But he was unable to summon it forth.

Still she did not pay him notice. Was she dead? No. Her chest was rising and falling.

Had the pain driven away the soundness of her mind?

No –

He was to soon discover the reason. Soon words did come from her mouth, in Hebrew, in the tongue of the Lord, amidst the tiny squeaks of the rats. "He wants to know where Father is. Do not tell him." Her voice came in unnatural tones, stripped raw by the fits of her wheezing and coughing and screaming. "He wants to know where Father's Caesarea house is. Do not tell him." Her eyes remained looking upward, then they closed. She had turned her thoughts inward again, to the steadfast resolve of not speaking to the torturer.

A voice barked from the darkness in back of Malir. "Aramaic! I wish to hear what she says in Aramaic!"

Mahlir delivered his answer in Aramaic. "She says she wishes to tell me she loves me and asks that I remember her the way she looked last, before I saw her this way."

Rachel smiled, because Mahlir had delivered the lie so convincingly, and probably because it was true, because those really were her thoughts. Then she coughed, an action that brought more pain, and more moaning.

Mahlir shrank from the horror of his nightmare, nearly collapsing again, wishing he could run backward in time. One day. Just one day.

So badly did he want to reverse that day that he almost made it possible.

A grotesque figure stepped from the darkness, a stooped old man, pleasant looking under other circumstances, kindly even, grandfatherly. But the things Mahlir saw him do to his wife turned the man's visage horrifically ugly.

"Ask her again," demanded the voice in the darkness. It was a voice familiar, but he couldn't tell from where. It must have frightened the rats, because the squeaks became louder.

"Where is your father?" asked the grotesque old man. It came from his lips not as a question but as an emotionless command, like he was unconnected to the task, bored with it, like he had done this a thousand times to others. He asked her first in Aramaic then in Greek.

Her chest heaved. No words came.

The grotesque old man went to work again, methodically, dispassionately, having no more emotion about it than a gardener pulling weeds. Mahlir couldn't tell what he was doing to her, just that it was bringing once again the screams, then the coughing and moaning.

Once more she said nothing.

"Ask young Mahlir," came the voice in the darkness.

"Where is your father-in-law?" the man with the flagellum asked, still holding the end of Mahlir's chain, still in control of Mahlir's every move, his every word, his life.

The question brought hope. Was that all he had to do? To gain her release? Eli himself, if he could know what was happening, would do no less. But Mahlir had to answer, "I don't know," for truthfully he did not. "I swear before God, I do not know."

From the darkness erupted more of the hideous laughter, from the unseen voice. Each time it burst out it was followed by a crescendo of the squeaks. The voice was that of the Tetrarch himself, Mahlir discovered. The king moved forward into the dimness of his vision.

"My Lord Archelaus," acknowledged the grotesque man, bowing, retreating back into the blackness.

"My Lord," echoed the man with the flagellum and the chain.

The king was dressed in purple with a gold diadem on his head and a purple cloak that flowed where he walked, giving him the appearance of an apparition floating on air. He stepped closer, close enough for Mahlir to almost touch, as if Archelaus were taunting him to try. Gold was on each finger. Earrings dangled beneath rows of braided black hair interwoven with thin ribbons of gold. Archelaus was a young man, and did not at all look evil or ugly, a handsome gentle look at first glance, until the laughter came out again, laughter as from the depths of a soul dark and twisted. From that moment on Mahlir's life's purpose changed. The enemy was no longer Rome. His devotion from then on was to the destruction of Archelaus, even if it be from beyond the grave.

"So finally I meet the troublesome young son of my father's nemesis Matthias," Archelaus said. "The young man who married the daughter of the Sadducee Eli who wishes me displaced by a Roman procurator." Mahlir lunged at him, instinctively, and felt again the cutting of the flagellum and fell to his knees. The pain from his knees on bare stone was worse than the sting of the flagellum, though none of it matched the pain in his heart.

"It is as you told me," smirked Archelaus, speaking to someone somewhere in the dark. Moving into the visage of the struggling light was a giant of a man Mahlir knew instantly. No one but Athronges was that tall. His arms hung like those of an oversized monkey. The robes he wore accentuated the anomaly. He was dressed in ceremonious purple like Archelaus, and like Archelaus, he had a golden diadem on his head, though of a lesser ornamentation "He is weak, a pathetic coward," Archelaus said to Athronges. The two stood next to one another, the Messiah and the King. An odd paring, the diminutive king beside the giant. How ordinary the king looked. It didn't seem right, that someone so ordinary looking could possess such vast power.

The Messiah spread his feet and folded his long arms, the ultimate gesture of supremacy – he always did it that way, feet first, then arms – as if the upper couldn't work without first being initiated by the lower, like he was too big for the earth on which he stood. You could particularly tell how tall and thick he was, standing next to Archelaus. "Hello Mahlir-of-Matthias," said Athronges, smiling, the silent spurts of laughter spitting out of his mouth. Everything was funny to Athronges, even the things that were not funny. Sometimes the things that weren't funny caused the most spurts. "Where is my crown?" he said.

"You must know by now that there is no such thing," responded Mahlir.

"This is a day of good fortune for you and your wife, as long as you make things right on your part. All you have to do, two things, tell us the whereabouts of Eli, who stirs up seditions against Israel, and tell us where the crown is. That is all you have to do. Then your wife goes free. There is danger in the world. But unlike the danger in the world, this you have control over. This you can stop at any time."

Spoke Archelaus, in support of Athronges: "At one time the Shepherd Messiah and I were enemies. Now we are united. He shall be formally anointed tomorrow as High Priest, with an acknowledgement that he is the Messiah promised by God. Together we shall conquer. We will have our blood. The eagle shall fall."

Athronges pointed to the wheel, and to Rachel all but beneath it, and to a device beside it, a second wheel conveying empty buckets, one of which was filling with sand streaming down from a spigot. "Each time a bucket fills it drops down and causes the wheel to advance. The time your wife has left is the time left for the sand to fill two more buckets."

Mahlir told them immediately, from his knees, in complete submission. What other choice did he have? "Eli's house is below Caesarea on the coast," he screamed out with breath nearly spent. "You will know it to be the home of Eli by the two palm trees that stand in front by the door. Two large fire pans light the way. They stand as sentries." God forgive him, but all he could think about was freeing Rachel. He would have said anything, done anything. "Now please, release her."

"And the crown?" said Athronges.

A sound was heard.

A cog in a mechanism had dropped, causing the wheel to advance a full quarter turn, bringing Rachel's stomach to within a razor's breadth of the spikes.

Mahlir thought they had not heard. He shouted for them to get her off the wheel, as though there had been a terrible accident toward which people would rush to help.

Of course no one did.

Mahir tore at the iron on his neck, and fell once more to his knees, ashamed that he had not exerted the strength to free himself. He tore at the phylactery on his forehead, accursed thing, and ripped it away. Relentlessly it had been chafing against his skin. The head wrap had offered no protection. The incessant itch was driving him to madness, boiling, festering, turning itself into a bleeding and scabbing sore the size of his entire forehead. He wanted to dig his fingers into the decaying flesh of it, but dared not, for fear it would worsen the sore, for fear that he had the onset of leprosy and that his captors would see. The writings encased by the phylactery now seemed as harbingers of his destruction, because of his evil, as the words themselves declared, encrypted in his own hand from the Scroll of Isaiah.

"...I will stir up the Spirit of a destroyer."

He had written the words in Hebrew, the language of Yahweh, a language in which words exist that have no direct translation into any other language. A single word may take an entire paragraph to explain. So it is with the word *"destroy." "To give oneself over completely to God,"* is the closest one can get outside of the holy text itself. *"To disappear into the bosom of the Almighty,"* could be another translation. *"To root out and extinguish, to trample under foot, to annihilate all that stands in the way,"* could be another. The writings had turned into weapons and had aimed themselves at Mahlir.

Archelaus burst out again in the offensive laughter.

"Quickly!" screamed Mahlir. "Release her! Quickly!"

"The crown?" repeated Athronges calmly.

"I don't know where it is! Oh God! You must believe me. The Essenes have it. That's all I know. They have it at their compound in the desert."

"Tell us where the compound is."

A stronger man would have protected the Essenes, gentle people with good souls. Athronges would find them, and he would kill them all, anything to get the crown. But Mahlir did not care. "I don't know. Oh God! I really don't know. It's somewhere between the Mt. of Olives and the Dead Sea. In the desert. That's all I know. If you search in that direction you will find it. Now please. Get it off her. Quickly."

And Mahlir was thinking they would. Archelaus and Athronges suddenly seemed as benefactors, two men of extraordinary power come to help, come to save. Not so many moments ago Mahlir had hated them, for what they had done; now he loved them, for what they were about to do.

Mahlir pleaded. "I have given you what you want. I have told you everything I know. Please. Let her go. Or if you must kill her, do so quickly. And kill me also, for I wish not to live without my wife. Why is it you do this to us?"

Archelaus proudly revealed the reason why: "The vastness of my father's kingdom should have come to me. All the territories, from north to south and east to west. All of it. And so it would have, but for the illness that caused him to go mad on his deathbed and divide the lands, giving only Judea to me; giving Galilee and Perea in the north to my brother Antipas, a man too cowardly to make a decision without first testing the whims of the people; and giving the upper most lands and the lands to the east to my older and tired brother Philip, who cares for nothing but to get through the day so he can ease his aching bones at its end; and giving the southern part to my father's sister Salome, who is a senseless old woman. He was surely mad when he declared these changes to his testament. Do you know how it was for him when he died? He was eaten by worms. Do you know what it is like to be eaten by worms? Let me tell you. It is no wonder he went mad. It is an inward pain that lives like a demon in your belly and colon, like hot coals ulcerating your entrails. Anyone would go mad. An aqueous liquor settles itself about your feet and at the bottom of your buttocks. Your privy member becomes swollen and black. Worms fall from its opening. Each breath is labored and quick. Those in the room can barely stand to be there with you, because of the odor that emanates from your mouth. You are forced to sit upright to draw breath. Is it any wonder he went mad and gave away his kingdom? No matter. I will bring the land under my rule, all the land, all four corners of it, because I will curry the favor of Rome, and I will place my supporters in the priesthood and in the Temple government."

Archelaus looked at Mahlir with eyes of intensity that Mahlir could read even in the darkness. " –and I will purge from my midst all those who disfavor me, along with all the members of their families, as is God's will. I have known for some time about the things the Sadducee Eli says in the Temple, how he plots among the members of the Sanhedrin to have Judea annexed by Rome. He is a traitor. Think you a traitor should live? Your father-in-law, since he loves the Romans so, will die the death of a Roman. By crucifixion. With you alongside him. Blessed be the Lord, the god of Israel, he who shall vanquish his enemies. In time we shall conquer Rome, and once again we will be the great nation that Israel was under David."

The words drove the burn of the itch deeper. Mahlir's hand flew to his forehead, but he stopped, remembering that he didn't want Archelaus to see the lesion, lest he think it leprous, fearing that it would show through the head-wrap if disturbed.

"If I have displeased you, then take my life. I give it willingly, subject me to the torture," Mahlir pleaded. "But let my wife go. And my unborn child she carries."

The statement humored Archelaus. It brought more of the laughter.

But it was Athronges who responded, stepping further forward and opening his mouth to speak. "Your *un*-born child? Your *un*-born child is no longer un-born," he said. Mahlir realized then that Rachel's stomach was flat. He realized that somewhere in the horrors of that nightmare, there within the dungeons of Antonia, she had brought forth their child. The tiny screeching and squeaking sounds he thought were from rats were coming from a baby's mouth.

Rachel's guttural screams ran throughout the tower and across the Temple courtyard as the Messiah, High Priest of the Jews, displayed a newborn baby boy, holding him up by the head like some trophy won in the arena. Until that moment she must have thought the child was dead. Athronges took the razor edge of a sword that had been tucked into his waist scabbard – a sword gilded with ceremonial gold – and with almost gentle courtesy traced a red line the length of the babe's torso, from top to bottom, from chin to loins. The skin yielded immediately to the touch, though not enough to expose internal organs. That would be the next slice, Athronges was seeming to say, by the twist of his smile.

The child's living skull was like a toy within the palm of the Messiah's hand. Its body was flush red, as is a babe's when recent from the womb. Each tiny limb was twisting and wriggling. Its mouth was warped wide by the shrieks of thoughts unimaginable.

There was no one there to help his son but Mahlir. No one in the entire world. And Mahlir was in chains.

As Athronges dangled the child in front of him, doing so for no more reason than the pleasure of it, as he put the tip of his sword again to the child, to again trace the wound, saying, "Choose, priest, your son or your wife; do it quickly, for the final bucket is almost full," a desperate idea came. Mahlir ripped the cloth from his head. "Unclean! Unclean!" he shouted and scratched at the sore. "Touch me and you too will become leprous! You may already have it!"

Athronges dropped the child and staggered backward, then dropped the sword.

The jailer peddled backward as well, with such haste he tripped over his own feet, dropping the chain in the process, its sound echoing off the walls.

Mahlir saw the bucket tottering, sinking.

He ran for his son and the sword, and gathered them up in almost the same instant the bucket dropped.

Mahlir would never speak of the horror of what followed. He would never even be able to bring it to mind. He would leave it entombed within cavernous depths. Such a depository exists within all human minds. It is a place wherein slumber the most vile of thoughts and emotions, and fears too intense for experience, and memories too dreadful to be recalled, imprisoned there, but nevertheless exerting their influence, driving us, motivating us from their unseen levels. Suffice it to say that as the wheel rolled forward, as Mahlir saw the final look on his wife's face, as he heard her screams, he fairly lost his mind. And his faith in God.

With his son in one arm and the sword in the other, and the end of the chain wrapped around his forearm, he ran from the Tower, down halls and through tunnels, not knowing where he was going, shouting, "Unclean, unclean!" No one stood in his way. Guards, priests, soldiers, common people, all parted a path for him.

He had also seen something else. Athronges had been standing close to the wheel, and when it advanced the fabric of his trailing robe became caught up by one of the spikes, and as the wheel rolled forward it caught Athronges with it and flipped him to the stone floor beside the wheel. As strong as Athronges was, he was not as strong as that cloth that bound him to that wheel. The very robes that defined him as priestly were the robes that clustered now around his neck to become his executioner, to force upon him the fate of dying beside the very person he was executing. At first it was nothing more than an annoyance, and he yanked at it as if to rip it to shreds, trying at the same time to scramble to his feet. But the effort only pulled the cloth tighter in its grip around his neck, and smashed his face harder against the splintery wood, a humiliating way to die, and the look of anger was overtaken by fear. "Help me," he gasped. It was a demand at first – then – "…help…help, quickly, please." – as its intensity dropped to a near muted pleading, and blood began to ooze from his eye sockets.

The grotesque old man ran up with his knife to cut the fabric, but King Archelaus put his hand up and shook his head. The grotesque man stopped, confused, unsure of what to do. He came close to doing it anyway.

"Quickly, please, quickly," rasped the once great voice of Athronges.

Archelaus shook his head no again.

The last sounds to be heard that day from that terrible place called the Praetorium, named also the Tower of Antonia, were the sounds of the Messiah pleading for help, then in his anger calling upon God to curse all those in the Kingdom of Israel.

CHAPTER 18

SURVIVING THE WILDERNESS

ISRAEL – THE DESERT WEST OF THE DEAD SEA

The acrid scent of wilderness air during the heat of mid-day, the scent of good soil moistened by spring-water, the cool spray as it tumbles down a mountainside, these are the things of an oasis, the things of Mahlir's salvation.

No water is as clear, as pure, as refreshing as that which bubbles up from beneath the desert. The child smiled with the whole of his mouth as Mahlir dipped him in. The pool was high up and small. It collected water momentarily then sent it spilling down the tree-lined canyon toward the Dead Sea. The babe pumped his little arms and legs as he felt the water wash over his hot skin and lift away the dust and the dried film of his excrements, as he felt its cleanliness work its way in amongst the reddening scabs of a long gash that lay the length of his torso, chin to groin cut by the sword of the Messiah, the mark of God. Almost instantly the redness went away.

Mahlir was ankle deep, having just drunk his fell. The babe also quenched his thirst. Mahlir was surprised that it was possible for a newborn to drink.

Mahlir splashed some of the healing water onto his neck where the sun had concentrated its rays to burn a blistering circle around it. The pain left immediately, replaced by numbness, a sensation still present but no longer painful.

En-Gedi was exactly where he had always been told it was, thirty Roman miles south and east of Jerusalem, by the rocky cliff-shore of the salt-plagued Dead Sea, leaping out of the desert to welcome all, giving her life to Jew and Gentile alike. She was an emerald twinkling in the midst of a scarred land of browns, whites, and yellows, a strip of pure green rolling up from the rocky seashore to the stream's mysterious source. Every type of plant grew there, every type of tree, every fruit. The rocks and cliffs themselves sprang forth with things green, so appreciative were they of the water that tumbled over them.

Mahlir partook of some dates and figs that had been laid out on a palm leaf by someone, and of some mangos. Then with the child in his arms he climbed to the top to see if Archelaus' soldiers were still following them. They were not. Nothing could be seen but the meandering of a slow-moving caravan – camels, horses, people on foot. Then he sat with the babe on his lap and let the water carry them away. Father and son went shooting down the moss-covered spillway into another clear pool, the front of which rolled into another, and another, and another. He felt cool and free as they went tumbling over them, as if they could take flight and soar to the sun-splashed clouds distant on the eastern horizon.

The water was making bearable the aches and the blisters on his skin. It terraced seven times before reaching the bottom, cascading into seven pools. The last was the Dead Sea itself.

The oddest thing – when they plunged into the Dead Sea, they found they could swim beneath its surface, in water so saturated with salt that to do anything but float is impossible. More peculiar still was the fact that a newborn infant was swimming under water! Holding his breath! Smiling. Playing. Tumbling in circles. Beckoning Mahlir to do the same.

So he did. He began playing with his son, rolling in the water, holding the child's tiny hands, chasing him, letting the boy chase him.

They were able to hold their breaths forever, it seemed. The salt was further balm to their wounds and blisters, and to the painful circle around Mahlir's neck.

The rocky bottom was sloping off into reaches unknown, depths of fathomless blue. They followed it.

There was a large, geometrically round boulder in front of them, between them and the open sea. Beyond it the slope dropped away into nothingness. "Don't go there," Mahlir warned his son. A frightful essence appeared to be emanating from it, something that seemed to want to pull them into it, to absorb them.

But the babe's little arms and legs were kicking, stroking toward it.

In a moment Mahlir saw why. The innocent child had seen its mother, and had recognized her. Rachel was standing atop the boulder, her black hair fanning outward and shining like obsidian from the sun streaming through the water. A crown of twelve stars was upon her head. Her tunic clung tightly to her body; and her colobium, whiter than the wings of a morning dove, hung in slow flutters on the drifts of the current, the current that was trying to sweep Mahlir and his son out beyond the boulder, out into the nothingness, the nothingness that was everything.

His beautiful wife called to him. She was unblemished, as though the torture of two days ago had not happened at all.

Mahir was in such a state of elation at seeing her that he forgot all about the dangers beyond the rock, and, like their son, he too began swimming toward her.

The child got there first. She took him in her embrace and held him close, then handed him back to Mahlir. "Take care of this out child," she said. "Circumcise him on the eighth day, as is our custom. He shall be called Matthias, in honor of you my lord, and in honor of his grandfather. He shall be proud of the name. And he shall do great things."

Mahlir had things to say, but there was no time. She was leaving, floating up and backward into the blue, fading into it, into the nothingness. Instead he asked a silly and completely irrelevant question. "What's it like to die?"

"Nobody has it right," was the answer, then she went on to say, "It's different than anything you've ever heard, or read, or imagined, or..." Her words were gone, faded into the nothingness.

And the blue turned to black.

And the rock became a scraggly bush, leafless, twisting out of the chalky, white dirt with just enough sturdiness for him to rest his back against. He had found it the night before as the scorching sun sank behind the cliffs of the backside of Olivet.

And the healing circle of blisters around his neck opened up again, as the heavy iron collar materialized. And the decaying flesh of his face began to pulse once more with pain.

There were stars overhead. No rain that day either.

The babe was warm on his chest. That was good. Sounds were still coming from its mouth – that was good – rapid pulses of breathing, broken now and then by attempts to swallow, then little cries when it discovered it could not, little cries only, for to cry too long would take effort away from the process of breathing. In the beginning Mahlir cringed each time he heard the cries. Now he cringed when he did not hear them. He wondered if the child too had been given the blessing of a pleasant dream.

A sound startled him. A scraping in the sand. He looked and saw that a black scorpion was sharing their shelter. He moved to grab the handle of the short-sword, but changed his mind. The scorpion had children too, soft and transparent, clinging perilously to her back, totally dependent on her.

"You take the spot," he told her. "We must be moving along anyway, before the sun breaks. Soon Archelaus and his soldiers will be advancing on us." Mahlir envied the scorpion. Though she had enemies, none of them were committed to the pure purpose of searching her out and her alone, and destroying her. The enemy of the scorpion, the viper, the desert fox, would be satisfied with any scorpion.

The days and nights were consumed in heat, an ever-present essence hanging in the air, but at night there was a wind, not quite cool, but moderate enough to wash away the heaviness. They had spent two of them in the wilderness, two days and two nights. The rainy season was late in coming, and he had no garments to protect them from the sun, or from the chill at the first part of morning. He had taken his tunic and torn it into pieces for the child's swaddlings, and had foolishly discarded the wrappings when soiled, all except two. Necessity had taught him that if he took a soiled wrapping and rubbed it thoroughly with dirt, then hung it from his waistband to dry, he could make it almost come clean by pounding it against rocks and flapping it in the air.

If only he could do as much for his infant's hunger. If only there was something to put in its mouth – the water from a storm, the juice of a fruit, the squeezings from a plant, anything, even the blood of an animal, at this point, though it be against the Law.

Blood? Of course. Why had he not thought of it before!

He sliced his palm and let the blood drip into the babe's mouth. The baby coughed and spat it out. Mahlir tried soaking the end of one of the swaddlings and putting it in his son's mouth, hoping he would suck on it. For a time it worked. He seemed to be taking it in; there seemed to be relief in his eyes. Then his mouth released it and twisted up in a cry.

So they walked.

They just kept walking, stumbling sometimes, the chain dragging behind him like a creature alive with fangs of fire buried into his neck, tugging, wanting to pull him into the white-hot powder of the soil, the abyss. Almost a substance of safety, the abyss was, soft almost, because if he allowed himself to sink into its serenity he would not have to struggle anymore. At times Mahlir carried the chain, until it was too hot to hold; at times he felt the collar turn itself into a newly forged blade, glowing, tipped in molten yellow, slicing through his neck so that his head could float painlessly above his body.

They could not travel the roads; Archelaus had his men posted. They could not enter the cities; the men were there also. If Mahlir looked over his shoulder he could see a cloud of dust from soldiers scouring the desert for them. He moved mostly on the steep slopes, child in his arms, and hid in the caves and in the cracks of the rocks, hoping for rain to wash over them, and to cleanse their mouths and cool their throats, hoping for an animal to come close enough to kill, or for a fruit tree.

By now they were lost, hopelessly disoriented. Even if the soldiers went away, even if the rains did come, they would be doomed. It was a matter of time.

By now the soldiers were at Eli's compound. If only Mahlir had the power of a sorcerer, to pick up a stone and gaze into it, and speak to Eli through it, warn him. "I am sorry, my beloved father-in-law," Mahlir said, speaking to him nonetheless. "Had I known the king was not going to release her, I never would have told."

The Wilderness had all but consumed them. The dust of the ground had become the grit of his mouth.

The iron around his neck was now a part of him. It had melded itself with him. The pain was now something he accepted.

His only wish was that his son would die first.

There is no terror like that which fills the soul of a father who realizes he is incapable of protecting his child. No fear is as intense. All Mahlir had to offer was the protection of his own body, and the putting forth of one foot in front of the other, perhaps leading to somewhere.

Once, Archelaus' men passed so close he could have touched them, had he reached his hand out. He was hiding in a jagged crevice. He could smell the stink of their unbathed bodies and the sweat of their horses. As the soldiers passed he thought of moving out into the open, of letting it end right there. But habit forced him on. And over the next rise there came to his eyes a sight that would forever change his life.

He saw jackals circling something, heads down, their cautious and hungry eyes fixed on whatever it was that had become their mark. The impatient younger ones were whining and yapping. The leader was holding back, waiting for the right time. It was the Ibex doe they were circling, Mahlir's scapegoat. Her tether cord was still tied to the rock. The predators circled closer and closer, then sniffed at the hapless animal, a harmless looking movement, like friendly dogs looking for a pat. Soon they would be ripping her to pieces, never growling, just ripping and tearing and gulping, calmly devouring the poor thing before her own living eyes, entrails first, because they were easiest and softest.

Mahlir took stones and drove them out of sight. For a time. They would be watching. Waiting. Waiting for all three of them, for the right moment.

The doe was on her knees, trying to get to her feet, relieved that her shepherd had returned. An idea came. Mahlir took the child and held him beneath the goat and placed one of her teats in his mouth.

To take back a scapegoat, to use it for any other purpose, is blasphemy. But when Mahlir saw his infant son begin to feed, and when he saw that the Ibex was allowing it, that she had given up trying to stand and had rolled sideways to bear her underbelly to the child, he did not care. God – if he did exist – could come down and strike him dead. God could demand that he release the goat back into the wilderness and he would refuse. Abraham should have refused, when told to take Isaac up to the mountain. Jephthah should have refused, when following through with his foolish promise to God to kill his daughter.

At first all the child could draw were drippings. But that was enough. Soon full milk began to flow, with Mahlir's help. He had to massage gently. Too much tended to choke the babe.

Then Mahlir drank.

Then he fashioned a bowl out of the Ibex's tether cord and let her drink. Yes, of her own milk.

Nourishment and strength brought a return of Mahlir's sensibilities. Rational thought now forced a realization that he and his son were still doomed, if not by the vengeful sword of Archelaus, then by any common man or woman they should encounter, because of his face. The itch had now turned to pain that sunk deep into his skull, pain terrible and constant. The affliction had now consumed the entire right side of his face and neck, just the right side, as if the demon had drawn a line dividing east and west and had decided to curse only that one portion. Mahlir resolved that he and his son would go where they should have gone in the beginning, to the place where their kind gathers, where they would be welcome, where maybe a wet nurse could be found for his son. It is a place near Jerusalem where lepers live in isolation. The government provides for them. And there, with hills and cliffs surrounding them, they live out their days. For a time Mahlir and his son could exist in peace. Until the affliction consumed them.

If along the way they should be caught and killed by Archelaus' soldiers, or stoned by villagers, so be it. It would be just as well. Better perhaps.

The resolve gave Mahlir actual physical strength. But the Ibex still could not walk. He draped her over his shoulders and carried her, though she weighed as much as a man, holding the goat's feet with one hand, his son with the other, and wrapped the chain around his forearm. He carried them to wherever the direction in front of them would lead.

Sometimes the pain of the chain's searing heat on his forearm would be too much to bear and he would unravel it and throw it angrily away, thinking in his madness he could do it, only to discover, like the living thing it surely was, that it had latched itself again onto his neck.

Eventually he decided to simply let it drag.

He tottered under the load, and stumbled sometimes when the chain would catch on a rock or in a crevice, but moved forward always, ever forward, up a hill, down a hill, counting his steps. Five hundred steps, then rest, five hundred more, rest. His legs burned and his breath came hard.

Up another hill.

On its crest he found himself looking down into something that could very well have been another dream, or at the very least an illusion born of the substance of what is seen by dying men in the desert. This, though, was no dream. This was no illusion. This was a valley carpeted in green, fed from the aquifer beneath the desert floor, broken by an occasional patch of parched brown and dotted with thousands upon thousands of wildflowers. An east wind began to blow and tousle his hair; he could smell the Dead Sea minerals on it. At the valley's far end, near the stone housing of a well, were the camps of several families of shepherds whose flocks were grazing throughout the flora. A paradise. As much so as the En-Gedi of his dream.

Of course for Mahlir it would do no good. A place where there were people, for Mahlir, would not be paradise. Because he was a leper.

He proceeded on anyway, through the flowers, through the blooms of the wild mustard and squill, saffron and poppies, and the blooms of the Nazareth Iris. A falcon was circling, meaning small creatures were below hiding in the grass and among the flowers – rabbits, hedgehogs, mice, lizards, snakes. Sunbirds danced and played in the air.

He was far past his five hundred steps, and kept walking. The ache in his back and legs was no longer noticeable. The burn in his lungs felt pleasant. As the scent of the flowers filled his head, as the breeze cooled and caressed the rotting flesh of his face, he began to deceive himself. He began to convince himself that this valley, with all its beauty, could not possibly bring harm to anyone.

But mankind inhabits this valley. Soon a crowd had gathered, encircling them, keeping their distance, never closing in. Mahir continued to walk. The circle moved with him, backing away, falling in behind. Fear was in their eyes. Some began picking up stones, bending quickly to gather them, never averting their eyes, as if Mahir and his child were serpents that would strike the moment they looked away.

Little children also held stones. What a foul place this world is, where even children are taught to kill.

Finally Mahlir sank to his knees and wept. The doe fell from his back and floundered in efforts to get to her feet, unable still to stand on her own.

He drew his sleeping child in close; it was for him he wept.

He closed his eyes. "Hush, my little one," he said in the tongue of his fathers. "It will be over soon."

"My religion is very simple. My religion is kindness."

The Dali Lama

Part II

THE MAN WITH THE PROPHET'S EYES

Years 51 to 52 of the Calendar of Pater Patriae Gaius Julius Caesar
Year 0 to Year 5 of the Gregorian Calendar (0AD to 5AD))

CHAPTER 19

THE SHEPHERDS OF THE DESERT

ISRAEL – AN OASIS NEAR THE DEAD SEA

He was crouched over his infant son. Two stones landed on his back, one on his shoulder.

That was all.

He opened his eyes and lifted his head, and saw as many as thirty people with their stones raised, halted from throwing them by a man standing in protection, his palm up. The man had the beard of a priest, long and untrimmed, soft brown streaked with gray, and he had the eyes of a prophet. He was a man of compassion, said the eyes.

He was also a fool. He laid down his crook-topped shepherd's staff and knelt to give Mahlir water. Mahlir particularly noticed the bright colors of his woolen cloak that draped his left shoulder, representative of his family, red, blue, and purple. And he noticed how clean he smelled, like he had just stepped out of a mikvah.

Mahlir handed him his son, because he trusted him.

Mahlir was then taken and bathed in cold, clean water from the well. Then he was led to a tent and given the comfort of a large divan, barely higher than the floor.

And that night there was peace in his soul and warmth on his face, a tingling type of heat that seemed to make the pain of the leprosy bearable, even pleasant to experience. How long he slept he didn't know. Days maybe.

When he awoke it was nighttime. Incense was circling the top of the tent, and a lamp flickered from close by.

By his side, seated upon a low bench carved from the wood of an Acacia tree, was the man with the prophet's eyes.

"Where is my child?" were the first words from Mahlir's mouth.

The man offered water from a hollowed out wooden ladle.

It purified Mahlir's insides as it went down, and cleansed his skin as it dripped down his beard and his neck. Someone had dressed him in a clean knee-length tunic. He also noticed that the chain and the iron collar were gone. These were all things that had happened to him without his knowledge, during the unconsciousness state of his exhaustion.

"All is well," said the man "Your son is being cared for."

"I must see him."

"Of course."

When the man returned, he brought with him a woman with a baby feeding at her breast, Mahlir's son. The child was mellow in his sleep, his mouth open, resting against the woman's nipple. He jerked, half waking, and began to suckle again, then fell back to sleep. His little cheeks were red with vivacity. A tuft of black hair stuck straight out from the top of his head. The woman smiled down at the babe, then with loving care placed him in Mahlir's arms.

A rush of something unexplainable rose, a warmth, a feathery kind of bliss akin to the effect of wine on an empty stomach, a connection between father and son.

Mahlir opened the swaddlings to examine the scabs of the baby's wound, cut by the sword of Athronges. They were completely healed. Remaining only was a scar, smooth and un-festered.

There was dirt around the baby's left eye. Mahlir took his hand to brush it away.

"A birth mark," the woman said. Terror seized him. He hadn't noticed it until now. Its reddish-brown color had made it seem like dust from the desert, or the imprints of the sun that had blistered their skin. Leprosy?

"It is merely a marking," the woman said. "Nothing more. He is healthy. It will fade with time." It was the near perfect shape of an arrowhead, pointing upward.

The baby jerked again, then once more fell off into sleep, oblivious to the peril that surrounded him.

Said the man with the prophet's eyes, seating himself again, "Tell me, how is it that a priest from the Temple, and one so young, comes to be found wandering half dead in the desert carrying a new-born babe?" He smiled inquisitively, like he was going to laugh, and ran his fingers through the length of his beard.

The question startled Mahlir. "How do you know me to be a priest?"

"The speech of your sleep gives you away."

"I flee from Archelaus, who wishes me dead."

"You are safe here."

"He will not rest until he finds me. I must go. I will take my son and leave at first light. I have nothing to offer in return for your kindnesses. I have no money. I have nothing. Even the clothes I now wear are yours." Mahlir held up the long sleeves of the tunic they had provided him. Its softness and its cleanliness felt good on his skin. "You may have my goat, on the condition that you not kill it, that you use it only for its milk. Beyond that I have nothing."

"We want nothing."

Still sleeping, the baby opened his mouth like he wanted to feed.

Mahlir looked at the woman.

She took the baby into her arms and opened her tunic.

Mahlir was immensely grateful and thanked her with his eyes.

"Let us care for the child," the man said. "Abigail has just given birth and has an abundance of milk. She will care for him as one of her own."

Abigail smiled in affirmation.

"Go to Elkanar the Essene," the man continued. "Tell him Simeon sends you. You will be safe there. When the time comes when Archelaus no longer seeks to persecute you, you may return here and live with us, and work with us for your keep, be a part of our family."

"So that is your name? Simeon?"

"Yes. And this is Abigail. For many generations my family has dealt in the trade of sheep and wool. Outside you will see the tents and fires of my sons and their wives. Abigail is married to my second son."

Mahlir had no choice. Without the breasts of Abigail his son would die. And if he stayed, and if Archelaus found him, likely all would die. "I will go," Mahlir said, standing, wanting to reach for the child, wanting to touch him one last time, wanting to grab him and run back into the desert, remembering the last words of Rachel – "…care for our son."

Instead he shouted at Simeon to take the boy away quickly. "…before I change my mind," causing the child to come awake with a start and begin to cry.

Simeon motioned to Abigail. She hurried away through the curtain with the baby.

Mahlir called her back. "Wait. There is one thing I must do first." He didn't know if this was the eighth day or not. In the desert he had lost count of the hours, and of the evenings and the mornings. "He must be circumcised. I will do it myself." As a priest he possessed the vested authority. "One promise, at least, that I can fulfill."

So with his child's hands and legs held out like the points of a star, and with a ceremonial blade procured from Simeon, Mahlir marked him forever as a son of Isaac. The last time his son saw his face, instead of closing his eyes in security, instead of smiling at the warmth, he was crying out in pain.

Then the child was gone.

Mahlir asked for his sword.

Simeon's face formed sadness. "Why will you have need for a weapon?"

Mahlir did not answer. He asked instead for sharpening tools.

After the sword's edges were honed, he took it to himself and began to remove his beard, that which represented his priesthood, everything that used to be meaningful to him.

"Why do you cut the symbol of your devotion to God?" asked Simeon.

"God? God has no interest in the affairs of mortal man, if God even exists," was Mahlir's answer.

"Words I would not expect from the mouth of a priest." The look Simeon gave Mahlir was one that spoke as though he had been personally injured by the act, as though Mahlir had taken the sword to his very neck.

"I have to travel back to Jerusalem. I have to warn my father-in-law. Archelaus searches him out as well. Without my beard I will not be recognized."

"Then do it for that reason, and for that reason alone. Not as blasphemy to God."

"You mean the god of the Jews?" The statement came from Mahlir's lips in tones of anger. "The god who watches over his chosen people, as David so often poeticized with the enchantment of his words?" Mahlir was looking at the wall of the tent as he spoke, as he shaved clean his beard with the awkward instrument, and it was there that his anger was directed, toward the wall, or some unseen entity beyond it, not toward Simeon. "This god of ours, who supposedly exists, who supposedly watches over us and protects us, watched dispassionately as my wife was tortured and killed, and as my son was tortured. You want the truth? I will tell you the truth of life. By men's weaknesses they bring misery upon other men, and they justify it by saying and by writing down that this great being that no one ever sees blesses them in those actions, even directs them in those actions." Mahlir's hand jerked, and he dabbed a finger at the point on his face where a tiny red bubble was rising. The fact that he had nicked himself calmed him for some reason, and softened the anger, turned it into a type of morose sarcasm that seemed to say he was thankful that he had this unseen entity beyond the wall to talk to. "Not too long ago I ended a brave young soldier's life, robbed his family of his presence forever, because supposedly this great being told us to make war against the Romans. I am responsible for that, not God. Me. No one else." Mahlir nicked himself again and it caused the sarcasm to morph into a type of distant introspection. "And the goat I gave you? Did you know that was supposed to be the animal that would bear my sins? Funny, isn't it, that it turns out to the be the animal that saves my life. How absurd, that we are unable to accept responsibility for our own sins, and because of that, an innocent and gentle animal is made to suffer. Time was, I was more devoted to God than anyone. My phylactery was filled with passages of God's promises of deliverance and of the coming of the Messiah. Musings of dreamers. The sayings of weak men needing to reach beyond their bonds, needing to believe in deliverance, needing to believe that once again a Moses or a David will come."

Simeon's eyes fired bright with enthusiasm. "Ah – but my child – you are wrong. The Messiah is here. He walks the earth as we speak, perhaps not far from here."

"Well, if his name is Athronges, the world is well to be rid of him. I saw him die."

"The name of our messiah is Yeshua-ben-Yosef," said Simeon. "A carpenter and master stone mason, by trade, from Nazareth." Gentleness remained on his lips as he spoke, and the certainty of what he was speaking was ever present in his eyes. "Let me tell you a story of something that happened to me," he said. "It was in the second year before the death of Herod-the-Great. My family and I were living in the herdsmen's village of Beit Sahura. We were pasturing our flocks on the slopes to the north. It was one night when the wind was still and the sky clear. The grass on the hillside was thick and green, though its color was sparkling silver from the midnight dew. The irises were budding, preparing for the morning. The sky above was the color of a million diamonds. Nay, ten times that. A hundred times. It was so bright the night had all but disappeared. Then, as the others on watch over our flocks can testify, the sounds of the night came suddenly silent. The jackal, the wolf, the owl, all ceased to be heard. The dome of the sky, so vast, so distant, so lonely, moved closer to the earth that night, and the blackness behind the stars turned to white. Man in all his days has never seen such whiteness. It was like noonday with the stars still out.

"Then, in front of us, there appeared a woman, or what I at first thought was a woman. She, or he, or whatever divine personage it might have been, quite purely formed from nothing. One instant she was not there, the next she was. It was that quick."

Simeon paused to look at Mahlir. Mahlir was still drawing the sword's edge over his smooth and youthful skin, feeling with his hand, redrawing it over clumps he had missed. The soft facial hair was finally giving way to a different look. He had no remorse.

Continued Simeon, "There was brilliance in which she stood, a light that looked to be radiating from her body. Her long robe – maybe it wasn't a robe; maybe it was a part of her body – was fluttering, no, flowing, smoothly flowing, and the bottom of it was gradually fading into an ethereal mist. It was as if her feet didn't touch the ground, if indeed she had feet. And her hair; she had the most unusual hair, long hair. It was being blown in the wind, up, out and away from her translucent body, in a circular motion, like the horns of an Ibex. Yet – there was no wind.

"Then it was that I realized this was not a woman at all. Its face, though pleasant to look at, was not the face of anything that walked the earth. It was long and thin, and the eyes were placed oddly close together, though not in an unattractive way.

"I realized that I was standing before an angel of the Lord, and that what I thought was hair had actually been a powerful type of energy emanating from the great being's shoulders, the very thing others before me had mistaken for wings.

"It spoke, calming me, saying, *'Fear not: for behold, I bring you good tidings of great joy, which shall be to all people. For unto you is born this day in the City of David a Savior, which is Christ the Lord. And this shall be a sign unto you. You shall find the babe wrapped in swaddling clothes, lying in a manger.'*

"It spoke first in Greek, then in Aramaic. There was a Greek child working with us on the hillside that night who spoke very little Aramaic. That, I can only presume, was the reason it spoke in Greek, so he could understand too."

Simeon paused once again, eyeing Mahlir, testing his reaction to the tale. Mahlir was barely hearing him. All he could hear was the distant crying of his son. Because the boy needed his presence? His comfort? Or because he was still in pain from the circumcision?

Simeon continued. "Then other angels appeared, first two, then three, then three times three, then so many they couldn't be counted, each one radiating its own brilliance, some white, others streaming with color. It was a sight impossible to look upon. We prostrated ourselves and covered our heads. And the heavens above us gave birth to a great noise, a thundering of voices as the sky came yet closer, as the angels, hundreds of them, thousands, maybe hundreds of thousands, sang over and over in many languages, *'Glory to God in the highest, and on earth peace, good will toward men.'*

"Bethlehem, the city where David was born, the city foretold by Micah as the birthplace of the next true king of Israel, could be seen to the west of us, less than a single Roman mile below the hill where we stood. We thought of waking the others, but decided against it, lest they think us daft. We drew lots to decide who among us would stay to keep guard over the flock, then set out on our journey. It was a short journey, five thousand footfalls. Though the angels were gone, their glow remained, in the sky and over the cover of the earth. Everything our eyes fell upon, from inanimate stone to living thing, from the low rock fences to the thick scrubs of grass, from the mushroom canopies of the Oaks and Terebinths to the solitary owl perched upon a pine, from the dust of the ground to the vastness of the sky above, was enlivened with color, though the night remained. When we reached the entrance to the town, we noticed someone following us. The man we had left behind to stand guard. Under any other circumstance we would have admonished him and sent him back – but – he also deserved our discovery. He also had been invited by the heavenly hosts. He assured us that the flock would be fine, saying that he had left it in the care of the Greek shepherd boy, who was quite capable.

"By chance – or was it chance? – the first place we came to was an inn, dark with all guests asleep, save for the flow of light coming from the hillside entrance to a cave close by where animals were stabled. I recognized the place. Once, when walking by it as a boy, my father told me it was the very spot where King David was born.

" 'We have no gifts,' I said to the man at the entrance. He was on one knee feeding a fire, sending warmth back to where a woman was sitting on her ankles attending to a child, while smoke drifted the other way out the cave's mouth and up into the night, a night still alive with its strange and subtle luminescence. 'We are not family, nor are we friends,' I said. 'But lowly as we are, we would like to offer a prayer and a blessing for your son.'

"The man stared at us for a short while without speaking, then formed a smile of welcome and rose and gestured for us to enter.

"The fire's flickering shadows adorned the rocky walls of the stone enclosure and danced calmly upon a feeding trough at the rear wherein lay the babe. A dozen or so beasts of burden were in silent observance, guardians. The woman was half asleep next to the trough, leaning against several sacks of grain, the slender fingers of one hand resting atop the babe, as though warming it.

"Our movements startled her. 'Good woman,' I said. 'We are here to celebrate the birth of your child. If you would have us.'

"The young mother, doubtless exhausted, moved a length of hair from her face and flipped it over her shoulder, and made embarrassing motions to straighten her clothing. She looked to be pleased that we were there. The birth of a Jewish baby is an important occurrence, attended by many, with much merriment and feasting, and midwives, and procedures to be followed. But for this mother's celebration there was no one, only us, simple shepherds, and the curious oxen and horses of the guests at the nearby inn, guests who were all fast asleep and unaware of the incredible event that had just taken place. There had been no time for preparations and procedures. This baby had come unexpectedly while the family was traveling.

"'How did you know of our child?' she asked, sleep clouding her speech, eyes moistened with happiness, because she had just received the greatest gift of all, public acknowledgement of the most significant event in a Jewish woman's life. 'Birth was only a short time ago. There were no witnesses. There was no one to go out and make an announcement.'

"We explained that there was indeed an announcement made. The smile she returned to me, after hearing the story, moved through me like a warming fire, and for a time, God forgive me, I felt like I too was her husband. That is how close I felt to her, and to the child, who opened his eyes and looked up at me, then closed them again, to lose himself once more in delicious mounds of sleep. Like the angel had said, he was wrapped in swaddlings of white linen, and lay in the trough on cushions of straw.

"'We would be grateful for your blessing,' affirmed the child's father.

"The mother asked me if I would like to hold him.

"That such a thing be possible, that I should be the first above all others in the world to hold the future king, above others who are much more deserving, turned my limbs weak.

"I explained that I was not a priest, that I was only a shepherd. As I was speaking, as I was making my protest, she placed the child in my arms.

"His mouth opened. I thought he was going to cry. It was a yawn instead, a peaceful, wide yawn. Was he aware that someone other than his father or mother was holding him? He looked at me, eyes half open. 'What do those eyes say?' I asked myself. 'Do I frighten him? Does he understand that I am the one who stands in awe of him?

"Whatever his thoughts, they were clearly not ones to cause him concern, for he soon closed his eyes again, and twitched and wiggled to make himself comfortable, and was off to sleep once more.

"I gave the blessing and kissed the child.

"And something happened. Words come difficult at this point; I am only mortal man, with only my voice to explain the unexplainable. It happened the moment my lips touched his forehead. The best to describe it – though the analogy falls far short – no – I don't know how to describe it."

Simeon stopped to assess Mahlir's reaction.

Mahlir had finished shaving off his beard, with only two cuts to his face, both minor, and was sitting on the edge of the divan, listening, and growing impatient. "I must be on my way soon," he said.

Simeon took a deep breath, like he was searching for words. "I saw the face of God," he said simply, as though he had giving up trying to explain it beyond that elementary statement.

"For a moment I stood on holy ground." Simeon was almost whispering the words. "For a brief moment, a veil was lifted. I was awake, for the very first time. I noticed then that the Greek shepherd boy had come down as well. But I wasn't concerned. With an entire legion of angels guarding the flock, what was there to be worried about?"

Again Simeon paused. Mahlir remained silent with him.

"The father told me he was a craftsman, traveling from the north, and that there had been no room in the inn. The stable was the only shelter available. I inquired of his plans.

"His response was, 'On the eighth day we will have him circumcised. Then, after the 40 days of my wife's required purification, we will journey on to the Temple and present him to the Lord.'" Simeon was finished. "He would be about six years of age," he finalized. There was disappointment in his face, as he looked at Mahlir. "Still you don't believe me, even now."

Simeon was wrong. Those were not Mahlir's thoughts at all. He had remembered something Rachel had told him, about how ten years earlier the soldiers of Herod-the-Great had slaughtered all the children in Bethlehem. The child that Simeon thought to be the Messiah would have been among them. Either way the Messiah was dead, be he Athronges or the babe in the manger.

So Mahlir said nothing.

"I have delayed you too long," Simeon said. "You should be on your way. And remember, after you have warned your father-in-law, go then to Elkanar in the compound of Qumran. You will be safe there."

A partial laugh came from deep in Mahlir's throat. "You think Elkanar would welcome me? Who but you is so foolish as to take in a man unclean? A man whose face is leprous?"

Simeon smiled and took Mahlir's hand and guided it to where the itching sores had been.

It was smooth!

There was no pain, no itching.

Mahlir was dumbstruck.

He also felt his neck. There were no lesions there either, where the iron had been.

Simeon explained. "When I kissed the child, when the Spirit of Yahweh moved through me, I was left with a certain condition. Things I touch become whole. An injured bird. A sick child. A pierced wound. Your face. Your son's wound."

Again Mahlir put his hand to his face. Smooth! And yes, his son's scabbed over and infected neck-to-loin gash had been healed over to a mere scar! Mahlir had been so absorbed in the moment, and in the rapidity of events, that he had not stopped to assess the obvious, that things in this little hamlet were very different.

"Go then, if you must," Simeon said. "And know that I will watch over your son, and care for him until you return, as if he were my own. My promise to you." Mahlir believed it to be so, such was the power carried by the words. As he left the camp, he could hear a lute being softly strummed, and a voice as sweet as a lark at noonday singing to his son. Mahlir envied the child, and the ever-present loneliness sank deeper.

On his approach to Jerusalem, he thought he could hear the sounds of torture, distant sounds, unholy shrieks that echoed and blended with the pleasant blush of a gentle desert breeze, and with the sounds of the nightingale, and the sound of a barking dog. It shivered his skin, and made him wonder if it was Eli, or just an illusion born of the fears of his imagination. He entered the city through the Joppa gate on the western side, the opposite of where Archelaus' soldiers would expect him to be, fearful nonetheless that he would be recognized, beardless though he was, and cloaked though he was in shepherds' garments, a long plain tunic without tassels, no phylacteries, with a keffiyeh covering his head, robe over his left shoulder, a shepherd's crook, and a sword hidden beneath it all.

He made his way through the crowds – crowds were good, a way for him to hide without hiding – and came to the Temple, to the gate of the Chamber of Hewn Stone on Tyropoeon Street. He would inquire there. There, within the halls wherein sits the Sanhedrin could be found friends. A place of safety for one like Mahlir.

Only a single person was there, a man sitting in one of the ante-rooms that served as offices and study rooms for the Sanhedrin members. Mahlir halted his steps when he saw who the man was. Joseph. Husband of the woman with whom he had carried on his indiscretions. Of course Joseph knew nothing about what Mahir had done. Mahlir was preparing to turn and walk away, unnoticed he was hoping, when Joseph looked up and welcomed him.

The Chamber of Hewn Stone was not what its name implied, as being literally hewn from solid rock. Its walls were circular and built of blocks to form its enormous inner oval. Curule type seats for seventy-two, for each member of the Sanhedrin body, were scooped out of stone and tiered into rows, U-shaped risers that ringed the entire rear of the enclosure. The study rooms were carved from the massive wall blocks themselves. They were barely rooms at all, more like decorative archways cut against the stone, antechambers, the members called them, just large enough for one person to sit within. Along the walls were shelves upon shelves of scrolls.

Joseph recognized Mahlir even without the beard. Joseph's eyes were full of pain, at first Mahlir thought because of the past, because of what Mahlir had done. But Joseph was unknowing of it. The look was because of what he was about to tell Mahlir.

CHAPTER 20

THE CROSS

ISRAEL – JERUSALEM

"Eli has been accused of crimes against the state," was what Joseph told him, "and was taken two days ago to Golgotha."

The rocky crest of the hill to the northwest, Golgotha, the Skull, so called because of its cavernous resemblance to a human skull, was above the quarry and was bisected by the main highway westward. Various foot worn paths angled off to wind through the killing grounds, around large rocks and boulders. Golgotha that day was bathed in shades of yellow and white from the setting sun. There were low lying clouds just above the hills. Their puffed edges, outlined in black, exploded in light that streamed downward in wide beams, ladders from the sky. And, as a shadow against the brilliance, stood the ultimate symbol of darkness, the most extreme form of execution ever devised by man, the cross. Its victim had been there two days, and still lived. He still rolled and twisted to free himself from his agony, each motion bringing unimaginable pain.

No other executions were being done. Just that one. Two children were coming down the path, running and laughing and playing. Then an old man came, then three women. They may have climbed the hill out of simple curiosity, these onlookers, young and old, or maybe out of some perverted kind of compassion, or, as some always do during a crucifixion, to torment the condemned. So often this is the worst part of such a death, the things done by those coming to see.

Spikes had been driven through his ankles on either side of the upright timber, the only support for his quivering fragile legs, his only means of keeping from sinking into suffocation. Six or seven bees were circling his head, attracted by honey that had been smeared on his face by someone. One was crawling across a fluttering eyelid.

Two guards sat in watch, consumed in boredom. Neither recognized Mahlir as one who was also an enemy of the state.

Just prior to the ordeal, as the nails are being driven, the victim thinks he will be able to end it by sliding down into suffocation. But the body will refuse, no matter the will, no matter the pain. Its reflexive urge for survival will force endurance. It drives one to absolute insanity. It robs all the breath from the body, except for that minimal needed for the next agonizing moment. For hours this continues. Days sometimes. Until exhaustion overcomes. Even then the body will refuse. It will muster the strength to raise itself just one more time to wheeze in just one more breath. If the executioner is skilled in his art, if the positioning of the arms and legs on the cross are in the right places, these last moments of death can be multiplied by the thousands.

Limbs quiver, pain streaks through every appendage, every organ, muscles knot and cramp. The throat is parched and dry.

Eli recognized his son-in-law even without the beard. In a barely audible and strained voice, yet a voice of precision, he spoke to him. He had to prepare for each thought he delivered. He had to gather strength, hold his breath before speaking, like one would do before lifting a heavy object. He could not move his head down to look at Mahlir – to do so would choke off air – so Mahlir moved away a bit, in order that Eli's eyes might rest on his while they talked. Mahlir could hear the things Eli said; his feet were only at chest level to him. Mahlir wanted to reach out, to impart by touch the things he felt, the love, the sorrow, the regret. But he didn't want to be like the children. Children sometimes play games, take dares on who has courage enough to touch a condemned man. The bees were still there, assembling systematically, more and more of them, but unlike their more advanced human counterparts, theirs was not a motive to injure or humiliate. They were laborers only, and remained unafraid, unthreatened in their duties. At one point there were so many of them they looked like a mantle cloaking him, at times crawling in and out of his mouth. But Eli had some things to say. Even bees would not deter him. He simply waited for them to crawl out again, then delivered his words, slowly, calmly. It almost seemed like the bees may have come in efforts to protect him, for indeed they did him no harm, and in time, when realizing that nothing alive, man nor beast, could save him, they left.

Here is what Eli had to say to Mahlir: "They tell me my daughter has been put to the torture, and that she now lies dead in Gehinnom. They say she gave birth in her death throws, and that my grandson is also dead, and that his body also rots among the corpses of the unclaimed."

What Mahlir did next was wrong. He just could not bear to tell Eli the truth. "My good lord," he said. "Rachel is safe. Your grandchild is safe, in a protected place among shepherds."

Eli's mouth turned up a smile, relief overwhelming.

Black streaks were traveling up his legs from the abscessed wounds holding his ankles to the uprights, venomous creatures, quivering his body each time they advanced. "You are a good man, Mahlir, my son-in-law," he said. His undeserved praise wept in Mahlir's soul. "Take care of her for me. And take care of my grandson, my legacy. Let me tell you a story." He paused again to gather strength. "This is a story of great kings and great kingdoms. It is a story that illustrates the importance of family. First there was a kingdom that encompassed all the habitable earth. No one could conquer this king and this kingdom. Because this king had the ability to unify his family and his generals and his people. That is why. But death came at an early age for this king. And without the king to unify them, the people and the king's generals could not keep the kingdom together. Nor could their descendants. They were left vulnerable to a family of simple farmers who rose up and took the kingdom for themselves. Many said these farmers were blessed by God, for in the final days of their victory their lamps burned for eight days, though they had oil enough for only one. It was a miracle, the people said, a sign that the new kingdom would last. But it did not last. The simple farmers could not get along either, brother with brother. The new kingdom also began to falter, and thus became vulnerable to a beast from the north who came like a thundercloud in purple. And the older brother among the farmers schemed against his younger brothers, because the beast in purple had promised this older brother the crown for himself, in return for his betrayal. For this the wrath of God was brought down, and the crown ended up on the head of the scheming older brother's lowly servant, who then passed it to his own son, who also turned against God's ways and became the worst of them all. For here was Herod-the-Great.

Mahlir understood him to be speaking of Rome's conquest and the campaigns of Pompey, and he understood the first king to be Alexander of Macedonia, and the scheming older brother to be John Hyrcanus II of the Maccabean line, and the lowly servant to be Antipater of Idumea, Hyrcanus's political ally and advisor, father of Herod-the Great.

"Let there be a lesson learned from the mistakes of our ancestors, my son-in-law. You are now my legacy, my only heir. Do not fail me. Remember, there is nothing as important as family. A family united will triumph. A family faithful to the principles of the Law will triumph. Protect my daughter and my grandson, and promise me you will raise him to be faithful to the Torah, and to the brothers he will have. Then our family will triumph. Then I shall have my legacy." His voice was distant and strained, because at this point he barely clung to life.

"I promise," said Mahlir, the blasphemy burning upon his lips.

Mahlir resolved to let hm die believing his wishes would be fulfilled.

Above the cross, on the very top of the upright timber, was nailed a sign. Inscribed in Aramaic was the sentence,

"He who dared stand against a king."

It is said that Archelaus himself drove the nails that attached the sign, and shouted as he rode away, "An example to those who dare to petition Rome for my demise!"

Said Mahlir, after listening to Eli, after promising to honor his wishes: "I am sorry."

Eli did not know what Mahlir was apologizing for.

Then he asked for Rachel.

Mahlir knew not what to say, so he said nothing.

Responded Eli, thinking he knew the reason for Mahlir's silence. "Ah, she stays away because she is in hiding, of course, because you are protecting her. My senses leave me, I fear. It is better anyway, that she not see me like this. How fortunate I am that you came into our lives, that I have you as a son-in-law, as the protector of the family and the bearer of my legacy. How fortunate indeed." The words, as they passed through his swollen lips and parched tongue were surprisingly distinct. He asked Mahlir to break his legs, a request that could not have been honored even if Mahlir did make the attempt. The guards were too close and would kill anyone who tried. Only the king could order such a thing, for without the support of the legs instant death would result, an immediate end of suffering. But death came anyway, almost in that very moment, as rain began to fall, little puffs in the dust that looked at first like they were bursting forth from realms below instead of falling from the heavens, then a rushing downpour, to prove that they were indeed from the heavens.

Mahlir hung his head. As he stood wondering what he would do next a sound startled him, a whimpering, like that of a newborn. Jesus-of-Sie! The dog was curled up beneath the cross, beneath his master. The pitiful animal looked like so many of the inanimate stones and boulders dotting the hilltop, curled in a ball, head buried in his water-soaked and quaking fur. His eyes were turned upward toward Eli. He would have given his life for his master if it would have done any good. He seemed to know that it wouldn't.

There came another sound. Mahlir looked and saw one of the guards cutting Eli's bonds and ripping his hands from the spikes. At last an end to suffering. The body fell forward and thumped face first into the muddy and watery earth, snapping the bones of his still attached legs, staying there until they could pry the feet loose. It was an unnatural sight, with Eli's neck protruding out of his shoulders at an awkward angle, rainwater pooling up around his head. The guards laughed at the sight. But Mahlir saw something the guards had missed – a mouth that was open and drawing air, half drowning in the pooling water, and eyes that were wide and filled with demons unimaginable. Lord God, he was still alive.

Unseen by the guards, in the few minutes he had available, Mahlir placed his hand over Eli's mouth, and wept bitterly. "Good-bye, my beloved father-in-law," he whispered. "My friend, my mentor." Eli welcomed it, but even then struggled against it as his body instinctively thrashed about, refusing death. Would this also be a burden Mahlir would carry? Four souls now, whose life he had taken?

The guards, two of them, castoffs from Archelaus' regular army, filthy gray beards tied at three points by leather thongs, drew their swords and poked the useless shell that until a moment ago held Eli. One of them jerked back the corpse's head by the hair to view its face. Satisfied that they had completed their duty, they turned to a crouching, shivering man – Mahlir had not noticed him earlier – and told him he could now claim the body for burial.

It was Shammah, Eli's dumb servant. Shammah gave a denarius to each guard and bowed in humbled courtesy, and bent and attempted to lift his revered master.

Shammah was old; the effort was useless. "Let me help you," Mahlir offered. The guards allowed it, not having the slightest idea that the nameless, beardless young man giving the assistance was also a criminal hunted by Archelaus. Eli and Mahlir had spoken to one another only in Hebrew, a tongue not known by the guards. Shammah had with him a cart for the purpose. There were no horses or oxen; it had to be pulled by human hands. Mahlir's hands. Shammah could never have done it alone.

Jesus-of-Sie lifted himself and followed after them, head low, tail in a purposeless droop.

Eli's cross stayed in place for days, with its sign – *"He who dared stand against the king,"* – empty, stained in blood turned black, as a warning to the people.

But it had the opposite effect. Instead of filling the people with fear, it infuriated them. Thus it was that Mahlir's anger, his hate for Archelaus, his determination to avenge Eli, found sympathetic ears in the halls of the Temple, as he solicited for a newfound purpose. Within him was a resolve that he would gather the leading men of the land, and with them travel to Rome and stand in front of Caesar, as Eli had done unsuccessfully a decade ago, as Eli had dreamed of doing again, and petition for annexation. He would see Eli's dream fulfilled. Mahlir talked only to those he knew he could trust, and only in secret, Sadducees mostly, friends of Eli, those who had also been brutalized by Archelaus. Several times he disguised himself as a beggar and passed notes to those he wanted to recruit. Each time he cautioned the person not to involve the high priest, knowing the priesthood was loyal to the government. Mahlir organized the opposition in small groups of fourteen, twenty groups in all, meeting with them late at night in the Kidron Valley below Olivet, among the tombs, with no torches or lamps or fires. And he wrote to the principal men of Samaria and asked them to join with the cause. Sometimes even enemies will unite if a greater enemy threatens them both. Mahlir made three copies of each letter and sent them by three separate couriers over three separate routes.

Never a thing in his life had he done with as much precision, with as much power and confidence. It must have showed, because he suddenly found himself a leader of men, in spite of his youth. Men three times his age, men with far more wisdom in life's ways, became dependent upon hm. The risks were high – if they were caught their fate would be as Eli's – but Mahlir felt no fear. The possibility of failure never entered his mind. His confidence inspired the others, hundreds, Jews and Samaritans alike, and in less than thirty days they were prepared to leave, none imagining defeat.

The caravan departed before the light of day, under the guise of a pilgrimage to Rome to share their faith with the Jews living there, and to take them badly needed funds and supplies. The journey was financed by the wealthiest of the Sadducees. Grain, livestock, ships, food, water, all was provided.

And Shammah and Jesus-of-Sie would come as well. An old man and an aging dog. Because they were family.

CHAPTER 21

PETITIONING FOR ANNEXATION

ROME

The morning sky was clear and powder blue, the sea swells rhythmic, as Mahir and his train of ships glided toward Rome's shore and a coastline now becoming more than just an obscure haze. An array of colors opened up – greens, reds, whites, staggering to the senses in their boldness – dark green tufts of trees, mellow green stretches of grasslands and hillsides, countless red rooflines, the white sides of houses and buildings, the gleaming brilliance of Temples and flora.

Mahlir stood on deck in amazement. "Rome is beautiful," he said aloud.

Shammah laughed and shook his head and made motions telling his master this was not Rome, telling him Rome was far grander. Shammah's gestures and mouth movements were becoming easier to understand. Jesus-of-Sie fairly trembled with the excitement, running back and forth, yapping, tail arched over his back. Bothersome dog, he always slept the night with his head on Mahlir's stomach.

Someone nearby spoke. "Rome is thirteen miles inland. This is the port city of Ostia."

Said someone else, "There has been talk of dredging out the sand here at Ostia and building deep port walls. One of the Emperor's engineers suggested that the entire harbor be enclosed in a hexagonal shipping dock with a canal connecting to the Tiber."

Another sailor scoffed. "A simpler task it would be to reconstruct the great tombs of Egypt."

As they got closer Mahlir could see twenty, maybe thirty ships anchored in deep water, and twice as many tenders oaring out to load up cargo. "The tenders, when filled, will row up the Tiber," one of the sailors explained, pointing to the smaller and more maneuverable freight taxis that dotted the blue-green waters like hungry fish swarming to a meal. "Or be towed by oxen."

At the mouth of the huge river, pushing back the waves of the sea, was a grain barge tilted to one side, stuck in the sand, the wind and surf battering it from the western side, the force of the swift-moving Tiber from the other. Water rolled over it from both directions, washing away its precious cargo. The ship was utterly devoid of life. Sailors, passengers and deckhands had long since left or been drowned. No one came to help, no one dared. The grain was lost, as was the ship. Did it belong to a wealthy merchant who could well stand the loss? Or perhaps it was the property of a newly liberated freedman who had gambled his last denarius on a business venture, someone who was not able to afford the added expense of the ferry tenders, someone who had to risk running the river directly.

Another barge had navigated around the hidden sandbars silting in from the great river's wash. It was a boat long and narrow and flat-bottomed. Its stern was tall and carved into the head of a lion that looked back on its crew in protection. Its cargo was an enormous pillar of porphyry marble. "From Egypt, likely," volunteered the sailor. "Destined for Rome and one of the Temples. Caesar's building program, you know."

The wind was becoming stronger the further in Mahlir's boat ventured. The center mast groaned under the immense red and white sail, billowed full, driving the bow through the waves with slapping thuds that shook every timber. Mahlir gripped the side railing and wondered in apprehension if the pilot was intending to shoot the main channel too, only to end up like the grounded grain barge.

The sandbars, created by the river's unpredictable rush, changed and moved daily, raised, lowered, shifted. No sailor could possibly know for sure how far he was from disaster, not even an experienced captain, until the fateful scrape and crunch was heard. "Proper navigation depends on the wind and tide, and the time of year," said the helmsman from his high perch on the stern, a grin of confidence besmirching his face, and he shouted out for the fore and the main to be swung around. Bare-chested bodies scrambled, lines whistled, sheets filled and popped. He slammed the rudder hard right, aiming directly at the river's blue-green confluence. He *was* going to run it. "It's late in the afternoon," he shouted out. "The spring flow of tributaries is strong, so the sand will be far out. The wind is from the southwest, so the channel will be on the right side. I watch the current and the color of the water." He laughed, as though drunk with the pleasure of terrifying everyone, and spoke loud enough for all to hear. He had come from one of the wealthier Sadducees who used him regularly to pilot cargoes of grain to Rome. "I shall get you there. I have never run aground yet."

His confidence did in fact do him well. They entered the river's mouth and felt its surge against the hull; he ordered the sails lowered and the oarsmen to drop and pull water. When they were fully inside the channel, lines were strung through the bow and hitched to oxen on each shore. So began the long trip to Rome, winding left, winding right, the powerful current foaming against the timbers, a current deceptively smooth and calm when left undisturbed, furious when opposed, at times bringing the ship nearly to a stop.

Twice the ropes broke, sending the vessel sideways until it could be rescued by the oarsmen. An Egyptian corn barge was behind them – enormous – Mahlir had never seen such a vessel, one hundred eighty-five spans in length, forty-five at the beam. They came close to colliding with it both times. The swarthy half-naked stevedores on board laughed at the near tragedies.

The entire day was spent struggling with the river, and well into the night. A light flickered from within the blackness ahead of them. They paid it no mind at first, but it grew and sharpened, and as it did voices came to be heard. Nearly at the point of a head-on collision, Mahlir saw coming down the river an Imperial Navy trireme, three tiers of oars, eighty-five to a side, a torch tied to her eagle carved bow. Her precision oarsmen drew back against the current and brought her to a dead stop in the water, a mere fifteen spans away, to tower over Mahlir and the crew. Mahlir's men cast the lines down and the oarsmen drew steady as the huge warship edged by. Her golden breast-plated soldiers with their plumed helmets and capes of red looked down, as if in protection, for in fact that is exactly what their duty was, to protect the visitors. In the era of Augustus, with its building programs and its commitment to peace, the Navy's entire purpose was to protect the river and guard the port against pirates and local insurrectionists.

The rise of the sun revealed that they were still not at Rome. It sifted its sunbeams through a sky of purple and gray, and through pillars of fog, disappearing smoke over the countryside, and brought forth colors bold and magical. Buildings of white danced in splendor, perfectly square with roofs of red. Green farmlands patchworked themselves over the expanse, each section separated from the next by dark green hedges or by rows of trees, some bulbous, others spiring like arrows. A hundred different types of trees grew there, or so it seemed – oak, spruce, date palms, trees cloaked in blooms of white, others in red. No wonder the Romans thought it home to the gods. Villages, villas, farms, chickens pecking about, people gathering vegetables for sale in the city – this was suburban Rome, becoming more dense the further in they traveled, becoming more painted with imprints of roads, and with embossings of sloping aqueducts crawling down from the hills, all leading to Rome. Mahlir was amazed, spellbound by the beauty. He had never seen greens so green, reds so red or whites so brilliant.

A road was being built along the riverbank, or rebuilt, according to one of the workers who yelled back at Mahlir when he asked what they were doing. Mahlir was surprised they could hear over the clatter of the toil, and the chortle of birds nesting in the riverbank greenery that had been trimmed back to allow for the lines and the oxen. It was the "High Road" they were rebuilding and widening, the worker said in brisk Latin, the Via Ostiense. He must have been a foreman. He was one of a number of men standing in supervision over five gangs of loin-clad laborers with bodies tanned from the sun. The first gang was digging deep down; the second, a distance behind, was laying crushed rock. A third, a distance further back yet, was laying down large stones, then more crushed rock, then more stones, then more crushed rock. A fourth was topping it off with flat stones that were mortared and rolled by a fifth group pulling huge round millstones.

Mahlir had slept in brief intervals throughout the night, Jesus' soft head on his stomach, Shammah by his side. The corn barge was still behind them, towering above them, and behind it were the other two vessels from the Jewish fleet. "Just around the next bend," said the helmsman, then laughed when the next bend came and Rome wasn't there. "Like I told you," he said, "just around the next bend," as if the city would magically spring forth like some mushroom. In truth it came upon them gradually, first with more roads, two from the south, one from the north, converging, laden with long lines of clattering freight wagons. Then came stone embankments on either side of the river, then dredged-out quays, one of which the corn barge tied on to, then tall windowless structures of gray concrete, the horrea, the helmsman explained, grain and corn storehouses. The largest was the famed Horreum of Augustus. Then there appeared great complexes of offices, then the porters' barracks. Stevedores scurried along the docks, as did the sailors and various merchants and vessel owners, with their various complexions and attires indicating the various countries whence they came. Virtually every quay held a ship; the corn barge was by far the largest. Most vessels of her size stayed anchored off Ostia.

The oxen pulling Mahlir's ship had by now been replaced with porters who soon would tie up and unload the grain. Slowly, laboriously, they pulled the boat around another bend – amidst the busy people about their many duties, amidst the idlers, and the beggars, and their many and varied languages, Latin and Greek being the most prominent. They pulled the boat to a quay to the south of a grand seven-tiered bridge. Beyond that, barely within sight, was an island around which the Tiber flowed. In the foreground an object loomed, one nearly as monumental as the Temple in Jerusalem. "That," said the helmsman, "is the Circus Maximus. Many a game have I witnessed there. Many a race."

Flowing to the senses were rushes of odors, some foul, some pleasant. The helmsman noticed it in Mahlir's face and laughed and pointed. "Near the Circus is a cattle market. Also nearby – those buildings there – are storage repositories. Oil, flax, lumber, wool, spices, wide-ranging are the goods that are stored in those silos." A bakery must have also been close by. The unmistakable aroma of freshly baked bread filtered in amongst the others. From another direction drifted the stench of open sewage.

In the near distance spired the glory of Rome, in more splendor than the poet could put to pen, a great jeweled crown – the rooftops and the red brick of the public squares being her rubies, the green of the meadows and trees her emeralds, the twinkling of the fountains her sapphires. Upon seven distinctive hills she sat, and in rolling valleys and ravines. Truly a crown. Of seven pinnacles. Same as Jerusalem.

The group was forced to stay the night on the outskirts because of a law prohibiting horse-drawn vehicles inside the city. Mahlir had just rented six wagons from a merchant on the wharf who very well knew of the ordinance. Now they were going to have to unload and hire porters, and there was not the time to do it all before sunset. It would have to be done tomorrow. That night they would share the company of drunkards and wharf slaves. The leaders of Jerusalem, whose rituals of cleanliness were as much as part of their religion as the doctrine itself, would drink and eat shoulder to shoulder with men whose foul breath and stale body odor was heightened only by the smell of the cheap wine they drank, in a city where bathing water was as plentiful and as free as sunshine.

Virtually every inn and drinking house in the Porta Capena held members of the Jewish traveling party. The Inn of Janus was the name of the place where Mahlir and the twelve from his boat were staying. It was on Aventine Hill by the Circus, where the Appian Way begins.

Mahlir bought two meals, one for himself and one for Shammah – two hot cups of calda, two cups of boiled peas, some pulse – and paid for them with six bronze asses, three times what the non-Jewish guests were being charged. Jesus-of-Sie, as always, was content to stay outside, curled up in his ball of self-protection, nose buried in his tail. Mahlir bargained with the proprietor for some leftover meat scraps, and walked out and put the food down in front of the loyal beast. Jesus slapped his tail in thanks.

The guttural whisperings of the Jewish language, and the accent it gave to the group's attempts at speaking Latin, and the clean piety of their clothes, which they washed daily, and their bearded faces, save for Mahlir – he continued to shave every morning – provided the unsavory tavern crowd with an irresistible source of amusement. The Jews of course had the discipline to ignore the taunts and the crude tongues; Mahlir had chosen for this mission only those with strong wills and even tempers. Nothing must deter them from their goal.

A ruffian walked up to Shammah, calling him "Jew Beggar," an epithet the crowd seemed fond of hurling, a term confusing to the Jews. The least of them held more financial worth than the entire tavern crowd combined.

"Come, Jew Beggar," he said, standing over him. "Share a meal and some drink with us."

Mahlir and Shammah were seated on a circular stone bench surrounding the cook-fire. Flames licked at the bottom of a cauldron, then vanished to reappear as a thin line of smoke just below the concrete ceiling, blackening its way outward to open air beyond the wall-less side of the drinking cubicle. From the steaming cauldron the sweet aroma of calda rose up, the mix of wine and water and spices that so warmed the heart and lightened the soul on a cool evening.

"He does not speak," Mahlir said, trying in his best Latin to explain that Shammah was mute.

The short and portly ruffian, oozing the stench of intimidation, pulled Shammah dancing in the air to the back wall where he and three other nameless drunkards had gathered around an empty hogshead barrel eating pork sausages. He speared a half-eaten grease-dripping chunk with a stiletto blade and drew it back and forth beneath Shammah's nose. "Eat, Jew Beggar," he goaded, knowing Jews were prohibited from eating the meat of swine. "Share our food and you shall walk away unharmed."

Shammah winced, doing his best to resist, his aging joints crackling in pain.

Mahlir's fingers folded around the handle of his short sword. Discipline. Hold steady. Not yet. A fight would cause their expulsion from the city, or worse, would land them all in the Tullianum. He had to wait. Resolve the matter another way. Nothing must deter them from their goal. Muddling it further, further slowing his response was that dark spirit of non-violence that had overtaken him of late, a strange visitor that desired well-being for even those of evil intent. He shook his head to rid himself of it, as one might do to chase out the fog of sleep…

…and waited, his hand firm but light on the handle, as he had been taught, the protectiveness growing, the moment building, his arm tensing, the anticipation growing. The charge would come from inside his chest, as he had been taught, not from his arm. The arm, the sword, would only be a part of the fluidity of the entire movement. The attack would be instantaneous, would surprise even those of his own crowd, who knew nothing of his early training at the hands of the Temple guards.

The ruffian rammed the sausage into Shammah's mouth with force enough to cause blood to flow.

Shammah spit it back at him, blood and all, bringing from the brute a stinging backhand. Shammah crumpled under it, stunned but conscious.

The ruffian picked him up with a huge hand encircling his throat – the ruffian's hands were oddly large, like his head, despite his diminutive stature – and slammed him again against the wall, turning Shammah's head so that he might view the gods and lares that had been painted into the wall's pink stucco, barely visible from the faraway flames of the firelight and the flickering of a lamp on the hogshead barrel. "If the gods forgive, so will I," he chortled. "Pay homage, Jew Beggar. Kneel and ask the mighty hosts of heaven for mercy."

Mahlir jumped to his feet.

But before his sword could come visible, a clamoring rose from the crowd. "The bucket men are coming!" someone shouted. In the same instant four soldiers clomped in with their heavily strapped hobnailed boots.

The room fell silent.

"They are Men of the Watch," whispered one of Mahlir's colleagues, a hushed tone of combined fear and respect timbering his voice.

One of the soldiers stepped ahead of the rest and threw his cape over his shoulder, and sneered at the thug. "Calvus," he said. "I see you finally found someone you can best."

"This is not business that concerns you, bucket man," quipped the ruffian, still pinning Shammah to the wall.

"Business of the Emperor *always* concerns the Praefectus Vigilum," the soldier fired back, and pulled from a sling on his back the oddest looking weapon, like a javelin with a hook below the point, a thing not unlike a shepherd's staff. He thrust it onto the ruffian's neck, forcing his face sideways against the stucco. Shammah slid from his grip and crumpled to the floor.

Another of the soldiers held up a tallow lantern and cast its dancing light on the scene, and held a hand out for Shammah, helping him to his feet.

"Here's the problem –" the one with the hook said. "These fellows you are bullying are ambassadors. The emperor is receiving them tomorrow. Woe be it to the man who harms a hair on one of their heads."

The words shocked Mahlir. Then came relief, not only because Shammah had been rescued – certainly he was grateful for that, but because he now knew his messages had gotten through, and that Augustus himself was intending to grant them his time. Mahlir had dispatched two messages to the Roman government. Neither had been acknowledged. Mahlir had set out on the journey hoping to arrange the audience upon arrival.

The letters had said nothing of the specifics of their purpose, only that, *"The prominent men of Jerusalem, including the most respected leaders of the Sanhedrin Council, do pray for an audience to discuss a matter of utmost importance to both our countries and our peoples."* Then in Latin characters double the size of the others, Mahlir had written, *"We implore that this correspondence be held in the strictest of confidence, and that our king, the most royal and exalted Archelaus, not be advised of this letter, lest we all perish."*

Mahlir came to discover that the Men of the Watch, the Praefectus Vigilum, bucket men for short, were feared, ridiculed, and respected all at the same time. Organized and deployed by Augustus, some seven thousand strong, these were the men entrusted with the protection and security of the citizens and guests of Rome and charged with the duty of fighting the ever-present fires plaguing the crowded and poorly built apartment buildings, some four and five stories high. These were the men who patrolled the black-dark streets and alleyways the night through, rounding up thieves and troublemakers and dispersing unruly crowds. The nickname "bucket men" came from the equipment they carried, buckets made of rope and waterproofed with pitch, and hand pumps, and hooks – the weapon used to pin the ruffian to the wall was a firefighting tool – and axes and ladders. In Rome water existed everywhere, in the wealthy and poor sections alike. Fountains and pools and basins poured forth on every corner, and in the middle of every street. The same people who mocked the bucket men as they rushed down the street with their buckets full of water were the same who applauded their courage and daring once a fire had been extinguished, or a citizen rescued. They were the same who ran in fear when doing mischief, the same who cheered when it was another who was caught in the midst of a dirty deed. The Men of the Watch were divided into various districts, each district being under the direction of an army centurion, with a tribune at the top, the City Praefect, his title. The men were not actual members of the army – most were freedmen – but were under the control and direction of the army. Most unique, this system of Augustus', of protection and justice. Each district had a facility where the criminals and lawbreakers were detained. For petty offenses they were tried on the spot before that particular district centurion, the Praefect of the Watch. Those committing larger crimes were sent to a central location, where, for a certain sum of money held as security, they were allowed their freedom until appearing for trial before the Praefect.

In some ways the bucket men looked humorously like peddlers, with their equipment and gathered up lengths of rope, but the fact that they held unsheathed swords gave sudden power to the look.

The bucket man nodded at Mahlir in respect, and clanked out, followed by the rattling of his crew. The crowd was silent until the bucket men were gone, then their conversations rose to mumblings, then laughter, directed of course at poor Calvus. Mahlir worried that that in itself would incite a quarrel again. But then something happened that took the attention away from the Jewish guests. Someone else walked in, someone in a snow-white toga with a garland of ivy on his head.

Everyone in the place got up to flock around this new personage. The mystery man raised a goblet and announced he was there to enjoy an "aequa libertus," a night with the lower class. "Good Proxemus," he called to the tavern owner. "Bring in every rascal in the neighborhood. Tonight I will drink with cut-throats and thieves. Tonight the dregs of humanity will share my goblet." The crowd forgot all about the Jews. Within the hour all were sprawled about on their way to a drunken stupor, happily availing themselves of the young nobleman's offer of free food and drink in his game of "doing the rounds," a favorite sport among the adventuresome youth of Rome's upper crust.

The following morning, after a good breakfast of cheese and bread dipped in wine and sprinkled with salt, Mahir hired the porters and the entourage set out for the homes of the brethren in the Jewish sector.

What a sight Malir and his group were, trudging along the popular Aurelian Highway in their colobiums, with their tassels and phylacteries, piously plodding, dozens of them, followed by as many porters. Some of the porters carried sacks and baskets, some of them pushed carts. Each basket, each cart was filled to overflowing with grain sacks for the Roman Jews, and with gifts of gold and precious items for the emperor.

More unusual yet was the sight Mahlir himself must have presented, clean shaven and not yet thirty, leading a long procession of Jewish holy men, his hands folded in front of him as he walked, head bowed in reverence to a god he was not sure he believed in anymore. One of the porters, for a modest fee, a quadrans for each footfall, had agreed to take them by the shortest route to the Jewish sector. Citizens gathered on street corners and came out of buildings and shops. Some laughed, some watched in respect, others in awe. Shammah was next to follow, as Mahlir's slave. Behind Shammah pranced the affable and ever-loyal Jesus-of-Sie, obedient to Shammah's every move, stopping only occasionally to lap water from one of the fountains, running then quickly to catch up. Behind Jesus-of-Sie was the porter to give directions. Mahlir found it hard to believe that the streets of a city could be so crowded, so alive with people, people from such divergent social strata, more so even than Jerusalem during Passover. It was particularly crowded in the forums – streets that opened into huge squares of polished marble and towering colonnades – beauty for all to enjoy, rich and poor. In some places people were shoulder to shoulder with one another. There were children at play, running in and out amongst the monolithic columns; there were old men sitting on the edges of fountains spinning tales; there were families strolling together; peddlers walked with pots and pans strapped to their backs; shop-owners were barking at passersby, their storefronts propped open, their wares sprawled out into the streets; children were playing "robbers" upon chalk diagrams scrawled on the marble paving stones; there were senators and wealthy citizens on their way to the public baths, or leisurely walking together discussing business, or hurrying to make appointments. There were beggars and there were masters and matrons, and there were slaves, some attending to the masters and matrons, some doing nothing at all, because at the time their services were not needed.

In looking at it all, in watching the people move aside for the procession, some staring and pointing, others ignoring them altogether, Mahlir's thoughts took an odd course. He began to think of the dream held by so many of an army gathered by the coming Messiah to plunder Rome. Such a shame it would be, to destroy these peaceful and happy people. Mahlir wondered if the streets of Jericho had looked like this when Joshua descended, unsuspecting, full of life.

He would have no part of it, if the Messiah did exist, if his intent was the slaughter and conquest of these people of beauty.

They passed through the Forum Julius with its statues and the great Temple of Venus rising out of its center. Julius Caesar, it is said, paid a hundred million sesterces for just the bare land. They crossed an expansive plaza that glittered from thousands of sections of stone and variegated marble, and from columns fronting the surrounding porticoes and shops. Square pedestals, many topped with statues, posted a pathway through the plaza where there was a second Temple to another deity, Mars the Avenger, its colonnades rising in heights to rival the Temple in Jerusalem. A flame burned vigilantly inside, awaiting anyone willing to climb the steps. Unlike the Temple in Jerusalem, all people were invited to enter here, the monument erected by Octavius after the great war-god helped him avenge the death of his father Julius Caesar by giving him victory over Brutus and Cassius, and over Mark Antony and Cleopatra. They passed into another tenement section, another of the many closely built blocks of apartments that jammed the city's lowlands, which were looked down upon by those living in the mansions on the hills. Here in the lowlands color also abounded. Color was everywhere, green mostly, from the scented things of the earth that grew on every street corner and along every curb and in every window box, and from the vines that climbed the walls and hung from doorways and windows. Shops and storefronts were painted in shades of green.

Marble columns and curbstones were patterned in swirls of green and rose. And the fountains sparkled everywhere. Fountains were the only source of water for the apartment dwellers. So numerous were they that a person had only to reach a cup out to be refreshed. And in Rome there existed monuments and statues everywhere, monuments to gods, to statesmen, to philosophers, orators, things offensive to these strange visitors who have vowed to have no graven images set before them.

One would never guess poverty existed in Rome, but for the people. Although, strange as it was, even in poverty the people of Rome carried about them a type of aristocracy, a type of artistry, a type of beauty common to rich and poor. The beggars and idlers possessed it. The old men and off-duty slaves possessed it. The women possessed it, walking alone and unveiled. The peddlers with their donkeys laden with wares and wine possessed it. The shopkeepers possessed it, their vegetables and freshly killed poultry hanging down. The cookhouses possessed it, out of which drifted laughter and the aroma of calda. The tall and cracking apartment buildings decorated with drifting flowers and vines possessed it. All was beautiful.

Then the Jews walked a street that ascended a hill, past something enormous being built. Workers swarmed its structure. Soldiers, Mahlir was told. In peacetime soldiers were builders.

The buildings on the hill, the Temples and the homes and the storefronts, were of a different class than those below. Magnificent – no less word would describe them. Each building, each stone, was the substance of fantasy. The curbstones, the mighty columns, the sun rich streamers of clouds above, it was all the stuff of dreams, of things pure. The streets on the hill were wider, and the people that trod them were more courteous to one another, and to the Jews. A man crossing the street stopped so abruptly for them that his personal slave, who had been shading him with a sun umbrella, bumped into him from behind. A crowd lounging in front of a barber shop immediately withdrew to the curb so that the Jews might pass. Unlike the section below, where the walls of shops were often no more than curtains rolled aside, the front of this shop was made of imported cedar – Mahlir could tell by the scent – and was polished and painted in floral calligraphic designs and was propped open from hinges on top. Even the curbstones, all perfectly square, were painted in painstaking detail. Here were the beautiful people. Togas, wreaths, short hair, clean-shaven faces. Next to the barber shop, high on a pedestal, was a statue of Augustus saluting from the horse, a reminder to the people of his promise of peace and prosperity. On the side of the pedestal, in chalk, was scrawled a writing. Rome was full of wall writings, in poor and wealthy sections alike, announcements, news items, notes to lovers, critiques of tribunes and senators, people expressing themselves in many and varied ways, in crude ways mostly, on occasion in ways resembling fine literature, more crudely in the valleys than on the hills. This writing, on this wealthy hilltop, was perhaps the crudest of all, and revealed another side to the gentle people.

All the good people of Rome
And of the Habitable Earth
In the Circus Maximus, and on the Tiber between the Two Bridges,
Each day from the 17th to the 30th of the month of Sivan
THE GAMES OF CLAUDIANUS LICINIANUS
Beginning with the rise of the sun at the sixth hour
Morning – Animal Fights and Beast Hunts
Afternoon – Executions of Criminals, new to the games,
To be carried out in the manner of their specific crimes.
On the Tiber witness a reenactment of the naval battle at Actium
Where criminals will die as did the naval soldiers of Marc Antony
TO BE FOLLOWED BY THE FIGHTS OF THE GLADIATORS

Ironic, that the announcement should be there, beneath a statue of Augustus, who on more than one occasion had publicly expressed his distaste for the games, allowing them nonetheless because the people loved them so.

Suddenly, ahead of them, from the opposite direction, soldiers appeared, a front-riding legate on horseback followed by high-ranking footmen, tribunes first, six of them, then a centurion. Behind the centurion marched his men, a hundred of them, ten abreast. Mahlir's heart lay still in his chest. Everyone in the street made way. Likewise did the Jews begin to move aside. The strangest of all things then happened. The legate, after raising his hand and shouting out a signal, dismounted and removed his helmet, and tucking it under his arm walked up to Mahlir. He threw aside his red cape to reveal he was carrying a rolled-up papyrus. Said he, as he handed it to Mahlir, in clear unspoiled Latin. "The emperor will receive you at the convening of the Senate at first light tomorrow. His Magnificence sends a full Century to greet you, in view of everyone, so that the citizens will see the respect he has for your visit and your people." After handing Mahlir the papyrus, he struck his chest, and in response every man in like manner saluted the Jews. He asked Mahlir their destination. "The Jewish sector," Mahlir said. "We must be coming to it soon. We have been walking a long time."

The legate's face turned into a scowl. It was a look directed at the porter who was Mahlir's guide. The porter shrunk from it. Said the legate, looking at the porter but addressing Mahlir: "The services of your guides and porters will be free of charge. Is that not correct, Marcellus?"

The porter bowed his acknowledgement.

"How much did this buffoon want to charge you?" the legate asked Mahlir.

"Two hundred and thirty denari, for the full three-mile journey."

"Three miles?" The legate snorted out laughter. "It's less than a half a mile from where you were staying on the Porta Capena. I wondered why you were going in circles. Marcellus had you traveling over Palatine, and over Esquiline, and through the Suburra, and the mighty lord Jupiter only knows where else. Your destination is right over there. Do you see that bridge? The Jewish sector is on the other side. Right there. Neptune's trident points the way." The enormous statue of the sea god was one of the many in the Forum, and the three points of his lance were indeed pointing at the Aemillius Bridge, one of seven spanning the Tiber.

"I carry with me a set of chains," the legate said, nodding toward his horse and its saddle bag, "for the next time someone tries to cheat guests of the emperor. Now finish your duties, Marcellus, and guide our guests to the doorstep of their destination, and make a sacrifice and thank the gods that I am not going to lash you."

The porter's neck wobbled on his shoulders in subservience, like it was going to flop away any minute and go bouncing down the street. "Thank you, thank-you, thank-you, my good lord Vitelius," he spewed. "It will never happen again." He raised his hands shoulder high and bowed low to the legate. "My lord, I am but a humble Stoic," he rattle on, "And as such am your servant. Thank-you, thank-you. I always say, whenever speaking of Praetorians and the guards of Caesar, that Vitelius is the best of them all, and as such has a good heart. I say that. I truly do. You can ask anyone. May the gods honor and hold and keep you. May the hearth goddess herself bring you and your family a thousand and one blessings." He bowed again and again, as he babbled on, his head waggling away. "Pax tectum," he finalized, bowing one long and last time. "Peace be with you. Peace. Pax. Pax."

The legate rolled his eyes and told Mahlir he would come to the Jewish sector in the morning to escort them personally to the Senate Chambers, and, saying no more, he turned and walked back to his horse. The purple plume of his helmet fanned itself in a momentary breeze as he put it back on and smoothly remounted.

Again he shouted a signal, and another strange thing happened. The legionnaires split, five rows to the left, five rows to the right, fifty soldiers on the left, fifty on the right, moving in strict unison to form for the Jews a symbolic gauntlet of protection, spears lifted and pointed inward, creating a canopy. The first soldier to be passed, plumed helmet, sectioned shoulder and breast plates, was holding the standard of Imperial Rome, the eagle of power within the wreath of peace, perched upon twin lightning bolts – peace backed by power, S.P.Q.R., Senatus Populusque Romanus, the Senate and the Roman People.

Mumblings rose behind Mahlir, and he held his breath, hoping his brethren would not embarrass their hosts. As Mahlir began to pass he turned and saw indeed they had not followed. They were milling in circles like moths caught in the midnight glow of a flame. Mahlir walked to the legate, and with courage summoned from somewhere thanked him for the honor, and explained that it is a belief of theirs that one must not bow before any graven image. "We mean no disrespect. We gladly accept and appreciate the protection of Rome, and have the deepest respect for her emperor, but we are forbidden by religious statute to bow down before or to pass beneath any image or representation. It is a belief of ours from ancient times."

To Mahlir's surprise the legate understood and signaled the legionnaire to lift the standard and move five paces back – and the Jews walked on through, every one of them.

And so the Jews proceeded to the section of the city where their people lived. On the crest of the bridge, overlooking the homes and tenements of the Roman Jews, Mahlir stopped the procession and read aloud the papyrus the legate had given him, so that the people in his party could hear and know what the great Caesar had to say concerning their visit, before proceeding into the valley within the hearing of their Roman brethren. Better it be that the Roman Jews not hear the words. Some of them would have loyalties to Rome, others to Archelaus, and there was no way of knowing which would be which.

Witnessed this 17th day of Sivan
Caesar Augustus, Emperor of Rome, has willing ears for the concerns of all the people of Rome and for all those in each of Rome's provinces.
The Emperor has received your correspondence and welcomes you.
You will be received tomorrow morning at the convening of the Senate in the Curia Julia at the Forum

Peace be to you.
Caius Julius Caesar Octavianus Augustus, Maius Imperium.

"It is sanctioned by the emperor himself," Mahlir shouted. He held it up. "Look – here is his seal."

Then they proceeded across, and Mahlir knew why they had been called "Jew Beggar" back at the inn. He saw it in the face of a small girl as she held her hand out for food. She was dressed in ragged clothes, though clean clothes. Her face was gaunt, though clean. It was full of hope.

"Yes, child," Mahlir said. "We bring food."

She followed them, gibbering in a mix of Hebrew and Greek, holding out her hand, not understanding that what they had was only grain, that it would not be food until tomorrow. Her mother came and hurried her away, scolding her for bothering them. This part of the city was very much like the Suburra, the other low-income section, only worse, narrower streets, more crowded, tall tenement buildings without water, the only water being the fountains, bone skinny dogs slinking from door to door, the odor of sewage pervading, beggars pleading, some who looked like criminals – where there is poverty there will always be crime – others who looked like good and pious people – even in poverty there will be good people. Mahlir's group left some of the gold, entrusting it to the officials in the synagogue to be used for the people, not to ornament the synagogue. Mahlir was specific.

Soon there was the rasping of millstones, a sound familiar in Rome, now as loud in the Jewish sector as in the rest of the city. Later that night Mahlir found the little beggar girl and personally gave her the loaf made for him.

That was the last he saw of her, because come morning Mahlir and his group were in the Curia watching the Fathers trickle in and take their seats, each in snow-white wool togas hemmed in purple.

CHAPTER 22

THE EMPEROR

ROME

Six hundred in all could be seated in the Curia. First were the consuls and praetors in their rows of backless curule chairs inlaid with gold and ivory. Behind them, in the tiers of carved benches, curving around in an enormous semi-circle, sat the ex-consuls and other former government and elected officials, ex-praetors, aediles, tribunes, and quaestors. The final rows were for the pedani, those senators who have never held elective office. And Jesus-of-Sie was outside by the entrance steps, curled up in a circle nose to tail, being watched over by one of the emperor's praetorians, such was the courtesy being afforded the Jews by the most powerful government in the known world.

Soon the Fathers had all taken their seats. Several were old men requiring the assistance of slaves. Retired dignitaries, someone said, who show up on very special occasions. All were in place, except for those to occupy an empty row of curule chairs in front. Each senator had cast the Jews at least a quick glance, a look of welcome and respect.

In the middle of the floor, from where the senators pleaded their cases, stood the statue of a winged woman, her feet resting on a globe, her hands stretching forth a palm branch and a laurel crown. She, the goddess Victory, the deity of successful conquest, stood there to silently bless the gathering. In front of her was always an altar of smoking coals.

Mahir was hoping she would not be noticed by his people; she was blocked from their view by the barrier. If they were to come forward to his vantage point, surely they would be offended and leave, and all would be lost.

A lictor came out with a bundle of wooden rods bound together around an axe, and signed with it, symbolic of strength through unity. A single rod is easily broken; the bundle is difficult to break. The chattering and the socializing ceased, and the assemblage all rose together. The ten magistrates to occupy the front chairs walked in, led by the presiding consul, the tenth magistrate. One chair was set apart, an eleventh, on a platform to the right of the statue. It was bigger and had more gold encrusting it, and more ivory.

The ten magistrates stood with their backs to their chairs, facing the statue. The consul cast a handful of incense on the altar. A cloud of pink fragrance filled the hall.

A voice sounded. "Bring forth the sacred fowl."

Two attendants appeared on the mirror-smooth floor with a golden cage, which caused the assemblage to rise in apprehension. Inside, two chickens scrawked and fluttered. Holding the cage between them by ivory handles carved as a camel's head on one end and a lion's head on the other, they carefully sat it down so as not to cause the slightest bump. An elderly senator carrying a ceremonial staff walked out and took from the attendants a dish of grain and bent down to the cage and slid open its two latticed doors. The chickens fluffed their wings. The senator spread the grain before them, which the chickens devoured with such fervor that the kernels went scattering out of the cage and onto the floor. Pleased, the senator straightened himself and announced, "There is no evil in sight. Affairs human can begin."

Murmurs of relief reverberated as the senators all reseated themselves.

Again the council that governed the known world began its business – first a request from the proprietor of Sicily, a senatorial province, that taxes from the peasant farmers be abated because of the conditions brought by a recent drought. The Conscript Fathers agreed, granting the measure by rising and walking to the right. Next came a petition from a border village in the Armenian region that soldiers be sent to offer protection from Parthian raiders, in reinforcement of the regular border patrols. Again the Fathers move right. Then a measure was introduced that offered to expand the free bread dole program to non-citizens who had lived in Rome for over fifteen years. This time, after much and eloquent debate over the economics of the issue, and over fears of the privileged being deprived, the majority moved to the left. Then the consul put forth a request from the emperor that the council decide on the need for more soldiers and more funds for the completing of an aqueduct project in faraway Gaul. Augustus, as Rome's first emperor since the Republic, often chose to pass decisions to the Senate, as it had been in the days of the Republic. The Senate approved. They also gave approval to a building program for improving sanitation and sewage systems in the Emporium district.

Then – the consul rose and announced the emperor. The body of the Senate also rose. Most of the Jews were still standing, though they straightened in apprehension. The others came to their feet, thankfully. Last night Mahlir had advised that they all show respect, in the Roman way, though it was at times offensive. To show respect is not to offer worship, Mahlir stressed.

Augustus appeared suddenly, walking briskly on elevated shoes, but with a mild limp on his left side, the effect of an arthritic hip that tended to plague him on certain mornings, an embarrassment, said the firm-set jaw of his expression, an annoyance he was trying his best to hide. Mahlir didn't know it at the time, but Augustus shrank from extravagance, even passed laws against excessive spending, among them a limit on the amount that could be spent on a wedding. Still, the toga had an elegance about it, clean, regal looking, flowing behind him as ripples in the air, catching now and again the shine of one of the many lamps hanging from stands and wall posts. Ranked on either side of him, walking in the same hurried pace across the blue and white patterns of squares and rectangles, floor mosaics of intricate detail, were two of his Praetorian guards, their heavy open-toed boots echoing in rhythm through the cavernous chamber, their armor clattering. Praetorians were different than soldiers, more powerful. They were the emperor's personal bodyguards. They were taller and stronger than soldiers, more colorful than soldiers, having elaborate helmet designs and pointed visors, and plumes of red and gold that were longer and taller and thicker than those of the regular army. Swirls of red and white draperies covered their breastplates and were cinched in at the waist with blue cords, giving the resulting broad-shouldered look a touch of gentility. Three purple tassels tipped in gold hung from each of their waist-cords. Their skirts were knee length and ceremoniously hemmed in etchings of bronze and gold. They walked past a piece of graffiti painted upon a balustrade lampooning the emperor for his laws against adultery while he himself was rumored to be unfaithful to his wife. It must have been done only the night before, otherwise the attendants would have removed it. Augustus paid it no mind, believing in the freedom of the people to speak their minds, having just days ago vetoed a law prohibiting people from writing political diatribes into their wills. "It is the right of the people to design their wills as they please, no matter who it offends," he maintained, in his impassioned speech before the Senate.

The left hand of the mighty Augustus held the folds of his toga. The other was free to gesture. He held it up to the Senate, much the same as the high priest would do in giving a blessing, palm forward, and spoke the words, "Civis Romanus Sum." Then he asked that the members be seated. His speech was clear and precise, never rambling, never halting, each word enunciated almost to the extreme, almost to the point of being unnatural.

He was shorter than Mahlir expected, even with the elevated shoes. At first it looked like he was wearing a crown. Then Mahlir saw it was a laurel wreath, fresh and green, only thicker and taller than the ones worn by the Fathers. Mahlir was able to catch the faint drifting of is aroma, the crisp scent of evergreens.

In the emperor's face were lines of age, but they were lines well suited to him. They gave to his countenance a look of wisdom and fairness, as was his reputation. At once Mahlir knew they would be successful. Augustus, it was said, had been known to hear cases far into the night, even during times when he was ill, even from his bed at home, rather than let the accused sit unfairly in prison.

Spoke the man who brought peace to the empire, the man who made the streets of Rome safe with his police and fire protection systems, the man who brought prosperity to his people, the deeply religious man Mahlir hoped would be tolerant of their own religion as well, "The representatives from Judea have journeyed far –" He gestured in Mahlir's direction. "– and we welcome them. I open my ears. I implore the Senate to do the same, so that I may have the benefit of its wisdom in making my decision regarding this matter of their concern. The Jewish leader shall have a period of four water clocks to speak." He looked directly at Mahlir. "You may begin. Please." He gestured for him to come forward.

The attendants brought in a glass vessel – glass was expensive, more costly than gold – and sat it upon a three-legged table and filled the upper chamber with water. The water began its slow trickle with a whisper, bringing Mahlir's throat tight with fear. He had rehearsed a hundred times the things he would say. But now the thoughts had left him. Now his mind stood useless.

He turned first to his people and explained what Augustus had said, speaking to them in Aramaic, since some did not know the language of Rome. Then trembling, he made his way toward the center of the floor to where Augustus was standing in welcome. Augustus was smiling, motioning with his hand. Mahlir didn't know how to address an emperor, what to say, what to do. He had forgotten to inquire of it.

He looked at Augustus briefly then dropped his eyes with a slight tuck of his head. "Thank you, Your Magnificence," he said.

A surprising look of reproach came from the emperor, albeit a gentle one. "He wishes not to be addressed in so formal a fashion," explained the consul.

But the consul did not let it be known exactly how the emperor should be addressed, so Mahlir simply said, with the utmost respect, "My Caesar." Mahlir learned later that Augustus lived in a small home atop Palatine, with furnishings less splendid than those of most commoners, and that he preferred to be seen as an equal among the people, which to Mahlir seemed odd, in the face of the widely known story concerning his parentage, that he was of divine birth, that his mother Atia had been taken into a trance one night and that the god Apollo had come to her in the form of a snake and deposited within her his seed, after which Augustus was born, a birth accompanied by prophetic tellings among the astrologers that here was the child that would someday bring peace and prosperity to the world. A gift from the gods. A savior.

The look Mahlir cast him, brief as it was, was sincere. Augustus had to have seen that.

The emperor seated himself in the elevated chair and adjusted himself to listen. The Fathers did the same.

Instead of speaking, instead of saying what he had come to say, Mahlir stood in silence, struggling to recall the words he had so carefully rehearsed. Sounds of impatience grew from the rows of the Fathers, whispers, an occasional cough, the scaping of feet shuffling. Why was fear gripping him? Robbing him of his final and only opportunity? He had to do it. He had to do it for Eli. He had to do it for his son. He had to do it for the Jewish people. To give himself courage he placed in his mind the image of Eli dying on the cross. And the words came, not in the order he had planned them, but come they did, and powerfully so. "Ten years ago," he began, speaking in slow and deliberate Latin, hoping his accent would not mar his words or cloud their effectiveness, "Archelaus, the son of Herod-the-Great by his Samaritan wife, to whom had been bequeathed that one-quarter portion of his father's kingdom that is our homeland, the land of Judea and Samaria, stood before you and asked that his father's will be set aside and that he be given the entire kingdom. So also did his brother Antipas plead for the entire kingdom, to whom had been bequeathed Galilee and Perea. And you, O Caesar, in your wisdom, decided to let the will stand for a time, and to assess from afar how the divisions would fare. The governments did indeed run smoothly, but only in the other kingdoms. All was not well in Judea and Samaria. Archelaus' misdoing and the disarray into which he allowed the region to fall caused my father-in-law, a good man by the name of Eli, and fifty of his fellow Jews, to make the journey to Rome and stand before Caesar, as we do now, and ask that Archelaus not be allowed to continue to rule over us, and that Judea and Samaria be made a part of Syria, that we be under the governorship of a procurator appointed by Rome, as it is with Syria.

"And so Archelaus prostrated himself before Caesar a second time. A second time he pleaded for his kingship. Nicolas of Damascus spoke on his behalf. And you, O Emperor, being a fair man, adjudicated that Archelaus be given another chance, on a trial basis, with the title of king being withheld until such time as he could prove to be a wise and effective leader. Please, I question not the wisdom of Caesar in that decision. The fault is not Caesar's. It is a wise ruler that allows the lands over which he rules to flourish on their own, by the hands of their own governments and with the strength of their own cultures. And indeed it has been so with the other portions. Galilee and Perea had been given to Antipas, a wise decision to let that part of the will stand. The northern section of Gaulonitis, Trachonitis and Paneas was bequeathed to Philip; I am told the land prospers. The hills and valleys of Ashod, Pastelis and Jarnnia was given by Herod to his sister Salome; another wise decision. It is only Archelaus against whom we have grievances. Archelaus alone is to blame for the things that have happened, for not having the character to rule as Caesar would rule, for not fulfilling the obligations and duties entrusted to him by Caesar." Mahlir took a breath. The Fathers leaned forward. "Eli, my beloved father-in-law, died on the cross at the hands of Archelaus, a method of execution to be applied only by the authority of Rome for those who have committed the most heinous of crimes. Eli's crime was that he was planning again to come and stand before Caesar, as he had done those years ago, and ask again that Judea be annexed. That is all. He stole nothing. He killed no one. He only wanted his family and his people to have the benefit of Caesar's fairness and of Rome's protection and prosperity." Again Mahlir paused. "My precious wife Rachel – she also died at the hands of Archelaus, killed by the torture. And my newborn child was also put to the torture." Mahlir looked at Augustus and could see anger in his face. Not knowing where the anger was directed, at him or at Archelaus, he pressed forward, first pointing at the Pharisees and Sadducees and businessmen who made the journey with him. "Each one of these men, leaders among our people, have stories to tell of the evils of Archelaus. Good Fathers, I thank you for granting me the time of four water clocks, but I don't need it. I defer my time to my colleagues." Mahlir gestured toward them. "Very simply, we request what my father-in-law requested. We beseech the emperor and the Senate that our homeland be made a part of Rome. The little I have told you should be sufficient for you to consider the matter in our favor. But if not, if you wish to hear more, please, allow me to bring forth one of my colleagues, and another, and another, until you are convinced." Mahlir turned to them and held both his hands up, speaking first in Latin then repeating the words in Aramaic. "Is it not so, what I have said? Is it not true that I speak your words? If it is true, then say so by stepping forward."

Rumblings of Aramaic could be heard rippling through the Jews, then they all murmured loudly in the affirmative and stepped forward. Thankfully, none looked over to see the statue of the goddess.

"Let me close by saying that we make this journey to Rome at the risk of our lives. If we fail, if you grant us not our request, we will surely die, as did my father-in-law, as did my wife, as did so many others.

Mahlir was finished. Before seating himself he gestured to the porters, and two caskets of gold and silver were brought forward. Herod-the-Great years ago had bequeathed gifts and large sums of money to Augustus.

Archelaus had bestowed upon him gifts and money. Likewise had Antipas. Now Mahlir had done the same. In Caesar's eyes these Jews today who stood before him were equal in the power of their intent.

Caesar rose to his feet, anger still flushing his face. And the body of the Senate rose. It was clear that Augustus was not going to ask for more testimonials. Nor was he interested in the opinions of the senators on the matter. Proclaimed the consul, "Nihil vos moramur, Patres Conscripti."

Mahlir repeated it to the others in Aramaic. "We detain you no longer, Conscript Fathers."

Prior to their leaving that night, on the docks of the Emporium, as they readied themselves to board ship, not knowing if they had succeeded or failed, not knowing if Augustus viewed them as friends or foes, not knowing whether his anger was at them or Archelaus, two Praetorians approached.

CHAPTER 23

THE BANISHMENT AND THE KIDNAPPING

ROME

Mahlir stood consumed in fear as the guards of Caesar walked up to him, wondering what terrible mistake he may have made with his words, in speaking before the Senate and the man who in his youth cast the head of Brutus at the feet of Caesar's statue, who on the Ides of March back during the civil wars when he was still Octavius sacrificed three hundred war prisoners on the altar of the Deified Julius, slitting their throats and offering up their blood as if they were no more than animals, though they begged for mercy.

Mahlir should not have come. His first obligation should have been to his son. He should never have left him.

The Praetorians had instructions to detain Mahlir. He was to follow them immediately. Shammah came as well, though Mahlir told him he could have his release. "Your fate shall be my fate," Shammah said with his hands. Jesus ambled along right behind them; the Praetorians allowed it.

However, instead of prison, Shammah and Mahlir were led to an elaborate bathhouse surrounded by green gardens. Instead of being put into chains, they were given robes and invited to enter the steaming blue-green waters. Caesar was the only person there, lounging on the steps of the enormous pool, submerged up to his neck, sinking just enough to let the hot water drift into his mouth. Six of his Praetorians were posted, one at each entrance, feet spread, eyes forward. Slaves and attendants abounded, but retreated upon Mahlir's arrival, save for a young maiden seated on a marble bench playing a nablum. The maiden's nimble hands sent forth chords particularly pleasing to Mahlir, since it was a Jewish instrument. In honor of Caesar's Hebrew guest? Pleasing also to the gods; how could it not be? Said the emperor to Mahlir, after he and Shammah had joined him in the water, "I want to know these people of yours, these people of Palestine; I want to understand them."

So – for a length of time extending far into the night, Mahlir told Augustus about the culture of the Jews and about their religion. Mahlir assured the emperor that his servant was mute, and that whatever was said would never be repeated. Jesus-of-Sie lay curled up on the pool's edge on the heat-filled tiles, twitching his ears now and then as if he too were listening. The gardens were visible through the bathhouse windows, glimpses of spiraling dark evergreens and billowy puffs of yellow-green shrubs. Above the bathers – there was no ceiling in the bath house – shapes of complicated clouds tumbled slowly by. Later, by the light of the moon – they were there that long – the trees turned to shades of gray and the clouds to platinum. The gods and their hosts peered out from behind them, from high up in their home. Caesar named them for his guests. Mars. Jupiter. Mercury. Saturn.

"I wish not to offend," Mahlir said. "But we believe there is only one god, and that we are his chosen people. That belief, and the rules laid down by that one god, direct us in everything we do and say and eat."

Augustus began to laugh, a loud belly laugh, a sound new to the quiet night, to the yielding melody of the nablum and the lapping of the water and the purring of the courtyard fountains, not the least of which was the upward spray in the pool's middle, tinted with the color and scent of the lilac. "That is rather arrogant of you," he said. Though he was turning frail and though his skin was peppered throughout with blemishes of age, Augustus had quick movements and rapid speech patterns. In his eyes was enthusiasm, and curiosity was in his face, making Mahlir believe that the things being said were profoundly interesting to him. How human he seemed, how perfectly normal, how approachable. "There was a time when I would have found that statement to be offensive," Augustus said. "But I have mellowed, I am pleased to say, and I have gained some wisdom too, I hope, as do we all. Do you know I once commended a centurion for offering prayers to your god when traveling through your holy city? One god? And you are his chosen people? Indeed!"

"The people of Judea and Samaria believe it to be so. That is why I tell you. And while it may or may not be true, if you respect the Jew's right to believe it, and if you allow them their customs, they will give you no trouble."

"What is his name, this god?"

"His name is unpronounceable. It consists of twenty-two Hebrew characters. Most texts shorten it to only four, YHVH. *Yah'way* is as close as can be approximated."

Again Augustus laughed. "Wouldn't it be curious if that were so, if there were only one god. And wouldn't it be curious if he cared not what we call him, or how we image him – Yahweh, Jupiter – but only how we live our lives, blessing us when we lay before him our goodwill and our virtues, cursing us for our misdeeds."

A small speck was bobbing in the water, as would a boat in a storm. Augustus reached out and let it settle on his finger. To do so was difficult; the water on which it rode kept rolling.

He lifted it up, a small and delicate fly. Its wings, triple the size of its body, lay crumpled, pinned by the weight of a single droplet. "You have done a good thing for your people," the emperor said, examining the insect as it struggled to free itself. "A very courageous thing. Do you believe the words you spoke to the Senate?"

"I do."

"Then," said the emperor, "with pride I make you, as of this moment and forever forward, a citizen of Rome."

Augustus uttered the remarkable statement almost as an afterthought. His attention was fixed on the fly, which he still held on his finger. In time the water droplet of its prison vanished. It lifted one wing, then the other – it was a beautiful creature – then started moving its legs, then lifted its body, then began to walk. The moonlight and the light from the lamps and the wall torches passed through its wings like sparkles from a rainbow, enormous wings in comparison to its body.

Augustus leaned back and reached over to a marble bench and put his finger next to it. The creature, so delicate, so strong, walked onto it and held its wings high in preparations for flight.

"Come," said Augustus. "Join me in the cold pool." The cold pool was always Mahlir's favorite. Its sting gave vitality to blood and bone, like a mikvah.

And the fly took wing, delicate, powerful, courageous.

The cold pool was through a half-oval archway bisected by red pillars and down a hallway. Jesus-of-Sie pattered after them, tail arched high, ears forward. A pleading look was on his face, because Augustus was munching on figs.

There was a snarling.

The emperor stopped. A Praetorian materialized.

Jesus-of-Sie had his eyes directly on Augustus, teeth barred.

But the emperor saw through it and halted the Praetorian, who by now had his sword drawn. It was no doubt the oddest expression on an animal either of them had ever seen, lips trying desperately to curl around its teeth, tail wagging, smiling the way dogs do when happy, tongue hanging out and ears pasted back, but broken by the intermittent attempts to hold the growl, half whining, begging for whatever it was the emperor was eating.

Mahlir quickly explained, barely able to speak.

No explanation was necessary. Augustus laughed and patted the dog's head and gave him one of the figs. Jesus worked it down and waved a huge thank you with his entire body. Augustus was a little friendlier after that, a little less regal, treating Mahlir and Shammah almost as if they were children of his, and always stopping to rub the dog's head and play the game again.

The cold pool was smaller and was square and surrounded by green pillars. The Romans had squares and circles everywhere. The beauty of the city was designed around these two forms, square parks, square gardens, square networks of paths leading inward to circular pools and multi-tiered round fountains, square buildings with domes on top, oval archways, square windows topped with half-moons, square patterned mosaics upon floors, circular mosaics, everywhere circles and squares. The sides of the pools, be they square or be they circular, consisted of steps. No sides, only steps.

Sometimes Augustus and his two esteemed guests from the land of the Jews lounged in the pool, sometimes on the steps, sometimes on benches, slaves constantly bringing them water, massaging them, scraping them. The air was unusually warm, quite pleasant. Dawn was near when they finished talking. By then Mahir felt like Caesar was a personal friend. The emperor invited them to break fast with him, bread, raisins, and olives. Mahlir wondered if the reason for the simple meal was because Augustus did not want to offend, having learned that even the consuming of food is a religious ritual to the Jews. Augustus was either very sincere or very shrewd, both perhaps, because in his presence Mahlir found himself frighteningly unguarded, speaking things that were on his mind before he realized they had been said. Augustus himself was unguarded in speech, perhaps only as a tool to draw forth information, confessing with a look as if confiding in a close friend, that he was afraid of thunder because of nearly being struck by lightning once, that he had difficulty sleeping, and that if he awoke during the night, which was frequent, he would make a slave read to him or tell him stories, rather than lie awake in the dark, and that rising early was particularly detestable to him. And Augustus extracted the intimacies of Mahlir's inward being as well. Before the night had ended he knew the reason Mahlir had spoken so dispassionately, so objectively when describing the belief of the Jews and their views about their god. He knew it was because Mahlir had no belief structure himself anymore, that it had been ripped away by the horrific trauma that brought him to Rome. And he liked that in Mahlir. It meant he could trust him, and that Mahlir was telling the truth about the abuses of Archelaus. To the emperor it made Mahlir seem devoted purely to the benefit of the people, as opposed to a belief or a religion, which is all but impossible to counter.

Augustus told Mahlir and Shammah that he had instructed most of those in the Jewish group to return to Palestine. A few had been asked to stay and were being housed in the emperor's palace. "When the time comes," he said, "I will see that all of your people are escorted safely home. For now, you have duties in Rome."

Those duties he did not define, other than to say that it would be the completion of their journey, and that they had done right by coming to Rome. "Everything will be good now for your people," he said. The emperor had a way of stimulating confidence with his words; to hear him say it was to believe it was so.

Hundreds of miles away in Jerusalem, at that very moment, Archelaus was being forewarned in a dream of the fate that hung over his head. He was dreaming of ten ears of corn, full of wheat and perfectly ripe, that were being devoured by oxen. A silly dream to anyone else, but to the dreamer it was puzzlingly oppressive. So disturbing to Archelaus was this dream that he awoke and called immediately for his diviners. None of them could give meaning to it, except Simon the Essene, who asked first to be allowed to speak his mind freely. Each of the ten ears of corn, said Simon, represented a year of Archelaus's rule, because that is the length of time it takes for an ear of corn to grow. The oxen represented afflictions and a change of affairs, for an ox takes uneasy pains in its birth giving, and land ploughed by an ox can never remain in its former state. The time for the reign of Archelaus was at an end, said the Essene, having lasted ten years.

The wife of Archelaus was also having a dream at the very same time. She was a woman of considerable beauty. By name she was called Glaphyra. Glaphyra dreamt that she stood before her deceased first husband Alexander, the brother of Archelaus, to whom she had been married as a young girl, her husband having been slain by his father Herod-the-Great. Her joy in the dream was bountiful, at seeing Alexander, and she embraced him with great affection. He told her that he loved her still, and that he forgave her for marrying again, and that he was standing in wait and welcome. Two days later the beautiful Glaphyra departed this life.

A short time after that, while he was still in mourning, and while he was dining with friends, Archelaus received an urgent dispatch from the emperor to come to Rome to answer charges that he had not behaved in moderation toward the Jews, as had been his instructions.

Mahir was there when he walked in, standing beside Caesar and wearing the white toga of a citizen. He was there to see Archelaus' face torn apart by surprise. And the Jews that had stayed behind were also there, to give their statements of censure. Archelaus prostrated himself, as he had done twice before. But this time he had no great orators to defend him. This time all he had was the mercy of Caesar's good heart. After hearing again from the Jews of his barbarous and tyrannical ways, and being unable to give satisfactory explanations, Augustus pronounced upon him his fate, a merciful one. Said Caesar, looking with eyes full of anger, and of pain, and of mercy at the same time, "It is my decision that you be banished from Judea, and from Rome. From this day forward your place of habitation shall be Vienna, a city of Gaul. As of this day forward your money and your possessions belong to Rome."

It happened that quickly, as fast as it took the words to fall from the emperor's mouth. Archelaus looked like he wanted to plead. Augustus stopped him with a hand held up. "If you refuse my mercy, or argue it in any way, I shall set you before the Senate for them to decide your guilt or innocence. If they walk left, then your punishment will be of the old way."

Knowing the old way to be whipped and tied in a sack with a dog, a cock, and a viper and cast into the sea, Archelaus said no more. He rose to his feet and thanked Augustus for his leniency.

"You shall depart from Rome immediately," the emperor said, then turned his back on him.

And so began a new course of events for the Jews. The land of Judea was added to the province of Syria, and one named Cyrenius, a Roman senator of impeccable standing, was selected to govern specifically over the Jews, an office bearing the title Procurator, just as Mahlir and his group had requested. Augustus wanted Mahlir to stay on as a scribe and advisor to Cyrenius. Mahir thanked him for the honor, but told him he longed to first fulfill his responsibility to his son. The request was granted, and so with Caesar's seal in his possession as proof of his citizenship, he set out to reclaim his son, with a promise that he would then return to take up his post as the secretarial assistant and adviser to the new governor of Judea.

A hollow feeling was inside him, as the boat moved down the Tiber, as Rome became more and more distant, not because of the beauty they were leaving behind, but because of something else they had left. Jesus-of-Sie. Shammah had given his dear friend to the emperor. Even sleep was difficult, because that bothersome head was not there anymore on Mahlir's stomach. Shammah had seen the look in the emperor's eyes as they were leaving, the look of affection as Augustus bent on one knee to give Jesus-of-Sie another morsel and rub his head. Shammah signed something with his hands. When the emperor asked for an interpretation Mahlir almost didn't have the courage to say. "He says the dog is a gift to you," he finally revealed. Augustus was so touched that he made Shammah a citizen as well. The emperor considered Jesus-of-Sie a gift greater than gold, so said the eyes.

Mahlir should not have waited as long as he did to return to the shepherd's camp. He had rationalized that his months in Rome would not make a difference to the welfare of his son, that the child was being well cared for. He was wrong. There were no plumes of smoke rising as he and Shammah approached the valley of the shepherds, as there should have been from the cook fires. There was no echoing of laughter from the children playing. An eerie silence only came from the little-known oasis hidden in the nearby distance. Mahlir and Shammah, trudging the way on foot, crested the final barren and rocky hill and saw in their unspoken hearts what they feared they might see. Instead of peaceful meadows alive with the homes of the shepherds, they saw overturned tents and broken bed frames and lampposts, and piles of clothes and things ripped and smashed and soiled in blood. And they saw corpses, some with arrows stuck in them, some scattered to the ends of the valley. The odor of death was heavy and all pervasive, like an acrid dew, an invisible cloud.

No one was alive. Mahlir put his hand out to touch a small child, older than his son. He thought he saw movement. The body was far too mutilated to contain life, he realized, right before his fingers made contact. He touched it anyway. He didn't know why. He removed a spear from another body. He wiped his hand furiously in the dust. It wouldn't come clean. For days he would feel the glue-like slipperiness of the decaying blood held by that spear handle, a reminder of the incomprehensible savagery of man. And for what purpose? Could anything be so great a prize? Could any purpose be so grand?

Riders appeared on the hilltops, barbarians, Parthian raiders. They were still there. The carnage was that fresh. They rode toward Mahlir and Shammah, slowly, casually, silently.

"I've read the last page of the Bible, it's all going to turn out all right."

Billy Graham

Part III

BELTESHAZZAR

Year 52 to Year 62 of the Calendar of Pater Patria Gaius Julius Caesar
Years 6 to 26 of the Gregorian Calendar (6AD to 26AD)

CHAPTER 24

THE SCROLLS OF THE MAGI

THE PARTHIAN EMPIRE – ECBATANA

The raiders did not kill them. They took them instead to a city called Ecbatana, deep within the Parthian empire, close by a vast inland ocean called Vaurukesh by the Parthians, later to be referred to as the Caspian Sea. By day their hands were bound and secured to the horses they were forced to ride, by night to trees or rocks. There were other captives. Most of them were held in caged wagons pulled by enormous work-horses. Mahlir told the raiders immediately who he was and gave them the papers to prove it, documents affixed with the emperor's seal showing that he was a Roman citizen and showing that he was a priest of Yahweh, documents also commending him for leading the opposition against Archelaus. This he did in hopes the raiders would answer his questions and tell him if there was a child among the captives. But the language barrier was strong, and the desire among the Parthians to communicate was weak.

Sometimes Mahir thought he could hear the cries of a baby. The moaning of a wolf, likely, or some other beast. Or the shouting out of his mind's creeping madness? They traveled over steep mountain passes, through dark forests, over plateaus, across deserts, landscapes foreign, landscapes so high trees could not grow, so high the soil itself was made of fist-sized rock the color of a gloomy sky. He didn't count the days. There were many. As they entered the city, riding tethered behind a bare-chested Parthian clothed in flowing bearskin, with bobbles of gold and copper hanging from every fierce appendage, Mahlir heard him speak the name "Dey," which he knew from his studies to be the tenth month in the Zoroastrian solar calendar, meaning they had traveled for over one hundred and twenty days. The streets of Ecbatana were overflowing with laughter, and with the sounds of children playing, and with music. Such beautiful music he had never before heard, light and melodious, lifting to the soul, making the emptiness all the more profound. Most of the music came from what sounded like stringed instruments, like harps and lutes, only with a fuller tone, and from drums that gave forth the sound of distant thunder. He had heard tales of Parthian soldiers carrying their huge drums into battle. The unfamiliar rumbling was said to terrify opponents.

It was nightfall by the time they made it into the city proper. Torches and fires burned everywhere, and people were dancing in the streets. The aroma of scented sandalwood and aloe, and of myrrh and frankincense filled the night. To the fire-worshipping Parthians these were the only substances pure enough to be burned. The fires were built upon high pedestals so as to be kept free from contaminants. Nothing impure was ever allowed to touch fire in Parthia. Cooking pots were left one-third empty to guard against boiling over and spilling into the fire. Menstruating women were kept fifteen paces away from any fire, no matter how cold the high mountain air was. No waste or garbage was ever burned. Corpses were never burned; they were placed high in the air, away from fire, away from the earth, to be picked apart by birds.

If it could be said in truth that the Romans embraced the shapes of the square and the circle, it is truer still that Parthia loved only the square, in the boldest form. While Roman and Greek lines were delicate and graceful, Parthian architecture was sturdy and bold. Temples and fortresses jutted into the air with absolute certainty, square and thick, topped with spear-like choppings of balustrades and turrets, and sectioned with long rectangular windows, all of it put together with blocks of sand-colored stone.

The saw-toothed roof lines, and wall perimeters, all were in steppings of sand-colored brick.

That night Mahlir and Shammah were separated. Mahlir was taken to the holiest place in all of Ecbatana, the Supreme Fire Temple of the Magi, open to the air with a great altar at its center, tall and square, wide as the Tiber and as high as an aging cedar, with steps on all four sides leading up to the eternal fire, above which was a winged representation of the unknowable, the omniscient, Ahura Mazda. Mahlir felt the warmth as he passed.

The Temple itself was fortressed around the altar. Its walls were its buildings, tall, thick and square. He was led to the building that made up the back wall. Babylonian winged lions formed its roofline. Inside, through one of the arched doors, a flatter arch than those of the Greeks and Romans, squarish, plainer, not as ornamented – was – a woman?

A Parthian maiden?

Of beauty most exquisite.

She was adorned in translucent cloth from the Orient and in jewels and gold, and in the high headdress of royalty.

An illusion of Mahlir's exhaustion?

Form-fitting folds of her sheer gown fashioned themselves over her figure in intricate angular patterns, and on her long sleeves were colorful bands of triangular embroidery. The gown was neck high but gave such freedom to her breasts that it seemed like there was no covering at all. Hanging between them nearly to her navel, drawing tight the transparent silk, were jewel-laden medallions of black stones and of gold and copper.

She came toward Mahlir. The floor blushed with the flowing of her garment.

She came close enough for him to feel the warmth of her breath and to smell the mint of its scent – and smiled.

To avoid her eyes, Mahlir looked up at the ceiling, a structure patterned in squares within squares, dizzying whirling triangles disappearing into one another. Supporting the roof and spaced on either side of a long walkway were fourteen quadrilobate columns, seven on each side. Parthian soldiers in long tunics stood rigid beside them, bows slung over their shoulders. At the far end of the walkway, at a fifty-pace distance from where the maiden and Mahlir stood, was a fully robed and ornamented Magus, ever watchful of the maiden, ever watchful of Mahlir. The Magus was standing in another doorway, a doorway to oblivion, square, black.

Mahlir's first emotion was embarrassment, because he had traveled the entire distance from Judea unclean, without having bathed, clothed for warmth in the crudely tanned skin of a goat. On his feet were wrappings of the same skin.

At the end of a long silence dominated by the control of the maiden's smile, words came from her parted lips. Said she, in tones dressed in Parthian harshness, but of the Aramaic tongue, that which has its roots in Babylon and Persia, the land of Mahlir's great-great-grandfather's exile, the very land on which they now stood, "Welcome to our kingdom."

Mahlir put his eyes to the floor.

Her bracelets made music as her hand lifted his chin. At first she said nothing. She just looked at him, in a shy way, but strong also, like she knew the power her beauty had over men. Then, again speaking in Aramaic: "I know you are confused. Let that confusion rest in the knowledge that you are soon to become an officer in the court of the Great and Holy Saoshyant." Her smile curved upward more, with one corner of her mouth lifting higher than the other, as if to comfort, and to ask a question at the same time – why would you even consider anything else? – and her eyes widened as the smile widened. That's what gave her the beauty, her ability to comfort and protect with nothing more than the look on her face. "...for the Lord Saoshyant is the savior who will bring peace and truth to the world."

The Magus began walking forward, his hands held together in front of him in the dignity of his priesthood. "A king has been born," he said in Aramaic, with a far thicker accent than that of the maiden. It would have almost been easier to understand him in his own language. "Our prophets have written of his coming."

"What has happened to my servant Shammah?" asked Mahlir. "He was also taken."

The Magus ignored the question. "We are the Magi," he said. "We are the kingmakers, feared and venerated by all in Parthia. We are eighty thousand strong, and possess the power of the earth and the might of the heavens. We own vast parcels of land; we populate entire towns and cities which we govern autonomously; we are half the Parthian Senate. We are the ancient; we are the priestly cast of old; we go back beyond the time of Xerxes and Darius, back beyond the time when your people's blood mixed with ours, when your people lived in exile among our people. For all these years we have installed kings and have given them the blessings of Ahura Mazda."

"Please. My servant. His name is Shammah. I must know what has happened to him."

The Magus ignored the request again, and tipped his head forward, as if blessing Mahlir with his high conical cap, and continued on. "The Chaldeans tell us that the king was born in your land, the land of Judea. They tell us that he grows to manhood in a town called Nazareth. Our prophets have written of his coming; they have prophesied that it would be heralded by miraculous signs in the heavens. We have seen such signs, among them a great star that led us westward to shine its light upon his anointed head."

Mahlir began to speak again, but was stopped by a hand held up by the Magus. "He is the Savior Saoyshyant. Born of virgin woman from the seed of Ahura Mazda, as is set down in the stanzas of the Yast and the Bundahishn. There was a sign in the heavens that appeared within the star cluster known to represent Judea. The Chaldeans told us the meaning, that the child had been born in Judea. At first we thought their interpretations errant. Why would our king be born in a foreign land? But then there came also a heavenly body great and magnificent, an outpouring of light in the night sky a hundred times the size of a normal star. It began to move. Slowly, its movement perceptible only through our sky charts, it began to move westward. We followed it, over long months. The Chaldeans were correct. It led us to Palestine, to Judea, to a house in a town called Bethlehem, to the very doorstep of the child. There is no mistake about it. The Lord Saoshyant, for whom we have waited hundreds, thousands of years, has come to walk among men on earth, to rule over men."

"Please, I must know if my servant is safe. His inability to speak may be interpreted as insolence. It is not. He simply is not able. He was born without voice. He is harmless to you, and has a servant's helpful heart. There is no need for anyone to harm him."

The Magus stepped closer, his hands still held together in front of him. "Worry not. Your servant is safe. And we will continue to provide for his safety, providing you shall help us in our cause of uniting our two peoples once again, and of bringing them under the rule of the Great Lord Saoshyant. We know how influential you are among your people. Do as we ask, help us in our cause, and no harm shall come to your servant. Do as we ask, help us in uniting the Parthians with the Jews, as it once was in the days of Darius and Xerxes, and he shall be made servant in my own household."

By uniting he of course meant conquering.

"How could you possibly know anything about me?" questioned Mahlir. "What makes you think that I, a slave-captive dressed in simple animal skins, could have any influence at all with a government many hundreds of miles away?"

The Magus smiled before continuing. "The eyes of Parthia exist everywhere. In every city of every nation. We have eyes and ears within the heart of your own temple, within the court or the Roman emperor himself.We know of your hatred for Archelaus, young priest, and we know of your successful efforts to have him removed. Righteous hatred is sometimes a good thing. It can give one ambition and unfaltering focus. It can result in deeds to the benefit of men on earth. We find no fault in what you have done. It simply has to be carried to its conclusion of destroying also the kingship of Rome, and of installing the Lord Saoshyant, so that he may begin his infinite reign of peace." The Magus moved another step closer, and used his eyes to penetrate Mahlir like weapons unseen. "It is fortunate that you have been guided here to us. Help us in our cause. Your servant is safe. Do this for us, and I shall make him a servant in my own household. You shall return to Palestine, and work to align the people there in the cause of the great Saoshyant, those that have ears to hear."

Said Mahlir to himself, "Truth be known, I would agree – I would agree to almost anything – if the powers of their magic could restore my child to me, though his mutilated body lies in the dust of the Wilderness...."

The Magus heard Mahlir's words, spoken in silence though they were, and answered him with a smile on his face and fire in his eyes. Eyes of distinction they were, persuasive eyes, difficult to look upon. "If that is all you require," the Magus said, "then you shall serve the Lord Saoshyant, and Parthia, and the world, for the slave traders have children in their wagons. How old is the babe?"

Mahlir would have been terror-stricken, that one human being could have the power to pierce a man's mind and hear thoughts unspoken, but for the fact that here also stood the man with the ability to return to him his treasure.

Mahlir answered in whispered apprehension. "Less than a year."

The Magus clapped his hands and a servant appeared. "Go to the slave traders. Purchase for me all the children that look to be under the age of three; three years because age is hard to judge in one so young. Have them brought to me."

The face of the Magus then smiled victoriously, revealing that an idea had just come to him. "Here is what you shall do," he said, after taking a precious few moments for his thoughts to congeal. "You shall deliver the Nazarene boy to us."

"Huh? What do mean? What are you talking about?"

"You shall deliver him to us, so that we may make him a king. For this he came into the world. He need but accept his inheritance, for he has been born a king, a king of all the world. It comes so ordained from Ahura Mazda and the great kingmakers of Parthia. He would be thirteen years of age by now."

"You expect me to bring you a teenage boy? Are you out of your mind? And just how am I supposed to go about this?"

"You will do it. It is clear that Ahura Mazda has brought you to us for this purpose, and as such Ahura Mazda will set the way before you. Pray upon it. Ahura Mazda will show you how. We will then make an exchange – your son for the Nazarene."

"You expect me to return to Judea, then make my way to Nazareth in the north, find this boy and convince his parents to let me take him over a thousand miles to Ecbatana? A boy I don't even know?"

"Ahhh – but you do know him. He was the boy at the Temple of the Jews who wanted to speak to you, but that you refused, the lost boy who was pushing the cart. Our name for him is the Stone Gardner, because his duty that day was to keep the gardens of stone polished and free from dirt and grime. His given name is Yeshua-ben-Yosef. His father is a stone mason and carpenter."

"How could you have possibly known about that?"

"The eyes of Parthia exist everywhere. We do not care how you go about it, by be-friending the lad or by treachery – Ahura Mazda will guide your steps and give you courage – just deliver us the boy, so that we may make him the king he was born to be, and so that we may deliver to you your son, and so that both nations can be reunited once again, in conquest of the Roman Empire. Babylon rises. Prophecies fulfilled."

Hope jumped within Mahlir and turned his skin warm and caused his voice to tremble. "You need not bring every child," Mahlir told him. "Mine you will know by a birth sign of an upward pointed arrowhead over one eye, and by the scar that runs from his neck to his loins."

"There, you have heard it," the Magus said. "Got then and find me the child."

The servant left and the Magus proceeded to flow with homilies about destiny and about the Parthian conqueror known as Saoshyant, born a Jew, because it pleases Ahura Mazda that the two nations be united once again. Mahlir barely heard it. His mind was focused on the hope.

Finalized the Magus: "The very fact that you are standing here in our presence in the Royal Palace should suggest that you have a guided purpose. It is by the will of Ahura Mazda that you are here. It is by no accident that you traveled half the habitable earth to our doorsteps. Do you think it coincidence that a roving band of Parthian outlaws, thieves and slave-traders despised even by our own kind, should take you captive and travel with you these many miles to our very doorsteps? We were waiting, expecting another sign, watching for it. And so it was that your captors came telling us that they had in their slave cages one of the principal men of Judea, more than that, that they held the warrior who toppled the great Archelaus, and could prove it with the seal of Caesar. We paid handsomely for you. Think on it, young priest. Do you really imagine it coincidence that in all of Parthia, the vastness of which exceeds Rome and all its occupations, the slave traders came here to this place, to us? One moment we are appealing to Ahura Mazda for a sign on how to unite the two empires, Israel and Parthia, so that a pathway might be laid for his ascension, the next you are here."

"I will do this that you ask. Be assured. I will succeed. For my son I will do this. Be tender with him when you find the babe. I will return with the Nazarene boy." Mahlir resolved to mask his thoughts, in case the Magus truly could see into his mind. He had no intention of kidnapping a thirteen-year-old boy. How could he do such a thing? He would mask his thoughts, in case his son truly was alive, in case the messenger really did return with the child. He would do so by turning his eyes to the maiden. He began to picture himself in her arms, swallowing her breath, feeling her breasts against him, feeling her melt around him. The Magus with his mind-piercing ability would never be able to see through it, so powerful was the lust. He would never be able to see that Mahlir's true thoughts were to never again mingle in affairs political where men are divided against men, where blood flows in the name of governments, in the name of ideologies, for the sake of boundary lines, for the sake of a good name, for the sake of a different religious belief.

The Magus smiled, as though pleased at what he saw, or what he thought he saw, and gestured to the dark-eyed beauty, so willing, it seemed, to be given to Mahlir. "Take the virgin, young priest, and sleep well. May the blessings of Ahura Mazda be with you, and ever ward off the evils of Ahriman. On the morrow you shall embrace your child, the flesh of your flesh. And you shall return to the land of the Jews to bring the Nazarene boy to us – Ahura Mazda will show you how – and the pleasures of a thousand virgins shall be yours, in the great future of Parthia under the Mighty Lord Saoshyant."

The Magus formed again satisfaction on his bearded face, and tipped his head in Mahlir's direction and backed away. The Magus seemed in that moment to be harmless, worthy of trust, fatherly, in a regal sort of way, with his mustache so prominent and twisted into points, with his beard so straight and square, with his tall conical cap ringed about with images of the moon and stars, hair puffed out from beneath it in typical Parthian fashion, with his long-sleeved tunic of bright red over which was worn a purple cloak long to below the knees and fastened at the neck by a round broach of gold, and with his puffy white trousers fluted in stripings of purple, and with his necklace shining of stones and jewels, and with his armlets of silver and bracelets of gold. He backed up to the inner doorway and disappeared into its square curtain of black. A trail of incense drifted out the instant he passed, as if he had simply turned to smoke.

Mahlir was left with the virgin, and with the guards and their bows following. "What is beyond the door?" he asked.

"The Hollow of the Chaldeans," responded one of the guards reverently, fearfully almost. "No one enters there."

The virgin led him to a place on the mountainside where from a stone-wrapped veranda he could see the entire Ecbatana valley, in itself a mountain top, its rocky hills and rivers captured in low-lying clouds, their ripples awash in moonlight. And again he defiled himself with a woman not his wife. Again Mahlir placed his seed in someone else. Again he dishonored Rachel. May she rest in peace.

CHAPTER 25

THE HOLLOW OF THE CHALDEANS

THE PARTHIAN EMPIRE – ECBATANA

After it was over, as the virgin slept – though he doubted she was a virgin; she certainly wasn't one now – he made his way to the Chaldean doorway, hoping for news of his son. He could hear the sounds of the guards following him. He could hear the rustling of their tunics and the soft chafing of the bows on their shoulders. He could glimpse them now and then, though mostly they kept out of sight. They stopped outside the doorway, going no further than its entrance.

Seeing no one outside, Mahlir stepped into its blackness.

As the darkness enveloped him the scent of incense came, and it calmed, welcomed. A light was flickering from somewhere, a much smaller light than those illuminating the streets and the Temple halls where the shadows of the night had been almost all conquered by the many fires and torch flames dancing to Ahura Mazda.

He had no fear at that point, only the hope that soon he would see his son. He moved forward, a half a step at a time. The light grew brighter. He could see it was coming from a lamp on a stone table, wherefrom struggled a flame so fragile he thought at any moment it would vanquish itself. Then the ruler of darkness would have him. Ahriman? Was that the name the Parthians had for him?

The first thing the light of the lamp allowed him to see was an eagle perched upon a bust of King Phraates, Parthia's former monarch. The magnificent bird opened its mouth as if to screech a warning, though no sound came out, and arched its wings and powered a rush of air, a force that would have lifted it into flight had it not been anchoring itself with its talons. Then Mahlir's adjusting eyes saw, sitting at the table, a Magus, one much older than the first. This one had white hair and a white beard, though he was dressed the same, the same conical cap emblazoned with stars and half-moons, the same type of cloak, the same puffy pants.

This Magus was writing, copying the words of one half-unrolled scroll onto another.

Mahlir stopped when he was within an arm's length of the old man, afraid he might startle this whimsical character made ever the more comical by the flickering of the ghostly lamplight that only half illuminated the wrinkled forehead and the absolute snow white of his beard. But the Magus was the one to speak first, without looking up, causing the eagle to again power a rush of air. "Sit by my side, young Mahlir," he said in flawless Hebrew, with the tracings of an accent not quite Parthian, a more fluid accent, softer, as though he had learned the language from somewhere else. "I am Belteshazzar," he said. "There is a stone bench here to my right for you to sit on. Please. I wish to tell you a story. Let me first read to you from the Avesta, a tale you have heard before, though from different writings."

When Belteshazzar fixed his eyes on Mahlir it was with a gentle look, and with a grandfatherly smile that warmed the soul, as if welcoming someone who was a part of the family. He removed his cap, showing a bald head crowning tufts of white poking out over his ears. Then he lifted himself with care. With the lamp in hand, casting in front of him a wavering semicircle of its light, he made his way to a wall pocketed full of scrolls and removed another. "We begin this story by opening to the eighth fragment of the thirty-second stanza of the Bundahishn," he said, untying and spreading out the parchment. "– where an angel has been given a seed of divine origin:

"The angel Neryosang received the brilliance and strength of that seed, delivered it with care to the angel Anahid and in time will blend it with a mother. Nine thousand, nine hundred, and ninety-nine, and nine myriads of the guardian spirits of the righteous are entrusted with its protection, so that the demons may not injure it.

"Young Mahlir, that time has come. Ahura Mazda has chosen that mother. She is the Hebrew maiden called by your people Mary. She is the unsoiled Eredat-fedria –" At the very mention of the name the elderly Magus bowed his head and untied and retied his holy waist cord, an obsessive ritual of the deeply religious Parthians, and intoned from the Avesta:"'We worship the Fravashi of the holy maid Eredat-fedri, who is called Visap-tauravairi.'– and she has conceived and brought forth the savior. I will tell you a secret, young Mahlir. Though I am a Magus of high stature and have been so for many years, like you, by birth I am a Jew. Like you, I was taken captive by the Parthians, called then the Babylonians. Kings come and go, regimes rise and fall, and I rose and fell with them. I went back to Palestine for a time after I was given my freedom, because they were my people. But then I came back, because these too were my people. But I digress." Belteshazzar was speaking with disarming sincerity. His words were coming with a sense of honor, of trustworthiness, and with a twist of his gentle mouth that seemed to reveal he would rather be telling a funny story.

"From the beginning, our writings did foretell the coming of the Savior Saoshyant," he said. "The mighty Saoshyant, for whom the world pleads, walks among men on earth. He was born a Jew, in your land, young Mahlir, the land the Judea. This I know. For I have seen him. I have placed my feet within the sphere of his radiance." Belteshazzar raised a finger as if to impart an idea, with an unspoken hope that Mahlir might be the one to understand. "It is written that the Lord Saoshyant –" He dropped his eyes and untied and retied his holy waist cord. "'We worship the Fravashi of the Holy King Saoshyant the Beneficent One, who is the Holy Astvatereta. – comes as a conqueror, one against whom no foe shall be able to stand. Greater than Darius, greater than the Caesars, greater than the Macedonian. So great is he, with purposes so grand – "

"You need not say anymore," interjected Mahlir. "I already told the other Magus yesterday that I agree."

It confused Belteshazzar. "Mmm? Agree to what?"

"To return to Israel and bring him back. Somehow I will do it. I will figure it out. I just want my son returned to me."

Belteshazzar chuckled deep in his throat. "Bring who back?"

"Si-hoo, or whatever his name is. The one we are talking about. I was told yesterday, by the other Magus, that he would retrieve my son from the slave cages if I would travel to Palestine and bring back this man you call, uh –"

"Saoshyant," rescued Old Belteshazzar, with a chuckle that turned to full blow laughter. "I don't want you to kidnap him. I want you to learn from him."

"Agreed then. Whatever your wish. Find my son and I will be your servant. I will wash and kiss your ass, if it be your wish."

"Yeshua the Saoshyant comes to earth to be your servant. If only I could make you understand."

"Where is my son?"

"I will help you. But first you must tell me about yourself. I know nothing of you except through a dream. A Fravashi came to me while I slept and told me about you. He told me that the slave traders have someone from the land of the Hebrews in their wagons who has a destiny with the great Saoshyant in spreading the good news of mankind's inheritance. I told the others of the Magi about my dream –" He smiled and held his arms up and chortled again. "And here you are."

And so Mahir told the story, of how he escaped into the desert with his son, and of the desert shepherd called Simeon whose hands held the power of healing, and of how Mahlir went to Rome to plead for annexation, and of how he returned to find the camp pillaged, which was when he was taken by the slave traders.

Belteshazzar stroked his snow-white beard and spoke as much to himself as to Mahlir. "Mmmm. Could it be that I misunderstood? Could it be that the Fravashi was talking about your son, and not about you?" He stroked his beard again. "Yes, I think I might be able to help you," he said. And he picked up his pen and wrote upon a sheet of papyrus, then tore away the excess and rolled it into a very small scroll and attached it to one of the eagle's legs and said something to the bird in a language Mahlir did not understand. The eagle screeched and flew from its perch. With two mighty powerings of its wings it flew out the door and up through the open roof of the Temple. Someone from the outside looking at the doorway would have thought it a divine event, to see an eagle bursting out of the blackness and flying upward into the sky.

Belteshazzar then looked at Mahlir with kindness in his aged eyes. "All that can be done has been done," he said. "Now listen to my words. Let me try to explain. Sinaces and I are two very different people. He told you that the Saoshyant comes as a conqueror? Indeed he does, but not a conqueror of flesh and blood. So great is Saoshyant, with purposes so grand, with authority from realms so lofty, that most who await him will not recognize him. Even among the Magi there will be those who will refuse the gift he brings. So it is with Sinances, and others of his ilk who wish to entangle you in the political and military objectives of men on earth. Did you know, young Mahlir, that Sinaces traveled with me to see the child? But we saw two different kings, he and I, when we knelt before him and gave him our gifts. He saw only a king of men. Hear my words, young Mahlir. The Lord Saoshyant comes not as an earthly warrior to do the battles of mortal men. He comes from the realms of the Angels and Fravashis to lead us in battles of the spirit that will free mortal men, that will make men more than men.

He comes with weapons forged from materials not of this world. From the words of your own prophet Isaiah: "...It is I who created the blacksmith who fans the coals into flame and forges a weapon fit for its work. And it is I who have created the destroyer to work havoc; no weapon forged against you will prevail."

Belteshazzar laboriously lifted his body again and walked to the wall and replaced the scroll, then finished his story. "We saw his star. We followed it. This was thirteen years ago, as measured by the twelve-month calendar of Zoroaster. The child would now be approaching the strength of his manhood. The star led us to the very doorstep of the child. But as we were laying our gifts before him, King Herod was issuing a decree. Not knowing the exact age of the child, knowing from us only the approximate time of the star's first appearance, he decreed that all children under the age of two be killed. Had we known that Herod would have done such a thing, we would have stayed in Parthia."

That had been the motive! For the massacre that had taken the life of Rachel's younger brother!

Said Belteshazzar, in seeming response to Mahlir's thoughts, as though he too had the ability to go uninvited into Mahlir's mind, as though he had snared the remembrances of Rachel's tale of the slaughter of the innocents and had seen Mahlir's doubts about the child's survival, "The child escaped the wrath of Herod that day by fleeing into Egypt. His father was visited in a dream by one of the Holy Savior's Fravashis, who told hm to take his son and his family into the land of the Pharos until the danger had passed."

Mahlir was fidgeting, his mind absorbing only bits of the aged Magus' wisdom, but Belteshazzar continued, nonetheless. "We are the Magi. We have existed among our people throughout the ages. We make up half the Parthian Senate; the other half are the Sophis, the 'Wise Men' as they are called, the temporal chiefs of our land. Together with the males of the Royal House we rule, and we nominate and install kings. None in the land are so powerful and so revered, and so feared, as the Magi." He was not saying it as a person of power, but rather as a humble explainer, as if he were embarrassed by the status, maybe even a little amused. His lips tended to particularly quiver when he was amused at what he was saying.

Mahlir began to fight the sudden need to let his eyelids fall. It was overpowering. He had gotten very little sleep in the past few days. "Why do they call this the Hollow of the Chaldeans?" he asked.

Belteshazzar was disappointed beyond measure, spoke the look of his thoughts, that Mahlir's mind was so far away from the essence of what he wanted to impart. "The Chaldeans, as spoken of here, are those among the Magi who possess knowledge of hidden things, and powers of the awakening soul." He said it while breathing out a sigh. "But to bring forth these powers before the soul is ready is to bring about a torrent of evil, a demon uncontrollable. Sadly, such is the case with some of those among us. These false Chaldeans, while they in their deception think they are serving the highest in themselves, while they think they possess knowledge, in truth serve only Ahriman."

"I care not for such talk," was all Mahlir said.

"If a priest of Yahweh cares not for matters of the spirit, what then does he care about?"

"About my son. I care about my son."

"You are a good man, Mahlir-of-Matthias," said Belteshazzar. "I hope I have at least planted a seed."

Mahlir's head dropped forward seeking slumber, then jerked up again. His anxious anticipation had robbed him of all sleep the night before. Now his body was demanding it, finding it in the tormented slumber of misshapen images, each one having some type of visage of his infant son, and of the color yellow. Why yellow he never knew.

When he awoke, Belteshazzar was gone. Mahlir had no idea how long he had slept, ten hours at least, because it was night. He could see the puffs of it as he breathed, could see it drift through the light flooding in from the back of him. Light? Light? From the back of him? Yellow light! Not the diffused silver of the outer moon and stars.

"The Hollow of the Chaldeans is forbidden," came the voice of Sinaces. It had a strange quickness, revealing that he was thoroughly pleased that he had caught Mahir beyond the threshold. "Do you know what the Court of Parthia once decreed as just punishment for a man who transgressed the laws of our religion? The man was a keeper of the flame. There was a storm, and he allowed the holy fire of Ahura Mazda to be extinguished. He was stripped of clothing and bound hand and foot, and his skin was sliced, and he was tied in a treetop to be picked apart by birds. But you need not worry. We of the Magi will protect you. We will give you our promise not to reveal what you have done. You, of course, in your gratitude, will promise to help us in our cause and bring us the boy."

"I have already told you I would do that," Mahlir said flatly. "I have not changed my mind."

Continued Sinances, "And we will keep our end of the bargain. Your son shall be reunited with you." The Magus spoke this even as the servant was running up to him, having returned from his mission of finding the child. But the servant's arms were empty, and upon his face was fear.

"My Lord," the servant said. "The child you sent me after, the one with the birthmark over his eye and the scar from his neck to his loins, has been taken in by the Royal Household."

"Then retrieve him from the Royal Household!" bellowed Sinances.

The servant was speaking in Greek, because he was a slave from that land, which allowed Mahlir to clearly understand what was being said. "'Tis not possible," the servant replied, trembling out the words. "The queen has taken pity on the babe and has taken him to her bosom. She vows to raise the child as her own. The king has placed his seal on the matter. They have named him Orodes. It seems the queen is quite taken by the child. Being barren herself, she wants desperately to have a son. She views the child as an answer to her prayers."

Spewed Sinaces in the Persian tongue – Mahlir had learned enough of the language during the enslavement of his journey to know that Sinaces was saying something to the effect of – "Fool! Why do you speak in Greek? Do you not know that Greek is the universal language? Do you not know that the Jew hears every word you say?" And the Magus immediately ordered the servant's execution by a horrible means.

All was lost. In that single moment, in hearing of his son's good fortune, Mahlir's heart, his mind, his soul, passed away from him like smoke from a jar, in a single, simple breath, along with his life's purpose. Fate had brought to his son someone better. Clearly Belteshazzar was behind it. That must have been the message carried by the eagle, a request from the Magi that the king and queen take the child in. At first Mahlir was angry at the betrayal. But then how could he be? Would he deny his son a kingdom? And the safety of a castle and personal bodyguards? His son had become a prince. All was lost, yet gained. For certain his son was now protected.

Mahlir had not realized it at the time, but Belteshazzar had saved his son from harm. Sinaces had no such concern. Mahlir would not have been able to keep the child safe, even if he did return with the Nazarene boy. Apart from the protection of the royal household, the child would have been doomed.

The father would remember the son always. But not so the son. For the son there was a new father, someone better. Eli would never have his legacy. A promise broken. Nor would Mahlir's father, the great Matthias, have a legacy. The legacy now belonged to the King of Parthia. So it is when God punishes a man for his sins. It is swift and severe.

No more was there a need for Mahlir in this world.

The depths of the sea would be his home, but Sinances would not know of his plan of suicide, because Mahlir would mask his despair with the look of a man who has good fortune.

"But worry not," said Mahlir. "I will still keep my end of the bargain. I will still travel to Israel and return with the young son of the stone mason.

"Providing," he said, "that you guarantee the part of the bargain that you still have control over, the safety of my servant. I must know that my servant who is mute will be protected. Swear to me by the holy name of Ahura Mazda that Shammah my servant will serve in your household and be treated well. By Ahura Mazda himself I want you to swear."

Responded Sinaces, "By the holy name of Ahura Mazda I so swear."

A Parthian's word before God is irrevocable, especially the word of a Magus. Even if Sinaces were to discover that he had been tricked, that Mahlir's true thoughts had been something different, the Magus would still be bound by his promise. Even if Mahlir's four armed escorts were to report back what they had seen as they neared Jerusalem, Mahlir standing on a cliff overlooking the Dead Sea, then tumbling into the water from the thrust of his own sword, still the Magus would be bound to his promise.

CHAPTER 26

NINETEEN YEARS IN QUMRAN

ISRAEL – A COMPOUND IN THE JUDEAN WILDERNESS

Whatever lay beyond – nothingness, good, evil, bliss, pain, nonexistence – it had to be better than the chattels of life, of existence within the confines of a prison of flesh and blood, of existence within the inescapable walls of the human mind, walls built of demons, perpetrators of sorrow, indestructible, stronger than brick, sturdier than stone.

But where was this place called death? Still it eluded him. The strike of the water shook the breath from his body. When he was able to draw it again, he found he could take in only water. His lungs struggled against all sensibilities. Yet still he lived.

The salt stung his exposed abdominal cavity.

He tried to swim, tried to scream, but was unable to move, unable to utter so much as a sound, unable to see. A black cloud had roiled up to surround him – blood from his ripped open torso? – and shrouded him in its warmth, tried to take him, to wrap him in its tender darkness. But it could not, because of the salt, because of its buoyancy, and because of the sun; the sun's brilliance carved through to illuminate even death. Shock pulses were thudding through his body, swelling him, shrinking him.

The blessing of an icy current found him and tried to pull him to the bottom, a thing alive, a friend, but even that was not successful. Again because of the buoyancy. The current could do no more than hold him a hand's breadth beneath the surface. Mahlir was face up, staring into the blindness of the sun, its brilliance magnified by the crystalline sparkles he was looking through.

Not even plants grew here. Yet for Mahlir the Dead Sea was struggling to give life.

Soon there was no longer the need to fight for breath, a relief immeasurable. There was not even the sensation of cold. The blazing sun, knifing through the water, seemed to suddenly be changing the cold to warmth, and the pain to euphoria. The shock pulses were now pleasant to experience.

Swelling, shrinking, swelling, shrinking. His entire body was swelling and shrinking.

Then the sun and its streaming brilliance became the far-off face of a man, a man of power, a man of kindness.

Mahlir began to float upward – dead or alive he didn't know, didn't think to care, so pleasant was the experience – upward toward the visage. The face of Yahweh?

The man's hair and clothing were the rays of the sun, and his eyes were pure kindness. No other needs had Mahlir, than to look at this man. For a great length he did so – until he began to sink backwards, back into sensation, back into the pain, a dull thudding pain in his chest and stomach. He began to taste blood in his mouth.

But the image remained, of the man of kindness, with a long beard and with hair falling loosely over his shoulders, untrimmed like the Zadokites of old, the sons of Aaron who were forbidden by the Law to cut the edges of their beards or the hair at the sides of their heads.

Said the man, "For a time we thought you were dead."

"Better for me had I died," Mahlir finally managed, through pain now present. "And better for the world."

The man spoke kindly. "For those who die by their own hand there is no Shiva, no tomb, no remembrance."

"My deeds are better left un-remembered."

The man answered by introducing himself. "I am Elkanar the Essene. You are being cared for in our community. You are fortunate. Your blade pierced none of your vital parts."

For the next nineteen years Mahlir lived among the Sons of Light, protected from temptation, growing in body and spirit, replacing old beliefs with new. Through the solitude of his meditations he made atonement for his sins, as best he could. How does one atone to those no longer living?

"What is that?" Mahlir asked one day, after having passed it a thousand times.

"That," Elkanar said, "is the receptacle containing the Crown of Kind David."

To Mahlir's utter surprise, Elkanar picked it up and handed it to him, as if inviting him to look inside. It was not as heavy as Mahlir had always thought it would be. It had been sitting unceremoniously on a shelf between two scrolls, unguarded. No golden pedestal, no winged seraphs looking down. It was a chest of the appropriate size, for a small crown at least, if it sat atop the head, certainly not big enough to contain a crown of solid gold that encircled the head. Of Acacia wood, the chest looked to be. It was banded by strips of brass and polished to a shine. Other than that, it was nothing special. Mahlir held it for a time, then carefully put it back. It was sealed shut by an application of wax, so Mahlir didn't ask to look inside. But it sat there for Mahlir to look at every time he passed it, which was at least a dozen times a day, and became a reminder of the chaos he had left behind. No one among the Essenes had ever looked inside. "Then how do you know it's in there, if no one has ever looked inside?" Mahlir asked Elkanar. Elkanar shrugged. "Does it really matter?" was the answer, as if it were completely irrelevant to his life. In time it became irrelevant to Mahlir as well. In time it became as common as the chairs and the tables and the shelves that the eye sees but never focuses on. Once he asked Elkanar, "Is there really a talent's worth of gold in there, as the legend says?" Elkanar's answer was logical. "Of course not. A full talent of gold would weigh more than a man could lift, let alone wear on his head. It was the poet's way of saying its value is beyond what gold can measure." And he asked Elkanar about the Fire, the power that would strike one dead. "Is it true, is there really such a power?" Elkanar answered with a smile and a dismissive wave of his hand, as if to say, "Maybe there is, maybe there isn't."

In Qumran Mahlir learned things that cannot be spoken of, deep things that were not even taught in the Temple, things that are never written down except within the envelope of symbols and stories. He was ready, Elkanar told him one day. "How can I be ready?" Mahlir said. "And ready for what?"

Elkanar was silent, until his mouth curved into a smile and his head began to nod up and down. "For the next step on the journey."

"How can I be ready? – I'm not sure I even believe in God."

"People who believe in God have destroyed half the world in the process," replied Elkanar.

Mahlir grew to maturity there, apart from the world, safe. In Qumran no one was pressuring him to rise to a position of prominence. In Qumran all men were equal. There were no temptations of the flesh. There were no women. All were men, and all were priests, and celibate, and all lived by the Law. And none had weapons. Mahlir never bothered to ask what had been done with his sword. Perhaps it still lay at the bottom of the Dead Sea. No matter – there, within those walls, he had no need for it. The members were committed to nonviolence and to the brotherhood of all. The nonviolence extended to their animal brethren as well. The priests at Qumran practiced no animal sacrifice. They ate only vegetables and drank only water. In the words of Elkanar – "...in understanding that life must survive by the consumption of life, we choose to kill and eat the least sensitive form of life. As Yahweh himself declared, as written in the scroll of Hosea, "*...I desire mercy, not sacrifice.*" The Sons of Light used the products of animals, certainly, but not at the expense of the animals' wellbeing. They used milk from goats and wool from the bodies of sheep. From their hides they made clothing and scrolls, but only after the animal had lived out the natural course of its life. Within those walls Mahlir forgot about the struggles on the outside, of revolutions and wars, and of death and pain, and heartbreak.

He was free from the world and its sin.

But evil crept into the sanctity of Qumran just the same, shadows stealing through cracks and slipping under doorways to torment. Sexual desires. Emptiness. Longings for a wife and children. And, at times, jealousy, over the presence of two young men, men by law but boys in truth, lauded by the Essenes as destined for deeds extraordinaire. It seemed all men were equal in Qumran, the city of mysteries, the city of light, with the exception of these two boys, both in their latter teen years, both related to one another, one from Nazareth, the other from Jerusalem. The boy from Jerusalem was called John, Yohanan in the Hebrew, son of Zechariah. The boy from Nazareth was called Jesus, Yeshua in the Hebrew, son of a carpenter and master stone mason called Yosef, Yeshua-ben-Yosef.

It was in Mahlir's fifth year at Qumran that the boys arrived. The elders discovered them in Jerusalem in the Temple where they were being schooled to be teachers of the Law and announced them as ones who were much more than teachers; they were ones of many goings out. Here, according to the elders, were the expected Messiahs, the Anointed Ones themselves. The elders at Qumran were among those who believed there to be two Messiahs, one royal, one priestly, as it was in the days of David. The Qumran fathers believed the Messiahs would come from their midst, this because the fathers believed themselves to be the ones to whom Yahweh would reveal his mysteries, the ones to whom had been given the keys to all things hidden.

"*...the Lord shall raise up from Levi as it were a Priest, and from Jacob as it were a King, god and man. So shall He save all the Gentiles, and the race of Israel,*" states the scroll of Enoch.

Also from Enoch,

"The Most High shall visit the earth; and He shall come as a man, with men eating and drinking."

and,

"...a star shall arise to you from Jacob in peace, and a man shall arise from my seed, like the Son of Righteousness, walking with the sons of men in meekness and righteousness, and no sin shall be found in Him. And the heavens shall be opened above Him, to shed forth the blessings of the Spirit from the Holy Father; and he shall shed forth a spirit of grace upon you, and you shall be unto Him sons in truth, and you shall walk in His commandments, the first and the last."

Also spoken about was one called the Teacher of Righteousness. The Teacher of Righteousness was different than the Messiahs, and shrouded in mystery. He was to be the one who would lead the way on the final stages of the journey, *"where there are no guideposts," "where no teachers can point the way."* The students at Qumran never met the Teacher of Righteousness. Nor were they told who he was or would be, or when he might come, or how they would know him. "He comes when the student is ready," was all they were told. One time, when Mahlir was puzzling over the enigma of atonement, how one could possibly atone to people who are dead, Elkanar replied, "The Teacher will come and point the way, when the student is ready." Mahlir once asked Elkanar if he, Elkanar, was the Teacher of Righteousness. Elkanar just laughed and repeated again, "The Teacher will come and make himself known when the student is ready." The same answer was given when he asked Elkanar if the Teacher of Righteousness was Yohanan or Yeshua.

It deeply offended Mahlir, the adoration showered upon these boys, how far above the others the elders placed them.

Most annoying to Mahlir – Yohanan and Yeshua came and went as they pleased, at times staying away for months at a time, and always they were permitted to return, their priestly status held intact. Sometimes Mahlir thought Yeshua was someone he knew from somewhere but couldn't quite place, because of the smell of alabaster that hung in the air whenever he was around, like the purity that comes from freshly cut stone, like the way an artist smells while sculpting; but mixed with the sweetness of a Galilean hillside in spring. He had smelled that very thing before, from somewhere.

He did Mahlir no wrong, this Yeshua, in word or deed. That in itself made Mahlir's jealousy grow. And it made him ashamed. Mahlir wondered in his quieter musings if maybe Yeshua was the child the Magi had spoken of, for Yeshua had in fact been born in Bethlehem at a time when the Magi had seen the star.

Then one day they left for good, first Yohannan, going where no one knew, some said to live the life of an ascetic in the desert; then a year later Yeshua left, going also into the desert, where he fasted forty days and forty nights. This Mahlir knew because Yeshua told him upon his return. He returned just long enough to offer a final goodbye to everyone, and to thank the priests and the leaders for their graciousness, and for their friendship, and for their devotion and help, but what Yeshua was really doing was renouncing them, severing association with his brothers of light, brothers with whom he had spent twelve years of his life. Some said he had become ill in the desert, to the point of death, and that it affected his mind. But he looked stronger than ever, and in his eyes was a depth Mahlir had not seen in any man, and his face bore the countenance of a beauty beyond beauty, a softness, no, a radiance, no, that too falls short. A power? Whatever it was, it seemed to still Mahlir's jealousy. It almost seemed to be a thing of physical substance, a softness around his head, an ever so faint yellow haze.

Yeshua did one thing more before leaving. He asked Mahlir to come with him. Mahlir declined.

Less than a month later Mahlir also took his leave, but it was not to travel and live in the desert; it was to venture into the temptations of the outside world, away from the safety of the unassuming blocks of yellow stone that for more than half his life had been his home. To those on the outside, Qumran was probably akin to a prison, a beautiless cluster of buildings on a desert mesa wherein a man starves himself of the pleasures of life. An eagle flying overhead would see Qumran as no more than the domes of the landscape itself. To Mahlir, those sand-colored buildings were places of refuge from the pleasures of life. The twinkling of the water rolling through the ground-level aqueduct, pure and clean, and the ripples it made upon entering the wide pool by the entrance, and the wave of cool it lifted up, and the studious smell of the scriptorium where he spent hours upon hours copying documents onto papyrus and leather, sometimes etching them into copper, and the scent and feel of the desert heat in the early morning as it began to melt away the night, and the silent sounds of the wind, simple things, and so much more, were Mahlir's pleasures, his refuge. There in Qumran he gave no pain; no pain came to him. And the writings and the teachings of the inner mysteries were there, open and uncloaked, to give him comfort – true or untrue – to give him peace.

But Mahir left, and he did not even know why. Maybe because of the jealousy. It is a biting stinging thing, jealousy, and it brings no pleasure. The jealousy was there even after Yeshua left, because still Mahlir was nothing in the eyes of the elders. Mahlir was the one who was the Zadokite. He was the one who was the son of Matthias. He was the one who had been advisor to Caesar himself. He had been responsible for ridding Judea of the evil king called Archelaus. Yet at Qumran he was nothing, which is what he wanted to be, he thought.

He left for a place he had been only once in his life, a place of incredible green – long spires of dark green trees, puffs of lighter green, hanging vines, fountains – a place that would welcome him, because he was one of her citizens, if he could just get there. He had no money. He had entered Qumran with nothing, he departed with nothing…except for a little box on the shelf between the scrolls. Before he left he stopped to look at it, and as he did Elkanr handed it to him, and entrusted him with a responsibility. "Take this," he said of the box containing the crown. "Find Yeshua, your brother in light. Give it to him."

"But why?"

"Because it will be a reminder of who he is and what he must do." Elkanar was insistent, and so Mahlir agreed. There were steel loops on the copper bands that ornamented the box, allowing him to secure it to his waist-sash.

The journey to Rome was lengthy and fraught with poverty. Somehow the money and the means always came, from doing whatever he had to do, pottery, working in the fields, serving in the various Temples along the way as a scribe, sometimes as a stone mason, often for only food and a place to stay the night. Yeshua had taught him the basics of masonry, so he could at least serve as an apprentice. It was a complex science often involving advanced mathematics to calculate load-bearing limits. Mahlir was exceptional at squaring stones. When he came away with extra money, he used it for travel. Anything beyond that he gave to the beggars, because he was near to being what they are. And still he did not open the box. Just knowing that a fortune in gold lay within his grasp gave him the confidence to find a way. Sometimes it was hard, resisting the temptation to make use of the contents of the box, not steal it, invest it, triple its value. Then he could give twice as much to Yeshua, even have a smith make a bigger crown. That way he could give Yeshua a crown *and* money and have some for himself as well. Mahlir laughed aloud at the thought, troubling even to the sparrows that danced overhead, and said aloud to them, "Settle down now, I'm only joking. Besides, if it really is what it's supposed to be, it's protected by the Shekinah Fire, the very breath of God. Just to look upon it would risk death." Still he could not figure out why it was so light, if it contained gold.

In Joppa he consigned himself as a stevedore aboard a grain barge bound for Rome. The opportunity presented itself and he worried another may never come, though he had not yet found Yeshua. He'd just have to give him the crown later.

Things had changed in the decade and a half he had been away. There were more buildings in Rome, taller buildings, more magnificent buildings, more Temples, more fountains, more people. He approached the Praetorians of the place where he was told could be found the Emperor – his Latin had improved over the years, because of the extensive reading he had done while in Qumran – and asked to be announced to Augustus.

They laughed. Augustus died long ago, they told him. His stepson Tiberius was now emperor.

And they sent him on his way, in his poverty.

As he went he passed a great statue thrice its human size, of Augustus sitting upon a gilded curule chair. Inanimate. Frozen in yesterday. Next to Augustus on the same pedestal was a smaller statue. Of the emperor's beloved pet, Jesus-of-Sie, renamed Anchises, in honor of the mortal man who slept with the goddess Venus and fathered the grandfather of Romulus and Remus. Mahlir would have put his hand on the stone of the animal's representation – the urge to do so was overpowering – but it was up too high. He touched the pedestal instead, in itself the size of a small house. There was a spot on Mahlir's stomach that felt suddenly warm, something from long, long ago.

The golden domes and gabled roofs, and the bronze statues, and the gardens wherein strolled the Lords of the World, and the fountains of beauty, these things mocked Mahlir, because he had the audacity to think that their home could be his home. He was walking amongst it all, touching it, yet it was as unreal as smoke, as distant as the storm clouds far above, their jagged sun-splattered edges threatening yet beautiful.

He wandered aimlessly. Even the bread dole programs, available to all citizens, were useless to Mahlir. Without the testimony of Augustus how was he to prove he was a citizen? Rain started falling, huge drops exploding upon the stone of the pavement, glittering gemstones, like an ocean above had been turned upside down, thousands of raindrops, millions. They gave relief to the hot air, and to the emptiness in Mahlir's soul. They seemed to bind him to the people, to the throngs, the massive flow of heads moving through the avenues with no pattern or direction, and to the shopkeepers with their wares spread out into the streets, though he had no money to buy what they were selling. People were turning to one another and talking about it, this most peculiar and wonderful downpour, laughing about it. No one sought shelter or even attempted to cover their heads. In moments their clothes were wet and their feet ankle high in puddles. It was pleasant, cool enough to ease the heat, not cool enough to chill. Mahlir put his face into a pool of a fountain and drank to quench his thirst – and saw something. A name was written on the fountain's base as a part of a poem, an ode to a visiting dignitary. Long moments passed before his mind processed recognition of the name. The fountain's base was perfectly square at the bottom, then crudely sculpted into nonsensical shapes that evolved upward into the creation of two muscled gods of the sea holding upon their shoulders a giant clam's shell out of which rolled the purity of their essence.

On its base, dry because the water spilled over without touching it, were scripted and chiseled many things, as is common in Rome, writings, announcements, verses of the heart, political statements, among them these words:

Welcome Orodes
Great Wolf Prince of Parthia
With all your power,
Still you come to the
Children of the Gods for
Knowledge and Refinement.

His son, now a prince, was somewhere in Rome?

Better that Mahlir forget him.

He walked slowly away, aimlessly, his feet tired, his back sore. He had intended to turn right at an intersection but turned left instead, to give comfort to a wailing child that had tripped in play. He picked the child up and dusted him off and assured him that he was fine, then continued walking on down the same street to the bottom of Palatine Hill and found himself in an unruly crowd that had encircled a thing despicable, two men fighting. The people were yelling, taking bets, straining to see. The bucket-men, there to keep the peace and break apart such goings on, were a part of it as well, taking their bets, shouting, laughing.

Then he noticed something – one of the men fighting was a woman.

She was a black-skinned Nubian with handsomely straight features and high cheek bones and puffed out hair that hung mid-neck in beaded strands of stones and jewels. She had large almond eyes, as seen in paintings and etchings of Nubians. Mythical creatures, beautiful creatures, from the faraway land of Kush, the mysterious land below Egypt, the land of many gods, unconquered by Alexander, unconquered by the Caesars. She was taller than any woman Mahlir had ever seen. Her upper body was bare and her breasts glistening in the combination of perspiration and the water falling from above. She was clearly the better combatant. She circled her confused and breath-burdened opponent in flat-footed strides of purpose, wiping the water from her brow with the back of her hand, eyeing him, smiling at him, studying him, taking the moments to gain back her own spent breath. The confidence in each of her movements was unsettling to her opponent, a man shorter in stature, a man also bare-chested and wet with rain and perspiration, and speckled with three or four days' worth of beard. He had short Roman hair, graying, and was girthed with the paunch of middle years, and had a face of leather that spoke of hard living, like the men of the Emporium saloons. Mahlir wondered in the allure of his curiosity what had happened to this point, to bring about this most unusual of happenings.

The man lunged for her. They locked together with the ferocity of two rams charging. She was upside down, then on her feet, a cat righting itself, then they were tumbling, rolling, twisting. And in the brevity of moments an end was at hand, with the man's head locked securely between the woman's powerful legs, leaving the crowd to scream itself to a frenzy.

Mahlir feared for the man's life, such seemed the force of the Nubian woman's legs as she steadily leveraged them together.

She yelled in Greek for him to submit, which he readily did.

Then someone shouted in Greek – "Blood! I want to see blood!" The rattle of gold mixed itself with the commotion as a purse jingled. "Another fifty sescterces if I see blood!"

The woman leapt astride her exhausted and beaten foe and began pummeling him. In her expression was determination, also a kind of twinkling, a glow almost, like she was having fun creating the spectacle, raining down on him tiny blows that hardly took any effort at all, that seemed more to humiliate than to damage. Whenever he pleaded, she would just laugh and punch again, feigning first to watch him jerk, then connecting with the other, and laughing all the louder at the show she was putting on.

She turned her head to the crowd as if boasting, and they roared so much the louder. "More! More!" they screamed. She looked down and mouthed a mock expression of apology and cuffed him again. It would have been better for his wounded pride had it been the knees of a muscled gladiator pinning his shoulders to the ground.

When blood finally did show – it was a stream of red mixed with the rain rolling down his neck and into the street – she squealed like a child that had just won a prize, for in fact she had. She rammed his head sideways and pointed. "See? Blood!. Do you see that? Right there!"

"I see no blood" said the man who had made the offer.

Determination came strong to the woman's face. Another punch flew, a wide hard one this time, so quick it could hardly be seen, like she had been trained in the art of fighting.

Blood spurted from the tender flesh of the man's ear, easily to be seen, even amid the rain.

The sight twisted inside Mahlir in wretched fits of fascination and revulsion – opposites entwined, silk and steel – and he could not get the woman out of his mind.

When she finally did let the man go, when he got to his feet, he came at her waving a knife, unmindful this time of any rules – but the bucket-men intervened and restrained him until his humiliation had left and his temper cooled.

She began collecting coins from those who had bet against her, including the fifty from the man who wanted the blood.

The next thing Mahlir knew, he was being shoved into the circle and his long tunic was being ripped from hm, along with the box that contained the crown. "A denarius that the Jew Beggar lasts longer than the innkeeper," a voice rang out.

"God and man are of the same substance,
Only in different degrees of development."

Spencer Kimball, 12th President of the Church
Of Jesus Christ of Latter-day Saints.

Part IV

THE PRINCESS OF KUSH

Year 72 (26AD) to Year 74 (28AD)of the Calendar
of Pater Patriea Gaius Julius Caesar

CHAPTER 27

WRESTLING WITH A PRINCESS

ROME

The Nubian woman smiled and studied Mahlir with curious eyes. There were scars on her cheeks, three on either side, beauty marks carved into her skin at birth. Yellow stone earrings hung down, images of the fanning sun with dangling streamers. Gemstones were woven into her braided hair. Gold armlets wound themselves up from her wrists, resemblant of another culture, inlaid with jewels and centered by an image of a four-winged goddess with headdress and double crown standing on a sun-like blossom, symbol of the ultimate conquest, a child of the divine standing victoriously atop the thousand and one petals of the flower of Ultimate Knowledge.

The smile widened. For a moment it seemed like it was a game, as if they were friends from somewhere distant, two children about to tumble in play.

Mahlir was not quite sure what he was going to do.

Her smile twitched, a split-second precursor to the uncoiling of her body.

But it never happened. The outcome would never be known. Because in that same instant, right before they would have collided, two Praetorians stepped between them. Mahlir was taken in one direction, the woman in the other.

Mahlir's captors were the highest of the Praetorian order, palace guards, by the purple of their plumes and capes. Odd – he was not led away on foot behind a horse like a typical prisoner, nor was he thrown into a cage or dungeon. Mahlir's cage, Malir's dungeon, was the splendor of a gilded traveling carriage pulled by four white steeds. Draped over the backs of the horses were blankets of embroidered gold and red. Golden tassels hung from their necks and hindquarters. The spokes of the wheels were of the arms and legs of beasts, and the hub was the golden face of a lion within the bursting rays of the sun. Mahlir and his captors sat upon blue cushions. A curved tapestry roof protected them from the still falling rain, though the downpour was easing. And through it all, the sun was making its appearance, pink and lavender rays struggling through the stubborn cloud cover.

They rolled along smoothly over the tightly bricked road, and a breeze danced upon the skin of Mahlir's naked chest and fanned his face and hair. His tunic was back in the city on the street where it had been cast, as was the box with the crown, which was almost a relief, not to be burdened with it anymore, the bulk of the thing or the temptation it brought to look inside. In the back of his mind there rumbled the fear that maybe it did contain some kind of magical power that could curse him. He was better to be rid of it. Soon the raindrops vanished altogether, and the breeze dried his rain-drenched skin and hair.

The guards sat on either side, saying nothing, looking straight ahead. Neither spoke when Mahlir asked what the charges were. No matter what he said, or what he asked, their eyes remained fixed and their ears deaf.

The driver was a slave, and one of a gentle manner, by the look of him, by the simplicity and cleanliness of his clothes and by the non-threatening way the gods had chosen to sculpt his face.

In Mahlir's bones was quiet warmth, from the sun, from the heat still locked in the air, and from the stillness of the countryside. It was the mid-summer month of the Dog Star, a time when the Senate was not in session and the wealthy were on the move to their country villas. The carriage must have overtaken as many as twenty slave-borne litters and baggage wagons. Twice that many less distinguished folk were traveling in the opposite direction, driving makeshift two-wheeled carts into the city to set up their booths in the market. Some of the travelers were on the backs of donkeys. Some walked alongside oxen that were drawing wagons full of hay or produce.

Mahlir and his captors traveled most of the day, six hours at least, by the position of the sun sinking low behind them, having stopped twice for fresh horses. The Apennines were growing closer, their scent rolling over the thick forests, coming cooled by leftover snows and cold mountain streams. The ascent was gradual but becoming more and more noticeable, as the fields and vineyards turned to meadows jeweled with flowers, then to hills strung with laurel. Mahlir slept for a time, a disquieting sleep haunted by the color silver, why silver he didn't know, and by shapeless images and by the burden of his uncertain anticipation. When he awoke, the sun was going down, burnishing the western slopes in a haze of gold, and falling upon the most magnificent estate he had ever seen. They were turning into it. A small city, it appeared to be, hidden so well within the trees and foliage that he would have missed it had it not been their destination. Like fine garments did the trees and shrubs and flowering vines clothe the many buildings of the estate, buildings of marble and stone, just like Rome, and with domed roofs like Rome, and gilded rooflines.

A faint spray brushed his face from a fountain.

Birds called from within the trees, and water gurgled quietly from pipes and marble basins. The birds were louder than in any other parts of the forest, perhaps because they knew they were protected here.

The sudden barking of a dog announced them, as if the clopping of the horses and the rolling of the wheels on the driveway had not already done so. The paving stones, all of them marble, were as large as the ones Mahlir remembered from the Temple streets of Jerusalem – O how long it had been? – and they were buffed to such a shine they actually cast the reflection of the carriage, a habit from days of old when a ruler would polish walls and floors in order to see enemies approaching.

Mahlir saw that there was a man casually strolling. One of the Practorians left the coach and walked toward the man, striding with such immediacy and with such pomp that one would think he was approaching Caesar himself. The man was on a pathway of white crushed rock that encircled one of the fountains and had stopped to filter water through his hand in an absentminded fashion as would a fellow with a mind burdened. The Praetorian stood still before him. There was a brief discussion, then the Praetorian motioned for Mahlir to come forward.

A peculiar man, this man at the fountain, a man better suited to the Emporium docks than a country villa, from the rugged looks of him, other than the short white tunic he wore, which was fastened on the right shoulder by a clasp of gold and pulled in at the waist by a purple cord. His eyes were piercing, and his chin square and his neck thick. His nose was prominent and hooked, giving him the look of an aging saloon pugilist, though the thoughtful countenance born by his sunken mouth led one to speculate otherwise. Here was a man of education, said the look, and a man concerned with more than just the trivialities of life. His white hair was cut square and high on his forehead, so that the wrinkles of his aged brow could clearly be seen, but hung long in back over the nape of his neck. On his head was a wreath, which he removed and handed to Mahlir. "The smell of the laurel is a thing of beauty," he said. "Put it on, Mahlir-of-Judea, and be proud, for you are a citizen of Rome."

Confused, surprised, pleased that somehow he knew, Mahlir did as the man requested, and stared at him for a long while, until the sunken mouth turned into a smile.

Mahlir bent forward over the fountain so he could see his own reflection, see for himself the wreath on his head. The catch pool was deep, and if he looked just right the image was clear, barely disturbed by the water from the pool above, which fell only in misting drops, bubbling first out of the unfolding petals of a flower into a clam's shell, then trickling over a likeness of King Neptune, the great god of the depths, surrounded by, protected by, a circle of five sea nymphs, their heads tipped slightly downward and to the side, held in peaceful sway by the water rolling over their naked bodies to drip into the bottom pool, into Mahlir's reflection.

He was caught completely unaware by what he saw. He had not seen himself in over two decades. Looking back was the reflection of a man who was anything but Roman. The man looking back had a beard and hair falling to the shoulders. He was an Essene – he had forgotten – but the real surprise was the age in his eyes, and the lines in his forehead, and the beginning of gray in his beard. And in looking at his naked upper body he was embarrassed at how thin it had become over the years; the Nubian woman might in fact have been able to beat him. It had been a long time since he had fought with men, twenty and more years, and never had he fought with a woman. He smiled at the thought of it – in a curious sort of way he was disappointed that the outcome would never be known – and shivered as a gust of wind blew a spray of water over him.

It caused the man with the white hair to wave at one of the Praetorians.

"Yes, my Caesar?"

Mahlir was stunned. He *was* the emperor.

"A covering for our guest. Was I not clear when I said he was not to be treated as a prisoner? This man is a citizen of Rome. Why was he stripped of clothing?"

"My Lord, we did no such thing. We found him this way. His clothes lay in the street when we arrived."

The emperor gestured the Praetorian away. "Quickly, bring Mahlir-of-Judea a covering, and see to it that his personal belongings are retrieved and brought here."

The other Praetorian removed his cape and placed it over Mahlir's shoulders.

Mahlir was uncomfortable with the attention but expressed only his thanks. "I am appreciative," he told the emperor. "I am especially appreciative, and humbled, that you know me to be a citizen. I must admit, I am bewildered as to how you know. It was many years ago that I was granted citizenship, and it was a thing that happened in private between your stepfather and me. And how is it possible that you know my name?"

The emperor put his hand on Mahlir's shoulder. "Shortly before leaving for the villa today, word came of a lunatic at the gate demanding to see Caesar Augustus. They said he was a Jew calling himself Mahlir, and that he claimed to be a citizen, claimed to have been a personal friend of my father's. Everyone was laughing. Except for me. How could I forget the man who gave my stepfather his dog? He loved that animal dearly and refused to dispatch it even in the suffering of its old age, instructing instead his own personal physicians to care for it as if it were a family member. My father spoke of you often, Mahlir-of-Judea. He told of how courageous you were, of how you had a belief in the Roman system and of how it could better people, and of how you believed it would be the foundation for future governments. He told of how you led a group of Jews to Rome to ask that Judea be annexed and made a part of Syria. Did you know he searched for you? He wanted to make you an administrator. He had great respect for you. But you had disappeared. It was as though the earth had swallowed you." Tiberius was a tall man, at least a head higher than Mahlir, and had huge hands, one of which he used to pluck an apple from a tree. With an equally large forefinger, he bored out the core and sunk his teeth into it. He smiled down. "Your appearance at the gate was well-timed. A moment or two later and we would have been gone. I instructed that you be escorted here. We arrived ourselves only a short time ago."

The Praetorian returned with a knee-length tunic hemmed in blue and gold. Exactly like the one the emperor wore, also with a golden clasp. In addition to the tunic, the Praetorian had with him a laurel wreath for the emperor, to replace the one given to Mahlir, a wreath larger and thicker, not because Tiberius desired superiority in his dress, rather because he believed that the leaves from the laurel served as protection against lightening, and parts of the sky were still covered with ominous looking clouds.

"Come – walk with me, Mahlir-of-Judea. I have something I want to offer you. I am old. I am tired. There was a time when I looked forward to each new day and the challenges it brought. Now I look forward to the day when I will have this responsibility no longer. At my death, I fear."

Mahlir stood rigid. An idea had come to him. He was standing before the emperor of Rome. As sudden as a mid-winter blow, had come this idea, this opportunity, for if there was anyone in the world who could put him face to face with his son, it was this man who stood before him now, if Orodes was still in Rome. Perhaps the Teacher of Righteousness was guiding his steps after all. He would wait until the right moment. One must be careful in asking a favor of a king. And Caesar was one greater than a king. Mahlir walked beside him, though a bit to the rear, just a bit, so as to let the emperor lead. The only sounds were those of their feet on the crushed rock and the whisperings of the fountains. The birds and all the animals had stilled themselves in the presence of the mighty Tiberius. The emperor continued. "I have put my full effort into being an efficient and just ruler. If the will of a man could bleed my feet would be washed in the blood of the heart. Such has been the extent of my effort."

They strolled through gardens every bit as elaborate as those in Rome, and down walkways just as elegant. The difference being, Mahlir and Tiberius were the only ones there, though from time to time Mahlir's eye caught the gleam of a Praetorian's helmet from the foliage.

"And, might I say, the effort has borne fruit, much of it anyway. I am proud of the things I have done. I would like to think that the people in the empire live a better life because of those things. But alas, as of late, I have enemies." He stopped and looked at Mahlir with sudden seriousness and popped the final bite of apple into his mouth. "I trust I am not to count you among them?"

Mahlir was surprised at the challenge and said the only thing he could say. "My Caesar – I am your trusted servant, and a servant of Rome."

Tiberius pressed his lips together in an alarming way and looked hard at Mahlir. "Tell me straight away, if you are not. If you misspeak, I will see it in your eyes."

Words failed him, when Mahlir needed them most.

Would Tiberius take silence as his answer?

The confusing diatribe kept coming. "A wave of my hand would bring ten and twenty guards down upon you. Before you could move an eyebrow, you would be dust under my feet."

"My Caesar," Mahlir finally said. "I have no reason to turn against you. To the contrary. I have every reason to support you."

The look continued.

Malir was visibly trembling.

Maybe that was what the emperor wanted to see – Mahlir trembling – because as suddenly as it came, the look left, and the emperor was as before. Either he was testing Malir, or toying with him, or he was insane. Mahlir was later to learn that Tiberius in fact had been a good administrator. Many believed the provinces were never better governed than during his reign. He improved police and fire protection, enhanced the bread dole program, kept the army in strict discipline and managed the finances with restraint and generosity. It is also true that the latter part of his rule, that which Mahlir was entering, was marked by executions and conspiracies, real and imagined.

They continued walking, and the emperor went on with his dialogue as though he had no memory at all of what had just taken place. "I am good at choosing effective governors and administrators. An emperor must choose well his chain of command, making sure that those in authority are effective and just. This I am good at. Now I am about to make my boldest choice. Lucius, my Prefect of the Guard, will sit in my place in Rome while I retire to the coast at Campania. Lucius will see to the daily duties and responsibilities of the empire."

Mahir wondered in the troublings of his thoughts why Tiberius was telling him these things.

The answer came. "I have also appointed a new procurator for Judea. I have replaced Valerius Gratus with Pontius Pilate. Pontius Pilate is one of those good administrators. In the short time he has been there he has proven that. But the Jewish people can be difficult. In many ways Judea is the most difficult of the provinces." Tiberius spread his sunken mouth into a smile once more. "I sometimes wonder if my stepfather did the right thing by allowing you to convince him to annex Judea those years ago."

Mahir smiled also, in courtesy only, for inside he was still trembling.

"You Jews are a troublesome sort. Very hard to understand. Do you know what I want for Judea? What I want for Judea is the same thing I want for all of the empire. Peace. Paramount in my mind is keeping the peace and seeing that the streets are safe and free from seditions and riots. This is one of the reasons I placed Pontius Pilate in power. To this end he is good. As our Lord Jupiter knows, Judea has had its share of rioting. Let me tell you of something that happened only a few months ago. Pilate had determined that the army should be headquartered in Jerusalem instead of Caesarea, knowing Jerusalem to be the heart-center of Judea, as well as its geographic center. It is a place from which troops can be deployed quickly to any area. It is the city of festivals. It is the place where the Jews come to celebrate their religion. It is the center of all trade and travel routes. For many reasons, Jerusalem is where the soldiers should be. Very often a simple show of force is all that is needed to prevent trouble and keep a city safe. So the army was moved to Jerusalem, for the safety of the people. But were they grateful? No. Moreover, they rioted. The soldiers arrived in the most tactful of ways, in the night so as not to create the impression of a threat. Yet the people rioted. They came in multitudes to Pilate's dwelling in Caesarea and demanded that he remove the images and symbols carried by the soldiers. For many days they interceded with Pilate, and for as many days Pilate refused, because he feared that to have the images of the eagle removed would be to disrespect the empire and weaken his authority. Finally Pilate had had enough. On the sixth day he gave them an ultimatum, disperse or die, that simple, thinking the threat would end their foolishness once and for all." Tiberius paused, and again almost formed a smile to crack through his frozen expression of seriousness. "Do you know what the people then did, Mahlir-of-Judea? Your people? I will tell you what they did. They threw themselves on the ground and laid their necks bare, saying they should prefer death than to live among the images." Tiberius moved his head back and forth in an expression of bewilderment. "What am I to do with these people, Mahlir? Can you tell me?"

"If I might ask, my Caesar, what did Pontius Pilate then do?"

"What else could he do? He removed the images."

Mahlir breathed relief. This Pontius Pilate is indeed a good administrator. Archelaus would have killed them all.

"So tell me, Mahlir-of-Judea, is it the images themselves they find offensive, or the soldiers? And why?"

"The Jews fear their god more than any soldier. Let me tell you a story. In the time of your forefathers, when Rome had not yet expanded beyond Sicily, there came from the line of Alexander the Macedonian an evil offshoot called Antiochus IV Epiphanes, who made it his sport to try to force the Jews to eat pork, a thing forbidden by our god. Now it came to be that a woman and her seven sons were arrested and put to the torture, with a promise of release and riches if they would only partake of the forbidden food. One by one they refused, and one by one, while the remaining brothers watched, and in front of their mother, each was scourged and the skin pulled from their bodies, and their tongues cut out, and their hands and feet severed from their limbs. Pans were heated, and one by one each was thrown in to be fried. Even as the smoke of their burning bodies rose, they refused, to the very last. The mother in like manner was tortured, and in like manner she too refused, and was also thrown into the pans. These, my Caesar, are the people you are dealing with in Judea."

Said Tiberius after a pause, and another rare smile that almost broke into laughter. "I would have eaten the pork."

Mahlir returned the smile. "As would I, Great Caesar. But there was a time I would have died also, in the same brutal manner."

"The military symbols and standards? They too are forbidden by your god?"

"It is written in the books of our Law, from the time of Moses, in the very hand of God, '*You shall have no other gods before me. You shall not make for yourselves any graven image, or any likeness of any thing that is in heaven above, or that is in the earth beneath, or that is in the water under the earth. You shall not bow down to them, nor serve them.*'"

Said Tiberius, "When I was a young soldier in service against the Marcomanni, far from home, many times we crossed into the lands of other gods, and we would pay homage to those gods, so as not to offend them, and hoping also for their blessings, not imagining that our own gods would be offended."

"The Jewish people are different."

"This I am beginning to see."

"Have you not taken notice that there are no statues in Jerusalem? No monuments to our heroes and our forefathers?"

"And that is the reason why, because your law forbids it?"

"That is why."

"So it was not the presence of the soldiers that caused the rioting, but the presence of the images."

"Yes, my Caesar."

"And you, do you find these images offensive?"

Mahlir stilled his fear, because in his answer he wanted to be able to speak effectively. "I am of the sect of the Essenes and have been taught that there is a meaning beyond the meaning. There are many differences between us Essenes and our brothers of the Temple, yet not so many differences. Our brethren offer up the blood of sacrificial animals to our god. We do not. We have been taught to offer something deeper, something from within ourselves, and to spare the life of the animal. Our brethren of the Temple refuse to eat pork, as is the commandment of our god. We eat no flesh of any sort but would do so to prevent the suffering of others. Our brethren refuse to make themselves subservient to graven images, yet bow continually before the images within their own hearts. We were taught that if one destroys the images within the heart one need never worry about stone and bronze. These are the things we were taught in Qumran, these and other things. Words easy to say, words not so easy to bring to manifestation."

Tiberius was thinking, pressing his lips together, seeming several times like he was going to speak. Finally he did. "I have learned in my years in leadership that in order to effectively govern a people one must understand them. Mahlir-of-Judea, you shall help me understand these people. You shall live once again in your homeland, in the employ of Rome, as personal advisor to Pontius Pilate."

To refuse was not possible. Tiberius let that be known, by the look on his face and by the tone of his voice. Mahlir would have accepted the offer anyway, because here was his opportunity to reunite with his son. His life's purpose was now at the footstool of the emperor. "I will do my best to be worthy of your confidence in me," Mahlir said. "I am honored to be in the service of the greatest nation the world has ever known, a nation where even her enemies are welcomed through her doors." He drew a breath, then said it. "Which brings to mind something I saw in the city today. There was a wall writing telling of Prince Orodes of Parthia living in Rome."

Tiberius raised his eyebrows and answered as if asking a question. "For certain Orodes is in Rome. He lives in Rome in pursuit of the finer points of his education. He resides and studies with one of my tutors, as did Vonones, a Parthian prince of earlier times." The emperor seemed ready to ask Mahlir why he cared, but then there came a smile of introspection to Tiberius' face, and instead he lapsed into a philosophical diatribe about the sociology of Parthia, Rome's largest and most bothersome neighbor. "Although I am not sure it will serve him all that well. True enough, Prince Orodes will leave Rome a better man, but the Parthian people will cast him aside for it. The Parthians are barbarians. They reject anything that comes from the outside, as they did with Prince Vonones after he was sent to Rome for culture and refinement. They referred to their country under him as being no better than a Roman province and rioted. The Magi were forced to call upon another to be king. They offered the crown to one called Artabanus, who is to this day king of Parthia. Cheers went up everywhere. There were celebrations in every city and in every fire Temple. This would have been about the time you met with my stepfather, when you led the Jewish opposition."

Tiberius then uncaged his thoughts about Artabanus. "I would have much preferred Vonones as king, I can tell you right now. King Artabanus has caused me my share of sleepless nights. I came nearly to the point of an all-out invasion against Parthia because of it. But that would not have served the purposes of the people of Rome, or my soldiery. I was unwilling to send young men to their deaths over a personal grudge of my own. But tell me, Mahlir-of-Judea, why do you concern yourself so with Parthia? Do you know this young man? This Prince Orodes?"

"I spent some time in Parthia," Mahlir answered, "as a slave. My son and I were taken by raiders."

Tiberius' voice was stiff, a barrier holding back anger. "Do you have allegiance to King Artabanus?" Before Mahlir could answer Tiberius held up his hand to silence him. "You would be better off striking a bargain with a desert jackal than aligning yourself with King Artabanus. Never mind the wrath of Rome. Never mind what I might do to you. Even if I do nothing, Artabanus himself will be the ruin of you. Let me tell you a story about King Artabanus and his queen. There is this game they are fond of playing with one another. The queen is a woman of considerable beauty. She picks a young man of her fancy and calls him to her chambers. The young man of course comes – who would dare refuse – not knowing he is entering the bedchamber of a monster. She lies with him, while the king watches from a hidden place. It pleases the king to do so. He pretends to catch them near the end of their encounter. That is his pleasure. Then it is that the queen is allowed her pleasure, to torture the hapless victim, sometimes to death, sometimes only to the point of disfigurement. Then, their passions heightened by the bizarre act, they themselves lie together. This is the father of the man you are asking about."

"Your Magnificence, I have allegiance only to Rome. I was a slave in Parthia and escaped as soon as I had the chance." Now was Mahlir's opportunity. There may never come another. "Your Magnificence, if I may, I have a favor to ask of you –"

Tiberius straightened. "Do not call me Your Magnificence. I loathe the term. But speak. I have willing ears to consider this favor."

All Mahlir had to do was explain; and he almost did. He almost told the emperor who Orodes really was, and that all he wanted was to see his son, to embrace him, that his arms still ached to do so even after a quarter of a century, but the words would not come. Fear seized his throat and muted it. Although – it was not fear of Tiberius. The fear was of his own son. What does a father say to a son he has not seen since birth? Does the boy even know of his existence?

Tiberius leaned forward into the silence, confused.

Mahlir's mind began to rationalize why it might be better not to step through this gate that had been opened for him. The Parthian people would surely reject Orodes, worse, assassinate him, if they found out his blood was not pure. Caesar may well imprison them both, if he felt threatened by an alliance of blood between Israel and Parthia. Such an alliance was what the Magi hoped for; it was what Caesar feared. Babylon reconstituted. Prophecy fulfilled.

So when far too much silence had passed, when it became necessary to put something else in its place, Mahlir said only this, a thing that was on his mind anyway, "The favor I would ask, I would like to know what became of the Nubian woman."

The vacant look in the eyes of the emperor revealed that he had no idea what Mahlir was talking about.

Mahlir explained.

"A woman accomplished in the Greek skills of wrestling and boxing? Most curious."

Mahlir told him she had been taken away by the guards at the same time of his detention. "I wish to be of record that she did nothing wrong," Mahlir said.

"I will investigate the matter."

Tiberius was good to his word. Ten days later, after Malir had forgotten about it altogether, at the point of Mahlir's departure from the country villa, Tiberius told him of the woman's horrific fate. "She has been made a gift to Decimus Cluentius, this year's praetor of the games."

"What does that mean?" Mahlir knew exactly what it meant, but he needed to hear it from Tiberius.

"She is being trained by Publius Calvus. Publius is well known to the fans of the arena. He is the lanista of the Julius Caesar School. The best, say those who follow the games."

The thought of it was inconceivable, throwing a woman into such an environment. "To be trained to kill and to die, you mean?" The words came from Mahlir's mouth before he could stop them. One could endanger one's life, speaking thus to an emperor.

But Tiberius answered without anger. "She will be trained as a netter, until the games of Ludi Romani in September, when she will be placed in the wild beast hunts." His eyes pointed at Mahlir with momentary excitement. "Against a tiger? Or perchance a panther? A show the likes of that has not been seen since the days of the Republic. If she prevails, she will advance to the gladiatorial contests of the afternoon, matched up against a heavy-armored Thracian." Tiberius saw Mahlir's look of bewilderment, his complete inability to understand why a human being, any human being, could find pleasure in the thought of such a spectacle. "If she is as good as I am told," Tiberius said in his attempt to placate, "I am sure she will be victorious. And from what I am told she will do so honorably."

"Victorious? Honorable? May I have leave to speak freely my thoughts? My Caesar?"

Tiberius nodded.

"Forgive me. I am not familiar completely with the Roman lifestyle, but what would a Roman consider victorious? What would a Roman consider honorable? Being forced to take the life of another? For no greater purpose than the entertainment of a gathered crowd?"

The emperor drew in a breath as if he was going to answer but shook his head instead and pressed his lips together, the way he did when thinking. Perhaps even the great Tiberius had grown weary of feeding the populace its blood lust, a duty to be borne by all emperors, to stand in the reserved front benches with the priests and the Vestal Virgins, to watch as powerful beasts rend each other in frightened frenzy, a tiger and a bear, a lion and a bull elephant, and to watch as men do the same, as spectators yell, "'Occide! Occide!'", "'Kill! Kill!'", to the combatants looking up for instructions as to whether an opponent should live or die, and to watch as the ferrymen come to club the fallen before dragging them off with long hooks and ropes, lest they be feigning death, and to watch as the people become lost in their feverish screams of excitement.

Tiberius finally answered this way. "She could come away with her freedom. One day she could end up as wealthy as a senator. The games are not altogether barbaric. They offer opportunity to those who would otherwise have none."

"But Caesar, she will not last even the training. She will be set upon and defiled by every man in the academy, prisoners and trainers both. And if she does survive, she will have no chance against the likes of a Thracian."

"I am told she has bested every man she has faced."

"With respect, my Caesar, there is a difference between an aging and gluttonous saloon drunkard and a fit fighter trained for the arena. You may as well execute her."

"Nothing can be done at this point. Money has changed hands. I have no say in the matter. There is great expense in purchasing and training a gladiator. I am told that a large sum has been spent already on this one. It is anticipated she will please the crowd greatly."

"My Caesar. Is there no way?"

"None." Tiberius was growing impatient

"If I were to take her as my wife. I am a citizen. I have the right, do I not?"

Caesar sighed. "It is sometimes the little decisions that weigh the most on me. How I long for a life in the country, or at a seashore villa, where I can fix my own eggs, where I can pour my own wine and feel and smell for myself the wood of the red-stained cask."

"Do this for me, my Lord, and I will never again ask you for anything."

"Why would you wed a woman from a strange and far-off land, one whom you do not know, and whose family you have never met?"

"I myself wonder, is it the right thing to do? I do not know. By doing it I violate the very laws of our people and of our god. Once, in the history of our people, during the time of the prophet Ezra, there were men who married outside our blood and lineage. When discovered, they were forced by our elders to send their wives and children into the desert. There were a hundred and thirteen wives in all that were banished that day, along with their children."

"You Jews are a barbaric sort."

"The sect of the Essenes, of which I belong, whose colonies I have only recently departed, take no wives at all. They live in complete celibacy."

"And yet you wish to marry? Simply to save the life of this woman?"

"Yes, my Caesar. If it be at all possible. Yes."

"Be sure of it."

"I am sure."

The emperor forced a long silence. "Very well. I will order it. Understand that in doing so I shall mandate that a fair price be allowed for her. I shall pay it. It shall be my gift to you. But you shall do *me* a favor. I am told you are a scribe and do well with the written word and with mathematics. Rome is sending several caravans of goods and trade supplies to the eastern regions over the next several weeks. I am putting you in charge of its organization. I will have Sejanus supply you with a list of the various items and their prices. You will organize these caravans and provide for the receipt of payment. They will travel as far as Ecbatana to the east."

Mahlir looked surprised. "You want me to travel to Ecbatana?"

Tiberius nearly broke out in laughter. "Of course not. I only want you to organize it. I will provide all the materials you will need, pen, ink, funds, my seal, whatever you need. Just make sure it gets done. As long as the messengers and the porters and the drivers and the managers do their jobs, and it all happens successfully and without delay, I see no reason for you to move at all from your desk. You are the one in charge. You arrange it. You hire the porters and drivers, and arrange for sales and purchases. We sell the Parthians grain; they sell us iron and beer. Sejanus will explain it and provide you with my seal and the materials. When it is done, and when payment has been received – and a profit has been made – you and your bride will travel to Caesarea to take up your position there with Pontius Pilate in the land of the Jews."

"The Teacher of Righteousness will point the way," Elkanar had always said, "– and guide you in your decisions." "Opportunities will open themselves," he would say, "so that you may grow in the enfoldment of the joy of Yahweh. Be watchful for them. Just be careful not to allow the cloak of the Scoffer to blind you." Was this woman the cloak of the Scoffer? Mahlir didn't care; it was what he wanted to do.

Before Mahir left for the city, the Praetorians arrived with his tunic, and the box. They had recovered them both. "What a strange thing this is," said Tiberius, examining the box. He shook it. "What might it contain? It makes no sound at all, as if empty. But it is too heavy to be empty." Yet far too light to contain a fortune in gold, which had been troubling Mahlir for some time.

Dare he tell the emperor of Rome what it contains? Dare he not tell him? He decided the best and safest way to answer the question was with complete honesty. That way, the worst that could happen would be having Tiberius confiscate it for his own treasury; then Mahlir would be rid of the obligation. But even that didn't work. Still the thing clung to him, ever the tighter. Tiberius only laughed "A magic crown you say? And you never bothered to look inside?" He bounced it in his hands to demonstrate its lack of significant weight and handed it over. "What is it made of? Twigs? He must be a very different sort of king, this Jewish fellow. Here, take it."

And to the cages they went, Mahlir and the emperor, where the Nubian woman was found in training dueling with a net and a three-pronged wooden lance.

"Be sure," the emperor said, in one final warning. "Be sure before we approach. It is a human life you trifle with."

"I am sure."

There was no teacher in front of them, or to the side of them, or in back of them. Whoever he was, this Teacher of Righteousness, wherever he was, he certainly was not with Mahlir and Tiberius. So Mahlir knew not whether his steps were being guided by Yahweh or by the Scoffer, or by simple circumstance.

But he didn't care, because it was what he wanted to do.

CHAPTER 28

SAVED BY MARRIAGE

ROME

A man was oiling and wiping the square grated bars. Another was raking and smoothing dirt. Five pairs of combatants were sparring, among them the Nubian woman and a red bearded Norseman. A lanista was striding between them, Publius Calvus most likely, barking instructions, shouting inspiration. "The scum of society, all of you," he spewed, in words harsh and raspy and filled with the ground's rising dust. "Murderers, thieves, low class ne'er-do-wells. But mark me when I say, from this point on, life will never be the same. From this pit some of you will rise to levels of wealth unimaginable. One of many examples of the beauty of the Roman system." He interrupted himself to demonstrate technique, wrenching a wooden sword from the Nubian woman's heavy-helmeted opponent. He was speaking in Greek, because the cultural mix of the trainees was divergent, from many lands, many languages, and Greek tended to be spoken universally. "Thrust. One does not slice. One thrusts. Like this, like a Roman soldier. A Roman soldier never slices. It is not a brainless melon you are cutting; it is a thinking man with the ability to dodge a wide-armed slice." He pulled the net from the Nubian woman and swung it to sweep the Norseman hard to the ground. "See what happens when you cross your feet? In the arena that would have meant your life." He resumed his pacing. "You are better off as gladiators, all of you. Criminals, slaves, volunteers, the lot of you are better off. Those of you who are here as criminals, a swift death by the sword is better than a slow death on the cross. Those of you who are slaves are also better off, because here you can win freedom and your fortune. Those of you who are here of your own free will, even you are better off. The average life span of a Roman citizen is thirty years. Do you know what the average life span of a gladiator is? Thirty years. What do you know! You may as well be in the arena vying for your fortune and your fame, where you are fed and bathed as kings. And those of you who die, you will be providing the people a service. You will show them how to die with courage. By watching you they will learn how to face their own mortality. Although it may surprise you – most gladiators survive their fights. It is only on rare occasions that an opponent is given a thumbs down. Most of the time the lives are spared. It costs a great deal to train a –"

Silence came instantly at the sight of the emperor's entourage. Save for the breathing of the gladiators and the creaking of the large gate being swung inward, there was not a sound to be heard. The emperor was on foot. Tiberius was one to abhor being "carried about like an invalid." Litters and carriages were almost always waved aside for the favor of a good mount or of simply walking. He moved in measured strides, as if he was fighting the pain of aging joints, but move he did, briskly, behind the clanking of two Praetorians. A single guard followed behind him. Then came Mahlir, his box bouncing off his side to the rhythm of his walk, followed by two more Praetorians. A rush of pride prickled Mahlir's skin, because of the eyes that were upon him, watching this strange event that was unfolding.

No one was more surprised than the Nubian woman, in realizing that the emperor was walking up to her.

"I offer you your freedom," Tiberius said, without pretense, without introduction, holding a scepter in his right hand and grasping the folds of his purple gold-embroidered toga with the other. " –conditioned upon your agreement to become the wife of Mahlir-the-Jew, officium to Pontius Pilate, governor of Judea."

The Nubian woman simply stared.

"My Caesar," Mahlir said. "I believe she speaks and understands only the language of the Greeks."

Tiberius repeated his offer in Greek, apathetically, as if he was wishing she would decline.

She did not. The trident fell from her grip, then the net fell, and still breathing hard she looked first at the emperor then at Mahlir. The look she gave Mahlir that day after the surprise had waned from her face held in it more devotion than most men will see in a lifetime.

Over on Vatican Hill, halfway up on a forested knoll, there was the home of a senator who was away at his country villa. It was here that the emperor had made arrangements for Mahlir to maintain an office until he was married and his duties for the empire completed. And it was at this very door that the Wolf Prince of Parthia bade admittance and asked for writing materials. And it was in this forested area that Prince Orodes had chosen to hide in his attempts to elude the soldiers of Tiberius.

Serendipitously, he had knocked on the one door that would offer him help, the one door behind which was the one person in Rome not an enemy.

Mahlir of course knew that the man seeking admittance might very well be his son when he saw the birthmark, faded and pointing upward, and when he noticed that there was an animal in accompaniment, one that looked quite like a wolf. It was confirmed when Orodes and Mithra were running back to the forested area, by the smooth gait of the animal, its movements unmatched even by the grace of the Pan dancers. The fact that the emperor had put Mahlir in charge of the shipments to the Far East allowed him to provide a traveling pass for his son and his "dog." He knew that his son was in danger. He had heard of the strange happenings at the arena – everyone in Rome had heard by now – how the Wolf Prince of Parthia had bewitched the animals and the guards. He was hoping the wolf would pass for a large dog, as gentle and lay back as the animal seemed. So

Mahlir made the arrangements, and was careful to hide the boy's identity, and the relationship he had with him. Orodes himself did not know. Better that way. Safer for both. Mahlir got the pass to him in the most nondescript of ways, along with directions on how and where to intercept the caravan. He used Livia as a go-between. Livia was the slave girl Caesar had assigned to Mahlir during his stay of duty. Mahlir treated her well. He could trust her silence.

He was immensely grateful for the opportunity providence had afforded him of helping his son one more time, though the boy would never know, and he gave a prayer of thanks to the god he still wasn't sure he believed in.

CHAPTER 29

THE KNOT OF HERCULES

ROME

The wedding of Mahlir-of-Matthias took place in Rome in the garden of a domus atop the summit of Esquiline, at the very end of Mercury Street. Mahlir never knew for sure, but he always speculated that it was one of the homes held by the family of Tiberius, because it was Tiberius who gave the orders for the preparations, leaving instructions that the wedding be done according to Roman custom, and that the feast be limited to a cost of one thousand sesterces, as had been the law decreed under his stepfather Augustus. A Jewish wedding was not possible, Mahlir told him, since he was marrying one who was not Jewish.

There was no family of the bride to host the wedding, no dowry to be offered. The emperor supplied it all, as though it was expected of him. And Mahlir forgot to thank him, as though he too expected it of him.

Mahlir heard music as he followed his attendant through the atrium to meet the woman who would walk through life with him. Flutes. Hundreds of them. He was led past a pool out of which rose a fountain of sea creatures spewing jets of water from their upturned mouths, then past pale green columns that supported the roof opening above, then past wall frescos of fishes, fruits and birds, and of scenes of Greek gods and goddesses, and of pictures of the voyages of Aeneas, skillfully painted, strongly colored, works of art all. Mahlir noticed there was no sun above to shine upon them. The sky was covered with clouds. Sad, he thought, that it should be cloudy on the day of their wedding. They walked past the tablium over a floor of colored stone, minute pieces tiled together to form jeweled patterns of the campaigns of Alexander.

The music grew louder. They walked past busts of unfamiliar people, family members probably, dating back to the time of the Republic, and past a full-size water clock beside which stood a slave whose duty it was to call out the hour of the day. They walked past a sign written in Latin, "No slave is to quit the house without permission of the Master. Penalty, 100 lashes."

They emerged finally into an enormous outer court sculpted in small hills angled through with stone pathways, and centered by a silver-smooth pond, fresh and clear, and surrounded by vine covered high walls. Hidden throughout were the flute players, half visible in the trees like curious animals. Mahlir followed his guide to the pond's edge and saw across from him an island of beauteous green, large enough for two people only, bride and groom. The still water surrounding it was home to many living things – lazily moving fish, lily pads, ducks, dragon flies flitting about, and, who knows what other creatures of beauty, said Mahlir's guide, nymphs perhaps, hiding, playing somewhere just out of sight. Mahlir felt a few drops of rain. He wondered if the wedding would be spoiled. Just then the cloud cover split and sunshine came streaming through to color the still falling raindrops, tiny prisms dangling and twinkling in the air. And, appearing on the island in the very same instant, stepping into the sunlight from a bridge on the other side, was his bride-to-be, her one-piece yellow garment aglow in the radiance. A ghost from the past arose, because it was the exact same thing that had happened when he married Rachel, sun streaming out of a cloud cover to bless the event.

The Nubian's neck and arms were bare, and of soft brown where sunlight fell, and of shiny black where shadows blended. The garment was drawn in at her waist by a golden cord and secured with the complex Knot of Hercules, to be untied only by the groom, lest ill fortune befall the marriage, and wherefrom comes the expression "tying the knot." Upon her head was a thing more expensive than gold, a veil of translucent cloth from the

Orient, that mysterious land beyond Parthia. A garland of tightly woven flowers held it in place, interspersed with sprigs of the sacred verbena herb.

No jewelry had she. None was needed. Adorning her body were instead the jewels of Juno, flowers and buds of all sizes and colors woven into her hair and fashioned into necklaces and bracelets.

Her shoes, now and again visible beneath the golden hem of her tunica-recta, were of white leather and covered with pearls.

Mahlir crossed the bridge and joined hands with his bride, not knowing even her name, and was struck by how very young she was. She had a face not yet enriched by maturity. Her enormous height and the roundness of her steel-like shoulders had been deceiving, had given her a look of womanhood that wasn't really there. While it was true that women often became brides in their early teen years, this was something he had not expected.

Her lips parted slowly upward into a smile that reached into Mahlir's soul. It was she who spoke first. "You are handsome without your beard," she said in well-spoken Greek, in words delivered with formality, and with a twinge of an unfamiliar accent.

Mahlir brought his hand to his face. He had forgotten. He had shaven it off and cut his hair.

"You look like a Roman," she finally said. She smiled as she said it, as if it pleased her.

"I am from many worlds," he told her. "I am a Jewish priest, and I am a Roman citizen, and I am of the sect of the Essenes. And now I am about to become a part of the world of the Kushites, your world."

"You look good as a Roman," she said.

"I am now in the employ of Rome, so I will dress as a Roman. We will be traveling to the land of Palestine, to a city on the coast called Caesarea, where we will live in the palace built by Herod, where I will be personal advisor to the governor of Judea, who makes it his home. It pleases the emperor that I dress as a Roman. To him it shows loyalty. So dress as a

Roman I shall. And you will be by my side. So you see, you will enter new worlds as well, through me."

Suddenly Mahlir became aware of many people watching, more than the flute players and the attendants. Guests? Clients, more likely, those common Romans who show up hoping to become preferred servants for the day, perhaps of being invited to dinner. Payment of a hundred quadrantes is expected at the end of the day if a client is lucky enough to obtain a full day's service.

"My name is Mahlir, son-of-Matthias," he told her. A strange way for a man to address his wife at the point of their union.

"I am Amanerinas," she reciprocated.

Then came a soothsayer, old and bent with long robes trailing. He was leading a ewe to the water's edge, and abruptly killed the animal. Mahlir didn't know what was coming, or he would have put a stop to it. There was not so much as a cry from the poor creature, so quickly did it occur. Then the soothsayer opened its belly and examined the spilled contents, entrails still quivering with the flow of life, able well to tell their story.

The flute players stopped. The buzz and noise of the crowd came to a hush. Some could be heard gasping, because the soothsayer had not immediately pronounced the entrails free of omens.

"Are the signs not favorable for this wedding?" someone whispered.

A troubled look was indeed upon the face of the soothsayer, who eventually did stand and cry, "Bene! – Good!" What else could he do? He was presiding over a wedding of a friend of the emperor.

"Bene! Bene!" the crowd roared in response.

The tablets of the marriage contract were brought forward and read and witnessed and signed with the seal of each.

Then Mahlir asked, in Latin, looking into the face of his bride, "Will you be my mater familias?"

She affirmed in Latin she would, then asked of Mahlir, "And will you be my pater familias?"

"Ita, immo sane," said Mahlir.

There was an altar in front of them. Together they placed a cake of coarse bread upon it and uttered in Latin dedications of the food to Jupiter and Juno, and to the gods of family union and childbirth, Tellus, Piccunus and Pilumnus, all of whom would bless the estate of the new couple. The rest of what they spoke to each other was in Greek, the tongue most familiar to Amanerinas.

The wedding feast was small. Only the most prestigious of the guests were present, and a handful of more presentable clients. The rest waited in the garden, for the ceremony was far from over. There were nine couches, each with purple cushions embroidered in gold, and twenty-seven guests, three reclining to a couch, and each couch surrounding a small and elegant citrus wood table, perfectly round and supported by three legs carved in the shapes of lion's paws. Slaves brought appetizers of salads on silver dishes, along with mushrooms and eggs. Drinks of muslum were handed out, wine sweetened with honey, served in handsomely embossed cups of silver. A small sip warmed the heart. Too much befuddled the senses. How unpredictable this thing is called life. A month ago Mahlir was destitute. Today he was feasting with the emperor of Rome. Unknown to Mahlir, Tiberius had motives deeper than altruism. Tiberius was using the occasion and the power of the muslum to loosen his tongue. To Mahlir it was a feast; to Tiberius it was an interrogation, of the subtlest kind, and of the most powerful kind. In the guise of friendship, he plied Mahlir with questions about his family, his philosophies, and his loyalties. Like flowing water, Mahlir let it all out. He told Tiberius about how at one time in his life his single passion was to serve Yahweh and the coming Messiah, but that his efforts had resulted in his being an unhappy man, confused and uneasy, and that the more he experienced in life, and the more he learned, the less he seemed to know. He purposely avoided telling the emperor anything at all about his son, because that would lead to questions, and he had already determined that secrecy would be the safest policy. Instead, he told Tiberius about himself, that he was living in constant search of recompense, because his deeds included the betrayal of the one he loved most in the world, who was now dead, and included also the taking of human life. He told him of his hardships and how he came to question the very existence of God. "By the Essenes I was given a new life," he said. "And a new understanding of its mysteries. There I took vows of celibacy and undertook to work for the sake of work and began to explore the dimensions of my inner being. You, my Caesar, have conquered the world, but have you conquered the world within? What of the process within that searches for security, that screams when lonely, that struggles for power, that dooms itself to an existence of inflicting misery upon itself and upon its fellow man? Have you conquered that?"

Tiberius had finished his mushrooms and salad greens. He dipped his fingers in a water basin held by a slave, then wiped his hands with a towel and asked, "Do you find me lonely and insecure, with a need to injure others?"

"I find all human creatures insecure, with a propensity to injure others. You, my Caesar, are a good man, and a good king."

"How do you know that? Until a month ago you did not know who I was."

"I have known other monarchs, and from what I have heard from you, and from what I have seen, you are a good king." By then Mahlir realized that the probing of the emperor had been more than elements of idle conversation, and he was terrified at where his quick tongue may have taken him. To recover required only the truth. "And I am proud to give you my loyalty," he said. He had not told him about the Battle of the Temple, that he had been among those revolting, and that he had ended the life of a Roman, maybe many Romans in the tipping over of ladders and the casting down of stones, deeds that also carved away at his well-being.

"It is, however, a loyalty second to your god," said Tiberius.

"Of the mysteries of our religion, of the strange and deep things taught in the inner circles, perhaps the strangest is – all alive on earth serve my god, whether acknowledging it or not, whether knowing it or not. You, the emperor of Rome, serve my god. Likewise do your gods serve my god."

Mahlir pointed eastward. "Your stepfather once asked me how it is possible to know what our god looks like, if we are not allowed to make any likenesses of him. If you wish to see the face of God, simply open your eyes and survey the things that surround you. If you want to feel the heartbeat of God, simply walk out and bathe yourself in the warmth of the sun."

Tiberius was silent. The slaves and servants brought more water and more towels, then served the main course, rare sturgeon from Rhodes garnished with vegetables, which Mahlir ate rather than offend his host.

Continued Mahlir, speaking more of the inner mysteries to the willing ears of the emperor of Rome, "It is written in our holy writings that the god of all people formed all that exists in seven days. The Essenes believe, true or not who can say, that we are embarking upon the journey of that seventh day – a day measured not by the rising and setting of the sun, or by the filling of water clocks, but by the works of God as those works rise to their completion – and that during that seventh day, a day which God has declared as holy, the human soul is unfolding to heights unimaginable."

Tiberius, when he finally did speak, shook his head, bewildered but unoffended, and when a smile did cross his face he said, "A most unusual people indeed." Satisfied that Mahlir would be loyal in his position, that he would work to prevent and quell riots and seditions, not fuel them, Tiberius set his mind free from his most troublesome province and its hard to understand citizenry. With a broad smile wrapped around his aging face, he called for the wedding cake, made of finely powdered meal mixed with costly wine and served upon bay leaves. It was delicious. Mahlir ate it in small pieces, allowing each to linger in his mouth, washing it down with a smooth sip of warmth from one of the silver goblets. After everyone had eaten their fill, and before the wedding procession began, where torchbearers would lead Mahlir and his bride to their chambers, the emperor of Rome disappeared. It would be many years before Mahir would see him again.

The procession was a grand sight. First went torchbearers, then the flute players, then a young woman carrying the bride's spindle and distaff, then Amanirinas herself with the wedding torch. Mahlir walked behind her and tossed walnuts to the children in the gathering crowd, walnuts because walnuts symbolize the outer layer of a man and a woman, within which is the purity of their souls that will be touched and bonded by marriage. Behind him were the slaves and would-be clients where normally would follow relatives and friends. Then there followed strangers, townspeople drawn by the sounds of the merriment, by the gleaming torchlight and music. "Io Thalassie!" everyone was shouting. "Hurrah for Thalassus the marriage god."

When they reached their chambers, Mahlir entered first, as was the Roman custom. It was a large guest-of-honor room at an inn at the bottom of the hill near the Circus, from where they would depart tomorrow down the Tiber to the sea for the long voyage to Caesarea. Amanirenas stopped outside to wind the door pillars with bits of wool, and to touch the door itself with oil and fat, a symbol of plenty. One of the slaves lifted her over the threshold. An ill omen it would be if she were to walk over it herself and stumble. Mahlir was waiting inside, there to present her with a cup of water and a glowing firebrand, representative of the fact that she is now entitled to his family Lares – household guardian spirits – the Roman equivalent of angels. Then they spoke to one another the words of the age-old marriage formula: "Ubit tu Gaius, ego Gaia. "*Where you are Gaius, I am Gaia,*" a pledge meaning *You will never walk alone. Where you go I will follow.*

The guests came inside and Amanirenas took out three coins. One she offered to Mahlir, a symbol of what she brings to the marriage. She spoke in Greek, "Beyond this simple coin I bring no money, no possessions," said she. "I bring to you something greater. I bring my goodness and a heart filled with love, pledging with this coin my devotion forever and throughout all eternity." The second coin she laid on an altar for the Lares of her new home and family. The third she cast into the street as a gift to the Lares of the Highway that would guard the door.

Mahlir put a golden ring on her finger, the third finger of her left hand, wherefrom a nerve runs to the heart, and as he did he looked at her and said, also in Greek, because he wanted to be sure she understood the exactness of his words, "I vow to you that I shall be your husband, and be devoted to you, in trying times as well as in good times, in times of your devotion as well as in times of your antipathy, in your health and in your sickness. Look to me not as a savior, or as a superior in anyway, but as a partner, a friend, an ally, for that is when a man and a woman are at their best. That is when the union is at its strongest. That is when their love has its greatest meaning. From this moment forward you shall never walk alone."

With long and tapered fingers she reached up and touched his face. "Likewise do I vow the same to you." Her voice was low in pitch, near to being harsh, smoothed with a silvery quality. "I wish also to express my devotion with a symbol. Upon my thumb is a stone ring. Wear this." She slipped it off and in the same manner placed it on the third finger of his left hand. It fit perfectly. She closed his hand inside both of hers – her hands felt cool – and squeezed. A tear formed in one of her eyes and bubbled up as if it was going to burst and flow, but instead it stayed, full and growing, right there in the corner of her eye. It seemed to sparkle. And a smile came, illuminating the happiness inside her heart. She squeezed his hand harder – he was surprised at her strength – pressing the thumb ring painfully into the bones of his other fingers. "The one who wears this ring need only look at it to know that with it comes my unfaltering love and devotion throughout eternity. Never take it off, my love, no matter the adversities that may come to confront us. It was given to me by my father as a blessing of good fortune. It has indeed brought me good fortune. It brought me you. Wear it always, as a symbol of the thread that unites us. Through that thread it shall continue to bless me. It shall bless us both. For I am a part of you."

Mahlir acknowledged that he would wear it.

Then Amanirenas blew out her torch and threw it into the crowd, where it was scurried after by the young people. The one to retrieve it would have good luck. Mahlir and his bride were then led to into the bedchamber and the door was shut. Outside they could hear the people singing. In the music there was beauty, because it reached to the hearts of the two lovers.

Amanirenas had been quiet the entire time, save for the lines she delivered for the ceremony. During the banquet she had said not a word. But as she lay in her husband's arms she told the story of her people. Her mother's mother had been the supreme Kandake of the Kingdom of Meroe, the queen who drove back Augustus sixty years earlier from the borders of Egypt. "Ours is the country to the south of Egypt," she said. "Egypt prior to that time had been ruled by the Greek called Ptolemy, and had recently been conquered by the Romans under the emperor Augustus, who was then called Octavius. Octavius had gathered his finest soldiers and set them up along our border, and demanded we pay tribute. The Nubians had always enjoyed peaceful relations with their neighbor to the north under the rule of Ptolemy. Now this peace had been breached. My grandmother was angered. A young woman at the time, she consulted with others in the royal family, and finally decided in favor of a military strike." The sound of Amanerinas' voice, husky, resonant, jeweled in soprano tracings, was healing to the wounds of Mahlir's soul. And her skin, the color of the still and starless night, was cool against him, and it sent blood quickening through him. Her leg began to fold across his stomach. She was rolling her fingers through his hair as she spoke and tracing her fingernails across his cheek. "But my grandmother knew she had to wait for the right time. That time came when the Romans had to withdraw the bulk of their forces to send needed reinforcements to the far-off land of Arabia. My people mounted their offensive, carrying ox-hide shields, axes, spears, and swords, and defeated the Romans, and left behind a message that they would not be taxed by a faraway government not their own. They took with them the head from a life size bronze statue of Octavius. My grandmother buried it beneath the doorway of her palace. Each time she would enter she would step on it. She would stop for a moment, her foot in place over the spot where the head lay, her full weight upon it, and invoke the power of Apedemak, the god of war, a deity that holds elephants and lions on leashes and grants us our victories. And each of those times she could feel Octavius beneath her foot becoming weaker, and her own form stronger.

When Octavius heard about the defeat of his troops he marched with fresh legions to engage us in battle. My grandmother personally took charge of her troops and marched them out to meet the enemy, confronting them at the city of Casr Ibrim south of Aswan. The Roman general Petronius surrendered before a single blow was struck, and told my grandmother that Octavius was willing to lay aside arms and negotiate a settlement. My grandmother agreed. Representatives from both sides met on the Greek island of Samos, where my people obtained everything for which they asked. Octavius even remitted the taxes he had previously levied."

The movements of Amanerinas' leg, the tracing of her fingers, the sound of her voice, brought forth Mahir's seed before he had even entered her, and it spilled out unfulfilled. Twenty years, it had been, since he had known a woman. His embarrassment was extreme. She laughed and finished the tale while moving astride him to let his newly erect penis ease up inside her to engulf him with her warmth, to absorb him with the coolness of her body. Her weight was solid upon him, proportioned equally from her breasts to her waist to her hips, and was as a narcotic to his senses. In the kingdom of Kush, to be large was to be beautiful. And indeed it was so.

They must have conceived that very night, for in the days to come Mahlir began to hear life within his wife's belly.

CHAPTER 30

LIFE WITH PILATE

ISRAEL – CAESAREA

The caravan returned from Parthia with the money from the sale of the grain, and with the iron and beer, and a profit was made, and the emperor was pleased. The incident at the arena with the Prince of Parthia and his wolf became humorous folklore, the subject of stories that grew and transformed themselves far beyond the truth. Tiberius himself was amused by the stories, and told his own augmented version, and laughed out loud every time he told it.

For the longest time Tiberius never knew what had become of the Parthian prince after his daring escape. He eventually was informed that he made it back to Parthia, but he never knew how he got there, never did find out that it was under the protection of his very own soldiery.

And Pontius Pilate was informed by the emperor that he would soon be receiving a man who would act as an advisor and liaison.

Life for Mahlir and his Kushite wife in Caesarea was an odd mix of luxury and poverty coexisting. Their quarters were in Pilate's palace, Herod's palace more properly, the coastal mansion built by Herod-the-Great that stretched out over the rocks and surf. They walked destitute in the midst of sparkle and grandeur. They barely had enough money to feed and clothe themselves.

Yet there was gold on his waist. "Why not sell it if there really is gold in there?" Amanirenas would sometimes ask, speaking of the box that bounced in rhythm to every footfall. And Mahlir would tell her the story all over again of how he came to be its courier, that it was not his, that it was supposed to contain the very crown worn by King David, and that he had made a promise to a dear friend to deliver it to a certain Galilean Rabbi, and he would underscore the superstition that had attached itself to the box over the years that the Shekinah Fire was affixed to it and would strike dead any thief who even so much as looked at it. So those who knew of the superstition did not touch it, and those who did not soon stopped paying it any mind, because the box eventually became so much a part of Mahlir's attire that it became as normal as the purse he carried on his other side.

Outside the bedchamber was a veranda enwrapped in a pillared railing overlooking the entire harbor of Caesarea. But as magnificent as the view from the veranda was, and as beautiful and spacious as their quarters were, the rooms were ones of bare stone, because the furnishings were their responsibility to provide, and Mahlir's remuneration was pitifully small. For the longest while all they had were two beds and a couch.

Mornings were good for Mahlir, because the day was new and free from problems, and the air fresh, its scent pure. Before the break of dawn, a cock would crow from somewhere in the city. By it he would rise, and he would shave with a razor, as does a Roman, but he would bathe as a Jew. Forty years of habit. Soon he would be joining Pilate to discuss the previous day's difficulties, and to talk over the puzzlements of the day to come, but first he would immerse himself in the iciness of his mikvah. Then, his skin prickling with vitality, he would stand on the veranda and watch the gray of dawn gradually turn to violet and begin to consume the twinkling lights of the beacon torches. And he would listen to the calming roar of the sea, and the squawking of the gulls, and the melodic morning chants from the synagogue. And he would breathe in the sea-born mist and savor its scent, always freshest in the morning – one could smell its coolness – and look out at the harbor as it speared out crescent shaped from the southern end of the city to hook northward to the open sea, where it became a breakwater built of hewn stones the size of bull elephants, making of itself a mole as big as a mountain, springing forth with towers and arches and lodges. At any given moment the silvery blue within would be dotted with the whites of a hundred billowed sails. Up close by the port seawall, as one waited for the rowboats to arrive with passengers and cargo, the blue waters transformed themselves to dirty green, and were scattered throughout with planks and wood splinters. Outside the breakwater, away from its protection, the naked masts of ships bobbed and swayed, waiting for the signal from the beacon-tower to enter, two torches at night, two flags by day. And somewhere in the distance, as the eye swept southward, hidden just beyond a barrier of coastal rocks and trees, lay the crumbling remains of a house once owned by a man called Eli. Now and then Mahlir would stroll among the exposed ruins and reflect, and whisper his regrets to the ghosts that walked there.

Directly below, open at the top, was Pilate's heated bathhouse, built among the rocks and the breaking surf. Now and then waves would spray over onto a bather. But its walls were sturdy against the water, even amid a storm.

Soon Pilate would come and slowly settle himself in the heat and look up, and Mahlir would hurry down. Pilate was a brilliant and complex man, able to carry on multiple conversations and give his complete attention to each. Often he would be listening to Mahlir's thoughts on a matter and at the same time be going into detail about something else with another aide, and never have to ask either to repeat themselves, retaining it all. The curious thing about Pontius Pilate – his brilliance was roughened by a self-taught education in the back streets of the Emporium. "I left home when I was eight," he boasted. "From then on there was only me to take care of me," he would say. He had struggled through his boyhood years sleeping on the docks, working for food, begging sometimes, fighting off bullies, many of them full-grown adults, until a wealthy freedman took pity on him and allowed him to be one of his clients, a position Pilate devoted himself to furiously. From that position Pontius Pilate rose to money and power and military fame – but even in Rome brilliance has its limitations, able to carry one only so far. As Pilate himself put it on more than one melancholy occasion, "If I would have come from noble stock my life's work certainly would not be one of administering to savages a world away." Then he would look at Mahlir and qualify the statement – "You know of course what I mean. By savages I mean the other Jews –" – speaking to Mahlir as if he were more Roman than Jew. Perhaps he was. Then Pilate would make some comment about how he would soon see to some changes. "These savages will soon be enjoying a better life," he would say. "They live amid squalor and disease, with poor drains and insufficient water supplies. This will soon change."

Pilate was a short, portly man who seemed much taller than he was simply by the way he carried himself. On most men a girth bespeaks physical weakness. On Pilate it gave a look of power and authority, though it hung in front of him like a keg of wine, and though his hairless head was fringed like that of a monk. The extra pounds looked like they were made of steel. Well they fit into his cuirass, plain though it was, with leather breastplates and knee-length kilt. Little more than the dress of a common legionnaire. Except that with it he always wore a purple cape and a civic crown of oak leaves. He swaggered when he walked, as though daring someone to refuse to step aside for him. Every now and then someone would refuse, an aide, sometimes a servant, and a wrestling match would ensue, often escalating to fists and sword play, with the offender never being disciplined, being instead respected all the more. Pilate probably thought of Mahlir as cowardly, because he never allowed himself to be drawn in by such fool's play. Twenty years ago Mahlir would have taken the bait, but not now, not today. Today Mahlir was like the elder King Solomon. Solomon as a young king had penned his proverbs with aggressive and dogmatic enthusiasm; as an elder king his more ecclesiastical writings poetized how he had mellowed with age, and how he had grown in his wisdom, practical wisdom which often told how to accomplish a task and stay out of trouble at the same time. Mahlir was strong when he needed to be, when the occasion called for it, when he truly thought Pilate was making a wrong decision. "I want to build a water system," Pilate once said. "I want to finance it from the Temple treasury." Pilate was a man of logic. To him it was painfully logical that the money the people gave to the Temple be used for the benefit of the people, for their health and welfare. To this Mahlir protested, to the point of Pilate's anger, to the point where Mahlir thought Pilate was going to strike him. "The people will resist," Mahlir stressed. "Do this and you will have a sedition. The money is given to God, and it must remain so. It is our way. It is the dictate of our religion. Our religion is the one thing you can never change."

Pilate was furious. "Then the people need to be protected from their religion," he bellowed, his face nearly touching Mahlir's. "I will not allow my citizenry to destroy themselves when they have the ability to do otherwise, any more than I would allow my children to walk among vipers. And what of this god? What kind of a god is it who would prefer his people amass gold and silver to no benefit other than to ornament his Temple and feed the extravagance of its priests, when water is needed, when sewage and drainage systems are needed?"

The most difficult thing about dealing with Pilate was the uncertainty of when an outburst would occur, and not knowing what would trigger it. The best thing about him, and a rare quality it was, was the fact that he never carried the anger beyond the moment. The eruption would happen, he would exhaust himself of it, express all he was thinking, sometimes in favor of Mahlir's recommendations, most of the time not, then it would be gone. And with a fatherly hand on Mahlir's shoulder he would be on to another subject. With Pontius Pilate, you never had to concern yourself about whether or not he was brooding over an issue, or whether he was holding resentment. He always said what was on his mind. If he disliked something someone said, it came out of his mouth immediately. And, perhaps the most remarkable thing about the governor, as belligerent as he was, as boyishly immature as he tended to be – he was razor-edged honest. He had his own brand of ethics, a moral code that depended on no one, on no thing, no government law, no religious deity, no dogma, and he defended it furiously. If the law conflicted, he stood on the side of what he thought was right. "Perhaps that right there is why I have been banished to the far reaches of the empire," he once jokingly commented. One time he was called to resolve a dispute between a peasant farmer and a landowner. The farmer owed the landowner money and had pledged himself as a slave for the debt for the customary seven years. During the term of his servitude the farmer had taken a slave woman as his wife, and she bore him three children. At the seventh year, the year the farmer could choose to take his freedom, the landowner refused to allow the man's wife and children to go free with him because the wife was a lifetime slave. The man's only alternative was to have *his* ear pierced with the awl and also become a lifetime servant. He appealed to Pilate.

Pilate counseled with Mahlir in private: "The landowner is correct," Mahlir told him. "To keep the woman and her children is his right. Because she was the landowner's slave from the beginning. By the laws of our god she still belongs to him, as do her children. It is his right."

"Then it is a right that is wrong!" Pilate shot out.

Most respectfully, Mahlir reminded him that he is under orders from the emperor not to interfere with the Jewish religion and its laws.

That was all it took. The veins popped out, the monk muttons shook, and Pilate's face turned as red as a pepper as the anger spewed forth. "Your god is wrong! And the emperor is wrong if he sides with your god and your religion!"

Mahlir reminded him that he was taking the chance of turning public sentiment away from him.

"The man's debt is paid!" Pilate thundered. "There is no reason his wife and family should suffer!"

"It is not unlike your own laws in Rome regarding slavery," Mahlir pointed out.

"That custom is also wrong," Pilate stated, quickly and flatly. His mind was made up. He walked back in to where the two disputants were waiting and granted that the man and his wife and children be given their freedom, with the words, “While I understand and respect the right of this landowner to his property, it is a right outweighed by the right of a man to his family and children, and by the rights of his family and children to their father, and by the right of a man to be able to provide for his family.” Using a reasonable rate for services rendered, Pilate calculated how much of the debt had been worked off by the time the seventh year rolled around – all of it, as it turned out, then some – and directed that the remainder be a debt the landowner owed the farmer – then calculated the value of the wife and the three children and declared the reverse debt cancelled. Both adversaries left scratching their heads, satisfied somehow, in their confusion.

Typically, the mornings with Pilate were smooth and free of tension. Typically, he and Mahlir would lounge in the warm water and talk, first discussing problems and issues, then things unrelated to business, like two friends talking. Then he would fix Mahlir breakfast. Pilate preferred to prepare it himself. Each morning breakfast was different, consisting of various combinations of pulse and bread. Mahlir was living as a Roman, but still his diet was absent meat, and Pilate respected that. Sometimes Amanirenas and Pilate’s wife Claudia would join them.

One brilliantly sunny morning Mahlir shall never forget, a fifth person came for breakfast. He came unannounced, asking for Mahlir.

“What does he want?” Pilate asked.

Responded the guard who had answered the call at the gate, “He says his name is Joseph. He hails from Arimethea, a town formerly known as Ramah.”

Numbness pulsed through Mahlir. There were many men in Judea named Joseph, many whom Mahlir knew, but only one Joseph-of-Arimethea, his friend from long ago, the husband of his adulterous lover.

“This man Joseph is a member of the high Sanhedrin council,” the guard said. “He is in the city seeing to some business affairs and is staying close by at a house he owns. He wishes that your administrator, Mahlir, the son of Matthias, be his guest for dinner on the morrow after next.”

“Do you know this Joseph?” Pilate asked Mahlir.

"He is an acquaintance from days of old," Malir responded.

Among Pilate's acute capabilities and talents was an ability to read human emotions. He knew instantly Mahlir had a secret.

Said Mahlir to the guard, "Tell him I shall be pleased to attend, if he shall give me a time and a place, and if I may bring my wife Amanirenas." Malir had told Amanirenas everything, about the adultery that changed the course of his future, about his abduction by the Parthians, and about his infant son that is now a prince, everything. She marveled at his cleverness when he told her how he made his escape by tricking the Parthian mind readers into believing he would kidnap a child for them. And she listened intently as he told her about the reclusive sect of the Essenes on the cliff shores of the Dead Sea, and about their secrets, and about his many years with them. She told him she was glad he had been filled with the unexplained need to move on, to travel again to Rome, because it was there that destiny decreed that he meet and marry her, so that they could have children together, so that they could forever remain bonded. He was her one and only true love, she told him. A destiny. And likewise did the child within her belly have a destiny.

Although – she did tease him mercilessly about his little box, the mystery container that enclosed the crown of King David, supposedly. She would balance it on her head and pretend to be a queen with magic powers. "Poof, let the sun rise," she would say and point to the horizon – it would be at the break of day – "...and lo, the sun rises." "Bow down to me," was her favorite, after putting the box on her head. "I am the queen. Tell me how wonderful I am." It was a punishable offense for a Jewish wife to speak thus to her husband – but who would ever know.

She never opened the box, though she threatened to. She would try to convince Mahlir to look inside, though she knew he never would. And she respected his reasons. "Why didn't you ever deliver it to this Yeshua person?" she asked.

"I told you, I tried, but I couldn't find him. Then I ran out of both money and time. So I guess I'll just have to wait until I have the money and time." Many times he had been tempted to open it himself and end their poverty once and for all, but for whatever subconscious reason, his hand would not move in that direction.

"Tell Joseph we will be there," Mahlir repeated to the guard. "He need only dispatch a message as to where and when."

"Nonsense," said Pilate. "We shall be pleased to have this man Joseph as a guest here at the palace, for breakfast tomorrow morning. Tell the messenger we shall expect his master at the first rays of the sun. We shall also be pleased to have the messenger as our guest. Tell him that." As the guard turned to depart Pilate changed his mind. "No, wait, tell hm we shall be pleased to have him as our guest today, this very morning, this very minute. He shall have the guest of honor place on the couch. We will wait." Pilate's greatest obsession was perhaps his greatest weakness. He had a need to control and dominate. As powerful as his need to breathe, it was. It was a need to dominate every person in his presence, and to have knowledge of every aspect of the lives of those people. The fact that there was something hidden in Mahlir's life was ulcerous to Pilate. The control Pilate needed, the dominance, was not of the physical kind where people were made to stand before him in chains, but rather it was a control of his mere presence that he craved, power given by his charisma. The ultimate in control to Pontius Pilate would be to have a brilliant and powerful man submissive to his will solely out of choice, out of a simple recognition that he, Pontius Pilate, was the better and wiser man. To have a servant that is more than a servant.

CHAPTER 31

BEFORE THE PARTY

ISRAEL – CAESAREA

Time had been kind to Joseph. In the nearly twenty years since Mahlir had seen him, he seemed not to have aged at all. He did seem taller, but maybe that was because his face was thinner. His beard was as white as the snows of the Apennines. Had it been that white before? And he seemed more dignified, though maybe it was because his aging frame was carrying him a bit slower

Mahlir wondered what would be said after so many years.

He had just finished telling Pilate about the debt he owed to Joseph, the transgression that had put a blot upon his soul. Pilate's skill with the spoken word and his art of persuasion had drawn it forth. Pilate's only comment was a simple one, delivered with a barely perceptible smile, a paternal expression, right before Joseph was announced. "A man doesn't get between another man and his wife; he's not much of a man if he does," was all he said.

Pilate rose and greeted his guest and pointed to a silver cushion marking the empty third place on the middle couch, the "Consul's Post."

Joseph accepted by giving a small bow. He acknowledged Pilate's wife with the same gesture.

"My wife, Claudia Procula," said Pilate.

Claudia nodded.

Then Joseph looked at Mahlir. There was no sign of ill will. But why should there be? Joseph didn't know.

Mahlir was unsure of how to respond, whether to treat him as a guest, with formality, or as a friend.

He simply rose and faced his old friend, doing and saying nothing.

Joseph came forward and offered the traditional embrace and kiss of friendship.

Mahlir accepted it stiffly and returned it, the symbolic exchanging of two spirits. He gestured toward the other woman on the couch, her clothes ablaze with the orange and red of a sunrise, ever the more beautiful now that she was so close to giving birth. "My wife, Amanirenas."

One aspect of Joseph, in particular, was different from what Mahlir remembered. His manner of dress. Instead of the formal and expensive attire he used to wear, the robes and golden tassels and high turbans of the Sadducees, he wore a single ankle-length tunic and a cloak across one shoulder. His hair hung loose and unwrapped. It was a freeing kind of appearance, one that gave him the look of a young man.

Joseph seated himself and reclined back on one elbow. A slave brought a wreath of flowers for his head, their fragrance powerful to ward off drunkenness from the strong wine being offered, and sprinkled him with perfume from a vial of alabaster, and offered him a goblet.

Seasoned eggs were prepared in front of everyone upon a smoking brazier by Pilate himself. Two slaves set out breads and salt, and olive oil for dipping.

Said Pilate, as he reclined, "I hope you will forgive the sparseness of our morning foods. In Rome the main meal is dinner. We eat mildly in the morning, fast during the day, then gorge ourselves at night."

All ate, but very little was said. What did Joseph want? Nothing, it seemed. He and Mahlir talked only of unimportant matters. Pilate just listened. Mahlir spoke of his experiences and journeys. Joseph talked of his life over the years, of how he had risen to prominence within the Sanhedrin, and of how well his children had done in their schooling in the Temple and of how he had become a follower of the Rabbi Yeshua. He spoke nothing of his wife, Mahlir's adulteress. The question of what had become of her suddenly began to burn within Mahlir, but he didn't ask, and pushed the curiosity from his mind. Even as the two of them walked alone in the garden Joseph spoke not of her. Only of Yeshua, Jesus in the Greek. They were speaking in Greek, since it was a customary tongue for Mahlir, because of Amanirenas. Jesus had become a legend by now, speaking words profound and bringing about acts of the supernatural, elevating him beyond even the folk-hero status of Cronin the Circle Drawer, the babbling rabbi who could make it rain by scratching symbols in the dirt. Whenever Mahlir heard the name – Yeshua, Jesus – something uncomfortable rose within hm. Envy still, perhaps. And of course it all reminded him of the promise, yet unfulfilled, that he had made to Elkanar about finding Yeshua and giving him the crown.

"I know him," Mahlir said, as politely as possible, after hearing as much of the name as he could stand. "I studied with him. We shared meals together. Trust me, he is nobody different from you or me. He's the son of a stone mason in Nazareth, nothing more. He's not even of the priestly line. The entire time I was with him I never saw him do one thing miraculous." Then came to mind once more the absurdity of what he was carrying on his hip, the box that was so light it could contain little more than a feather, certainly not a talent's worth of gold reserved for the anointed head of the Messiah. He suddenly became aware of it, still attached to his belt, riding easily on his hip, bouncing lightly between steps, a part of him. He thought of just giving it to Joseph and having him deliver it. Elkanar didn't specifically say it had to be handed over by Mahlir. Mahlir thought about it, almost did it. His hand reached back and touched it, almost closed around it and brought it forward...but didn't. His right side would be empty without the feel of it there.

Responded Joseph, a sickening smile of admiration warping his face. "May I tell you the story of how I first met him? You can rely on my word in what I am about to tell you, for you know me as one who does not lie.

I was visiting friends in Nazareth. I was invited to speak in the synagogue there. I was given the righthand seat of honor, as is the custom for visiting priests and teachers of the Law. Have you seen the synagogue in Nazareth? It is a building shining with ebony splendor, a star of brilliance among the black basalt of a very common town, with very common people. In many ways that synagogue is one of Israel's finest, with a broad nave running the length of the interior. Double stone benches are built against the wall. Two seats are carved into the upper rows in the southeast and southwest corners. These are the seats of honor, one on the right, one on the left. They have curved and comfortable backs, like the Sanhedrin chambers in the Temple. It was in one of these that I sat. Across from me, in the other seat, was a second honored guest. It was announced that this person also was a teacher of the Law. It was announced that here was the Rabbi Jesus, the one from Capernaum who performs the miracles and speaks with insight to the crowds that follow him. He was introduced as having studied many years in Jerusalem in the Temple under the most learned of teachers. He had grown up there in Nazareth, it was proclaimed, and now, as he had done as a boy in this very synagogue, he would read from the texts. An attendant reached into the Ark of Scrolls and pulled forth the Book of Isaiah, and held it out for him, along with a tallit, which he wrapped around himself.

"He took the scroll and walked to the center pedestal and found the place in the 61st chapter where it is written – you know it well, having read it many times:

> *The Spirit of the Sovereign Lord is on me,*
> *Because the Lord has anointed me*
> *To preach good news to the poor.*
> *He has sent me to bind up the brokenhearted,*
> *To proclaim freedom for the prisoners*
> *And recovery of sight for the blind,*
> *To release the oppressed,*

To proclaim the year of the Lord's favor.

"The rabbi's speech was fluent and precise, and his voice warm. His words came with authority, and the eyes of the people were transfixed upon him. He rolled up the scroll and handed it back to the attendant. The service paused at that point, while the eyes of everyone followed him back to his seat. The seats of honor are places that can been seen by anyone from anywhere in the synagogue. After settling himself hc looked at the people. Was that it? Was that all he was going to do? Read a simple paragraph from the text without offering explanation? Anyone could do that. He looked at each one of us separately, looked right into our eyes, one by one, causing us all to sit a bit straighter. Then he said something while still seated that shocked us to the extreme. 'Today this scripture is fulfilled in your hearing,' he said, and he said no more.

"The people began mumbling to one another. Some were stifling laughter. 'Isn't this Joseph's son?' came a voice.

"Another voice rose. 'Is he saying that he has been called by God, that he has been anointed?' There was more laughter. A cry came up out of the people, a question by a man sitting somewhere in the congregation. 'Little Jesus, who used to play robbers with my own little boy, is he telling us that he is the Christ?' The last of the man's words were swallowed by guffaws of his own laughter.

"Jesus then said to them, 'Surely you will quote this proverb to me; Physician heal thyself! Do here in your hometown what we have heard you do in Capernaum.'

"There was more whispering and mumbling, and more laughter.

"'I tell you truly,' Jesus then said, 'No prophet is accepted in his hometown.' He reminded the people that when Elijah healed the leper, he healed a leper from the Northern Kingdom, not one from his own land. The implication was clear. The Rabbi Jesus would not be doing his wonderworks in his hometown, because of their ridicule and disbelief.

"The people were angry. They seized hold of him and took him to cast him from the brink of a cliff at the edge of town. I tried to dissuade them, as did several others, unsuccessfully. I thought surely I would be a witness to his death. Instead, what I witnessed was another of his wondrous works. Just as he was about to go over, he looked at one of the men grasping him and the man let go and backed away. That was all Jesus did. Just looked at him. That's it! As God is my witness, the man released him and backed away, as if terrified by what he saw in those eyes. Then Jesus looked at another man, and another, and another. Soon they were all backing away. Without uttering a word he walked through the crowd to his freedom. They were unable to lay as much as a finger on him.

"I followed him. I followed him all the way to Capernaum. On the Sabbath he went to the synagogue there and taught the people. And we were all amazed at the things he said. He is less than half my age, yet he has double my wisdom. What I am about to tell you is true. By our God I swear it. In the synagogue, there in Capernaum, as he was speaking, a man fell to the floor and began crying out at the top of his voice, yelling things unintelligible, and was shaking and convulsing. Jesus stopped his speaking and looked at the man and said something to him that I couldn't quite make out. The man instantly became calm. The demon had come full out of him. That was not the only thing I saw him do. He told a paralyzed man that his sins were forgiven, that he could take up his mat and go home. And guess what! The man did just that! But what I find so compelling about this man is not what he does but what he says. From his lips come concepts I have not heard spoken anywhere, or seen written by anyone, sage or prophet, past or present, concepts so simple, so basic that they are profound. Love your enemies, bless those that curse you, pray for those who mistreat you. One would think him insane, were not his concepts so insightful. Some do think him insane. Perhaps he is." Then Joseph looked into Mahlir's soul, making him squirm with the gaze, making him wonder if maybe he knew after all about Mahlir's most grievous sin. "Forgive and you will be forgiven, is what he says. Be merciful, just as your Father in Heaven is merciful.'"

Joseph allowed the words to settle and germinate, and just as Mahlir was about to confess it all, Joseph went on with his dialogue. "But alas," he said, "I fear that among my Temple colleagues I am alone in my admiration of him. Many of them quite despise him, because he is openly critical of the priests and teachers and scribes of the Law, in ways I must say that are deserved. He speaks nothing of us that is not true."

The sun was up now, warming the open-air garden through which Mahlir and Joseph were strolling. A fountain they had just passed was beginning to collect doves in its top basin, birds of beauty, fluffing their white feathers in the spray, walking the edges picking out insects. Joseph was tiring. "May we sit for a time?" he asked, and eased himself onto a low balustrade and leaned back against one of the columns supporting the outer roof. Two single vines of yellow-green ivy entwined it. In front of him hung a hundred more from the sloping red-tiled roof. On the marble walkway were curls of leaves, brown, red, yellow, heralds of a season change from trees brought in from Rome that do well if given constant water. An urn of silver and bronze sparkled beside them, showing the gleam of overnight dew. Out of its top bloomed the soft purple of Roman Columbines, bells with stars.

Mahlir sat opposite Joseph. As he looked at his friend, he knew for sure. He knew that Joseph knew. The sadness in the droop of his smile, the heaviness in his eyes, as he babbled on about the Rabbi Yeshua, about doing good to those who do harm to you – that's how Mahlir knew. Joseph was a man confronting his demons.

"I have transgressed the Law," Mahlir finally said. "I have injured you."

"Yes," Joseph acknowledged.

"I have a debt to pay to you. But I have no money. I have nothing to offer you. You are wealthy, I am poor. There is no way for me to make you whole."

"But there is." Joseph leaned closer. "Extend a hand to one who has less. And forgive another. That is how you can do it. For we are all connected. A wound to one is a wound to all. To lift one up is to lift all."

Then a terrifying thought came. Joseph's wife must have paid the penalty! An adulteress is stoned. It is the Law.

Mahlir asked.

"No, Jael is fine. She has repented and has been a good wife over the years, and a good mother. A grandmother now. I told no one. There were four people only who knew, and it stayed that way."

"Four?!" Mahlir trembled at the implication. Jael, Joseph, Mahlir, and… "Rachel?"

Joseph nodded. Yes. Rachel knew."

"But she said nothing. Ever."

"Then she suffered in silence."

How could she possibly have known?

Joseph answered the question, though Mahlir had posed it only in his mind. "She was a witness. She saw you two together one morning. She had gone to visit Jael that particular morning, thinking Jael was alone and in need of company, thinking you were in service at the Temple. She was intending to surprise her friend." Joseph looked then at Mahlir, teacher to student, friend to friend, brother to brother, with eyes of power, eyes of authority. Not the look of accusation, or even of pain, this was a look that came from eyes that seemed to be hoping to impart a truth. "God has forgiven you," he said. "This is what I learned from the Rabbi Yeshua. And I have forgiven you. This is as the Rabbi commands."

"But I have committed adultery, and I have done so in the name of God, using God as my alibi. Even for this, Yahweh forgives?"

"Even for this."

"And Rachel knew all along?"

Joseph nodded.

"This cannot be happening," Mahlir whispered, barely able to push forth the words.

Said Joseph, "Many an hour I spent in prayer asking how I should deal with the matter. By the Law? So that she be stoned? Or should I simply put her away in private by divorcement? Then the hand of the Lord directed me to the writings of Hosea. I was walking one day near the Temple, on the wide streets of Tyropean, when a scrap of papyrus blew between my feet. It was a torn piece of a scroll, from the scroll of Hosea as he wrote to the brothers of the Northern Kingdom of the things God spoke to him. *'Go show love to your wife again, though she is loved by another and is an adulteress. Love her as the Lord loves the Israelites, though they turn to other gods and love the sacred raisin cakes.'* I had my answer."

Rachel knew? Demons danced inside Mahlir's head, shameful creatures that fed themselves on the substance of his guilt. Each of those nights that he stole away, with the excuse of going to the Temple to study to pray, to councel others – she knew? Yet she said nothing? The night the soldiers came – she knew where Mahlir was? The day she died on the wheel, the moment she cast her final look at Mahlir – she knew where he had been? The vision of the Dead Sea, where she came to him from the afterlife and spoke only words of love – she knew?

"How can I possibly atone?" he whispered. "She is dead. Her bones are scattered in Gahenna."

Again Joseph said, "Forgive another. That is how. For we are all connected."

The confusion inside Mahlir melted the sturdy features of his chiseled face and gave it a sudden look of innocence, of wonderment and fear, as a child might display when looking into the face of someone wiser and more powerful.

Joseph nodded, in reinforcement of the eccentric words. His breathing seemed easier, as if a burden of his own had been lifted.

Mahlir asked him to tell him about the affairs of the world. Twenty years Mahlir had been in Qumran. Now, it seemed, he had stepped through a door in time.

"Many things have happened in the Eastern regions since you have been gone," Joseph began. Some Mahlir knew of, some not. He knew that Vonones had been recalled from Rome and installed as king of Parthia, and that that the Parthians rejected him and installed Artabanus instead. And he knew of how Germanicus, Rome's general for the Asiatic regions, had fallen mysteriously dead, at the hands of Artabanus it was suspected.

"Those close to the affairs of Parthia say that he was seduced by the Queen of Parthia," said Joseph. "They say that he lost his life in the Queen's bed chambers. For a man is never as weak as he is in the hands of a beautiful woman. And it is said that the Queen of Parthia is stunning in her beauty." Joseph leaned forward and spoke softly, as if in fear of creatures listening beyond sight. "It is said that the Queen of Parthia has dispatched many a powerful man from within her chambers. She beds them then she kills them, as a spider would do." A nod of Joseph's head affirmed it as fact. Then he said something that caused Mahlir's heart to stand still. He said it almost as a throwaway comment that meant nothing to anybody anywhere, except Mahlir: "Perhaps you heard," he said, and there was a smile upon his face, as if he was about to say something humorous. "The games in Rome, detestable in the eyes of God and of all things decent, were interrupted by the son of Artabanus, the one they call the Wolf Prince. Who knows how it really happened, but the story is that the boy freed the wolves and all the animals. They say he did it by sorcery. However he did it, it was a good thing. The devil himself could have freed them and I would call it a good thing."

CHAPTER 32

AN URGENT MATTER

ISRAEL – CAESAREA

Of the sons of Herod-the-Great who charted the destiny of Palestine, one was about to bring it to ruin. Antipas, ruler of Galilee, was having a love affair with the wife of one of his brothers. Joseph widened his eyes and chuckled, but it was not a laughter of humor; it was more an expression of puzzlement. "You might say the Herods like to keep it in the family," he said.

"And now," Joseph began, "he has taken her into the palace as though she were his legitimate wife. It is an entanglement that threatens to tear apart the tetrarchy. Such debauchery has been known in the annals of history to bring about civil wars and to have toppled empires."

Mahlir remembered what Eli had said while hanging on the cross, about how whenever royalty feuds, kingdoms fall. "It is something we cannot allow to happen," Mahlir whispered.

"It becomes worse," continued Joseph. "His legal wife happens to be the daughter of the king of Arabia. And she has gone back to her father. War is probably developing as we speak."

A lonely looking owl, a captive within a hanging cage, blinked at Mahlir from its prison, as if to say it heard what had been said, and was casting an ill omen upon the situation. By Roman superstition the very sight of an owl brings bad luck, though everyone knows true bad luck comes only from owls in the wild. This owl was a pet, seen every day on walks, a creature kept but never comforted, fed but never stroked.

"There has been a dispute of border boundaries between the two countries, Arabia and Galilee," Joseph went on, "ongoing for many years, kept quiet only by the marriage of the families."

Above, in the morning sky, between long and slender slivers of lavender, was the white outline of the moon, in full daylight, another bad omen. Suddenly Mahlir felt very displaced, very empty. Suddenly he became aware of the things surrounding them in this enormous garden embraced by the ocean and palace walls – busts and statues of gods and athletes, a Penelope that looked in every detail like the Scopas original, a series of statuettes presenting the myths of the god Bacchus, busts of Tiberius, Octavius, Julius Caesar, Pompey-the-Great, Marc Antony, and others, many Mahlir did not recognize. As he looked at them the emptiness grew. "Am I powerless to do anything about this?" he asked, speaking as much to himself as to Joseph.

Pilate confirmed Mahir's fears. "I cannot order the man back to his wife," he told him. "My duties are to keep order here in the province of Judea. Outside of its boundaries I have no jurisdiction."

"Then let us inform Caesar," said Mahlir. "So that he may prepare himself to take necessary steps." Mahlir asked Pilate to send him as an emissary to negotiate between the two countries.

Pilate didn't answer, but seated himself instead. Pilate often used silence to think.

It was Joseph who spoke next. "There is another matter of concern." He said it softly, but in a voice that in the quiet sounded like thunder. "One more problem exists, that threatens peril. There is the matter of the Baptist."

"The Baptist?" questioned Pilate.

"He is another prophet of the people. Some say he is Elijah returned. Others claim him to be the Messiah. He performs ritual washings in the Jordan, a cleansing of the body to symbolize the purification of the soul. Antipas has imprisoned him in the castle Machaerus, a horrible place on the borders of the lands of Galilee and Arabia."

The ever-present, ever-slight skew of Pilate's smile wormed its way into the anticipation of yet another crisis in the governing of these impossible people. "Who is this Baptist?" he wanted to know. "Where does he come from?"

"His name is John. He is reported to be the son of a Zadokite, a Temple priest called Zechariah."

The answer stunned Malir. "I know him, this man. He too was with me at Qumran. He is not dangerous. The washing is an Essene ritual, done by gentle people for gentle purposes. Call him what you will, lunatic or fanatic, perhaps he is both, but he is not a man of violence. It simply is not true. This man would never bring about rioting." Mahlir looked at Pilate. "We must intercede on his behalf."

Pilate straightened and rested his hand on the hilt of his sword and shrugged, after first issuing a smile of quiet authority "There is nothing I can do. Philip's and Antipas' lands are theirs to rule, by the emperor's wish."

"As long as they rule in such a way that is peaceful," Mahlir reminded. "And not burdensome to the emperor. I full on guarantee you, what Antipas has done *will* burden the emperor. The arrest of a man considered by the Jews to be a prophet, while Antipas may have done it in the interest of peace, will have the opposite effect. Plus, a renewing of the border dispute between Galilee and Arabia will very much burden the emperor. Antipas has committed the gravest of errors by imprisoning this man called the Baptist; and not to mention – he has taken as a lover his brother's wife, while his own wife is afar in her father's kingdom stirring up the bitter brew of war."

Pilate narrowed his mouth with a look a parent might have while giving in to a persistent child.

And persist Mahlir did. "Send me as an emissary. Let the emperor express his concerns on the matter through me."

Pilate finally agreed. A dispatch was sent by sea to Rome, which came back in the affirmative, authorizing Mahlir to travel to the palace of Antipas as an official representative of Caesar.

In the interim, Amanirenas gave birth. Her child-bearing months had been ones that would forever be among Mahlir's fondest memories. He and Amanirenas had become very close. She had become the other half of his heart, of his soul, of his mind and body. He shared with her everything from his business dealings with Pilate to the mysteries of Qumran, and found that she possessed a surprising ability to grasp it all, even the Hidden Knowledge, and that she had a keen intellect when it came to the affairs of men and governments. She was his equal. It had been his destiny to meet this woman, to travel to Rome and walk down that particular street that particular day. The Teacher of Righteousness had been guiding his steps after all.

Their child was a girl. They named her Tabitha, Aramaic for gazelle, because the gazelle was Amanirenas' favorite animal, swift, delicate, strong, beautiful. Tabitha was the color of almond brown, sweet child, a shade darker than Mahlir's own olive skin. Her hair was so black it gleamed. And her eyes were large and brown like her mother's. She was a beautiful child. The birthing had been hard for Amanirenas. Mahlir worried for a time that she would die, and that she would take Tabitha with her. But sometimes God is merciful.

Or is he? Shortly after the birth, Amanirenas' milk dried up. At first they didn't know why Tabitha was constantly crying. The dear child was starving, bit by bit. She was attaching and suckling, but hardly anything was coming out. And the milk supply was lessening by the day, until finally, one night, long before the rise of the sun, in the absolute darkest hour, Amanirenas could no longer try. Cracks and infected sores had developed on her nipples. Nothing would come out, not so much as a trickle.

Mahlir was dumfounded, and frightened, and spent the night walking through the dangerous streets of Caesarea with a baby in his arms, looking for a mother with a breast. Memories of twenty-five years earlier came ripping into his mind of when he was forced to wander the desert with his day-old son. Strange, Mahlir felt more protected in the desert than he did here in Caesarea with houses all around. He was turned away from every door he approached, because he was a Roman. He explained that he was actually a Jew, a priest, of the Zadokite line. They only laughed. At least in the desert he had sustenance for the child, be it only a goat.

With each banging upon each door the child's cries grew louder, then her agony became lost in breathy gasps, and into disappearing respites of brief sleep…

…until they came upon a beggar woman sitting under the cover of a dripping roof. Rain had begun to fall. The woman was shivering, clutching a baby of her own. Unlike Mahlir's baby, hers was asleep and unaware of its peril.

"Good sir," said the woman upon seeing Malir. "Can you give a poor soul money for a crust of bread and a place to sleep?"

"Woman, I am carrying no money with me," Malir responded honestly. "But there is something I would ask of you."

It was such an odd feeling for Mahlir, to be looking down at a beggar and knowing that she possessed something more valuable to him than all of Solomon's gold, something he would have given a hundred talents for, had he the money. He would have given all he owned. But this precious woman bared her breast and offered it for free. Mahlir bent down and put Tabitha to it. It was then that he realized her own baby was dead, though she held it as tight and as lovingly as if it lived.

Mahlir put his hand out. "Come," he said. "If you follow me I will see to it that you have shelter and food, and a place to entomb your child."

And so it was that Mahlir and Amanirenas acquired their slave. Esther was her name.

At first Amanirenas was unaccepting of Esther. She wanted Mahlir to find another woman to nurse Tabitha. She wanted him to find a nurse not as young and not as pretty. Mahlir refused. "Tabitha needs milk now," he said. "And Esther needs a home now. She stays."

Amanirenas was furious, spewing forth epithets in her native tongue, leaving Mahlir to shake his head in almost amused confusion, having not the slightest idea what she was saying. She went so far as to threaten to end their marriage over the mater, and that she did in Greek so that he could clearly understand. Usually when they argued, over the little things, disagreements coming now and then in moments of anxiety over life's complexities – over the way she spent money, or over Mahlir's lack of ambition to rise further than his position with Pilate, or over her complaints about their indebtedness – he always acquiesced. With those issues she was correct. Amanirenas deserved to have a husband who could provide her with a comfortable lifestyle. They had hopes that things would get better. Pilate had recently created a shipping company for ferrying wheat and grain from Caesarea to Rome, of which Mahlir had been promised a percentage in return for his assigned duty of keeping its records. But what Amanirenas and Mahlir thought would bring them large sums generally brought very little. They were no better off, and Mahlir was working twice as hard. She was within her rights to complain. But this was different. This argument was about practicality and safety. "Do what you will," he said. "Leave if you want. I'll talk to Pilate and see if we can arrange passage for you back to Kush. Or, if it better suits you, go back to the arena. You can go as a free person. Perhaps you can win your recognition and your fortune." He said it because of something she had once said when money was short and stress high. She had mumbled, "I should have stayed in the arena. At least there I would have had a chance at money."

Mahlir walked out, his threats burning on his tongue, regretting having said any of it, feeling emptiness deep down in his soul. He had let frustration, not intent, from his words. The marriage bond is a sacred covenant with God and should be held so by the people it unites. Even though theirs had been a Roman ceremony, even though the prayers had been to Juno, still it was sacrosanct. If it be a sin to break that sacred covenant, it is an even greater sin to use it against a spouse as a threat to win an argument.

When Mahlir returned, Amanirenas was dressed in an elaborate Kushite costume, long and white with folds of colorful linen. In her hands were flowers from the garden. In her eyes was the look of an apology. In her embrace was healing. "You are right," she said. "Esther should stay. Our daughter needs her, and Esther needs us. And you and I need each other."

"I too am sorry," he said. "I deeply regret the words I spoke. They were spoken thoughtlessly. I didn't mean them."

She scolded him with the angular beauty of her smile and forgave him with the same look, and the melodic softness of the words she always used when she wanted to fix things. "I ought to humble you, you know that?"

"I'd like to see you try."

"The only thing you would see would be the bottom of my foot right before it came to squash you."

"You mean right before I tip you over onto your head?"

"Someday maybe we'll find out," she said.

"Some day."

Their lives were back to normal, other than the occasional squabble, as any couple has, no family is immune. Their lives were once again a fit, just as good of a fit as Abraham had with Sarah and Sarah with Abraham. They were true friends to one another. And they were kind and giving to their servant girl Esther. And they were kind and giving to the people of Caesarea and to the children that played in the city streets. During the day, while Mahlir was with Pilate, Amanirenas devoted every waking minute to Tabitha. She played games with her, and read to her in five languages, Greek, Meroitic, Latin, and Aramaic, and in Hebrew to honor her husband. She taught her things and took walks with her, and showed her the animals and the birds and the insects, and the many flowers that grew in amongst the dense brush of the forests that ringed Caesarea Bay, and a hundred other things that a child's growing and curious mind thirsts to see and experience. And she welcomed other children into their home, to the aggravation of Pilate oftentimes, and set out figs and fruits for them to snack on, and included them in the games she would play with Tabitha, and read to them in the same five languages, all of which the children learned to a greater or lesser extent. Blessed it was, that Amanirenas walked the earth, and proud Mahlir was of the woman he had taken as his wife. There was no one alive Mahlir honored more than Amanirenas. She was his bonded heart and soul.

Amanirenas also involved Esther in the play with Tabitha and the children, and the two women became close friends. The child was blessed to have so much love in its life.

The mornings always found Mahlir caring for Tabitha, getting up with her when she cried, carrying her to Esther's breast, bathing her, changing her wrappings. Esther was willing to do it all – more than willing, obsessed was more accurate – but Mahlir needed to do it. Out of those times in the morning grew a special bond between father and daughter. Sometimes Mahlir would carry her in to Amanirenas and lay down beside them both. Amanirenas' mouth would curve upward into a smile of inward peace, and she'd nestle the child in close and reach over and touch Mahlir and drift off to sleep again.

In time Amanirenas' breasts healed, though she still had difficulty lactating, so Esther continued to do the feedings.

Esther's duties were undefined. They were duties of her own choosing. By her own choosing she rose at dawn to cook and clean, and keep Mahlir's letters and messages and documents, and to tend the garden and feed the animals. Once, Esther painted a fresco of a Caesarean sunset on one of the walls, a large orange ball sinking westward into the flat edge of the Great Sea. A month later, on the opposite wall she painted a fresco of the rising sun, fanning its stream of brilliance upward to the ceiling. The astronomer Aristarchus was correct, Elkanar used to say, a smile of arrogance on his face to corroborate the famous thinker's radical ideas that the sun was a ball of fire around which the earth revolved, and that the rising and setting of the sun was in reality the rotation of the earth around an imaginary axis. Moreover, Elkanar used to say, each of the twinkling stars in the night sky represented the streaming warmth of yet another sun but far, far away, with life growing and maturing there in a cycle of its own, some lesser than ours, others far more advanced. On the ceiling Esther painted blue sky and clouds. It was beautiful. Mahlir watched her as she painted, and felt troublesome emotions, a quickening in his chest while his eyes beheld the snowy white of her tunic being stretched around her diminutive frame, form-fitting itself around her large breasts and small waist. The fault was not Esther's. It was just the way she was stretching that caused his heart to leap, and the way her waves of curly black hair were falling down her back, sprinkled in splotches of pigment from her paintbrush, and the way her plain but expressive lips were pursing in thought. Harmless. Because she didn't know. Nor did Amanirenas. No one knew how dangerously close Mahlir was to committing the same sin. Clouds within his mind only. He would allow it to go no further.

As the days turned into weeks, as the weeks folded into months, Mahlir and Pilate became close friends, as it should be. An assistant to a governor needs to be close professionally as well as personally, to be truly effective. It was not uncommon for them to discuss issues late into the night. One such night found them doing so while lounging in the pool, lamenting their problems and listening to the sounds of midnight – the silent and menacing waves spilling against the rocks and the pillars, the ominous single cry of an owl, the far-off call of a wolf…

Commented Pilate, as he listened to the mournful call, likely the cry of a pack member that had lost its way, "I heard it said that the Hebrew Rabbi your friend Joseph keeps talking about can call the wolves to him right out of the forests as if they were his personal pets. You suppose that's true?"

"Who knows."

"One soldier told me that an eagle materialized out of thin air and landed on his shoulder. A very strange man. I've even heard stories of him restoring sight to the blind. Do you suppose any of it is true?"

"Who knows."

Pilate reached out and took hold of the box, which Mahlir always laid beside him at the pool's edge. "What's in this thing, anyway?"

"Supposed to be a golden crown." Mahlir went on to tell him the story but only because it sounded so absurd that he didn't figure Pilate would believe him.

He didn't. He held it to his ear and shook it, as though expecting to hear something. "There's no crown in here. There's nothing in here."

"Maybe not."

"So why haven't you delivered it to him?"

"I haven't seen him."

"Why not just give it to Joseph, have Joseph give it to him?"

"I might."

Pilate shook it again. "Here, let's open it up."

"Go ahead," said Mahlir. "But don't blame me if you fall over dead."

Pilate spurted out a weak laugh, the wine having amplified the superstitious part of him. "Hand me my dagger over there."

Mahlir reached over for it – he being closest to where the clothes were laid out – and handed the dagger to Pilate. Pilate made a feigned motion to slice open the seal. "Hmmm?"

"Go ahead." Mahlir was almost laughing, at seeing the powerful man wilt under the influence of nothing more than an uncorroborated story. "Go ahead. But let me move away a bit."

"So what's it supposed to do?"

"Like I said, it was supposed to have been worn by King David himself, his golden crown. It became lost the day of the king's adulterous sin with Bathsheba. Legend has that it waits for a pure soul."

"There's no gold in here."

"So open it up. I'm curious myself. I just don't want to be the one to do it."

"So what do you think will happen?"

"Maybe nothing, if you're the Messiah."

"And if I'm not."

"It will melt you like a blacksmith's furnace."

"Bullshit."

Mahlir smiled and shrugged. "So open it then."

Pilate put it back down and threw the dagger so that it stuck in the wood of the door post, its hilt twanging, as if to show he had not been intimidated by the thing, that no story could scare him – "I haven't got time for child's tales," he said – and with that he was back to talking business.

Mahir departed immediately for Machaerus when the approval from Rome came, taking Amanirenas, Tabitha, and Esther with him. They began the journey early. The sun had not yet broken as they boarded the rowboat that would ferry them to the ship, and the air was still, except for the waves slapping against the concrete port wall, and except for the calls of the gulls and the morning conversations of the other passengers milling about, and the strains and grunts of the burly Egyptian stevedores loading bundles of wheat and flax, all sounds that were somehow separate from the beauty and quiet of the morning.

Mahlir loved the sea, the mystery of going out beyond where the eye can see, beyond what is known.

The three women, Amanirenas, Esther, and Tabitha boarded first, helped and steadied by Pilate. Mahlir smiled. The writers of history will surely record Pilate as the strangest of all leaders, surrounded by guards and servants yet utilizing none of them. Half the time it was he who assisted them. With Pilate it was a matter of pride. He was continually boasting of how he was stronger than the lot of them and could do anything they could do, only better.

Mahlir boarded last, so that he could receive last minute instructions from Pilate, and guidelines for diplomacy from Joseph, who was there for the task at Pilate's request. Joseph knew better than anyone the complications of the tetrarchy because he had been close to it while Mahlir had been away in Qumran, and because he was a part of the Sanhedrin. It would never be said publicly, but many a Roman official had come to respect the Sanhedrin as being more powerful than Herod-Antipas and Philip combined, more powerful than Rome, because the Sanhedrin controlled the people by tradition. Rome and the Herods controlled only by force. And with the stubborn Jews, so often force was pitifully ineffective. "Promise him nothing," Pilate said sternly, quickly, in his way of saying so much with so little. "...except the swift response of Rome if any of his actions bring about an uprising of citizens or a border conflict with Arabia." The position of Rome was clear. At this point it would not interfere. Any concession Mahlir was able to get from Antipas would be by persuasion only. Mahlir was free, however, to point out to Antipas that he was there as king by the grace and goodness of Rome, and by appointment of Rome, and that if he couldn't behave himself Rome was prepared to remove him. Rome was still the father and would act as a father acts.

Mahlir's friend John, with whom he had shared quarters and studies, could depend on him only as far as his powers of persuasion could carry him. Mahlir remembered the day John left Qumran. He remembered watching him walk away into the desert, watching until he had disappeared among the huge rocks and boulders that cluttered the landscape, strewn about in an almost unnatural way, as though God had shaken them from the sky. Elkanar walked up and stood beside Mahlir, and they watched together. "For John, the Teacher has come," Elknanar said, referring once again to the illusive Teacher of Righteousness.

Mahlir had been surprised at the statement. "But Master," he said in response. "Does it not seem that John lacks the discipline to continue on with us? Why else would he leave?"

"No," had been Elkanar's simple response, shading his eyes from the direct sun in efforts to catch one last glimpse of him. "John leaves at the Teacher's behest. The Teacher is leading his steps."

"I see no teacher," Mahlir said. "I see only John. Where is this teacher?"

Answered Elkanar, the same answer he always gave, "Do not worry, my young friend, when you are ready the Teacher will come. When the final steps to be take are upon terrain so rocky and so steep none can travel, it is then that the Teacher will come. When the journey is on a path where there is no path, where there are no guideposts, where none can lead, where only the disciple can go, it is then that the Teacher of Righteousness will come with his lamp and light the way."

A year and thirty-seven days later, Yeshua left. Elkanar said something that day that puzzled Mahlir even more, as they both watched, in the same way they had watched John leave. "Does he also follow the Teacher?" Mahlir had asked.

"For him no teacher is needed," was Elkanar's reply.

Joseph brought Mahlir's mind back from his inward thoughts. "To review once again," he said, "here is what has transpired with Herod Antipas, tetrarch of Galilee. Antipas has proven to be a moderate ruler, though at times unwise in his decisions. He built his capital city upon the graves of our ancestors, on the shores of the Sea of Galilee. At first no one would enter. He had to populate it with slaves he liberated on the condition they not quit the city. He named it Tiberias, in honor of the emperor.

"He took as a wife the daughter of the king of Arabia, one of his wiser decisions, and as a result tensions with Arabia subsided. But then he fell in love with the lady Herodias. When his wife learned of the illicit affair, in fearing for her life, she secretly slipped out and went back to Arabia and her father. At about the same time, Antipas arrested the Baptist, supposedly for activities in stirring up the people and creating unrest. But I think the real reason for the Baptist's arrest was that he angered the Lady Herodias, because he publicly condemned her for her adulterous ways. And that is as it stands today. Antipas' wife, the legitimate queen of the Galilean tetrarchy, is in exile with her father the king of Arabia, and Antipas is living with his brother's wife."

Pilate hooked his arm inside Mahlir's arm and brought up the corner of his mouth, a very slight smile. "You be careful. I'm sending Praetorians with you in full Roman dress to stand by your side, to sanction the fact that you speak with the authority of Rome."

Continued Pilate, "Happening in seven days is a banquet in honor of Antipas' birthday. In attendance will be many important people. Philip the tetrarch of Paneas. Artabanus king of Parthia. Artaxias of Armenia. Others. And you shall be there as the representative of the mighty Tiberius Caesar, the greatest of them all."

Added Joseph, "It couldn't be any better if there had been scheduled a summit meeting of them all, of these leaders of nations affixed together by common borders, all of whom stand to be affected by this foolishness of King Antipas, by his love affair with his brother's wife."

Pilate gave Mahlir final instructions. "You will be sailing south along the coast to the port of Joppa. A caravan will be waiting and will take you inland toward the castle Machaerus. Machaerus was built years ago by Antipas' father Herod-the-Great atop the peak of a mountain and surrounded by deep ravines so that those approaching would be visible from all sides. It serves now as a place of response for Antipas. Many a day does he spend there. He thinks of it as a holy place, because it is shadowed by Nebo, the mountain from where Moses looked down into the Promised Land."

"Notables from kingdoms throughout the known world will be there," Joseph reiterated. Mahlir wondered if King Artabanus' favored son and heir to the Parthian throne, Prince Orodes would be there. "Likely not," said Joseph. "Reports reaching us from the east say that Orodes will be heading up the Parthian Army's border forces in the distant region of Iberia."

"…you pray for the hungry, then you feed them. That's how prayer works."

Pope Frances

Part V

A VOICE CRYING IN THE WILDERNESS

Year 74 (28AD) to 75 (29AD) of the Calendar
of Pater Patriea Gaius Julius Caesar

CHAPTER 33

THE PARTY

ISRAEL – THE CASTLE MACHAERUS IN THE DEAD SEA DESERT

Mahlir's vision fell first on Herod-Antipas. Mahlir knew it to be him from the purple he wore, and from the place he occupied on the center couch, and by the tiger tethered to his hand with an enormous chain. He had heard that Antipas had a penchant for making pets of wild things. Monarchs from distant lands made gifts of them to gain his favor. The beast's heavy sides quivered as it panted its breath. Its expression of contentment yielded to nervousness when serving plates crashed and clattered or when loud laughter came suddenly to its ears. Occasionally a curious merrymaker would throw a morsel for it to snatch up.

Another in the room was the king of Parthia, Artabanus. He also was easily recognizable. All Parthian royalty had sleepy eyes and mouths that refused to smile from beneath their square beards, beards that stuck out from their faces as if carved from stone.

There was a woman reclining next to King Artabanus. The Queen of Parthia, no doubt. Mahlir took an instant dislike to her, to both of them. He should have been grateful; they had given his son a kingdom.

Long and heavily cushioned couches gave repose to those present. The couches were equal in size to beds, so that the dinner guests could lounge full length and eat propped up on one elbow, or just sit upright, as the Parthian king and his queen were doing. Her bare feet, manicured and jeweled in baubles of gold, were drawn up onto the king's lap. The end of the couch was a roll of upright marble upon which she rested an arm so that she might lean over to the table in front of her. A slave in a long tunic was carefully pouring wine into her goblet from an ornamented stone decanter. With her fingers she was eating from a platter of delicacies artistically arranged in the patterns of flowers.

The Queen of Parthia had chosen to fix her eyes on Mahlir. Her mouth formed a smile. Mahlir could not tell if it was one of disdain or simply an expression of vague curiosity. Could it be that she knew who he was, that she knew he was the blood father of her son? Not possible. Could it be she fancied him? He turned to see if someone was in back of him. There was no one. It amused her to see Mahlir squirm under the stare. Amanirenas, by his side, tall and black and lovely, prettier than any queen, sensed his emotions and stiffened. One of Mahlir's guards must have felt something too, because he placed his hand on the hilt of his short-sword, or what he thought was the hilt of his sword. He had forgotten in the moment that weapons had been confiscated at the palace entrance.

"Quite delicious," the Queen of Parthia said, clearly speaking to Mahlir, her mouth full of the viands she had just placed there with the jingling of her gold bracelets. "The Shield of Minerva. A collage supreme to the taste. Made of the livers of char fish, and the brains of pheasants and peacocks, and the tongues of flamingos and the entrails of lampreys. You should try some." Indeed it was Mahlir she was speaking to. There could be no doubt. "I am told that King Herod sent his ships as far as the Aegean to collect these." Her accent was harsh as her tongue tried to grip the guttural roll of proper Aramaic.

Mahlir simply smiled politely and bowed in courtesy. The slave who had led them through the palace corridors announced them, also in Aramaic. "O Great King Antipas, to whom all present pay homage, Tetrarch of Galilee and Perea, son of Herod-the-Great, I present Mahlir-of-Judea, representing the emperor Tiberius. And his wife Amanirenas." Barefoot maidens rushed up and placed wreathes of roses on their heads and reminded them to pass the final threshold right foot forward.

Mahlir did so, acknowledging the superstitious custom that emanated from ancient days, then sank to one knee. Amanirenas fell behind, in respect of another custom, that wives walk ten paces behind husbands. Mahlir shook his head in silent protest and waved her forward. She was his equal and he would honor her as such. Gasps and whispers could be heard, as the tall and ebony skinned beauty from the South of Egypt came to walk beside her husband. She entered with her left foot forward, having not understood the Latin instructions from the slave, exposing therefore the entire gathering to bad luck for the evening. More gasps came. Surely something evil would happen before this party dispersed. She did remember to sink to one knee and bow her head, as anyone would before a king. Their two guards, Praetorians, stout and in full dress, stood straight to remind all present that there existed a greater king. "The emperor sends regrets that he was not able to personally attend," Mahlir said, "and asks me to extend his best for your birthday, and for many years to come."

For a time Mahlir forgot about the strange look the Queen of Parthia had given him.

Antipas waved them to their feet and responded, not to Mahlir, but to Amanirenas. "Amanirenas," he mused, saying the name slowly, puzzling over it, like it was one of the exotic things that had been brought to him from afar. "Tell me my dear, are you royalty? You must be. You are too lovely to be anything less."

Mahir could see Amanirenas blush at the flattery. The jade black of her face was turning to a shine.

"Might you be related to that great Kushite queen by the same name? Of whom tales are told of how during the Civil Wars she buried the head of Caesar's statue beneath the threshold of her palace? So that each time she entered and stepped on it she would gain magical powers, and was able therefrom to defeat the Romans when they invaded?"

Amanirenas' large brown eyes swept the floor. "She was my grandmother, O King."

"Indeed!" Antipas gestured for her to walk forward. "Come. You shall eat by my side, granddaughter of the empress who defeated Caesar."

Spoke Amanirenas in response to the invitation, "O Great King, your kindness flatters me. Let me say first, our only regret is that we were unable to arrive at the beginning of the banquet. Please forgive us. The fault was mine."

Replied Antipas, "How could a creature so lovely have any faults?"

"Again you flatter me, but undeservingly. I was taken ill this morning and thought for a time I would be unable to attend at all. Fortunately the illness was only temporary."

Mahlir did think of turning back, upon realizing they would be late, but he had a duty to the empire and a stronger duty to his friend from Qumran. Delaying them further had been a surprise they had not counted on, the difficulty of approaching the castle itself. The ravines surrounding the mountaintop were wider and deeper than they had expected. Absent having wings to soar across them, the only alternative was to travel the paths cut from the cliff sides, and on cracked stone bridges beneath which fathomed the depths. The final climb upward was agonizing, taking the length of many hours, and the evening was upon the little group before they were able to draw close. They could hear sounds of merriment from inside the castle's white walls, intense above them under the splashes of the setting Dead Sea sun. The pathway torches sparkled almost as gentle stars in the twilight sky, terrifying them. It is better not to go at all if the alternative is being late to a king's banquet. Night had fully descended by the time they arrived.

Repeated Antipas, gesturing with his ring laden hand, "I insist, granddaughter of the queen who defeated Caesar, join me at my side."

She moved one foot hesitantly forward, unsure of what to do. Fine linen lay upon her body, tight to follow the fullness of her form, white to show the purity of her black skin, colorful weavings draped thereon to speak of her heritage and homeland, browns, reds, greens. In her hair were braids laced through with colorful stones, and on her wrists were snakes of gold. On her ankles, hardly visible beneath the white linen, were anklets of golden stars. Thin-soled sandals of the finest leather adorned her feet and were traced with sapphires. A garland of roses interlaced itself upon her head, bejeweling her as stones never could. The three scars on each cheek truly did seem like marks of beauty, in that moment, as she stood before the king, bewitching him.

"How does a man like your husband," Mahlir could almost hear him thinking, "without money or power, come to have such a wife?" Dressed as he was, studiously, plainly, Mahlir hardly seemed a suitable mate for anyone, let alone royalty, in the knee-length tunic of a lowly scribe, single red stripe angling over his shoulder, symbol of his service to Rome, and with no beard on his face to hide the creeping of age.

"Come," coaxed Antipas, nodding his head in reassurance, gesturing her forward.

A woman reclining on an adjacent couch – three couches to a table, Roman style – turned visibly red. In Herod's face was a kind of satisfaction, like he had been angry with her for something and this was recompense. Here was Herodias, surely. The faltering light from one of the many lamp stands that supported three flames, hanging, swaying, added mystery to the features of her Jewish beauty, slender face and nose, triangular lips, olive dark skin, long black hair the sides of which sparkled from see-through tracings of gold, and high cheekbones that gave her eyes a fairylike quality, eyes that said here was a woman that cannot be conquered, so let no one try, least of all her husband. She looked to be tall, the mark of an Idumean. Indeed this was Herodias, the woman who had seduced a king, who held within her the power to crush Mahlir where he stood, with a whisper of a word and no more. More effort it would take for her to press down her sandal on one of the centipedes that were alarming no one, that were as common as birds in the sky, that wicked men and women took careful steps to avoid harming, that were finding their way in and out of the tight crevices of the marble floor stones.

Suddenly Mahlir realized he had to speak. The moment he had feared for days had arrived. Its apprehension had invaded his sleep and dominated each of his walking hours. Many times he had envisioned he would let the moment pass without acting. He was under no obligation, no orders from Pilate or Tiberius to do this thing; he had merely been granted permission.

Tabitha was with Esther outside the palace walls and would likely be safe and able to return to Caesarea, should something happen to him. But would Pilate care for them? Probably. In spite of his difficult demeanor and outbursts of temper, Pilate was a man of ethics, a man of responsibility. If Mahlir could depend on anyone to do the fair and right thing, it would be Pontius Pilate.

Mahlir's body and mind were frozen. His head began to spin.

This was the time. There would be no other. And, if he spoke now, witnesses from many nations would hear and be aware of the grave nature of Antipas' actions. It would be as if he were speaking it out to the world. If ever there existed an opportunity to spare the Baptist's life, it was now. If ever there existed an opportunity to spare his people from war, it was now.

"Come," Antipas repeated, making room for Amanirenas by sitting a bit more upright.

He clapped his hands for a slave. "Bring more couches, and another table for our new guests, and more lamps. But the granddaughter of the queen who defeated Caesar sits with me."

This was the time.

Mahlir's mouth opened. Somehow speech came forth, amid the beating of his heart. "O King. I thank you for your hospitality. Would you grant first that I might speak? I am bound to express not only the good wishes of Caesar, but also the concerns of Caesar over a matter. If I may. If it please the king."

Antipas grew serious and sat completely upright, and leaned forward, his eyes driving right through Mahlir, as if to say, "Don't you do this," but telling him that he must, now that he had begun.

"O King. A matter has come to the attention of the emperor, concerning the client state over which you have been appointed, and the neighboring land of Arabia, the land of your estranged wife's father..."

As Mahlir drew in the courage to continue a noise came from above, slaves opening a portion of the fettered ivory ceiling to let the starlight in, and to shower the guests with garlands and to spray down sweet scents, unaware of the inappropriateness of their timing. No matter. No one paid attention to it, because of the confrontation the king was about to have. When the rest of Mahlir's words finally came, the enormous room drew quiet. All had focused their attention on Mahir and what he was about to say. The multitudes of hanging oil lamps seemed to dim their gentle flames in anticipation. Harps and flutes had been playing, their volume growing right along with the raucous sounds of the guests, but now they were silent. On corner stages between pilasters of Hymettus marble were dancers and jugglers, and magicians who breathed fire, handsome men and women all, displaying, along with their skills, unclothed bodies of youth and beauty. Now they were silent and motionless, as still as the uneasiness in the air.

Antipas leaned further forward, and took his fingers, each of which bore gold, and combed the ends of his speckled black and gray beard. His eyes dueled with Mahlir and dared him to continue.

Mahlir did, barely conscious of what he was saying, words he had rehearsed many times. "The emperor hopes that you and your estranged wife will resolve your differences –" Mahlir had to say it exactly as Pilate had instructed. "The emperor cares not how many wives you have, or how many concubines, as long as it does not threaten the security and peace of his borders. With war as the alternative, it would be better in the emperor's eyes if you repaired relations with your wife, who is the daughter of the Arabian king. I am constrained by duty to respectfully remind the king that he sits on the throne by the will and good grace of the emperor."

Antipas twisted his mouth in frightening seriousness but said nothing. Mahlir took the opportunity of the silence to finish what he had come to say, while courage still was with him. "It would also please the emperor if the king would release the Baptist."

Antipas' expression changed with the mention of the Baptist, in the span of that single instant. His mouth dropped open in a look akin to shock. Not anger. Something else. Herodias began to laugh.

Mahlir continued. "Perhaps the king's good intentions are to keep the Baptist away from the people, to keep him from stirring them into a sedition. The emperor has concerns that it will have the opposite effect. He is concerned, as are we, that the people will riot *because* the Baptist has been arrested."

Herodias laughed again.

Antipas looked dumbstruck. It was as though Mahlir had driven him through with a javelin, the look he had. And Mahlir was left in his confusion trying to figure out why, and to figure out what he should do or say next.

Herodias was the one to speak, at long last. As she did she waved Mahlir over, saying, "Mahlir-of-Judea – is that your name? – come sit with me." And she looked at Antipas, a look of victory.

Dare he do it? Dare he not do it?

Antipas saw Mahlir's confusion. "It is all right," he said in reassurance. "You may sit with the Queen." But it was a veiled reassurance, spoken, Mahlir feared, by someone who felt he had no other choice. Antipas looked again at Mahlir's beautiful wife and gestured to her once more. "Come. You have a king's invitation."

Mahlir nodded to Amanerinas.

Nervously, they both ventured forward, stepping aside the tiger. The beast threw back its head, and did nothing more.

A young girl moved to allow Mahlir's positioning of reclining next to Herodias. Salome, likely, the daughter of Herodias, named after Salome the sister of Herod-the-Great, the woman who saved the men of the Jewish nation when Herod, on his deathbed, decreed that they all be locked in the hippodrome and executed at the point of his death, so that the countryside would morn. The girl was lovely, though more of a child by chronology, barely entering her grown-up years, and had a resemblance to Herodias that would have made her a twin had it not been for the age difference. In the child's expression was innocence. Such creatures of God can find pleasure in the simplest of things, like a sunset, or the flight of a dove, or the crisp scent of early morning dew. Here was a person who could as yet do no evil, were Mahlir's thoughts as he watched her move to one of the empty couches, a person still unspoiled by the hands of adulthood. Mahlir knew it not at the time, but she was the promised future wife of Philip, the tetrarch of the northern regions.

Herodias' fingers came to rest uncomfortably on Mahlir's thigh. Said she, "We have had our cooks prepare something special for our guests representing Rome." Again she cast a look of victory upon her husband. "Have we not my dear?"

Herodias whispered something to a standing slave, who then hurried out of the dining hall to do whatever it was he had been instructed to do, to bring them their dishes, Mahlir was assuming. Perhaps the hosts had been told he ate no meat. Present at all of the other tables were trays and platters filled with steaming preparations of every wild thing imaginable, pork, duck, pheasant, hare, venison. One guest was heard expressing satisfaction over the tase of turbot, a rare fish from the Adriatic. Mahlir had made his mind up that he would eat whatever was set before him rather than offend his host, particularly on such an important occasion.

The tension between Herodias and Antipas increased, unspoken, veiled in politeness, in this bizarre game of bettering one another that Mahlir and Amanirenas had been unwittingly trapped within. Antipas' jealous eyes were upon Mahlir. Mahlir could feel them. Antipas was studying the two of them, as Herodias was running her hands over Mahlir's leg and chest, talking of things Mahlir hardly heard, asking questions he was barely cognizant of answering, about who he was and what had been his background, and how he had come to be in the service of the emperor, all of which he answered, unaware of the peril it was bringing.

Mahlir had two choices, both of which were suicidal. Stay and anger Antipas. Leave and anger Herodias.

So he decided without deciding.

He was relieved when the slave boy came with the platter. Now he could eat and occupy himself.

The slave boy, Roman wreath in his short hair, long-sleeve tunic to his ankles, laid the platter before Mahlir and bowed and backed away, a look on his face so void of emotions it almost seemed like terror.

Whatever was on the platter was hidden beneath a large silver bell.

Beneath it were sounds, like the buzzing of fruit flies. From it was coming the odor of dead flesh, uncooked, like the smell of a tanning house.

Herodias smiled and gestured. "For you. Our guest. Please."

Mahlir reached for it.

It was cold to the touch.

He knew what was there. He knew before he saw it.

The flies roared furiously as he lifted their enclosure, whirring in circles and banging themselves against its insides.

He turned his gaze away from what he was about to see, and looked first, for a brief moment, at the faces of those around him. They also knew what was under the bell. Some were amused, most had expressions of disgust. Some seemed horror stricken. Oddly, one of the latter, with expressions of horror, was Herod-Antipas. Mahlir saw for the first time how many people were there, thousands maybe, three to a couch, three couches to a table, nine couches at some of the larger tables, hundreds of couches, and twice as many slaves scurrying about with wine jars and plates of food. All their eyes were on Mahlir as he was lifting the bell. Some were on their feet stretching to see. The rumbling din of conversation and laughter had completely ceased. The flute players and harpists were peering out from behind the curtains. All knew what was beneath the bell. The tiger was twitching at the silence. Its nose was sniffing the air, catching the odor of death freshly let.

Mahlir looked back down at the platter...

...and saw the severed head of his friend from long ago, with whom he had studied and learned, John-son-of-Zacharias, called now the Baptist. Confusion flowed from Mahlir's heart. And anger. And grief.

How is it that the Teacher of Righteousness, whoever he is, could have led John into such danger? Did not David write of God as being a caring and protecting shepherd? *Yeah though I walk through the valley of the shadow of death, I will fear no evil, for thou art with me?* Surely if anyone was holy and deserving of protection, it was John.

The condescending sound of Herodias' voice came to Mahlir's dulled hearing. "Had you not been late, Mahlir-of-Judea, had you come but a moment or two earlier, with news that Caesar wished my husband to spare the Baptist, you would have saved him." She looked over at Antipas, though she was still speaking to Mahlir. "For I do believe my husband would have welcomed any opportunity to spare of his life. Yes? My dear?" Her voice turned bitter. "For I do believe my husband had a fondness for him, even though he spoke to my ruination, even though he sought to have me deposed. I would not at all be surprised if they were lovers. Why else would my husband steal off alone to his prison cell?"

Then, for the amusement of the guests, she took the head into her hands and with it did things unspeakable.

Someone laughed.

Such deeds as were done that day at Machaerus, and the fact that human hands could bring them about, women, mothers of children, children themselves, turned the contents of Mahlir's stomach foul.

And therein was the excuse Mahlir needed to remove himself. He ran. He ran to an expanse beyond the curtains of the dining hall and fell there to his knees and vomited onto the floor, and wept, and tried desperately to keep from choking on his own breath.

The laughter resumed, louder than before. And the dancers and the flute players and the harpists started up again, with more intensity.

The head became an object of morbid fascination to the guests, being passed from one to the other. Those having the courage to hold it showed off their bravery in imaginative attempts at one-upmanship – juggling it with apples and fruit, pouring wine into its mouth, women drawing back and running from it, squealing in mock horror when it came their way, dropping it to the floor and kicking it away.

"A party to be long remembered!" one voice yelled.

And Mahlir wept some more.

He felt the comforting hand of Amanirenas on his shoulder. She lifted him to his feet and spoke to him in Hebrew, as a gesture of respect. "My love," she said, doing surprisingly well with the words and the accent. "You are a good man. The vile creatures here tonight are not worthy to walk the same earth with a man like you."

Also by his side were his weaponless guards, standing like statues, saying nothing, ever watchful, doing their jobs. Dogs without teeth, Herod had laughingly called them when they first arrived, boasting of how useless they were within the palace walls where were posted hundreds of his own guards

Then into Mahlir's presence walked one called Agrippa, who was also repulsed by the spectacle, who also gave comfort. He said he was the brother of Herodias and had lived in Rome many years with the family of Tiberius, and had heard the emperor speak well of Mahlir. Strange that this Agrippa was so sensitive, so gentle, because his features would indicate otherwise – narrow faced with the beaked nose of a bird of prey and the bulging watchful eyes of a mongoose, and a voice that leached out from thin lips that always seemed pursed and ready to pronounce judgement of some sort or another, as would a king on a throne, though this man was far from a king. Agrippa was beardless, like a Roman, and his hair was short, and around it he wore a leather band tied in back, warrior style. He told Mahlir of what had transpired before he and Amanirenas had arrived. "I am greatly distressed at the behavior of my sister," he said. "She dishonored her marriage to Philip, my uncle, who is her rightful husband."

Agrippa took a moment to explain, upon seeing Mahlir's look of confusion," No no no, not the Philip who is tetrarch of Paneas in the north," he clarified. "My father sired two sons named Philip, each by different mothers. The Philip I speak of is the one who lives in Rome. Under his very roof in Rome, while he slept, my sister, his wife, shared herself with another man. Now she has taken up abode with that other man, King Herod Antipas, while her husband still lives. And the Baptizer? The one whom the people considered to be their prophet? He was a fool. He spoke openly against her. He denounced her to the public and to her face, and to Herod, shouting outside of his window. 'It is not lawful for you to have her,' he would shout. She was furious. To pacify her, Herod had him arrested and bound and thrown into prison, put into the very dungeons here at Machaerus."

"Herod resisted my sister in her persistent requests that the Baptizer be done away with," Agrippa went on, "partly because the people looked upon the Baptizer as a prophet, and partly because, I do believe, he also thought him to be a holy man. There were times that Herod had the Baptizer brought before him just to talk, because he was greatly puzzled by the things he said, and because he liked to hear him speak. This infuriated my sister. So then he would steal away to the Baptizer's prison cell in secret, not wanting to raise her ire.

"Finally my sister's opportunity came at the birthday banquet, which drew attendance from high officials and leading military men and commanders everywhere. Salome, daughter of my sister by her rightful husband and the betrothed of Philip the Tetrarch, danced for Herod. He was so pleased that he said to the girl, 'Ask me for anything you want, and I will give it you.' He promised her with an oath that he would give her up to half his kingdom. But my sister told her to ask for the head of the Baptizer, which she did. The king was deeply distressed, though he didn't refuse her, because of the oaths he had made before his prominent guests. He sent an executioner to the prison chambers, who returned promptly with the Baptizer's head.

"And that was what happened prior to your arrival, at the beginning of the party."

Every one of Mahlir's limbs felt weak at hearing the story. He moved to sit on one of two gold embossed couches nearby. The couches faced each other; Mahlir sat on one, Agrippa the other, peristylium couches, short and decorative. There were as many as forty of them scattered throughout the deserted peristylium, set together in pairs along the outer walls by the torches and columns, and beneath the hanging vines and oil lamps, and amongst the flowers, places for quiet conversation, each of their locations marked by a golden menorah stand, solitary symbols of a supposedly Jewish king in a palace spoiled by so many things Roman.

Amanirenas sat beside Mahlir, laying her always gentle hand on his shoulder.

"Yours is a precious wife," Agrippa said. "She comforts you in your grief. She stands by you. My own wife Cypros is such woman. I am the magistrate of the great capital city of Tiberias that the king built, wherein the king himself resides. I am the second most powerful man in Galilee. But it was not always so. There was a time, not so very long ago, when I had nothing. Let me tell you my story, so that you may take heart in it and know that one day, like me, you shall rise from your misery."

What type of man was this? Speaking so boldly of things so private? Some men speak thusly to be boastful, others out of deceit, because they scheme for something in return, some only because it is their nature to speak unfettered. As Agrippa talked, Mahlir wondered which one was he. "You see, my Jewish brother," Agrippa began. "Though Jew by birth, I too am a Roman citizen. I was raised in the household of Tiberius and was as a brother to his favored son Drusus. When Drusus succumbed to an illness and departed this life – some say by the hand of Sejanus – Caesar put me out. I had spent my inheritance on gifts of extravagance for Caesar and his friends and freedmen, never imagining he would abandon me. They happily received my gifts and my money, then when none of it was left they blamed me, calling me irresponsible. I had nothing. No more than the beggar in the doorway." Agrippa's movements, the gesturing of his hands, the uncommon way he sat upright on the back of the couch, the darting back and forth of his head, the bold and unreserved expressions of his mouth, his harsh and rapid-toned voice, the wide eyes from which leapt his enthusiasm, or from which spilled his troubles, were the mirroring of a man of intensity. "Caesar took me into his family, told me he thought of me as his son, then when I came to believe it, and when I had no more of my own money, he rejected me." Agrippa looked at Mahlir, anticipating what he might be thinking. "Foolish? An unwise use of my inherited assets? Yes, no doubt, but I thought I would always have a home there. I thought I was family." He looked at Mahlir as if to extract sympathy. When it showed in Mahlir's eyes he continued. "My wife Cypros and I sailed to Judea. The shame followed me, as did my creditors. I had made plans to take the only way out, but right before I was ready to thrust the sword into my heart, Herod-Antipas summoned me, my uncle, and asked for my help in the stabilizing of his capital city, the city he built with his own hands in honor of the emperor. I am honored that he recognized my skills in leadership. So you see, as Solomon in his wisdom said so long ago: to everything there is a season, a time to mourn and a time to dance. Today you mourn, tomorrow you shall dance."

And with that, Agrippa, the magistrate of the city of Tiberias, left. Perhaps his only motive was no motive at all.

He walked no more than ten paces when he whirled around and said one thing more, and revealed the motive. Proudly throwing aside his long cape, which entangled his legs as he turned, he said defiantly, as if Mahlir were the one who had done him the injustice, "Tell the emperor that the son he cast away is now the magistrate of the largest and most productive metropolis in Galilee. A worthless embarrassment? Because my family's fortune was not large enough to sustain me in the fashion to which Caesar's friends are accustomed? Well, you may tell him that his worthless embarrassment who could do nothing apart from the breast of Caesar is now the magistrate of the city that bears his name."

Mahlir did in fact include it in his report to Tiberius.

Agrippa did not return to the party. He disappeared instead into the shadows of the peristylium's torch-lit beauty, into the complexity of its colorful greenery and fountains and statuettes, away from the madness.

The mania in the dining room had grown to mammoth proportions. The walls were shuddering. People were fighting, throwing things, climbing over tables. Merriment had mixed itself with evil.

Mahlir saw Herod Antipas standing on his couch, and heard him utter a loud and desperate cry. "It is enough!"

Then Mahlir heard a snarling from the tiger. There was gnashing of its teeth and screams from the people. The people trampled one another to get away from the beast, so great was the panic.

The party, for which Antipas had paid over 400,000 sesterces, had been spoiled. Antipas did his best to reassemble the guests. Some had been taken to the palace physicians, some had departed out of anger, some in fear. Left in the room were only half the numbers of the original. Amanirenas and Mahlir were two who returned. It was Mahlir's duty, as an emissary of Caesar. A terrible mistake. Said Antipas – he had a large voice that vibrated from the lowest timbers of his throat – in words that fairly thundered through the palace, as he stood before the guests, as he raised his large silver goblet, "Friends, citizens of the land of Galilee, esteemed leaders and guests –" The costly wine, brought in from the fields north of Rome, had settled in his brain, and had made his speech smooth and his eyes soft. He seemed almost gentle under its influence. "An age ago my father Herod-the-Great, ruler of all of the Jews, on his deathbed divided the kingdom into four parts, one north, one west, one east, one south, and bequeathed them to us his children. We tetrarchs ruled wisely, and the people lived in prosperity. Then there came a blight upon the land in the form of an evil priest who gathered together a band of treasonists and traveled to Rome to convince the emperor to make the heart center of all of Israel a part of the Roman Empire." The guests groaned audibly. "They petitioned that the land of our forefathers wherein resides the Holy Temple in Jerusalem, the land of King David and of Abraham and Isaac, wherefrom surges the pulse of our people, be handed over to Rome to be ruled by a Roman governor, as it still is to this day."

The deceptively gentle eyes looked in Mahlir's direction. "For years we have wondered what had become of that evil priest. One can only imagine my surprise when I discovered that he is here, this day, in this very room. Among you here today is the priest who betrayed his people and his god." Antipas thrust the index finger of the hand holding the goblet straight at Mahlir. The smoothness of the wine was gone. "He is Mahlir-son-of-Matthias. Our guest who represents Rome. His own tongue has exposed him. He sat with Herodias and told her of his past. He told her of how he spent many years as a celibate in the community of the Essenes on the shores of the Dead Sea, and how before that he had been a guest in the house of Caesar, and how before that he had been a guest in the court of the Magi in Parthia, and how before that he had wandered as a lost sheep in the desert. But it wasn't until he told of being a Zadokite in Jerusalem's Temple that Herodias realized who he was. When she told me, I realized that she was right, that here among us is that evil priest, a traitor to Jews, the man who gave a quarter of my father's kingdom over to Rome to be ruled by the Caesars forever. He is Mahlir-son-of-Matthias, personal secretary to Governor Pontius Pilate!"

In his triumph Antipas threw off his purple cape and cloak, leaving them in a heap on the floor, and paced back and forth in front of Mahlir. Mahlir was surprised at how thin he was. Rumors of his gluttony, of how he would eat six and seven enormous meals a day, always led Mahlir to believe Antipas would be big bellied. A telltale roundness poked out from his midsection, but that was all. Everything else, arms, legs, neck, was stick thin. Tales were told of how he would purge his stomach to be able to eat more. With his bulbous nose aglow from the wine, and with the very tip of his hairless head showing through the top of his diadem, with his short and well-trimmed beard quivering in his anger – or was it excitement? – he stood in front of Mahlir and delivered his denunciation. "My brother Archelaus, tetrarch of Judea, discovered the plot and had him seized. But somehow he was able to escape and flee into the desert, adding then murder to his crimes, taking the life of one called Athronges, known as the Shepherd Messiah. To have been able to do such a thing he must have had the hosts of darkness themselves as his accomplices."

Mahlir should have left when the opportunity presented itself, instead of returning to the banquet. Once again he was saying to himself, "Would that I could trade a moment's time for the past of yesterday."

King Antipas resumed his pacing, and his sipping of the wine, which had again taken hold of his personality to sooth his vane and angry eyes. Continued he, looking at Mahlir but speaking to the others, "Malir, Zadokite priest, Roman emissary, is a criminal guilty of treason and murder. Fortunate it is for him that he is under Roman protection. For because of this he will not be arrested."

Mahlir breathed immense relief.

Antipas raised the goblet to his mouth and took another drink, and let the sweetness roll warmly down his throat, remnants spilling deliciously onto his chin, then made a wide gesture toward the guests, sweeping the goblet before him in the air. "Mahlir-of-Matthias should mark me in what I say. Let him forever continue in the service of the emperor, for if he ever quits Rome, no place will be safe for him. Sleep shall he have none; there will be no place for him to lay his head. Let him not cross my borders. Let not his camels nor his horses, nor property of his of any kind come under my jurisdiction, should he ever cease to become Caesar's bond slave. Even now, even with the seal her carries and with his guards, he should be wary of dark places and of strangers approaching."

Agrippa came into the room, unaware of what he was spoiling, crossing in front of Antipas, interrupting his uncle's thoughts, unaware that he was stirring the anger of a man already unbalanced by rage, already brought to the point of irrationality by the day's circumstances. This was to have been a birthday extraordinaire. It was to have been a day of celebration unlike any other. Instead, it had been a day of embarrassment and humiliations. He had even been manipulated into killing a man.

And Agrippa walking by – it could have been anyone – brought the king to say things he otherwise would have held to himself. He pointed the goblet at Agrippa and delivered a stinging rebuke, in words calm but dark. “My bother-in-law, my sister’s affluent brother whom I rescued from the streets of despair, does me the honor of interrupting me as I address my guests. Here. Let us all give a cheer for the magistrate of Tiberias. He is a very important man. It is a very important position he holds, with many important decisions to be made. Each day he must decide which side of his ass to scratch.”

Sporadic laughter rose.

“Sometimes I help him in that very important decision. I advise him that it should be the side that itches.”

More laughter.

“Let me tell you the story of my prosperous brother-in-law, the magistrate of Tiberias. He grew up in Caesar’s house with his mother Bernice, eating off of silver and sleeping on jewels, sucking off whatever golden tit he could find, be it his mother’s, be it Caesar’s, be it mine. A fortune did Bernice possess, until the magistrate of Tiberias laid his hands on it. His mother was wise and beautiful – you can see straight away he doesn’t resemble her –”

The people roared in their laughter. A smile also was forming on Amanirenas’ face, which hurt Mahlir, that a woman he loved could find pleasure in another’s pain. But then that’s the way of the human creation, that it seeks by its nature to belittle others, that it is drawn, like a stone to the earth, to the infliction of misery upon its own sisters and brothers, hence upon itself. It is structured with a need to rise above them, to conquer them, to destroy them. Truth be known, Mahlir found the beast also within himself, bringing up its deceitful head, wanting to form a smile also on his face because of the artful way Antipas was molding his wit. It left Malhir wishing he could reach inside himself and strangle the thing, the substanceless beast that was himself.

Antipas continued. "My wife's brother Agrippa has a strong liking for the spending of money. His mother, while she lived, kept him on a close tether. But once she was dead and he was left to his own ways, he may as well have cast her coins from the roof tops. In a very short time he had reduced himself to poverty. Caesar threw him out and creditors chased him into hiding, where within the walls of a certain castle in Idumea called Malathia he conceived a plan to do away with himself." Sarcasm filled Herod Antipas' voice. "That indeed would have been a disaster. What ever would we do without our MAGISTRATE?"

Antipas drew the word out drippingly, and with it invited the laugher to come again and drown him out.

"Thankfully, his wife Cypros is more of a man that he is. She appealed to my wife Herodias, the queen, Herodias being his sister, that she might offer up help, that she might engage me in the cause. So we gave him a place of habitation in Tiberias, where nobody else would live because it was built over a graveyard, and we gave him some money for his maintenance, and gave him the title of MAAAGISTRATE –"

The laughter rose again.

The belittled man's eyes swept the crowd, searching desperately for someone who wasn't laughing, finding that someone in Mahlir, but looking away quickly, because the pity he saw was worse.

Agrippa stood inanimate, not knowing whether to recline or stand, not knowing whether to stay or leave. Finally he looked with pleading eyes at Antipas.

Antipas leaned forward and intoned, "MAAAAAGISTRATE."

The laughter rose again.

After the spasms of laughter crashing into his body became intolerable, withering it like a substance foul and poisonous, Agrippa ran from the room.

And that caused the laughter to come louder still, assailing his fleeing heels like horsemen from the grave.

A woman followed – Cypros.

The laughter climbed to a crescendo of thunder.

And – in the confusion of everything, Amanirenas disappeared. One instant she was there, the next she was gone.

CHAPTER 34

THE STRATAGEM

ISRAEL – THE CASTLE MACHAERUS

But for the disappearance of Amanirenas, the small entourage representing Rome would have left that night, as the full moon was rising behind the Dead Sea Hills, as it was casting its familiar silver onto the pale white landscape, as the foreboding gateways of the Arabian mountains to the east were emerging under its light…as the attack forces of Aretas were amassing along its borders.

The guests were beginning to dwindle in numbers, and still Mahlir was not finding her.

Finally the last of the guests departed; she was not among them. He wandered the halls in desperation, halls that resounded with the silence of their isolation. No one was there. Not his guards. Not the guards of Machaerus. No guests. No servants. Not even soldiers to arrest him for his intrusions. No one. He was a man small and solitary, among the maze of Machaerus, the castle with a thousand walls, each one flickering ominously with dim light from the wall lamps. The sound of his footsteps bounced off the walls in monstrous echoes; he could hear his breathing against the cold beauty of marble and limestone. He looked in every room, every doorway, all except the prison chambers.

Prison chambers!

But what was he to do? If that was where she was?

Whatever was necessary.

Trading his life for hers, if that be the price.

Mahlir remembered an opening to the right of the main gate. Could that have been the entrance? It was large, and from it had come the foulest of odors. Upon their arrival, soldiers from its pit had come to take away the weapons of Mahlir's two guards. The Praetorians had at first protested, but consented under Mahlir's order, when told that the weapons of all guests and guards were being held during the banquet, to be retrieved on departure.

Also by the entrance, on the other side, among the flowers and bushes of a beautiful garden, Esther was waiting with Tabitha. "I have seen many people leave, my lord," she told Mahlir. "But I have not seen my lady or her guards." Tabitha had fallen asleep in Esther's arms while nursing. Mahlir never could figure out how a woman so small – the top of Esther's head came barely past his shoulders – could have arms powerful enough to carry a child so effortlessly. Mahlir looked at the infant, half asleep, suckling Esther's nipple, and wondered what it would be like to be the child, to be so unaware of the world in its peril, to have one's biggest problems be the annoyances of noises and sudden movements. Mahlir wondered too, for a curious moment, what it would be like to be Esther, to be able to feel life coming from your chest. "Good woman, sit," he said, and directed Esther to a nearby bench. "Sit and hear what I have to say. Antipas knows me to be the one who led the Jews to Rome. I think Amanirenas may have been seized as a means to get to me." Mahlir pointed toward the gaping cave-like opening. "I believe she may be within the dungeons. I intend to search for her there."

"But my lord –"

"Shh. Listen to me now. If morning comes and I have not returned, here is what I want you to do. I want you to leave without me at the first light of day. I want you to go back home to Pilate." Sheltered close to the garden were the two camels and four horses they had used in their travels, being tended by the man Pilate had sent as driver and guide. He had a good strong Roman name, Horatio. "I have spoken to Horatio. He has my instructions to leave with you tomorrow morning at the point where the sun fully crests the Arabian mountains and casts itself in its totality on the castle."

Esther forgot herself and boomed forth with a protest that caused two birds on a nearby branch to take wing. Tabitha's arms flew out, as if the support beneath her had been pulled away. She recovered by sucking furiously on Esther's nipple. "Have you lost your mind?" Esther screeched. "To go into that place? You most assuredly have lost your mind! You will not return. You simply cannot do it!" Though circumstances had placed Esther in the role of a slave, her personality had never quite conformed. It kept continually bursting undisciplined through its barriers, sometimes in ways humorous, if not in ways downright dangerous, such as the way she often frightened Pilate. She could make the perfect sound of an owl. Pilate, like all Romans, had a superstition about owls in the wild. Portents of ill fortune, the Romans believed them to be. One time when a meeting was stretching out long after matters had been concluded, as they tended to do, with Pilate rambling on about things irrelevant, and when Esther thought it time for Mahlir to be caring for Tabitha, the sound of an owl came from the corridor. Terrified, Pilate ended the meeting and hastened into his private chamber to ask the gods for protection and forgiveness. After that it became commonplace for an owl to hoot during the meetings that had become burdensome. Pilate was never the wiser.

Mahlir became dependent upon Esther, too dependent, he often thought. He didn't have to worry about appointments. He knew Esther would remind him. He didn't worry about misplacing anything important. He knew all he needed to do was ask Esther and she would produce it. Sometimes he even consulted her on business matters. More often than not he didn't have to. More often than not she offered her thoughts anyway, most of which were valid, with ideas or points he hadn't considered. So when she issued her protest, especially in her loud and convincing way, he almost didn't go. "You are free now," she raved on. "You most certainly will not be, after going in there. If the king's design is to place you in chains with no repercussions from Rome, what better excuse could there be than to innocently and honestly say that you went in there of your own free will, and that it was the peril of the dungeon that took your life? My lord, a better plan would be to wait. Amanirenas may have been detained elsewhere. The castle is a big place. If you go in that cave and never come out, as will surely be the case, what good will you be to her then, when she does come forward safely, and what good will you be to your daughter? Venture not there, my lord. It is not a wise choice. Wise choices are born of careful thought, not from the rashness of emotion. It was you who told me that. Common sense, my lord."

"Shhh. I must." Mahlir's voice was soft, like he was talking in fear of someone hearing, though no one was around.

Said Esther, a final plea, "Again I must ask – what will become of your child? How will I care for her?"

"Pilate will care for you both. I know he will. He is an honorable man. He is a man of virtue."

Ester's eyes watered up, and her mouth formed itself as if to protest more.

Mahlir stopped her with a finger on her lips. "Shhh. I must."

And he turned and was gone.

Nightfall had completely hidden the dungeon entrance, even with the moon in full dress. When he drew close, he finally saw it, a jagged circle of blackness against the castle wall. Recessed within the cavernous opening were sentries and soldiers who paid Mahlir no mind when he walked inside, as if he were an apparition unseen. They were grouped together wearing their black leather breast plates and black helmets, playing gambling games and gathered around fires that shed light within their small circle only. Some had their armor stacked up beside them. Mahlir bolstered his courage and asked one if a Nubian woman had been imprisoned there. "Many prisoners are brought in; I don't see them all," was the reply.

"Then you have not seen a Nubian woman in these chambers," Mahlir pressed. "Tall, and with black skin?"

"No," he said. "But you may look for yourself." He swept his arm toward the darkness and laughed as Mahlir stared into it.

"Go on," the sentry taunted, sweeping again toward the hole with the same gesture. "Entering Machaerus is the easy part. Finding your way out again is another matter."

"Go," goaded another. "The rats have not been fed yet. Poor things."

Mahlir could still hear the laughter of the guards as the darkness swallowed him, as he walked into its bosom, as the guard's images became lost behind him. Wall torches appeared as Mahlir descended, illuminating dimly the area in front of him. The walls narrowed the deeper he went. And the angle of his descent steepened, turning eventually into steps hewn from the earth itself. The further in he walked, the colder became the air, and the more filled with moisture it became, and with the smell of mildew and other things foul. Some of the torches were entirely spent, causing Mahlir to stumble in blackness. He was trembling, from the cold partly, partly from the frightful isolation of the place. He began to hear mournful sounds and screams of pain. From a child? It was almost more than he could bear. How could Antipas allow it? A true king would not allow it, could not. A true king surely could not be happy on his throne above as long as even one of his subjects remained imprisoned below and in misery. But alas, such a king has not existed since the days of David.

He came to a junction. Stairs descended to the left and to the right. He went to the right because that was where the sounds were coming from. The passageway was barely wider than his shoulders, having no light within it, no lamps, no wall torches. There was a torch by his right shoulder, the final one, silently speaking to him on its upward rush of airflow to somewhere, offering itself in its near silence, if he dare. He pulled it from its receptacle and pressed on. Here at last were the prison cells themselves, on both sides of the passageway, all with narrow iron doors. The stench of human waste came from each, but not the sounds of life. At each one he called her name. From each there came no response.

He descended further, down more steps, along another passageway, and saw eventually, hidden within the absolute belly of the dungeon's depths, a light, and heard the whispered conversations of men.

And he heard again the screams of the child, louder, at the level of his face and from within a crevice in the earthen wall. Then the sounds burst forth upon screeching wings. Bats. Was all. Bats, screaming like a child. He almost laughed.

The voices stopped.

Mahlir doused the torch and stood motionless.

The voices resumed, low and deep, coming from somber men speaking serious things, unintelligible at first. He crept closer, toward its dim light. The voices were in an open cell. Six men there were, no seven, clothed in robes with cowls hiding their faces, gathered around a fire that burned in the middle of the chamber floor, like sorcerers casting a spell.

Speaking in Greek, each with his own peculiarity of accent, the men were plotting the overthrow of the mighty Roman Empire. By the God of Abraham and Isaac, that was what Mahlir-of-Matthias heard that day. If he were to be discovered, surely he would die.

He moved to within a single pace of the open iron door, as breathlessly and silently as a spider spinning in the air, and crouched. It was the last cell, cut from the end of the passage. A heavy drop of water fell on Mahlir's forehead. The smell of deep dirt was in it, and of rotten timbers and mildew.

Despots with dreams, nothing more, dangerous enough to him, but certainly no threat to Caesar. But then he recognized the voice of Herod-Antipas, and saw beneath the cowl of another the stiff beard of King Artabanus. The dampness shivered through him, and he listened – beyond belief was this that he was hearing – and felt the distant warmth of the fire. The flames were yellow and tall, sparking and crackling as if crisp cedar had been supplied as its fuel, and sprang upward toward some kind of natural vent in the stone. The ultimate torture, it must have been, for those that had occupied this chamber, to know that there was a corridor to freedom, to be able to feel its fresh air, perhaps to be able to see the sky above, the sun, the moon, the stars, if the crack be wide enough. Maybe some had escaped through it, or tried, their skeletons still entombed there.

Mahlir listened, and learned bit by bit of a conspiracy involving Parthia, Iberia, Galilee, and Armenia, reaching into Perea and Judea, crossing southward beyond the borders of Egypt, and stretching into the heart of Rome itself, to overthrow the Mighty Roman Empire and replace it with a fused government made up of the heretofore subjugated and warring governments. This that he was witnessing was no less than a powerful and highly organized movement made up of disgruntled factions from virtually every major nation, every political sway. All that was needed was a leader to solidify the movement, to bring everyone together, to make the many operate as one, a man with the gift of mesmerizing enormous masses, for then the recorded history of mankind could forever be changed to the betterment of men and women everywhere. "With him we could bring it about," someone said.

"We of the Magi have seen it in our holy writings," said another. "The writings point to him as the one."

Said another, "It is in the scrolls of our prophets as well. The prophet Micah, in writing to the people of Israel and Judah, points to him as the one, referring to him as an ancient one *whose goings out are from of old, from days of eternity,* though he is but thirty."

Said both, in unintended unison, vocalizing the same thought, as if a greater force were guiding them, "It then shall be him."

"Agreed," said the voice of an Armenian. Artaxias?

"Agreed," affirmed another voice, Pharasmanes, Mahlir speculated, King of Iberia.

Then came the voice of Antipas. "I must have under my governorship all the lands that my father ruled over."

Said Artabanus, "And I must have the lands formerly held by our people, those territories up to and bordering the Sea of Caspi, including Cappadocia, lands rightfully ours, territories that belonged of old to Macedonia and Persia." He paused to gather his thoughts. "Except of course

Iberia and Amenia, which I respectfully relinquish to King Pharasmanes and King Artaxias, since they are a part of our circle. But Cappadocia I must have. It is my intent to divide it into northern and southern portions and give them to my sons Gotarzes and Orodes. Gotarzes is my oldest. Orodes is my son by adoption, whom I have just made general of my forces for the northern border regions. I wish for the Magi to confirm that this condition will be met. This I must be assured of in order to give my complete support to the Magi."

"So it shall be," intoned a raspy voice, followed by the echoing of the others. The raspy voice was low, an almost whispered sound of authority, a Magus presumably, since the accent was Parthian.

Orodes, Mahlir's son, a prince, having a kingdom of his own? So be it. Mahlir had failed. He did not do his job as a father. So his son was plucked up by forces divine and given a new father, one who *could* do his job, one who could do more than the job, one who could give him a kingdom. It is what it is.

Reiterated Artabanus, looking at the specter wherefrom came the raspy voice, "I must have complete assurances that Orodes, though he is not of royal blood, will share in these lands. By origin he is a Jew. Parthian law holds that he has no claim to ruling rights or to royal possessions. Yet in my heart he is my son. I want him to have a kingdom of his own. I want him to be recognized as if he were royalty. I must have assurances of this. From the Magi themselves. Give him a portion of Cappadocia. That will satisfy me."

The raspy voice gave its pledge. "Rest assured. Orodes will have a kingdom, if not Cappadocia, then one of like splendor and beauty. It is the promise of the Magi." The Magus looked in the direction of another of the cowled figures and said this: "And you, Scjanus, upon Caesar's assassination, shall have all territories northward from Paneas, and westward to Gaul. And the world will bow at your doorstep, and finally there shall be peace, under one magnificent and priestly king, come from origins divine. The gods themselves will bow in subservience."

"Sejanus!" Mahlir whispered the name aloud in his shock. Aleius Sejanus, personal and trusted aid to Tiberius Caesar. Head of the Praetorian Guard. Tiberius did indeed have cause to be distrustful of those he trusted most.

Mahlir stood stiff in his fear. Had his whispered outburst been heard? Probably not, because the group was intoning, "agreed," in unison, in a type of sing-song.

Then there followed an oration from a voice of Jewish origin. Someone scholarly, likely, by the way he formed his words, someone of great religious learning, someone with degrees and certifications. "I am a follower of his," he said. "I have no doubt about it. This is our long-awaited Messiah. His kingdom will be the greatest rulership the world has ever known, or ever will know. The nations will link hands. Never to war with one another again. Each nation shall retain its own identity, yet be part of a greater identity, the identity of the one. The many shall become the one. E Pluribus Unum."

The one with the raspy voice nodded his cowled head in agreement. "Babylon reconstituted," he rasped. "Prophesy fulfilled."

"Also the fulfillment of what Isaiah said," continued the one of Jewish origin. "'*...and your days of sorrow will end. Then will all your people be righteous, and they will possess the land forever. They are the shoot I have planted, the work of my hands, for the display of my splendor. The least of you will become a thousand, the smallest a mighty nation. I am the Lord; in its time I will do this swiftly.*'"

Mahlir could not place the voice. But he knew the man was of learning and influence. This he could tell by the way he struggled to put the Holy Hebrew into the secularity of the Greek, attempts that frustrated him and caused him long pauses as his mind struggled to convey the accuracy of the words, some of which have no translation at all beyond Hebrew. "And of what Ezekiel said," he continued, "'*Fruit trees of all kinds will grow on both banks of the river. Their leaves will not wither, nor will their fruit fail. Every month they will bear, because the water from the sanctuary flows to them. Their fruit will serve for food and their leaves for healing.*' And of what Micah said. '*...you will tread our sins underfoot and hurl all our iniquities into the depths of the sea.*' It shall be so. He shall be given the crown."

"Let it be so," droned another.

"There is, however, a problem," the known Jew said. "He doesn't want it."

Surprise and anger toned the voices of the others.

"What do you mean he doesn't want it? How can he not want it?"

"Who would turn away a kingship?"

"Then he is not the one."

"But the signs?"

"You must convince him."

"I will."

"You must."

"I will."

"But if he is not the one?"

"He is the one," repeated the unknown Jew. "I have witnessed such things at his hands that no mortal man could bring about. I have seen him raise the dead. I have seen him heal lepers. I have seen him make the dumb speak and the lame walk. I have seen stormy seas yield to his command. He is the one. Moreover, he has said repeatedly – it is fundamental to his teachings – that the kingdom of God is for Gentiles as well as Jews, for Romans, Samaritans, Parthians, Egyptians, for all. It is what angers the Temple leaders most about him. For certain, he is the one."

"Then a will greater than our own shall prevail," said the raspy Parthian. "The Great Creator of heaven and earth will set him upon the throne. If he is the one, you will be able to convince him."

"He is the one," finalized the unknown Jew.

"Then the Creator will guide your words. Have faith, Judas, my brother."

"I will convince him. I am his friend and his most trusted disciple."

"So it shall be," the Parthian said. Then the Parthian spoke to himself, rasping, whispering in his native language: "*We worship the good, strong, beneficent Fravashis of the Mighty Lord Saoshyant, who is to bring fire to the world to destroy all its evil, which fire shall be as milk to the righteous."*

Sworn enemies. Brought together in fulfillment of ancient prophesies. In depths where demons dwell, shoulder to shoulder in a meeting never to be known. Different religions. Different cultures. Coming together. Cultures as vastly different as air is to water. Yet not so different.

Mahlir moved slightly and breathed in something, a spider web, a puff of falling dust, something. He swallowed to keep from choking on it and pushed himself to his feet, to continue on with his search for Amanirenas, stumbling in his blindness, feeling along the sides until he found another torch. The affairs of men on earth were secondary to him. He must find his wife.

He did not. He heard and saw unimaginable cruelties, before leaving the dungeons of Machaerus, but Amanirenas he did not find.

The prison guards allowed him passage through all the corridors and chambers, joking with him at times about why he was looking for a tall black-skinned woman. Better luck he would have finding a bear, they said, joking about Mahlir not being in his right mind, and about how they should save him from himself by putting him in chains. But never once did they make a move to restrain him.

At the gate, however, as sweet moonlight summoned, someone did seize him. A Parthian soldier. Other Parthians stepped forward. There was no chance of escape. Where they led him he knew not – a wrapping was placed over his eyes – somewhere within the palace, a room of splendor, finer than the triclinium. The bed quarters of a queen, it turned out. The guest suite of the Queen of Parthia. Because after a long length of time, deep into the heart of the night, with the guards watching over him to prevent his escape, with unseen eyes also upon him – one can always tell – the Queen came into view.

Said Mahlir in Greek, "Am I your prisoner?"

The Queen tipped her head in the direction of the soldiers. "They have no weapons. They came to you as escorts, not guards."

"What do you want of me, O Queen?"

She made a motion with her arm. The soldiers obeyed it and bowed and walked out, dropping a heavy curtain behind them, then pulled a door shut from the recess of the wall to further ensure privacy. Through the criss-crossings of the door's lattice, as the curtain settled itself from its sway. Mahlir could see their backs, standing silent.

And – in the silence wherein pounded his heart – the Queen of Parthia came to him. Her breasts brushed his bare arm, warm through the coolness of the blue silk. She wore a sun-shaped pendant. Mahlir felt its gold against him. It was smooth and mellow, like an exquisite food, something to be savored. The mint of her breath filled his head with desire, and he hated himself for feeling it. "Look into my eyes," she said. "Sip the wine of my soul."

CHAPTER 35

FATHER AND SON

ISRAEL – THE CASTLE MACHAERUS

Mahlir looked away, afraid the Queen would see the passion within him. "Why do you do this to me?" he asked, never allowing his eyes to return to her, feeling her hands on his shoulder, her breath on his cheek, her leg on his loins. "You endanger my life to the king, and my soul to my God."

"Am I so undesirable?" she whispered.

"O Queen – I do find you desirable." Dare he say anything else? "But Queen, tell me, how is it that you, the most powerful woman in a kingdom equal in size to the Roman Empire, could possibly find me desirable? I am in the middle of my years, and not at all comely like any one of a thousand men at your call."

Mahlir felt her hand on his face; still he was looking away. "Your jaw is strong and square," she said. His eyelids fluttered as her fingers brushed across them. "Your eyes speak of deep things. They tell tales of a man burdened, a man on a quest. Am I correct? A treasure, could it be? You remind me of my adopted son. Orodes is his name. He has the same eyes. In so many ways you look like him. Your cheekbones. Your smile. The way you part your lips slightly when you are nervous, like now. When I first beheld you I thought I was looking at him."

The mention of his son's name caused him to tremble deep down inside.

Her fingers found their way inside his tunic, with nails hard and smooth and dusted in gold. At their touch he became weak. There was strength in the demeanor of the Queen of Parthia. The allure of maturity maybe? When maturity is present, it enhances beauty. Confidence maybe? Power? Whatever it was, it was overwhelming.

She could perceive his nervousness and spoke to reassure him. "Do not worry," she whispered. "The guards beyond the door will not betray us." She could feel the object of her conquest losing control. She took Mahlir's hands and put them to her waist, and guided them over her hips. "Do you truly find me so repulsive?" A dozen oil lamps gave light to the room with their halting flames. They too were unsure of themselves, casting their motley shadows of foreboding to flicker against the tapestries of fruits and flowers, and against brightly colored wall frescoes depicting scenes of lovers, and of waterfalls, and of brides adorning themselves. There was an open receptacle on a table giving off scents. Within the light's spell were massive Corinthian columns of pink marble, and windows fitted with glass, a luxury seldom seen, and a fountain of bronze Tritons spewing sprays of water from outstretched hands, its basin overflowing with the vines of plants and flowers. In a gilded cage sat a colored bird from the land of Kush, the land of his wife's origin. "Salve, salve," it kept saying. "Be well, be well."

It was the bird that forced Mahlir to act. The bird from the land of Kush. He nearly took the Queen's poison and fed his senses with it. But the bird would not let him. "Salve, salve," it kept repeating, warning him, shaming him.

He threw the Queen back so hard she stumbled.

Her voice turned into that of a raging beast. Everyone in the palace must have heard her. "Fool!" she cried. "It would be better for you if you were a scorpion beneath my heel. For then you would die quickly."

The curtain! Mahlir thought he saw it move! Someone was behind it!

Then he remembered what Tiberius had told him about the game the king and his wife play, how the king hides and watches, then pretends to catch them near the end of their encounter, whereupon she is "allowed her pleasure," to torture the hapless victim, sometimes to death, sometimes only to the point of disfigurement. This was the fate Mahlir escaped that day. Instead of cries of pain from his gagged mouth, muffled sounds that would have been barely noticeable outside the thick bed-chamber walls, what the guards heard was the screeching fury of their Queen.

She began to tear off her clothes. "I will tell everyone you forced yourself upon me!" she shrieked. "Herod will give you over to us. Herod despises you. All he needs is an excuse. I will give him that excuse." The two Parthian guards came running in but were brushed aside by a third man who threw Mahlir against the wall and pinned him there with a stiletto dagger at his throat.

"Kill him!" screamed the Queen.

The man's hand that held the dagger was shaking as he looked into Mahlir's eyes, as if pondering a recognition he couldn't quite place. The man had the eyes and nose of a Jew. The puffed hair was Parthian, the stiff beard, the weathered skin, but the eyes and nose were those of a Jew, Mahlir's eyes and nose. The same young man Mahlir saw in Rome, the man who had approached his door with the request for writing materials. Around the young man's left eye was the discoloration of a birthmark, arrowhead shaped, faded but distinctive. The sight of it sucked the breath from Mahlir's body. It was him!

"Before you thrust the dagger," Mahlir told him, "or have me bound and taken to prison, hear my words, for once the deed is done I shall never see you again, and you will never know. Hear me out, O Great Orodes, for I made you with my own seed."

Orodes shook his head, scattering away the words the way a dog shakes away water, and re-gripped again.

Mahlir's voice was barely audible. "Look in my eyes, look deep and hear the story of who you are. I doubt even your mother knows. Let me tell you of your heritage. It is a distinguished one. You are of the Zadokite line of priests. Your lineage goes back to Aaron, brother of Moses, the first priest commissioned to serve the Holy God Yahweh."

"Kill him!" the Queen screamed.

"Your grandfather was Matthias, high priest during the reign of Herod-the-Great."

The Queen's screaming became deafening. "Lies! Lies! Lies! Kill him!"

"Go ahead and kill me, Orodes, my son. Then when the deed is done look again at the scar that runs from your neck to your loins, the scar you have seen each day of your life. I am the only one who can tell you how that scar came to be. Because I was there. It was given to you by the warlord Athronges, pretender to the Messianic throne, as a torture to me. I also know that you happen to be the only Parthian who is circumcised. I did it with my own hands."

"He lies! Lies! Lies!" screamed the Queen.

The dagger moved tighter as Orodes again regripped. One more thrust, the tiniest, and Mahlir would be choking on his own blood.

"I snatched you from the very arms of your assassin and ran with you into the desert. I protected you. You are alive because of me. We were both captured by the Parthian slave traders."

"Lies! Lies!" She probably truly did think of Mahlir's words as lies, for the slave traders had told the king and queen a far different narrative. Those who traded in human flesh were prohibited by Parthian law from taking children, so each child found in a slave wagon needed to come with a story – orphaned and starving, lost alone without parentage, or in this case, rescued from the sacrificial altar – and it seemed plausible to the Parthians, because historical evidence existed that the Jews did in fact practice child sacrifice, notably the story of Abraham and Isaac.

"Kill him!" she kept screaming, but when the guards moved to obey she halted them. "No, wait, I want my son to do it. It is my son's duty of honor. Protect my honor, my son, like any noble son would do!"

But Orodes just stood there, holding the dagger, and in the midst of his indecision, which in itself was a decision, Mahlir ran. He took one brief look at his son, and he ran, and found he was not as isolated as he thought. The bedchamber opened into the vast palace atrium. He ran into it, and his eyes saw the coming of a group of people on its far side. They were walking slowly, absorbed in their own conversations. They had not heard the commotion. Among them were Amanirenas and Mahlir's two Praetorians. Like angels descended.

Walking side by side with Amanirenas, talking with her, was a man with a red and purple robe and a diadem on his head.

Another king? Who was this new man of royalty who walked with his wife? In attendance were servants and guards. Jews, by their appearance and dress. This unknown king and Amanirenas were the only ones speaking. No one talks to a king unless being invited to do so.

Amanirenas was angry with Mahlir for having left her side. They had been looking for him, she said. Her anger became confusion when she saw running behind him the form of the bedraggled Queen and her confused guards, yelling out that Mahlir had violated her.

The Praetorians acted quicky. They inserted themselves between Mahlir and the pursuing Parthian guards. Hidden daggers appeared in their hands; likewise did daggers materialize into the hands of the Parthians, stiletto bladed like the one Orodes held to Mahlir's throat, looking more like needles than knives. The guards of the unfamiliar king also brandished weapons, though none were supposed to exist within the palace walls, and suddenly there was a standoff triangle of death. Romans, Parthians, Jews, poised, prepared to die, hoping for salvation from somewhere.

It came in the form of a servant running in to announce the existence of a more powerful force, the Arabians, marching on the castle. "They have destroyed the border divisions and are at this hour approaching Machaerus. Hundreds are dead –"

In that moment of hesitation, Mahlir and Amanirenas were hurried away by the Praetorians. The Jewish guards likewise led the unknown king to safety. And Orodes? He was standing at a distance, bewilderment marking his face.

The Praetorians helped to gather up Esther and Tabitha when they reached the garden, and the little group quietly disappeared into the western desert, leaving everything behind except the clothes on their backs.

The sun by then had risen. Following them was a cloud of dust, growing ever closer, its thundering becoming ever louder. The Parthians? The Arabians? They never knew. They took refuge in Qumran, in the buildings that looked to be no more than the rough of the landscape. Mahlir knew Elkanar would welcome them, even at risk to his own safety. The Praetorians acted as human shields for the women as Elkanar led to them to their chambers, while Mahlir and his guide watered the camels and horses then covered all tracks leading to where they were.

And that night they slept in safety.

But Mahlir's sleep was a disquieting one, filled with disturbing dreams.

In the midst of those dreams Amanirenas shook him awake, because she heard him calling her name.

"What were you dreaming, my love?" Her gentle voice was warming to Mahlir's soul. It was the first she had spoken since Machaerus. Since Machaerus, the only communication between the two had been her icy stare. She believed him, that he had been falsely accused by the Queen, that he had not done the evil thing of her accusation, but it took time for her emotions to calm themselves.

"I dreamed that a great wizard came from the north and took you away from me," he said, "and gave to you a kingdom, and made you wife to its king, because I was unable to provide for you the things you deserve –"

She shook her head and scolded him with the devotion of her large brown eyes. "You know what? I really do need to humble you."

The scriptorium's silence was broken by Mahlir's relief and by his laughter. "You? Humble me? You can't be serious."

"I am serious. I *would* have beaten you too. You are fortunate the Praetorians saved you."

"It was *you* the Praetorians saved," he whispered. "Believe it."

"Here's what I believe –" her silver-chimed voice soothed, "– that I would have placed my seal on your forehead. Your very own beauty mark. It would have been a pattern looking quite like the bottom of my shoe."

"I don't think so."

"Someday maybe we'll find out." She was sitting up looking down at him, stroking his forehead, moving hair away from his eyes.

"Some day."

"Some day."

That night in Qumran, Mahlir and Amanirenas became as close as they had ever been. He told her his secrets, knowing that what he said would never be repeated. There was no one alive he trusted more. He told her about the conspiracy, and he told her about his son and the strange quirk of fate that had made him a prince. As fantastic as the tales were, she believed them. And she told Mahlir some things about herself that were equally as fanciful, things she also had never revealed, of how she came to be exiled from the kingdom of Kush, and of how she ended up in Rome. She had fallen in love with a man not of royal blood and had conceived a child by him. And because of the shame brought to the crown, the child was cut from her womb while the man who fathered it watched; then he was killed, and she was sent into the desert to die, or to somehow survive, if it be the will of Apedemak. While she related the story, tears formed to moisten her eyes. "I don't even know if it was a boy or girl," she said. "They bound me and violated me in a way far worse than anything else they could have done." She put her shaking hands to her mouth, an effort to block the words before more came out, and looked upward into the blackness of the dark room where the midnight light from without could not reach. At night in Quman, when the moon is large and white and low, it transforms the wasteland into sparkles of ivory that dance on glowing beams of star shine. "They were my parents. They were the ones who were supposed to love and protect me."

Mahir touched her cheek again, amid the moonlight on her face. It caused her to blink, and a tear fell to settle in the recess of one of her beauty scars.

Her lips were dark like polished cherry wood and pursed into a triangle of child-like gentleness, of vulnerability. Her voice was deep, clear, like a flute, sky-blue if it were a color. "Such a brutal time it is that we chose to be born into," she said. "And such brutal people. Do you think we choose the parents we are born to?"

"I don't know," spoke Mahlir, as silent as a whisper, so as not to wake Tabitha.

"Could it have been that my child thought he was choosing a good mother, and it all just went bad somehow?"

"You may not have lost your child at all," he told her, "if Elkanar is correct. If Elkanar is correct, it is very possible that the child stolen from you by your parents is Tabitha. He once told us that if a soul's destiny is to enter a certain womb, it will happen one way or the other, the second time if not the first, the third if not the second. You are a good mother. Tabitha is a lucky soul. But go on. Finish your story."

So she did. She took a breath for courage, then continued and told of how, while still aching from the butchery, and having no food or shelter, or cloak for her shoulders, she was rescued by a wealthy Arab specializing in the training and trading of gladiators. "I was taken and taught the ways of the arena, as a novelty, because of my size. One day a visitor came to the camp from a far-off land and shared wine and stories with the Arab around a late-night fire. I could hear them talking. His best fighter, the Arab called me, a woman from the land of Kush who can beat any man, is what he said. Then they started to gamble, and somewhere during the night something happened, and I ended up the property of the visitor. I must have ended up as security for a gambling debt, or I was sold, something, because come morning I was taken away by the visitor. I had a new master." She looked down at Mahlir lovingly. "However it happened," she said. "I'm grateful. For it brought me to you. I never even knew his name, my new owner. All he told me was that I now belonged to him. He told me I would be fighting in front of crowds of thousands in the circuses of Antioch and Rome, in front of wealthy citizens and senators, not in the back country hamlets where those watching are moneyless peasants, as I had been doing. He said he was going to pair me always with opponents I could defeat, so that I would be assured of my eventual freedom. 'Before which time, my dear,' he said, 'you shall make me a fortune. Because none shall be more favored before a crowd than a beautiful woman who can best a man.'

"But I had other plans. I asked him if he would remove my chains and take me to his tent, so that we might celebrate our victory together. There I plied him with more wine, and I gave myself to him. Then after it was over and while he slept I stole away, taking with me a bag of money. I bought passage to Ostia, wanting to be as far from Kush and the deserts of Egypt as possible. Eventually my money exhausted itself. I spent my last coin on a crust of bread and a hot cup of calda in a tavern filled with men that smelled like they hadn't bathed since the time they were born. I didn't know where I was going to sleep, or how after that I was going to be able to feed myself, or if I would see another sunrise. The thought came that I might be raped and maybe killed by these men if I stayed another moment. But I had nowhere else to go. One of the men took particular notice of me. He was unkempt, and had a beard matted with stale wine and old food, and a large belly and breath as foul as a sewer. He was leaning on me and groping me and saying in Greek that he would be pleased to show me the pleasures a man can offer. I noticed that this man's arms were thin, and that he was shorter than I was, and conceived an idea. I told him he could have me, but first he must win me in a fair fight. If I lost, his price would be me for the night. If he lost, my prize would be money enough for food and lodging. The inn erupted in excitement. Men were backing me, putting up money for me, placing bets among themselves. It was amazing. I walked away with better than a hundred denarii that night. I had found my means of survival. After that I traveled from town to town fighting the curious and the drunken for money, always without weapons, always picking those I knew I could beat, and always watchful for the Arab and the visitor, neither of whom I ever saw again.

"Then I met you, my dearest, and my life changed. No longer did I fear the dawning of another day. I have learned the joy of living, and of loving a husband, and I have been given a new chance to love a child. After so much misery I have at last found happiness." A cloud darkened the moon and the white beams yielded. The luster of her face and the outline of her lips disappeared into the blackness. Mahlir reached to touch her cheek again and brought her down and pressed her body to his, and felt its heat, and felt the rise and fall of her chest and the beating of her pure heart. Though – there was no consummation. Flooding Mahlir's mind were images that he simply could not rid himself of, crowding in, poisoning the beauty, images from the stories she had told, of the incomprehensible savagery to which she had been subjected, and the savagery into which she was forced. He was unable to hold an erection. It had never happened before. The harder he tried, the more futile the effort became. He didn't know what to say. He just looked at her with apologies powerful enough to be seen right through the darkness.

She smiled and drew back her hand and slapped him. The surprise and the sting of it numbed his mind…and up rose his penis. She sank onto it, with a smile that widened to laughter, and leaned back in her victory, their victory. The simple scent of straw, and of ink and papyrus – their bedchamber was the scriptorium, where scrolls are copied – filled them like those of expensive essences. In a moment so quiet that Tabitha never woke or even stirred, Mahlir and his blessed wife bound themselves, after which Amanirenas said, in charmed silver whispers, as she stroked his body with the tips of her fingers, "Know this, my love. If you had an accident tomorrow so that you could never again satisfy my physical needs, still I would love you. Still I would be devoted. Know that I will love you regardless of circumstance. And know that never will I do you harm. If all others in the world were to become mortal enemies to you, me you could depend upon.

If all your possessions were to be taken from you, still you would have me. It will be all right."

The affliction never returned.

They stayed at Qumran until word could be conveyed to Pilate, who sent soldiers to escort them back to Caesarea. Before leaving, Mahlir confided in Elkanar.

"You should know, there is a conspiracy afoot," Mahlir told him. "A large conspiracy among many nations to march against Rome. They say they intend to make the Rabbi Yeshua their leader, by force, if necessary. They say he is the Messiah."

This is how Elkanar responded: "The Rabbi Yeshua is a slave to no man, yet a servant to all. He stayed with us for a time, but he belongs not to us. He studied also in the Temple, but belongs not to the Sanhedrin. The Parthian Magi offered him their wisdom. Neither does he belong to them."

Said Mahlir, "They say that it is the will of God, that it is the fulfillment of prophecy, for Yeshua to lead a revolt against Rome. But if it is God's will for there to be more war, more revolution, then I cannot do God's will. If to follow God and to follow the Messiah means the shedding of blood, then this, I think, is something I am not able to do."

Said Elkanar in response, "Perhaps it is that you have found the Teacher after all." And he said no more.

On their way home, escorted front and back by mounted soldiers sent by Pilate, Amanirenas joked about the unknown king Mahir had seen her talking to back at the castle. Every time Mahlir asked who the mysterious man with the diadem was, she would toy with him and tell him something different, the king of a make-believe country that she would give some fictitious name, or the risen ghost of Herod-the-Great, or the Messiah come to her first. She enjoyed the game immensely.

Soon enough it would be that Mahlir would find out who the man really was. He would be a person who would take Mahlir to lofty heights and to valleys low. He would be his savior and his nemesis.

CHAPTER 36

NEW HORIZONS

ISRAEL – CAESAREA

Mahlir's return to Caesarea found him facing Pilate's scathing fury. "I had to send an entire legion out to get you," Pilate roared, in the normal manner of his intimidation. In truth it had not been an entire legion – it had been a couple hundred soldiers at most – but Mahlir knew better than to argue. It would only lead him away from the issues at hand. Pilate was nose to nose with him. Backing up would only show weakness, a despicable trait to Pontius Pilate. "You put good soldiers at risk," he shouted, nearly touching noses. "You put me at risk, leaving our fortifications here undermanned. You weakened my position."

Pilate began to pace, hands behind his back, waist gear clanking, continuing his belittlement, but in a form more like muttering, as much to himself as to Mahlir. "I should have let you go ahead and get yourself killed. I should have let them pull you apart by horses, or whatever it is those barbarians do in Parthia." He came back and hovered over Mahlir again. "Do you know what would have happened if our soldiers would have engaged the Parthians within the borders of Judea? You would have single handedly plunged us into a greater conflict than the one you had been sent to prevent. You leave on a mission to stave off war with the Arabians and come back with the entire western region taking arms against us." He paused long enough to draw a deep breath, then raised his eyes, a doubting smile beneath them. "Then the thought occurs to me, perhaps no one at all was chasing you. Which means I sent my men out for no reason. We found no soldiers when we arrived, of any kind. Scouts were dispatched in all directions. No Parthians, no Arabians, no Herodians. What do you have to say to that?"

"We were told the Arabians were advancing on the castle. We didn't see them, but someone was chasing us. We barely eluded the dust clouds. I can only assume it was the Parthians, since it was the Parthian Queen whom I embarrassed."

"It most certainly was not the Arabians," Pilate spouted. "The Arabians never reached the castle. The skirmishes were contained within the border regions."

"Someone *was* chasing us."

Pilate went back to the pacing and muttering. "As the gods bear witness, I don't know what to believe. For all I know, all three nations were chasing you. I can tell you one thing, it's going to be a good long while before you travel outside these walls again. I can't afford the damage."

He came back nose to nose again. "Do you have any idea what happened here while you were gone? Where do I begin the list? Word of the Baptist's death reached here long before you did. There were people clambering about in the streets of every city; they were angry people, and there was no one here to talk to them. A mob came to the palace, crying out that I would see the vindictive hand of God. I don't know what they expect of me. The Baptist didn't die by my hand. What am I to do? Can I replace his head and raise him up from the dead?

"To make matters worse, I was petitioned by some of the leading men of the Temple about the traveling Nazarene Rabbi. What is his name? It escapes me."

"Iesus," Mahlir said quietly, since they were speaking in the tongue of the Romans at that moment. Pilate was multi-lingual, having mastered Greek, Hebrew, Aramaic, and Pahlavi, the language of the Parhians. It was one of the reasons he was chosen for the post. "Yehsua, is how it is said in the Hebrew language. Jesus in the Greek."

"Yeshua then. Whomever. They came to me and complained that he masquerades as a Temple teacher, but brings only trouble. They complained that he speaks against their law and that he is turning people away from them. They say people follow him in crowds of thousands, and come from as far off as Syria and Tyre. Why complain to me? Why to me? What am I to do?" Pilate was no longer yelling. He was now lamenting his problems upon a willing ear. "From what I hear, he spends more time in Galilee than in my jurisdiction, coming into Judea only for the festivals. What am I to do? What law has he broken? When they can show me evidence of him breaking a law, that's what I told them, a specific law of Caesar, then I will deal with him. Otherwise, bother me not. They asked me if I would consider it the breaking of a law if someone were to advise the people not to pay Caesar's taxes. Bring me evidence, I told them. Let there be ten witnesses, all of different households. Who is this man anyway? That people come from distant places to hear him? What do you know of him? Is he another of your prophets?"

"Some say he is the Messiah."

"Tell me again about this Messiah."

Mahlir explained that the ancient teachings foretold of the coming of a king greater than David, a king who would be enthroned by God himself, who would re-establish Israel as the ruling kingdom.

"These are such difficult people," Pilate said, ignoring Mahlir's veiled warning, dismissing it as only the fanciful wishing of a downtrodden society. "My campaigns as a soldier caused me less grief, when my very life was in peril. The other day I had to resolve a dispute between the Sadducees and Pharisees over which takes precedence, the Sabbath sacrifice or the Passover sacrifice, if they happen to fall on the same day." Pilate shook his head at the absurdity of it.

Mahlir said nothing about the conspiracy and felt like a traitor for not having done so. Where did his allegiance lie? Anymore he didn't know.

"Caesar detests me," Pilate babbled on. "He must. Otherwise he would not give me a position like this, the governing of an impossible people." He huffed a sigh. "A king. Indeed a king. A king with no gold. A king without a palace. It makes about as much sense as a king who has somebody else carry his crown around in a box on his belt." Pilate's mouth twisted itself upward into a mocking smile that would have made Mahlir laugh, had he not been its target. "Next thing you know I'll be having to deal with the ghost of your King David. Lord-Jupiter-All-Mighty! The way things are going I'm half expecting him to show up at my bedside wanting to know where his crown is. 'Sorry, Your Majesty, that would be my personal assistant you need to talk to. He carries it around on his belt.'" Mahlir thought he could see Esther stifle laughter as she busied herself with dusting things that didn't need to be dusted. "'But who knows where he is? My guess is, he's out somewhere making mischief among nations.'"

Then Pilate began to speak in a different tone, so low Malir barely could hear. "Also, there is the matter of the aqueduct," he said. "I made an error in judgement, I'm afraid." Pilate came again to stand close, but as a friend this time, as an equal, to use the power of his voice to dissolve anger at what Mahlir was about to hear, preparing in his sublime way to confess that he had gone against Mahlir's advice and had taken the Temple money and begun construction, and that he had slaughtered hundreds of Jews in the acts of their protests. So great was this gift of Pilate's, this marvelous gift of persuasion, that even when he was wrong he could be convincing that it was for the right reason, or that his mistake was understandable and excusable. He continued, a look of humility curving upon his lips, resembling almost a smile. "I started on the aqueduct. The people of Jerusalem need the water. As it stands now, the only ones with an adequate supply are the priests of the Temple. That just is not right. The people need the water to keep themselves free from disease, and to continue in their traditions of bathing. The design involves a distance of only two hundred furlongs from the stream's source. It's a bit complex, because of the hills, expensive, true, but doable, and a logical use of the sacred money. What is sacred money to be used for if not the welfare of the people?" He lifted one shoulder in a half shrug, a gesture of apology. "You were right. I misjudged them. These Jews, they are indeed a unique bunch. With them, the normal logic that exists in men simply is not there." Having first disarmed Mahlir with the angry onslaught, having then allied himself as a confidant, as an equal, Pilate was now ready to explain the details of the deed for which historians would have remembered him forever, but for an even greater leadership miscalculation, yet to occur. "Sometimes a leader of men is not able to properly control those under him. The quelling of a riot in the streets, where soldiers are under orders to exercise restraint, can be more terrifying to a soldier than the facing of an army fully laden in the field." Again he shrugged. "The responsibility is mine. The soldiers dealt the blows, but it was I who allowed them to do it." Pilate explained that when the people surrounded the compound, "throwing stones and threatening the lives of all of us," he sent soldiers into their midst disguised in the habits of the Jews, concealing knives. "I instructed them to exact only the blows necessary to disperse the people." He paused, pursed his lips, then said, "A great number were slain. Many others were wounded. I did not expect for that to happen."

Mahlir's response was quietly spoken, and completely unexpected. "It is pointless for me to be involved if you are not going to do at least some of what I advise," he said. "It is clear that I serve no purpose here."

That was all it took. Rage burst into Pilate's face. "Talk to me like that again and I shall be all too delighted to send you back to Caesar!" he bellowed. "You will be at his footstool pleading for work, right before he throws you back onto the street where you belong!"

"I expect Caesar would be quite interested in hearing about large numbers of citizens being massacred by one of his governors. I think, though, first, that I should speak with some of the Jews involved, before making my report."

The boldness of Mahlir's talk brought Pilate to near insanity. He whirled and called for his Praetorians, screaming until breath failed him, screaming that Mahlir was to be immediately removed from the premises, that he was no longer under his employ. "I want John out of here!" he kept yelling. Whenever Pilate's anger was at peak level he would always forget Mahlir's name and call him John.

Protested one of the Praetorians, "Governor, you cannot dismiss him."

"I can do anything I please within the environ of my own household!" Pilate bellowed back.

"Governor, if I may. This will not be good for your image. To dismiss your Jewish aide in the wake of such bloodletting would not be wise. If I may say –" For a guard to advise a governor would in any other province be unheard of, but with Pilate, with his unique form of rulership, his guards were friends as well as servants, advisors as much as guards, jousting partners as much as protectors.

Shrieked Pilate, stumbling over the words, "You may say anything you like, as long as it is said while you are putting the rascal out!"

"You cannot do this," pressed the guard. "No Jew will ever trust you again."

What Pilate did not know was, Mahlir had already been offered work elsewhere. The mysterious king that Amanirenas had been talking to had been Philip-of-Paneas, the tetrarch of the northern regions. She had told Philip of how Mahlir kept the books and managed the affairs of Pilate's shipping concerns, and of how little the compensation was. At first it had been only a joking matter, with Philip laughing and telling Amanirenas, "Send him to me. I shall partner with him and erect a shipping business and pay him twice that and still be getting a bargain." When she explained how Pilate's shipping business had flourished under Mahlir's direction in the short time of its existence, Philip's offer became serious.

Pilate was continuing to scream about how he would do as he pleased in his own palace and on the soil of his own province, when Mahlir looked at him squarely in the eye and said, with a voice calm and self-assured, "It was Caesar who installed me; it is Caesar alone who shall remove me, lest I do it myself."

Shouted Pilate – never had Mahlir seen him so angry – "You cannot remove yourself, because I have already removed you! It is already done!"

To which Mahlir calmly replied, with the power of logic and reason backing his words, which only fired Pilate's fury more, "It is done because I have chosen to do it. I shall resign and give a full report to Caesar as to the reason why. Perhaps it will be you who will be at Caesar's footstool pleading not to be thrown into the street. Or maybe there is another country he will conquer, one further away where he can put you and give to you another advisor whose advice you won't follow."

Pilate's open hand came up to strike Mahlir.

Mahlir didn't wince, fully expecting the blow to come crashing into his face.

It did not.

Instead, Pilate turned and used it to wave a gesture of frustration into the air. "Get him out of my sight. You may tell him also that I have just given him back his position, which I had previously removed from him."

"My resignation stands," Mahlir said quietly.

What followed then would have been humorous, had Pilate not been so furious. He whirled about and strode over to bark at Mahlir that he was not dismissed.

"I am," Mahlir shot back.

"You are *not*."

"I am."

"Not."

"Am."

And on it went until the sound of a hooting owl came from the corridors.

Pilate jumped and looked around. "Did you hear that?"

"What?" Mahlir said. "Hear what?"

"Shhhh. Listen. Quiet."

"I hear nothing"

"Quiet!" Pilate strained to listen to the air and the noises it carried.

There was no owl to be seen.

He looked at everyone around him – the Praetorians, Mahlir, Esther, who was now tending to the greenery adorning the corners and walls and columns.

The others pressed their lips together to keep from laughing, because they all knew the sound had come from Esther.

Pilate looked back at Mahlir, convinced it was his imagination. "And I refuse to allow *you* to dismiss you," he finalized.

Came the sound again, a tiny, "Whoo-hooo," Esther was so good at it she could do it without opening her mouth. An ever so slight smirk on her serene lips was the only clue.

"There it is again! Did you hear it?"

"No, Governor," spoke all the Praetorians, shaking their heads. They all knew, but they would never tell.

Pilate's eyes swept the room. "You didn't hear that?" He walked to the veranda to peer outside.

It came again. "Whoo-hoo." So scant of a sound it could barely be heard.

"I must go," he said.

As he walked away she did it again, scurrying him along like something invisible nipping at his heels.

Esther smiled broadly, and just for the danger of it did it one more time, boosting him along faster, while Mahlir was motioning for her to stop.

Pilate's boots echoed the sounds of his frightened footfalls as he disappeared, to make his peace with the gods, to put away the ill omen, muttering unintelligibly.

And so it was that Mahlir's short career as aid to Pontius Pilate ended. Until hearing of the aqueduct bloodletting, Mahlir had fully planned on staying. He had even drafted a letter to Philip turning away the offer. He destroyed the letter and wrote another to Tiberius. He wrote that he and Pilate had come to a parting of the ways.

It was a parting that was civil, surprisingly. Mahlir continued on with his immediate duties, performing them with responsibility and diligence, not wanting to cause Pilate or the province any undue hardships. Mahlir had been scheduled to depart on a business trip to Tyre to meet with emissaries on trade issues. He left for the business trip as planned and proceeded successfully to negotiate an agreement quite beneficial to the Judean Jews and to the Empire. Once Pilate's anger had been spent, and once he realized that threats and intimidation were useless in swaying Mahlir, he called him formally into his office and spoke to him as though it was Mahlir who was the man of power. In a voice of diplomacy, as kings would speak to kings, referring to himself in the third person, Pilate said, "Pontius Pilate is a gentle lion with a loud roar. Philip-the-Tetrarch is a lamb with the cunning of a fox and the bite of a viper."

Mahlir had been completely honest with Pilate about where he was going and what he was going to do, that he was going to partner up with Philip in the establishment of a competing shipping business. Pilate respected that. More than anything, Pilate respected strength and straight talk. "You are much better off with the lion," Pilate said. "With the lion you always know when you are going to get bit. With the viper, you never know, until the creature's deadly fangs have pierced you."

Good advice, Mahlir was soon to discover. At the moment, though, he did not believe it. "I have someone I wish for you to speak with," Pilate said, and whispered to a Praetorian who returned with the odd little man Mahlir had met at Macherus, Agrippa, grandson of Herod-the-Great, nephew of Philip-the-Tetrarch. Agrippa also tried to dissuade Mahlir, telling him tales of the criminal mentality of the Herod brothers, of the huge sums they extort from people, and of dirty deeds done for money, things not of common knowledge.

Said Agrippa, "A statement my uncle Philip once made to me: 'You can get anybody to do anything if you pay them enough money.'"

Put in Pilate, "My mistakes weren't purposeful; they were judgment errors. They were not designed to hurt the people I serve. This cannot be said of the Herod brothers."

"What he says is true," Agrippa reinforced.

Pilate signaled a servant to pour Mahlir more wine. Mahlir and Pilate were equals that day, along with Agrippa, lounging at Pilate's desk in curule chairs. Behind them was a wall of shields and swords. To the front of them was a window that swept out a full view of the azure blue sea and its narrow strip of white beachfront garnished by thick shore lands of forested green. Mahlir let a sip of the wine linger in his mouth – strong, Pilate's best stock – and allowed its tingle and its taste to rise up into his nostrils, and said to Agrippa, "It is good to see you again." Mahlir thought of him as a friend, because of the kindness he showed back at Machaerus. "What brings you?"

"Cypros and I, and our children, are on our way to Syria. Its president is now Flaccus. He was a great friend of mine during my boyhood days in Rome. Also with him, as a part of his government, is my brother Aristobulus. There will be a place for me there. Pilate, in his generosity, is allowing Cypros and me to quarter here for a time before we take up our journey again.

Pilate added, "What you witnessed at Machaerus was an example of what we speak. You have seen firsthand the behavior of the Herods – the beheading of a prophet, the public humiliation of a man on nothing more than a whim of irrational anger, and if I'm not mistaken, threats against your life. This is a family you wish to align yourself with?"

"The family is a network," Agrippa said. "Their criminal activity is linked by a common cord. It is very organized. If one has odds against you, so does the family. Deny it if you will, but it is true. I am happy to have finally broken away from them. I shall never return."

Finalized Pilate, looking hard into Mahlir's eyes. "A man such as yourself would not fit well within the business environ of the Herods."

Silence was Malir's response.

Realizing he had failed in his efforts, seeing it in Mahlir's face, knowing it in his silence, Pilate wished him well.

In the dispatch to Tiberius, Mahlir spoke of the massacre in terms as fair as possible. He wrote that it was his belief that Pilate did not intend for so many to die, that the fault was with his soldiers, that mass murder had not been the order given. Instructions had been to disperse those in the crowd, and to kill only if necessary. For matters personal, Mahlir wrote, "I implore to be released from my obligations so that I might pursue business ventures of my own. My plans are as follows, assuming the emperor approves. I will continue in the service of the Empire for another six months, during which time I will prepare for my journey to the northern kingdom of Philip-the-Tetrarch. It is with him as a partner that I intend to create my business. During this six-month interim period, I will work with the Procurator to find and install a replacement for me, and will of course continue to attend diligently to my duties here in Judea. Even as I travel to my new home in Caesarea Philippi, near the base of Mt. Hermon, I will be in the service of the Empire, for I shall be attending to a matter of some concern to the Procurator. There is a man called Iesus who travels in the land of Galilee, and is considered by many to be a prophet. At Pilate's request, I will visit this man, whose acquaintance is not foreign to me. On the occasions of the festivals this man Iesus comes into Pilate's jurisdiction and is very often at odds with the ruling members of the Temple and the Sanhedrin. Pilate has already been petitioned by Temple officials to have him arrested, which of course he cannot do, since this man has broken no law. But there could be trouble. There could be rioting among the people, since he gathers enormous crowds with him. I will speak with him. He will listen to me, knowing me as one who has greater wisdom. As my final act in service of Pilate and the empire, I will caution him of the trouble he is stirring, of which I am sure he is not aware. I will advise him to no longer speak out publicly against the Temple officials. He is an intelligent man. He will see the wisdom of it I am sure, for his well-being as well as for the Empire. And a potential for trouble will be eliminated. I thank you for the opportunity that has been given me to serve the Empire. It has been a gratifying experience, as well as one of learning. If the emperor wishes me to continue in his service, either with Pilate or elsewhere, I will do it. I recognize that I have no obligation to do so, being a free citizen and not being in a conscript capacity, but my deep respect for the emperor and the

Empire nonetheless demands that I offer. I await your response. If I don't hear from you I will presume you have no further need of me, and that you approve of my plans."

Mahlir said nothing about the crown, which he would also be delivering, a deathbed promise. No sense in alarming Tiberius. Word down from Rome was that the emperor lived in constant fear of seditions and revolutions, real and imagined, and that innocent people were being imprisoned and executed as a result. Nor did Mahlir say anything about the conspiracy, or about the border conflict between Antipas and Aretas. The conspiracy was something he should have revealed. That he should have revealed long ago.

CHAPTER 37

THE HILLSIDE

ISRAEL – NORTH OF THE SEA OF GALILEE

Mahlir never knew if Tiberius received the letter. No return reply ever came. He heard that Tiberius had retired to the island of Capri and had left the running of the Empire to Sejanus. Aleius Sejanus. His trusted Prefect of the Guard. The only man he trusted. Tiberius, in the uncertainty of his old age, was mistrustful of everyone and every deed. He saw plotted evil everywhere, except behind the eyes of Sejanus, the one place he should have looked. Reason enough for Mahlir to speak. But he would not. He and Amanirenas and the children would surely die if he spoke up, if not by the hand of Tiberius, then by the conspirators, one of whom was Sejanus.

Mahlir and Amanirenas had saved four thousand sesterces for the trip, which would be security for a time – except they did not now have it. Mahlir had loaned most of it out. Agrippa had approached him and asked to borrow three thousand of it for his relocation to Syria. The request caught Mahlir by such surprise that he said yes immediately. He didn't know how to say no to a man of influence. Agrippa promised to return the money once he arrived in Syria where funds awaited him. He would include a heavy rate of interest for the trouble, he told Mahlir. He told Mahlir to notify him at the headquarters of Flaccus, so the money could be forwarded. Pilate widened his eyes when learning of it and looked at Mahlir with a fatalistic turn of his mouth. "I'm afraid you have lost your money, and your mind," he said. "In many ways Agrippa is a good man. I like him. But as a dependable repository for money, he is not. The reason he is living so far from Rome is because of all the money he owes to so many people there, hundreds of thousands."

Amanirenas was furious with Mahlir, and he with himself. Would that he could walk up to Agrippa and ask for it back. But of course that was impossible. "Maybe it will be all right," he told Amanirenas. "Maybe it will work out to be a good investment after all."

But waiting for them on their journey was tragedy far worse than the loss of money. It happened in a remote area to the north not far from their destination, on the northeastern shore of the Sea of Galilee. They were purposely avoiding the towns and cities. They wanted to take no chance of being seen by Antipas or his soldiers, remembering Antipas' promise to throw him in prison if he ever left the services of Caesar. They traveled a route south into Idumea, then around the southern tip of the Dead Sea where the water is shallow and the salt spires tip the surface, a wondrous sight, then northward along the eastern shore through deserts and cliff shorn heights that rise up out of the water. It was a long and arduous journey. Often they traveled through lands where there were no roads at all. Then, to the north of the Dead Sea, they moved along the elevations overlooking the Jordan.

The Dead Sea, they say, was something scooped out hurriedly by the giant hand of God. If so, then the long stretch of the Jordan Valley to the north was painstakingly smoothed by the same hand. As they looked down upon the soft green lowlands and the ribbon of green running between the Dead Sa and the Sea of Galilee, they were reminded of how Moses must have felt when he surveyed the sight from Mt. Nebo, knowing he would never live to make it his home. Amanirenas kept a written account of what she saw. She copied the words down on rolls of expensive papyrus given her by the Essenes, using ink and a reed pen that were personal gifts from Elkanar. She was good with words. "*The Jordan Valley in the spring,*" she wrote, having learned the Hebrew from Mahlir in an effort to honor her husband, "*is a dichotomy of extremes. One comes upon sweeping hillsides of grass and wildflowers, and reckless gorges ripped into existence by wintertime flash flooding – wadis, they are called – huge fissures that snake down the otherwise colorful slopes and splinter around sturdy flat-topped plateaus that refuse to give way. Their jagged and dry riverbeds are pocked by year-round trees and bushes fed by the aquifer, water held just below the surface upon a table of impenetrable stone. Soon rocks can be seen, huge rocks. The soil is red, and becomes redder the further north we go, and rockier, strewn with boulders the size of houses, and always surrounded by grass and wildflowers. The soil soon turns white again. The Arabian Mountains lie to the east, their long flat peaks blue and hazy. Samaria is to the west, with its rocky cliffs. Cypress pines dot the valley, and date palms. The rocks are enormous now, multitudes of them, stacked one on top of another to form their own peculiar mountains. High in the sky a group of storks is circling, hundreds of them, like a swarm of bees. We are about halfway there, I am told. The soil is red once again, and the grass green. The olive trees are fuller and taller than the ones in Jerusalem and Caesarea. Still there are rolling hills, beautiful, and carved out valleys. Every tree I have ever seen grows here. Mango. Avocado. Cypress. Bamboo. Banana trees. Apple trees. The flowers on some of them are as plentiful as the leaves. We come now to what is called the Sea of Galilee. It is a marvelous blue color, deeper I think than any blue I have ever seen. It is encircled in green. The soil is now dark brown, a rich color, like in the land of Kush. There is a mountain ahead of us. It is brown and green and dotted in numerous clumps of trees. I am told it is Mt. Pan. In back of it, visible at times, is a larger mountain, treeless with a tip of snow on it. This is Mt. Hermon."*

"God has blessed me," she wrote, *"to have given me the beauty of this land for my home."*

Ever present in their travels was the threat of being set upon by thieves. Coming instead was a thief of a different kind. A man with a weapon is something one can fight. An illness, on the other hand, is an essence untouchable, less discernable than the slightest wisp of a wind. It is a mystery. It is a foe unbeatable. All one can do is wait and pray for the thing to take its leave. It struck Amanirenas just above the Sea of Galilee, close to their new home of Caesarea Philippi, within days of it. Mahlir had decided not to seek out Yeshua as he had promised in his letter to Tiberius. They would have had to have crossed the Jordan into Galilee, perhaps into the busy metropolis of Capernaum. Finding him even then would be uncertain, since Yeshua had no home, that Mahlir knew of anyway, no known place of permanent residence. The trip was precarious enough as it was.

They were on a lengthy mountainside when it happened. The Sea of Galilee was a distant ribbon of smoke below them. The rise was gentle, northward, toward a mounded peak where three full-canopied Tabor Oaks grew. Mt. Pan and the tip of Hermon lay somewhere beyond, hidden from view. Wildflowers – poppies, anemone, wild mustard – billowed their way in back of them down to the lake and a shore of trees and reeds that drank insatiably from the giving waters. Black porous rocks poked up along the way, more like gemstones than rocks; and lazy clumps of green bushes rose here and there. A desert wheatear tried to light on the fragile single blossom of an iris but took flight once it realized the petals wouldn't support it. The morning sun was settling in their bones, taking away the chill of the night. Tabitha turned her face into its warmth. She was riding Samson. A gentle beast he was, a double-humped aging camel Pilate had provided them, fitted with a crib bed so she could sleep to the roll. Amanirenas, Esther, and Mahlir were walking; they wished not to overburden the animal in his advancing years. Tabitha was hungry, but there was nothing anymore to eat, and there wouldn't be anything until they could take their measured funds to a town and buy bread. How foolish he had been to loan his money out. Giving it out, more properly. Throwing it away. Depriving his family. Misplaced responsibility so often forged the pathways of Mahlir's existence.

In the distance, on the crest of the hill, by the three Tabor Oaks, Mahlir saw a lone wolf, a portent, some say, of a change of events. Its head was visible only for a moment above the pink and red shadings of a sun splashed rock. Its face was also the color red, with markings of white, or maybe it was just the sunrise that gave it that hue. There was curiosity in its face, and a humbleness, maybe a look of loneliness before it twitched its ears and vanished, as if it were desperate for one more run with the pack, one more single play.

Mahlir looked over his shoulder, curious if Amanirenas had seen the animal, and saw that she was a full forty paces back, walking doubled over, being helped by Esther. Something was wrong. Terribly wrong.

He ran to her; Amanirenas was resting on one knee. Her breath was heavy, as if she had been running, though the hill was moderate. And a frightening thing Malir saw – blood – coming from somewhere, soaking her orange and brown cloak and the white linens underneath, and pooling onto the heavy sod of the ground.

He looked around to see who, what could have done this thing. His first thought was an assassin. Antipas. Or Pilate, angry that Mahlir had decided to actually leave. But there was no one. And there was nowhere for anyone to hide, just the three trees on top and the rolling slope of the hill and its multitude of wildflowers.

Esther knew the problem. She laid Amanirenas on her back and lifted her garments and took away her loin coverings. Her abdomen was convulsing, her muscles rolling. From between her legs was being pushed clumps of what Mahlir at first thought was the whole of her insides.

Tabitha began to cry.

In his helplessness Mahlir kneeled by Amanirenas and shaded her head from the sun – it was the only thing he could think of to do – and wiped her sweat-beaded brow with the hem of his tunic.

Said Esther, massaging Amanirenas' stomach, "My lady has been with child for the past three months. It is not the will of the Lord that it be born."

When shock allowed him voice, Mahlir asked of his wife, "Why didn't you tell me?"

She didn't seem to be in pain, just weak, as the life substance continued to pour out of her, well after the clumps had discharged themselves.

"Why didn't you tell me?" he repeated.

She used what strength she had to raise her hand and bring it to touch her husband's cheek. "I am sorry, my love," was all she said.

Then a shivering gripped her body, as if her clothing had turned to ice.

Mahlir tore off his cloak and covered her with it. The shaking only became worse, and the blood flow greater. Until the mid-point of day it continued to flow. Nothing would stop it. Her body was on fire. Mahlir and Esther tried cooling her face with water. They tried packing her vagina with rags torn from linens; the blood only backed up inside her. Nothing helped. It was running in rivulets down the mountain. Mahlir picked up Tabitha to try to comfort her, covered though he was in the blood of her mother.

And there on that hillside, in the midst of the beauty, beneath the heat of the sun, caressed by the cool of the upward breeze from the lake, Mahlir's wife, his love, lover, best friend, left him. She closed her eyes as if to sleep, and there was no more shaking. No longer did her chest rise and fall. Her jaw dropped, not much, only a little, to open her mouth into an awkward expression, a meaningless empty look. She hadn't even said goodbye.

Mahlir wasn't aware of what he did next. He must have shut his own eyes.

Because the next thing he remembered seeing was a hand on Amanirenas' abdomen. There was the smell of alabaster, fresh and powder pure. He looked up. And saw Yeshua, only as he had never seen him before. A haze of yellow was shrouding his head and shoulders, translucent, almost like it wasn't there, some kind of a trick of nature, like heat shimmers on a hot day. It gave him a certain warmth, softened him, or empowered him, words fail. It was unlike anything Mahlir had ever seen. It was him, yet it wasn't.

"Daughter," he said. "Open your eyes and sin no more."

Tabitha, still crying, still in Mahlir's arms, lurched and threw out her hands as if to catch herself, and stopped crying in the same instant, then fell straight away into sleep.

Amanirenas sat up and looked around in confusion.

Then Yeshua turned his eyes on Mahlir, preparing to acknowledge him. Did Yeshua recognize him, Mahlir wondered, as his friend from the Qumran years? He put his eyes on Mahlir with a look that rendered him powerless, but empowered him at the same time, eyes that stripped him of confidence, yet filled him with confidence, a look of welcome, but also a look of caution. They were eyes that invited him to speak, knowing he had a purpose to tell him something, eyes that said it was all right to say whatever it was that duty had bound him to say. But Mahlir was mute. Nothing came out. He simply turned his eyes toward the ground.

A thundering of people came into view, shouting, running up the hill, waving their arms. At first it frightened Mahlir – his thought had been that it was an army. The commotion was that great. The people, all types, Jews, Samaritans, holy men, wicked men, soldiers, rich men, poor men, women, children, entire families, came in such a horde that Mahlir worried about being trampled. What followed was a series of happenings that forever changed him, that left him in question of what he had seen, in question of reality itself.

There were other men there with Yeshua, separate from the approaching crowd. They must have been there all along. Guards? If they were, they made no effort to protect him, and they carried no weapons. It was as if they had seen what was about to happen a thousand times. Yeshua stood unafraid, and opened his arms and welcomed the throng, the thousands. They brought him their sick and dying, and he restored them. Then he spoke to them as one who had authority, and as such Mahlir did not doubt his words. He spoke about what he called the kingdom of God, and taught them many marvelous things. "Who *is* this man?" Mahlir whispered. The four of them, Amanirenas, Mahlir, Tabitha, and Esther, were sitting so close to Yeshua that Mahlir wondered if he heard him say it, because he turned for a brief moment and looked at him, this man Mahlir knew, yet he didn't.

When Yeshua had finished speaking he turned to one of the guards. "Philip," he said. "Where shall we buy bread for all these people to eat?"

Philip was astounded at the question. "Two hundred denarii would not buy enough bread for each one to have a bite!" he said.

Another of the guards spoke up. "Here is a boy with five small barely loaves and two small fishes, but how far will that go among so many?"

"Have the people sit down," instructed Yeshua.

Yeshua then paid the boy and took the loaves and gave thanks, and distributed to all as much as they wanted. He did the same with the fish. Tabitha ate as well, as did Amanirenas, Mahlir, and Esther. And Amanirenas drank from Mahlir's wineskin, filled with water that they had been carrying. Amanirenas was fairly gulping it down. "Let her drink," said one of the guards, seeing Mahlir make a motion to stop her. "It is well that she drinks."

The people in the crowd spoke among themselves as they ate. They spoke about what they had seen and heard, deeds greater than those of a magician, words more compelling than those of a king, words they had never before heard, confusing words, simple words, powerful words. Nothing else was on their lips. The rumblings of their conversations were almost as a hush, things spoken of in wonderment, rising upward upon the Galilean wind. Many were saying, "Here is the prophet Moses wrote about." And they were amazed at this picture he was painting of their god, as a deity of compassion, of forgiveness, of love for all, even Gentiles, and it filled their hearts with hope. Some were angry, because he seemed to be implying that their god was not exclusively theirs.

And the ghost of the young soldier rose once again, the boy he had killed in the war. Whispers were hushing through the crowd, because others must have had their ghosts as well.

"If you knew what I knew –" one woman said to Mahlir, telling then a tale of how she had met him once at a well. "He asked me for water. I reminded him that I was a Samaritan woman, and that a Jew should not be so bold as to ask for water from a Samaritan. He answered by telling me that if I knew who he was, and that if I knew the gift of God, it would be me asking him for a drink, and then he would give me *living* water. 'Everyone who drinks of this living water,' he said, 'will never thirst again.' I thought he was joking. You know how some people are – they can never talk straight – they joke even when you think they're being serious. So I answered back in the same way, joking with him, thinking he was a bit of a lunatic, you know, crazy in the head. I told him, I said, 'Sir, give me this water so that I won't get thirsty, and have to keep coming here to draw water.' Then he said, 'Go, call your husband and come back.' I told him I didn't have a husband. Then do you know what he said? He said, 'You are right when you say you have no husband. The fact is, you have had five husbands, and the man you now have is not your husband.' Well I'll tell you right here and now, in front of God who hears everything – what he said was absolutely true, all of it, every last bit of it. I *have* been married five times, and the man I was sleeping with at the time was not my husband. I knew then that he was a prophet. I could see it in his eyes – and he had this strange smell, the way men smell when they're really clean, only it was a stronger smell, and sweeter. I was afraid of him. I started talking about something else, just to change the subject. I started talking about the Samaritans and the Jews, about how they worship in different places, and how silly it is that the Jews insist we worship in Jerusalem, when our forefathers all worshiped at Mr. Gerizim. He told me I was worshiping what I did not know. And he started to explain to me about God, but he wasn't making any sense with the things he was saying. I told him the Messiah will make clear these things when he comes. Then do you know what he said? He said to me, he said, 'I who speak to you am he.'"

"Hmmm," said Mahlir. His lips were trying to disguise a smile.

"You don't believe me."

"I didn't say that."

"What then?"

"I have a question."

"What?"

"Did you give him the drink of water?"

"I gave him the entire bucket!"

When the people had all eaten, when each one of the many had been filled, Yeshua ruffled the head of a dog and said to his guards – there were twelve of them – "Gather the pieces that are left over. Let nothing be wasted." So the twelve gathered the pieces left over by the five loaves and the two fishes, and filled twelve baskets with them. Somehow it had fed the thousands and thousands of those present. By this time the crowd was dispersing, beginning to walk back down the hill. Some remained. Some, Mahlir heard one person say, followed him always. Those were in addition to his chosen twelve.

Mahlir looked over the hill and marveled at the sight. Colors abounded in the robes and adornments of the people as they slowly moved in waves toward Bethsaida and the other shore towns, far in the distance, three, four Roman miles away, leaving the hillside as clean and as pure as it had been before they arrived. The flowers looked not even to have been trampled, and the grass was full and flowing, not in the least matted down. And the lake below sparkled like millions of tiny jewels.

Mahlir was left a mere part of himself, wondering what his life would have been had he accepted Yeshua's invitation that day, when he asked him to come with him, when Mahlir said no. He asked someone next to him, "Where will Yeshua go next? Does he have a home? Where does he sleep?"

"He sleeps wherever his feet take him, wherever it is he chooses to lay his head," said the man. He pointed at Yeshua, still sitting in the same spot where he had delivered his oration, as people milled around him. "He will stay and speak with them as long as they are able to listen, and he will answer questions as long as they are willing to ask them."

There was a deep emptiness in Mahlir's soul. But then he looked at Amanirenas. And then he looked down at his child, sleeping once again. And he became filled. "Thank you," he said, in Yeshua's direction. And though engaged in conversation with someone else Yeshua looked back and smiled.

"He told you not to sin anymore," Mahlir mused. "What do you suppose he meant by that?"

The question puzzled Amanirenas. “He what? Who? What are you talking about?”

“Yeshua. When he laid his hand on you. He told you not to sin anymore. Has my love been untrue to me?”

The absurdity of the question formed a smile on her face. “I have committed no sin. Who are you going to believe? A stranger who has never met me? Or me?”

“You, of course.”

“I definitely need to humble you.”

“You better write home and get some of those ox-hide grass jumpers of your grandmother’s to help you.”

“The only help I might need from them is to help you get up off the ground while I’m running the arena with a palm branch.”

“The only palm branch there’ll be will be the one I spank you with.”

“Some day maybe we’ll find out.”

“Some day.”

“Some day.”

One odd thing, the one thing Yeshua did that stuck in Mahlir’s mind–when a man had approached Yeshua and sank to one knee in worship, Yeshua had pulled him upright with gentle words of reprimand.

The whole thing was so immense, so overwhelmingly powerful, that Mahlir forgot all about his purpose of giving Yeshua the crown.

CHAPTER 38

THE ROYAL PRISONER

ECBATANA – THE CAPITAL CITY OF PARTHIA

During the time Mahlir and the little family had been in hiding among the Qumran fathers after their flight from Machaerus, political and social change had been afoot. News had been spreading of the deeds and words of a young rabbi that can raise the dead and give sight to the blind. The news even reached the far-off kingdoms and the ears of one Prince Gotarzes of Parthia. Now that his brother had abdicated and gone to the land of the Hebrews to live the life of an ascetic, deserting not only his country but also the relationship the two of them had forged, a bond he thought was special beyond words, Gotarzes hid himself from his pain within the veil of military prowess and a newfound quest for power. He had learned something from his brother's letters, coming now with regularity from the far western regions, from the land of the Jews. What Gotarzes had learned, verified by travelers and traders, was of how very much the people venerated this simple man called Yeshua, this strange man to whom the Magi would soon offer a crown. They stood read to do his bidding no matter the call. They quite literally worshiped him. He also learned that Yeshua had no more than twelve guards to protect him, while he, Gotrzes, had the backing of the entire Hyrcanian army, two hundred thousand trained fighters in all and four hundred auxiliary units, well enough to conquer nations. Plus, he had the support of some of the more hawkish Magi. But he didn't need it. All he needed, in order to conquer nations, was to conquer one man, one isolated little man, Yeshua-ben-Yosef, who had no more than a group of twelve unarmed men guarding him.

Yet the abduction would not be without complications, warned the Parthian agents in Israel. Crowds of thousands follow him wherever he goes. It would have to be done at night, they told him. The difficulty would be recognizing the target, the agents said. He wears no crown and does not dress as royalty, doesn't even dress in the traditional robing of the Jewish priesthood. But Gotarzes had a plan for that as well. "Offer someone who knows him two hundred silver drachmae to point him out to us while he sleeps," Gotarzes instructed the agents.

"Does he have a mother?" Gotarzes wanted to know.

"Yes," came back the communique. "Her name is Mary."

"Find out where she lives. Offer someone the same amount to point her out. Does he have a wife?"

"He is frequently seen in the company of a young woman from a town called Magdala, on the western shore of the Sea of Galilee," came back the communique. "Her name is also Mary. Some simply refer to her as the Magdalene."

The return communique from Gotarzes went out. "Offer *four* hundred drachmae to have the second Mary pointed out," it said.

And so it was. For a total of eight hundred drachmae of silver the plan would be set in motion. And Gotarzes would see the fulfillment of his dream of conquest. The mighty Prince of Parthia and his army of thirty thousand men – thirty thousand would do for now – set out for the tiny kingdom called Israel, to find a king destined by prophesy to rule the world, and to persuade that king by any means necessary to proclaim Gotarzes his general – the leap from general to king is a but a small one – and history will be what history should be. In the annals of recorded antiquity, many a general has risen to the level of kingship. Busts of Gotarzes will be placed among the pedestals of kings and queens. His statue will grace the entranceways to Temples and meeting houses.

His legacy and power will be greater than that of the Macedonian.

Step by step this massive army began its move across mountains and plains, unstoppable, traveling by night under the cover of darkness. The footfalls of each horse and each foot soldier were purposely random, so as not to set the earth to trembling and thereby alert the masses, though surely the earth did tremble, as this colossus steadily moved forward toward its purpose. Gotarzes left the bulk of the army on the Arabian side. Roman border patrols had been spotted. He took only a small contingent into Judea. His spies had pinpointed the rabbi's location. And, it turned out, that was all that was needed. It was almost as if the rabbi had been expecting him and had acquiesced voluntarily to the abduction.

CHAPTER 39

AN AWAKENING

ISRAEL – SOMEWHERE NEAR THE SHORES OF THE SEA OF GALILEE

A young man with a strong face stood before the mighty warrior prince of Parthia, helpless, hands bound. A flame floated on oil in a brass basin between them. It was the only light in the tent, and it cast its shadows in a terrifying way upon the face of Prince Gotarzes. Although the young man seemed anything but terrified.

"Your name is Yeshua-ben-Yosef?" Gotarzes asked the young man in his best Aramaic, heavy with a Parthian accent.

"You know it is," said the young man.

It was early. The sun had not yet risen. Four Parthian guards stood at the tent's entrance, two inside, two outside. "I will get to the point," said Gotarzes. "We can be of mutual service to one another, you and I, as leaders of men. You have something I need. I have something you need."

Yeshua did not answer.

Gotarzes presented an image that truly would have been frightening to any other man – a long cape of deer hide flowing down over a sleeveless tunic of bear skin, a curved scimitar dressing his waistband, a bow in his hand he was using to gesture with, and a fully loaded quiver fashioned from a hollowed-out human arm, hand intact – but the look on this prisoner's face seemed to be one of sorrowfulness, like one might have upon finding a helpless and injured baby bird. Gotarzes motioned to one of the guards, and a woman was brought in.

The woman fell to her knees upon seeing Gotarzes and his prisoner. "Please release my son," she pleaded. "He has done nothing to you, and he is not wealthy. He has no gold or silver. He has nothing you could possibly want."

"Ah, but he does," Gotarzes said to the woman. "He has power. And now I have something he wants. I have you."

The young man was silent.

"I have something else as well." Gotarzes gestured again to the guard, though speaking to Yeshua. "I have yet another prisoner. Another woman. One you know quite intimately, I am told. But you need not worry. I will protect them both. They will be safe within the confines of my father's harem. No harm will come to them…as long as I am by your side as your first in command, as you conquer nations." Gotarzes was good at reading faces, and he saw nothing of what he was expecting to see in the young man's face, no fear, no desperation, just that same kind of brooding sadness.

"I want to become your partner in your quest to conquer nations," he went on. "That is all. Then both women will be set free. From what I hear, the people will follow you no matter the risk, no matter the objective. Merely say the word and they will follow. That is the kind of power I want. And keep in mind – I have experience leading men into battle. I will be of great benefit to you." He gestured with the bow toward the tent's opening. "Out there, just beyond the border of our two nations, is an army legion in size. My army. You, on the other hand, have but twelve men. I could make you kneel. But I won't. All I ask is that you appoint me General of your Horse, when you begin your campaigns. I shall be riding beside you as your –"

Footsteps at the tent's entrance interrupted Gotarzes. It was the guard returning with the second woman. He threw her stumbling into the lamplight. The sight of her stunned Gotarzes. He had not participated in the abductions himself. He had only given the order, trusting it would be carried out. Standing before him was the last person in the world he expected to see…

…his own sister.

Nahid was dressed in the habits of a Jewish wife, with a colored tichel wound around her head and flowing down over her left shoulder. He had never seen her as beautiful as she was that night, in that tent, adorned by the irregular light of a tiny floating flame.

When speech finally came to the prince, he roared at the guard for his mistake. "What have you done! Imbecile! I shall have you sliced and hung in a tree for the birds to feast on! Imbecile!"

The guard cowered. "My lord," he said. "We did as we were told. We seized the woman called the Magdalene."

Gotarzes slapped him with back of his hand and sent him tumbling. "Imbecile! This is my sister! Take those bonds off her at once!"

Gotarzes did not wait for the guard to pick himself up and untie Nahid's hands; he did it himself. "Dear sister," he said. "I am sorry for this. Forgive my guard. He shall pay dearly for this grave mistake."

"It is no mistake," said Nahid, as her brother was wiping the tears from her eyes. "The one they call Yeshua is my beloved. Release him, dear brother, and bend your knee to him, for he can point the way to a kingdom greater than any on earth."

"But –" said Gotarzes in his confusion. "Your name –"

"Yes, I have taken a new name. My name is now Mary."

Gotarzes looked over at the young man whose name was Yeshua. There was no need to untie him. The thongs that had previously bound his hands now lay at his feet. How was that possible? Gotarzes had tied the thongs himself. He had tied them so tight blood came. In fact he saw that there was dried blood staining the leather straps that lay useless on the ground.

Yeshua walked toward Gotarzes and reached out with his right hand to place it on his forehead.

The mighty warrior stood there, as if a statue frozen in eternity, so that when the palm of the young man's right hand made its gentle contact, the two men were looking straight across at one another, as if fused by some ethereal bond.

For the longest time there was silence.

And in those moments, in the very silence in which he stood, Gotarzes saw the face of a new world, in stillness so profound it pulsed through him as a living thing.

Gotarzes' was a soul in turmoil, though one would not guess from outward appearances and from the harsh speak of his words and the way he ground them out with profanity and things offensive. One would never guess that within this hard-boiled man of war there raged a war of its own, a brutal struggle between good and evil, where the Divine had become strong and weaponized through many goings out, rising now to the surface in near victory. A simple circumstance was all that was needed to move him to the noble side, the selfless side. It must have made the angels smile, that the circumstance to do so was the very one created by the dark side.

The menacing look on Gotarzes' face melted away and began to show all the wonderment and surprise of what he was experiencing. A veil had been lifted to reveal a reality heretofore unknown, a reality unknown to most, even to those of high learning. The Greeks had a name for it. *Apocalypse.* It means just that, "*The lifting of the veil.*"

Visible on the face of the brutal man of war was a sense of awe, cobalt blue, if it were a color, power, if it could be defined.

"I didn't know!" Gotarzes whispered. "How could I have known!?"

More silence.

Then came desperation, because what he was seeing, experiencing, was slipping away.

"How can I get it back? A lover has been torn from my breast. How? Tell me how?"

Answered the young man: "You cannot. It comes to you. And it comes not by works, but by the grace of God."

"But how? Surely there must be a way."

"Love your enemies, that is how. Pray for those that abuse you. Do good to those that do you harm. That is how. Mourn for those who suffer. Become as a child, forge within yourself a pure heart, wage peace not war, suffer righteousness in the face of evil, forgive those who do you injustice. Those are your weapons, in the greatest battle men on earth will wage. Do these things," he said, "and you *shall* inherit the Kingdom of Heaven. It is there for you. It is your Father-in-Heaven's bequeathal to you."

Gotarzes fell to his knees and wept.

CHAPTER 40

THE STONE GARDNER'S FIRE

ISRAEL – NORTH OF THE SEA OF GALILEE

There had been a familiarity about one of the men sitting close to Yeshua, back when he was giving his oration on the hillside, but Mahlir hadn't given it much thought, until the man turned. Recognition had been instant. It was Orodes. Prince of Parthia. The one who held a knife to his throat. His own son. Each recognized the other simultaneously.

There was silence when they came face to face, after jostling through the crowd that separated them. It was broken by Orodes. "Father?"

"Yes. I am your father, from a time long, long ago that you don't remember."

"At first I wasn't sure," said Orodes. "I had only seen you that one time, that time at the fortress."

"Twice," corrected Mahlir. "There was also the time in Rome when you knocked on my door and asked for writing materials, which you insisted on paying for."

"You? That was you?" Orodes broke into a wide smile. "Of course. Now it makes sense. And the mysterious woman who showed up that night in the forest offering passage to Parthia – you also?"

"Well, not exactly. That was Caesar's servant, who had been consigned to me during my service as steward of the trade caravans."

Orodes looked deep into his father's eyes, then nodded his head with approval at what he saw. "Father," was all he said, a simple acknowledgement.

Mahlir moved his head up and down in affirmation of the fact.

"My adoptive father had fashioned a rather gruesome image of you, said you had attempted to offer me as a sacrifice to Ahriman –" It was difficult for Mahlir not to break in with an immediate denial, but he had learned from Elkanar that the art of communication was best served by listening rather than talking. "– and that the Parthian slave traders rescued me at the very moment of the deed."

Said Mahlir then: "None of what they told you is true. None of it."

"I realize that now, but at the time it was believable to me, because the Jews have been known to have practiced child sacrifice in the history of their religion. There is the story of a man named Abraham."

"None of what they told you is true."

Father and son embraced.

Someone else was there with Orodes, a man tall and thick with a Parthian square beard. The man was almost a head taller than Orodes. Whereas Orodes was gentle looking, this man was the consummate image of a fierce Parthian warrior. "Father," said Orodes, gesturing to the man, "– my companion, my…" He was reaching for the word to explain who, what Gotarzes was to him, but such a word did not exist.

Gotarzes rescued him by introducing himself. "Good sir," he said. "I am called Gotarzes." His voice was such that it trembled the very stones of the earth.

"Gotarzes? This is Gotarzes? The warrior prince I hear so much about? Your brother?"

"My brother not by blood," rescued Orodes. "By my adoption into the royal family we were made brothers."

Added Gotarzes: "Things may be different now for both of us, since we are not going back. Since we are now followers of the Master. The royal family and the Magi will consider it abdication I am sure."

Gotarzes' eyes kept moving toward Amanirenas as he was talking.

"My apologies, everyone," Mahlir expressed. "I'm forgetting myself. This is my wife, Amanirenas."

Gotarzes roared in laughter. "Great Blue Balls of the Magi! This lovely creature is the mother of Orodes? Truly?"

Orodes bowed toward Amanirenas. "You must excuse my paramour," he told her. "While his soul belongs to the Lord, his outer shell remains a bit crusty."

The word *"paramouor"* startled and confused Mahlir. A mistake, he rationalized, had to have been, a word that lost meaning due to the language barrier. Parthians often struggled with Aramaic, even though it had its origins from Parthian history. He had to have meant "friend," "close associate." No other explanation was possible. Mahlir continued on the with the introduction. "She is my second wife. From the land of the Nubians."

"Any relation to the Great Kandake Amanirenas, the warrior queen who defeated Caesar?" Gotarzes asked.

"She is my grandmother," replied Amanirenas.

"Ah, a grand heritage," said Orodes.

A wolf loped up and sat beside Orodes, and Orodes was not alarmed, confirming the fable of the Wolf Prince. Orodes reached down and patted its head, as if it were no more than a dog, at which the wolf smiled with the entirety of its mouth and with eyes dilated full black, exactly like a dog, except that it was much larger than a dog, and stood on taller legs, and had a much larger head, triangle like, and a longer nose. "I think I may have seen that animal," said Mahlir. "As we were climbing the hill, a wolf popped its head up over the lip of a rock. Yes. I'm sure it was the same one. Yes. White markings blending into gold and red. Yes. I am sure. A beautiful animal."

"Mithra," said Orodes, and rubbed the wolf's head again. Its ears were pasted back against its head in its delight. "It was Mithra you can thank for saving your wife's life."

"Some have said that a wolf follows the Rabbi Yeshua. Where the wolf is, so is the rabbi."

"Mithra," he acknowledged, and patted the animal's head again. The wolf shook and settled itself into a ball at Orodes' feet, and curled its luxuriant black-tipped tail around its body. "The wolf follows me, I follow the rabbi."

"Yes, definitely. That was the wolf I saw on the hillside. I thought it was a wild animal."

Orodes went on to explain. "The Master was resting before speaking, preparing for the people, when Mithra came running to us, crying and spinning in circles, confusing to us at first. He was of course telling us that someone was in trouble and had need of the Master. He ran forward, then came back when we didn't follow, and whined and ran forward again. The Master understood. He patted Mithra and said, 'All right little disciple, let us go and see what the trouble is,' and followed as Mithra led."

"So I have a wolf to thank?"

"You have God to thank."

"How does it come to be that you have a wolf as a pet?"

"Mithra is not my pet, he is my friend. My loving and loyal partner. How is it that my father ended up married to an African princess?"

"It looks like you and I need to set aside some time for one another. It appears we both have stories to tell."

"Yes." Orodes paused for a moment, as if what he was about to say required courage, then looked over at Gotarzes. "First I need to explain who we are to one another, so you will not hear it through the ugliness of street rumors."

"What do you mean, who you are?" Mahlir began to realize what was coming, what was happening, because Orodes reached out for Gotarzes' hand and squeezed it lovingly, and Gotarzes responded with an equal look of affection. It was wholly unnatural and wrong. Mahlir was shrinking from it, looking for, hoping for another explanation.

But there was no other explanation. His son was a homosexual, and his paramour was his son's own brother. Mahlir staggered backward as the reality began to solidify. A forty-pound Gaulic hammer could not have stunned him more. He tried to speak, but gagged instead, unable to breathe. Words came as weapons: "I saved you from the sword of Athronges. For what? For this?" The words just kept coming, rolling out of his mouth uncontrollably. "Take care of our son, was the last of what was spoken by your mother when she appeared to me after she passed. I remember it well. For what? For this? I was going to name you after your grandfather. Something tells me he would not exactly be proud of the honor. After all these years of searching, praying, dreaming of finding you – it was my sole purpose in life – this?"

Mahlir looked at Gotarzes – "I blame you," – he spouted, and stabilized himself with a wide stance and shouted it out. "You! A savage! You are to blame!"

The old Gotarzes would have lopped off Mahir's head. This was the new Gotarzes.

Mahlir restrained himself from saying anything further, because people were within earshot, and people are of an evil bent when a homosexual is in their midst, because they know the Torah, and they know the law as it was given to Moses on Sinai, that a man who lies with another man is to be stoned. He may have already said too much. Now a new sickness began to assault Mahir-of-Matthias, a sickness born out of fear. As angry as he was, he did not want his son to die. So even though there was more to say, more of his anger to be spent, more of his confusion, he walked away. He stopped and turned as if to go back, but to say what? So he just walked away altogether.

Amanirenas followed after him and reprimanded him in loud hushed whispers. It was out of place for a wife to upbraid a husband in such a manner, and in public no less, unheard of in Mahlir's society, but Amanirenas was from another kingdom and another culture. "For shame, husband," she scolded. "This is your son, your flesh and blood, and a good man at that. You should be proud, for he is kind and gentle, and strikingly handsome, and he has done nothing at all wrong. To the contrary, the world is a better place because he walks it."

"Nothing wrong?" Mahlir screamed, after recovering from the shock of his wife's insubordination. "It is a violation of law!"

"For shame, husband. It may be a violation of your law, but it is certainly not a violation of what should be the law."

"Ah!" He was waving a finger at her. "But it is! That is where you are wrong. For a man to lie with another man is strictly forbidden by Moses."

"Moses? Who is Moses!?"

"Moses, woman! I have told you –"

"Yes, you have told me who Moses was. Moses was a flesh and blood man subject to the same fears and superstitions as the rest of the people, was who Moses was."

"Hush! You are speaking absolute blasphemy. God spoke through Moses. It certainly is the law of God."

Then Amanirenas spoke the ultimate in blasphemy. "If that is the case, you must go to a different mountain in your quest for your god, because the devil abides on the slopes of the mountain Moses climbed." And she told Mahlir of two males from her country. "Niankhkhum and Khumhotep, servants in the royal household whom the people so loved and respected that they immortalized the love and commitment they shared for one another in stone wall-drawings right in the midst of the city, and on their tombs when they died, where the two are embracing as lovers."

To that Mahlir did not respond, but continued walking. They walked together for a time, then Mahlir stopped at a flat place and suggested that they not continue on, that they make camp for the night there on the mount. As they were gathering wood and dried sage for a fire, a great noise erupted from somewhere in back of them, from beyond sight, from behind a small ridge he and Amanirenas had crested. Quarrelling? Laughter? The commotion was growing. Mahlir almost kept on with his duties – it was none of his business – but then he heard the howl of a wolf and saw its reddish blond body burst into view. Coming to ask for Mahlir's help? Mahlir turned and followed Mithra back toward the commotion, Amanirenas scurrying behind him. When they got closer they saw that a pit had been dug and that two men had been buried up to their necks. The act itself was enough to kill them, the pressure of the earth; but if not, the crowd itself soon would with the stones they were gathering. Some had already been thrown. Blood was obscuring the faces of both men. Mahlir recognized the other one first, because there was less blood to hide recognition – Gotarzes, the savage who had poisoned the mind of his son. Then the other one must be – he strained to see through the blood – yes, Orodes!

"Most are not throwing yet," huffed Mahlir, out of breath and stumbling, breaking his way through the crowd that had by now completely encircled the condemned. "They're holding back, just gathering. A stoning needs to be presided over by a priest."

"A call has been put out for one," said someone close by, bending over, feeling rocks, tossing most of them aside. "They have to be just right," the man said. "They have to have points all around." The man was creating a makeshift basket out of the looseness of his cloak. Epithets were being hurled – fags, fudge packers, butt-whores – but the crowd still held back from throwing their stones, waiting for the priest and his central signal. "Because the execution of a homosexual is a religious ritual," explained one lady.

Mahlir thrust his way into the circle and held his hands up. Mithra burst in at the same time, a golden blur soaring over the heads of the people. The animal kept its back to the two victims, protecting them, its enormous teeth ever present in front of all those who held stones. "Wait, go get Yeshua," Mahlir yelled out. "Yeshua can fix them. Someone, go get Yeshua."

"According to Moses, they must die," came a shout.

"No," Mahlir shouted back. "Do not do this. Yeshua would not want it. To kill them would be turning against his teachings."

"It is in the Torah. They must die."

"Where is the priest? Someone find a priest. It is time. They must die."

"Kill them."

"We do not need the priest. Kill them now."

"No, wait," Mahlir pleaded. "Yeshua can heal these two homosexuals. He can drive out their demons. He can change them. You have seen him heal the sick. You have seen it with your own eyes. I have seen him bring life out of death. He can do this."

Singular voices continued to rise up over the crowd's ever-growing din and rumble.

"Yes, let us wait," came another voice. "He is right."

"No, kill them," said still another. "It is the law laid down by God."

"You heard him just today say, 'blessed are the pure in heart, blessed are he peacemakers,'" came still another voice.

"Yes, let us wait," shouted out yet another.

Mahlir held his hands up in protection. "You have heard him say that you must love the man who sins even though you hate the sin."

"He is right. We must wait."

"Yeshua is gone. He is not even here."

"He *is* here!" Mahlir pointed to Mithra, still baring his teeth. "Where the wolf is, he is. He is coming. We only have to wait a short while!"

"He's right. The wolf is always by his side. We must wait."

"Yes. He's right. He healed my son of the runs." It was a man with a Samaritan accent. "And right before he showed up, I saw the wolf. Wherever the wolf is, the rabbi is soon to follow."

"Yes. Let us wait."

"Yes."

"Yes, we will wait."

But then someone let fly with a rock, and that was the trigger, activating a barrage of other stones, hundreds of them. Mithra shrieked as one hit him, a helpless sound like a child crying. Mahlir's head shook and rang as several hit him, and he slumped to the ground to be enveloped by a curtain of black. He saw the bloody face of his son right before losing consciousness, hardly a face at all, still living, still breathing, but crushed and ripped past recognition.

When Mahlir opened his eyes, he was looking up at Yeshua. "I'm thirsty," he said. Someone lifted a gourd full of water to his lips. It was Amanirenas. Tears were wetting her face. Mahlir drank it in gulps. He looked around. Orodes and Gotarzes were consoling one another, not a scratch on them.

Mahlir was confused – they were consoling one another beyond the way a man would console another man. This was the way a husband would console a wife, and it made Mahlir angry all over again. He struggled half to his feet and looked at Yeshua and asked him why. "You restored them to life, yet you did not take away their sin? Why?"

Others were standing by watching. They too were wondering. It was in their faces. Yeshua saw it and understood, and he taught them, answering this way:

> *"There was once a Master Mason who enlisted the services of his six sons to help him build a mansion, which was to be their inheritance. He sent them out two by two. He sent the first two out with a cart-full of mortar and a cart-full of bricks. He sent the second two out in like manner with a cart-full of mortar and a cart-full of bricks. But when he sent the youngest two sons out he sent them each out with a cart full of mortar only. The youngest sons were confused and wondered why their father had not given them any bricks, for a mansion cannot be built with mortar only. The older brothers laughed at them and put abuses upon them saying that their father did not trust them in their ability to transform raw stone into beauty. But when the six all returned after the day's work the father upbraided the older sons severely for their cruelty. 'But why then did you send them out with only mortar and no stone?' they asked their father. 'Because we have enough stone,' answered the father. 'What we need now is more mortar.'"*

"Are you saying we should not obey the Law of Moses?" someone shouted.

Yeshua answered the man, speaking with the authority of one who knows. "Woe be to you, for you are no better than the Scribes and Pharisees who profess devotion to God yet serve only mammon. Do you really condemn these good men for the deed of committing themselves and devoting themselves to one another, while you yourselves languish in sin? They commit no adultery. They do not steal off under the cover of lies to lust after another. They have given themselves only to one another, and have given up a kingdom to follow me, and I shall make them princes in a greater kingdom, for they are now soldiers of God." The man who had asked the question turned red with embarrassment. Then Yeshua turned his hard eyes on Mahlir. "You should be proud of your son. I am. I have renamed him Matthias, in honor of his grandfather, your father." Then he said this, though he had not been anywhere around when Mahlir had been admonishing his son. "And yes, his grandfather *is* proud that his grandson has his name." Yeshua looked at another in the crowd: "They have not murdered their mistress's husband out of jealousy." Then another. "They do not speak unkindly of family members behind their backs while lauding them with praise and pearls when they are around to hear." It was clear that he was picking their sins out of thin air, because every time he spoke, the person he was looking at shriveled under the gaze. "They have not cast aside their wives because their wives have grown old and have become disfigured with age." Some of the men he looked at flushed red with anger, because so many are unable to look at themselves. "They do not treat one another like slaves, ordering each other about. They treat one another with respect." He looked at a woman in the crowd. "They support one another's goals and ambitions." He pointed in the direction of Mt. Gerizim. "They do not wish death upon another man because he chooses to worship the Lord in a different way in a different place." Many now in the crowd were flaring with anger.

"You condemn these two men for having sex with one another in committed love," Yeshua went on, "yet you force yourself in a sexual way upon those unfortunate young men you take as prisoners, as did the reprobates of Sodom and Gomorrah." And somewhere within the crowd a man's face flamed up with guilt. Yeshua then looked at a man who had the appearance of a beggar. "They do not stand around lazily when work is available and allow their families to go hungry." He looked at the wives whose husbands had fallen on hard times. "These two men support one another. When one is unable to work, the other picks up the load and does so happily and lovingly." On and on he went, until the crowd dispersed, mumbling among themselves, dropping their stones as they went. With some, their hearts were changed. With others, their hearts had only hardened, and it was the beginning of the end for this strange yet wonderful man called Yeshua-ben-Yosef, this man with no credentials, no degrees, no titles, whose simple yet profound wisdom would soon change forever the way men and women live their lives and interact with one another.

Mahlir remembered he had forgotten to give Yeshua the crown. His fingers reached to unhook his belt but couldn't complete the move. So instead he just walked away, walked aimlessly to wherever in front of him his feet would carry him, angry, confused, embarrassed, for he had been humiliated in front of his wife and family. He climbed the hill and sat beneath the three Tabor Oaks and allowed his body to sink into the vibrations of his shamed and stunned body.

He leaned back against the biggest tree, because it had the thickest bark and his back itched. It was a great relief to rub it over the gnarled surface, and it allowed his body to go deeper into the vibrations. Amanirenas had not followed; he could see her down there with the others, circulating amongst those in the crowd that had not yet dispersed. She probably was thinking he had deserted her. Of course he had not. He just needed time to think. The shock of everything – his son's revelation, the extreme violence of gentle people, Yeshua's humiliating oration, the throbbing of his heart from the brisk uphill walk – all of it was pulsing through him. It was a strange sort of calm, akin to the serenity that sometimes occurs inside a raging storm, and within it there exploded a marvelous transformation. He saw himself as a huge ball of earth and stone suspended among the stars, within which was a fiery core. Were it not for the enwrapping crust, this core would fill all time and space. And this earthen mass that was Mahlir, this star unable to shine, was shaking and trembling as though a giant earthquake had gripped it. Heaving, shaking, cracking, was this thing that was Mahlir, spewing out fire and light from each of those cracks, as happens in the dark when the door of a furnace is opened. Hotter than the fire which forges steel, was this that was Malir, hotter, brighter. And with its escape came a tingling type of ecstasy. Then the fire and light blasted a hole through the crust and filled the entirety of space, and as it did his body tingled more with the ecstasy. The tingling fairly danced in his blood and in his bones. Then all was quiet. For a time. Until the heaving and shaking and cracking started up all over again, this time with more intensity, more heaving, more cracking, more holes, more tingling, more ecstasy, more of the light streaming out. It continued, holes bursting through, light streaming out, as if there were a catapult inside blasting out these missiles of fire, and of the tingling and the ecstasy, until he was quite sure he was going to lose his mind and forever be consumed by this that was streaming out to fill all space and time, on out to the extreme, the end of which is only the beginning, and on down to the infinitesimal, the smallest of which yields to a unit smaller yet, and includes every microbe and every cell, every atom of everything that exists, living or otherwise, and everything that *has* existed or *will* exist. And he understood it all in those moments, or that moment. Time had ceased to exist, and somehow it all made sense, in that moment, or moments.

Then it left him, left him struggling to recreate it in the form of a memory. It is an impossible task, the quantifying and labeling of an experience beyond the mind, because the mind must use the images of the mind, and so it grabs hold of whatever is available. In Mahlir's case it was the star. In John-the-Apostle's case, as he would write many years later on the Isle of Patmos, the images were of dragons and war horses in a scroll called the Book of Revelations.

And it left him a changed man. It left him calling out for his son.

CHAPTER 41

REDEMPTION

ISRAEL – NORTH OF THE SEA OF GALILEE

The change that occurred beneath the three Tabor Oaks had been instantaneous.

A change that occurs within the process of thought can take days, months, years to imbed and solidify itself, as when happens when one converts to a different religion. But when a thing is perceived directly, it moves from the realm of belief to the grasp of reality, such as happened with Mahlir on the little mountain beneath the three Tabor Oaks, or as might happen with a tiny ant on a tabletop that can perceive realty in only two dimensions, width and length, a story often told by Elkanar. At the time it made no sense to Mahlir. The ant encounters a man that rests the tips of his fingers on the tabletop. The ant, being able to perceive in only two dimensions, sees only five circles. He tells the other ants about the strange circles that suddenly appeared from out of nowhere. They all come to look. And they call the other ants to come and look. The wisest among them studies the circles and develops the Law of the Five Circles, that they can move outward a certain distance, that they can move inward to touch one another, but that the largest of the circles can never move in back of the other four. Now they know all there is to know about the five circles. One of the ants develops a belief about the circles – they are warm to the touch, so they must be pieces of the sun that have fallen off. It seems plausible to the other ants, so that particular ant is given authority over the circles, and he is given the title of a cleric, and the other ants study his writings and gain knowledge and receive certificates authenticating that knowledge. Other ants come along and reconstitute and change that system of belief, and sub-systems form themselves and come to be accepted, and the ants that study those systems are given their respective certificates of authority. Then one day one of the lowly ants, one who has neither title nor certificate, is able to raise his consciousness from two dimensions to three, and discovers what?, that the five circles are not separate after all. That they are connected inseparably. He knows this as a fact because he has perceived it directly. For him it has ceased to become a belief. He tries to tell the others, but is scorned and persecuted, because he has no titles or certificates. They ostracize the little fellow; ultimately they do away with him altogether, for having the audacity to challenge authority.

Orodes was still there. Yeshua and his group were still engaged with those left over from the crowd – hours later, even as the night was descending – answering their questions, talking, laughing. Mahlir surprised his son with an embrace. "I have made a terrible mistake," he told him, "and I am sorry." He looked over and saw Amanirenas and went over and embraced her as well, and did the unthinkable while the others watched. He apologized to his wife. A man simply does not do that. "I am sorry, good woman. You were right. I was wrong. I am lucky to have you as my wife."

"I ought to humble you, you know that?" she said, and happily wiped her teared-up face with the back of her hand. No more needed to be said.

He tried to explain to everyone. He should not have. Even the followers of Yeshua laughed. One called Thomas came up and said, through his laughter, "A ball of fire? Where in the name of the All Mighty did you come up with that?"

Mahlir turned red with embarrassment.

Thomas put his hand on Mahlir's shoulder, laughing still. "Balls of fire floating around in the sky?" Thomas laughed so hard he nearly fell to the ground.

NOTES:

Page 5 (6 lines down) *"...as the city rose upland from the shoreless Mazandaran Sea."* Known today as the Caspian Sea.

Page 15 (12 lines down) *"...a happening that was recorded in the journals of a Chinese stargazer, who had made note of a large comet that had appeared over the valleys and mountains of Hyrcania at the time of his birth, and whose course over the days and months had taken it westward to pass over Judea, so that doubtful future generations may read and believe."* Ancient Chinese records show a comet making an appearance in approximately 5BC traveling westward from China in the direction of Palestine. Humphreys, C. J., 1991, *Q. Jl R astr. Soci.*, 32, 389-407, and Tyndale Bulletin, 1992, 43.1, 31-56.

Page 28 (28 lines down) *"Imagine for a moment what kind of a world it would be if there was nothing to kill or die for ..."* Imagine, written by John Lennon & Yoko Ono, single released in 1971 in the US, 1975 in the UK.

Page 35 (15 lines down) *"...with the stars, and sip beer..."* Parthia's contribution to the alcoholic beverage. According to clay tablets discovered by historians, brewing beer was a well-respected craft in ancient Persia at least 7,000 years ago. https://renegadebrewing.com/beer-history/

Page 59 (26 lines down) *"...His goings out number as many..."* The terminology *goings out* in theological literature of antiquity refers to the concept of the transmigration of the soul, reincarnation, which was widely accepted during the time of Jesus, *going out* from one's home, as it were. The quote appears unredacted in the King James version, translated from the Hebrew (Micah 5:2), but was taken out of the New International Version

(1978, re-edited in 2010), replacing "goings out" with, "origins." The actual quote from the Hebrew, unredacted and unedited, is: *"But you, Bethlehem Ephratah, though you are small among the clans of Judah, out of you will come for me one who will be ruler over Israel, whose goings out are from of old, from ancient times."*

Page 60 (10 lines down) "*...a banquet will be held in honor of King Antipas, tetrarch of the Galilean regions.*" When Herod the Great died he divided the kingdom and gave each of four parts to his three sons and his sister. Philip was given the northern most region of Paneas and Gaulanitis, Antipas was given the middle portion of Galilee and Perea, Archelaus was bequeathed Judea and Samaria, and his sister Salome was given the southernmost portion of Idumea.

Page 123 (last line) "*...reflections of the insane lawlessness that pervaded the land, sect against sect, tribe against tribe..*" In those days the Jews and Samaritans were warring factions against one another, for reasons going back decades. But the primary reason was one of absurdity to the logical mind. The Jews believed God's holy place to be the Temple in Jerusalem; the Samaritans believed it to be Mt. Gerizim, and both were willing to kill each other over this difference. The Samaritans came from the intermarriage of Jews and Persians after Nebuchadnezzar captured the Jewish people (known as "The Exile") and forced them into Babylonian lands (Persian) where languages, religions, and cultures merged. The Aramaic tongue came from this language meshing.

Page 141 (20 lines down) "*...continuing on as tetrarch of Judea and Samaria...*" Tetrarchs were kings of an empire divided into four parts, each part being ruled autonomously.

Page 148 (19 lines down) "*...And I purified myself with the doves...*" Leviticus 15:19-33. Of the many laws laid down by God through Moses states that menstruating women must cleanse themselves by killing two doves and sprinkling themselves with the blood.

Page 151 (26 lines down) *"of man-made stone, the Roman invention of hardened ash, limestone, and water..."* Though the Romans didn't invent concrete, they were the first to use it on a widespread basis. It's first use can be traced back as far as 6.500 BC.

Page 207 (30 lines down) *"...The affliction had now consumed the entire right side of his face..."* Medical Science now recognizes this disease as Herpes Zoster, commonly known as Shingles. It's the dormant Chicken Pox virus. Intense emotions can activate it. It follows the nerve channels of one side or the other, leaving the other untouched.

Page 240 (14 lines down) *"... would land them all in Tullianum."* Tullianum was a prison in ancient Rome, horrific in its structure, a grated over hole in the ground through which prisoners were dropped, thought to be the place where Peter was imprisoned, now a tourist attraction.

Page 262 (25 lines down) *"...to the yielding melody of the nablum..."* The great grandmother to the modern-day guitar. You can Google a picture of it.

Page 364 (28 lines down) *"He is another prophet of the people. Some say he is Elijah returned. Others say..."* This in fact is confirmed by Biblical scripture, that John the Baptist was the incarnation of Elijah, Matthew 17:12-13. *Jesus replied, "To be sure, Elijah comes and will restore all things. But I tell you, Elijah has already come, and they did not recognize him, but have done to him everything they wished. In the same way the Son of Man is going to suffer at their hands." Then the disciples understood that he was talking to them about John the Baptist.*

Page 409 (29 lines down) *"...Fruit trees of all kinds will grow on both banks of the river. Their leaves will not wither..."* The Tree of Life is a map of the human soul. Refer to the Sefer Yetzirah, the book of Jewish Mysticism.

Page 439 (11 lines down) *"...Mt. Pan and the tip of Hermon lay somewhere..."* Mt. Pan was the cliff-shorn mountain forming one of the many foothills of the great Mt. Hermon. It is known now as Mt. Dove, named after an Israeli soldier from the 1967 war.